THE AQUARIUS
PROJECT

THE AQUARIUS PROJECT

B.A. CHEPAITIS

WILDSIDE PRESS

PART 1

PRELIMINARY DATA

The old woman stirred, feeling the shift of particular molecules somewhere far away. She listened, seeking the source.

It was not quite sunrise, and she hadn't yet tugged her ancient body out of bed, but she'd found that within the confines of flesh, this was a good time to be still and listen. The jagged edge of dawn cut through the crap of the day and told her what she needed to know.

As she listened, she sensed energy wrapped in a piece of matter known as Cali Spring, a young woman who sat in a science class and listened attentively while another piece of matter known as her teacher spoke about quantum fields. She was surrounded by energy the old woman knew as teenage girls—very restless pieces of matter. They were passing notes, because the piece of matter known as the teacher tolerated no talk. They had to avoid any disruption in the field of this classroom, but that didn't mean they had to listen.

The piece of matter named Cali Spring listened.

She was intrigued by the notion of the quantum field, and the irreconcilable differences it dealt with. She was, in general, intrigued by irreconcilable differences. Her interest was both intellectual and personal.

The old woman, who also rejoiced in the dance of irreconcilable differences, was intrigued by Cali Spring. Both she and Cali were momentary manifestations of intangible fields, which were the only real things in the universe.

She considered the infinite variety of those fields. She laughed, and listened to the echoes of her own laughter. Laughter was one way of admiring a universe that spit out many odd things, such planets, stars, aardvarks, a creature that would invent a word like aardvark. Things like Cali Spring, and herself, here to do the work of matter for a while.

The old woman got out of bed. She had many random and chaotic events to face, as the human population veered toward a change both great and meaningless. Great, because it would extend human boundaries beyond the discovery of fire. Meaningless, because no one knew about it.

Some of the results would be unpleasant, but all would lead to a moment when her field and the field that was Cali Spring might interact abruptly, in particular regions of absurd space.

Brownian Motion

Betty was watching Racer again, and Cali didn't like it.

She was asking herself how much she didn't like it when Lola tapped her arm. Cali turned to her.

"Pass the butter," Lola said.

"Margarine," Cali corrected, handing her the plastic tub. There wasn't anything as luxurious as butter at St. Ida's.

"Hey—while you're at it, pass the crap," Lola said, pointing at the dish of meat, and snickers went up and down the table.

They kept them low, knowing the lunch monitors moved in when things got noisy, whether the noise was good or not. Noise in general was a bad thing here, and though the lunchroom still looked like what it had once been—the cafeteria of a Catholic girl's boarding school—none of them ever forgot that this was now a medium security facility for bad girls between the ages of 16 and 20. Its school, dorms, gymnasium and yards were surrounded by electric fencing topped with barbed wire, and the fence guards carried guns and the dorm and school monitors had billy clubs, mace, and zappers. All the girls here had been convicted of felonies. Some of them would leave only to finish their sentences in bigger houses.

Cali eyed Betty, who was eyeing Racer, who was looking twitchy these past few days. Racer, Cali's roommate, was sent to St. Ida's on a charge of arson after she set the girl's restroom on fire. She was younger by a few years, and pretty easy to get along with except when her eye started its rhythmic twitch and her right leg began its tapping dance and her nails were chewed down as far as possible. All that meant she was ready to blow. If she blew she'd end up in solitary, maybe take a few girls with her. Cali liked to make sure things didn't get that far. She had only a few months left before she turned twenty-one and faced the parole board, and as the senior member of the group she also preferred things quiet.

"Hey," Lola said, poking at the meat portion of lunch with her fork. "What *is* this anyway? I mean, it's not chicken."

"Beef?" Mindy suggested. She was mousy, without much personality or imagination, tolerated rather than liked.

"Dog," Tibby said. "A long haired doggie dog." She mimicked a snarl, eyes flashing laughter. Tibby had energy, and used it.

"Nah," Lola said, tasting it. "Too tough. I'm pretty sure it's the Marilyn special."

This brought long slow smiles up and down the table. Marilyn was one of the older counselors, recently dead of a heart attack. Nobody was sorry to see her go. Nobody here would mind if they used her for lunch.

Tibby brought a forkful to her mouth. "Mmm-mm. Tastes good to me."

Lola's dark face split into a grin. She had the darkest skin Cali had ever seen. Even here, where the majority of the girls were dark skinned, she stood out like the night sky put against noon shadows. Lola liked to say that the darker the berry, the sweeter the juice, and she'd tease Cali that if she'd just get out in the sun more she might achieve a little more in that way. Cali didn't think so.

Her skin was a deep olive from her father's half-Nepali heritage, but it also had the influence of her Irish mother and no amount of sun would change that. Her eyes were coal black, though, as was her hair. Now it was cropped short, to avoid having someone grab it in a fight, but before St. Ida's she'd worn it long, and it poured down her back like night water.

"You better get yours while you can, girl," Lola said to Cali, pushing the meat toward her. Cali wasn't hungry but she took it to be sociable, to maintain a cordial bond with Lola, who had a tricky kind of temper.

Lola was sent to St. Ida's for breaking and entering into a rich woman's house to take a bath. She'd run away from home and was living on the streets at the time, and all she wanted was warm water. "What did I take?" she yelled at the arresting officers. "I took a bath. It's not like she didn't have plenty more."

Which would have been true, except that the woman, finding a pretty young black girl in her tub, assumed Lola was her husband's prostitute and attacked her. After years of defending herself at home from a drunk father and on the streets from everyone else, Lola was the better fighter, and the woman ended up with a cracked skull that almost killed her. Lola was only 16 when she was convicted of aggravated assault, and breaking and entering, so she landed at St. Ida's.

Most of the girls had less interesting stories. Cali thought hers was no great shakes. She was arrested on a charge of dealing meth. Simple and sweet. Of course, it was her mother who was dealing but that made no difference. Mom wasn't home when the cops showed. Cali was. And when Mom finally arrived, she was glad enough to give her daughter away.

Cali might have harbored anger about that, but her mother died of a heart attack soon after, probably drug related the coroner said. So Cali was here, had been here for almost three years, but she was alive and dependent on no drugs, no man, no woman for her life. She didn't waste energy on either yesterday or tomorrow. She stayed with today. And today Betty was eyeing Racer, and Racer was getting twitchy.

Racer had a lot of trouble that way. Her prettiness deceived people into thinking she was docile, and that made her vulnerable. She was white, blonde haired and blue-eyed, her turned up nose and big round eyes making her look younger than her years. And middled-aged, plump Betty, who breathed loud through her nose and had short red hair with gray roots, had her fill of tough dark girls. She wanted a new flavor.

They'd all had their turn dealing with her, and some had used the attention to their advantage, while others tried to reject it and ended up in solitary, or with extended sentences from her reports.

Cali had gone through her own brief turn when she first got here, found it boring and distasteful, and shrugged it off when it was over. The only real problem was that if you said yes to Betty the older girls thought that meant they'd have a turn, and once they had you, they kept you. Of course, some of the girls didn't mind that. They paired up, and established the same kind of relationships and dramas they might otherwise be having with boys if they weren't here.

Cali preferred to avoid all that. Once initiated by Betty, she made it clear she wanted to be on her own, and nobody contradicted her after Glory tried a few moves and ended up dead. Not that Cali killed her. She just died. Some freak stroke. But in the eyes of the girls here it made Cali into a kind of bad luck charm. They stayed away.

So did Betty, after her initial interest. "You got a bad look in your eye," she told Cali. "You just ain't much fun."

And that was that. Betty moved on to the next girl. And the next. And the next.

Nobody reported her. Nobody gave a rat's ass. The girls here were throw-aways, with dead parents, drug addict parents, parents too poor for anyone else to care about them. St. Ida's, once an expensive Catholic boarding school, was now a cheap closet, cluttered with second-hand girls.

"You got anything special today?" Cali asked Racer.

"Garden this afternoon," Racer said, casting a glance toward Betty, who worked as a monitor in the gardens. She'd go with the girls to get tools from the shed, and if it took a while to find them, nobody noticed.

"Is she still bothering you?" Cali asked.

Racer's lips set themselves in a thin line. "Not too bad. I'll handle it."

"Just don't handle it with a shovel at the back of her head or anything."

Racer turned her large baby blue eyes up to Cali, a confused mixture of expressions flitting across her face. She was so pretty, Cali thought, she might have walked off the cover of Teen Magazine. And of all the girls, Racer was the one most likely to end up dead of her own anger.

She'd earned her name from an incident in the yard when she first got here. That day Lana, head of the Aryan gang, called out names at Racer, who was talking to a black girl she'd made friends with. Racer kept smiling, talking fast about how she wanted some dope so bad she'd give her front teeth away for it.

Then they were called into line to go inside, and Racer, without losing her smile, ran so fast at Lana nobody even saw her until she had the rock in her hand and was about to bash it onto the girl's head.

Cali got there first and pulled her off before anything irrevocable happened, and all of them got solitary. After that, she kept an eye on Racer, learned the signs of impending disaster and tried to avert them. It wasn't always easy. Racer was a blur, only half in the world. When her brain got away from her she'd begin to twitch, bite her nails down to the quick, and soon after that she'd explode in a way nobody could predict and nobody, looking at her sweet face, would suspect.

"I'm not planning anything stupid," Racer said.

"You never are," Cali replied. "Listen, if she starts on you, tell her you're mine. Say it nice. Bat those big eyes and say you're afraid I'll get angry."

"C'mon, Cali. Everyone knows you don't—"

"—She doesn't know."

Racer put a finger to her mouth and chewed on the end of it. Cali pulled it down.

"Do it, okay?"

Racer shrugged, went back to her food. Cali gave Betty a look she hoped would support what she was trying to pull off.

She'd considered offering herself to Betty in Racer's place, but she knew Betty wasn't interested. Besides, she'd tried that before and it got her nowhere. When her mother started on the meth her boyfriend and dealer, Keith, was clearly as interested in the daughter as the mother. Cali, 16 at the time, made a deal with him. She'd do it with him, if he stopped giving her mother meth, put word on the street that nobody else could, help get her into rehab.

He agreed, but of course he didn't do it. He stopped her supply for a week while they were going at it, but then he lost interest, and she found her mother's needles, saw her face, knew it was all on again. She confronted him with it, but he just laughed.

That was Keith, with his blonde rasta hair and attitude and philosophizing. "I look at life and I see it's overvalued," he said. "We think everyone should live, but I say why? Look at the birds. Their death rate's enormous and as a species they been around a lot longer. Look at bugs. They're everywhere, and we squash 'em whenever we can. So what makes us special? Nothing I can see."

No, Cali thought. She wouldn't try that again. But she hoped Racer didn't make trouble because right now she couldn't afford it. She was too close to the possibility of freedom. When she faced the parole board they'd either send her to a halfway house, her record expunged, or they'd send her to Bedford to serve the rest of her sentence, depending on reports of her behavior.

Five more years, in a real prison. She'd do just about anything to avoid that. Just the thought of it made her stomach turn over.

A bell rang, and the lunch monitors shifted positions, taking posts at different tables and dismissing the girls to their next tasks, which varied. Some cleared the tables, some had classes or counseling sessions, some had garden or yard duty. St. Ida's liked to think of itself as a rehabilitative facility, though Cali never figured out how clearing lunch tables would make you a better person.

"You got lunch clean up?" Racer asked Cali.

She shook her head.

"Counseling?"

"No. They didn't re-assign me." Marilyn had been her counselor, and though her other girls were given a new counselor, she wasn't.

Tibby's mouth dropped open in exaggerated gape of surprise. "No more counseling?"

"Just some C and E, work placement."

"That's it?" Lola asked. "No more freak show? Don't they know you're crazy?"

Cali laughed. "Maybe they gave up on me."

"Where you working?"

"Maintenance."

Tibby whispered a sincere 'bitch' close to her ear.

The older girls, the one's heading out, had sessions in the Career and Education office—C and E—and work placement in offices, in classrooms, in the cafeteria. Maintenance was considered one of the juicier positions because you could get outside, do work on the grounds outside the fences. Besides, the maintenance crew was mostly male, and except for Larry Johnson who was old as dirt, they were young and cute and good for laughs.

"I'd kill you if I didn't like you so much," Lola said. "Who'd they give you to?"

"Jesse Halende."

The girls gaped at her. "Jesse? The man himself?"

"Mama," Lola declared, tossing her arms up. "You got all the luck and left us none. I filled in with him once and they won't let me near him again. I gave him the sweats."

"Other way around, girl," Tibby said. "Jesse never sweats. We do."

Cali offered a shrug and a grin that acknowledged her fortune and her awareness that she didn't deserve it anymore than they did. She knew everyone was interested in Jesse.

The girls often reported something broken in their rooms when they knew he was on shift. He could fix anything, and watching him do so was a pleasure. Racer once disconnected the innards of the toilet to get him to their room. She hovered behind him while he worked, but Cali just sat on her bed, reading a book about Chaos theory.

Before he left the room he nodded at her. "Good book?" he asked.

"If you like this kind of thing," she replied, not looking up.

"I do. Enjoy," he said, and left.

Racer gave her shit about it all night long. She'd worked to get him there, and all he did was talk to her, and leave.

"That sucks," Racer said now. "You get Jesse, and they're giving me to Judson." She wrinkled her face and pulled out her cheeks. "It's simply an issue of chemistry, young lady," she mimicked. "If you had better body chemistry, you wouldn't be here."

She followed this with a belch. Cali laughed. Judson, the counselor who was taking on many of Marilyn's leftovers, was a fossil. He smelled old, had dandruff, and didn't know crap about their lives.

"That's sad," Tibby said. "He's the only one who made Marilyn look good."

"I don't know. I kinda miss her. She made life interesting," Racer commented.

"I *do* know. That woman was pure evil. She only worked here to find more demons for her pack."

"Not a bad place to look. If the demons don't kill you first, right Cali?"

Cali had the honor of being Marilyn's last appointment before she was found dead in her office. For the girls that only confirmed her mojo. "Evil's more interesting than Marilyn," she said. "She was just an ordinary perv."

"Oh yeah. That for sure." Lola put on a serious face and licked her lips. "Do you like sex? What kind of sex? How often do you masturbate? Who do you have sex with? Do you dream about sex? Can you spell sex?"

"That's it," Tibby agreed. "The hurting bitch. She started that shit with me, I told her to get a life."

"She got dead," Cali said quietly. Next to her, Racer twitched. Cali cast her a glance.

"Yeah, but Jesse. Mm-mm good," Lola said, and that concluded the conversation because none of the girls said much about Jesse beyond that, which was unusual. Bad mouthing counselors, teachers, guards, that was what they had. They did it all the time. Very few were let off the hook. Jesse, Mrs. Henderson, and Harold, the only cafeteria cook who produced decent food. That was about it. They never got the treatment. Jesse, in particular, was immune.

"Yeah, Cali," Racer said. "Don't kill this one, okay?"

She grinned. The girls on lunch duty got up to clear tables and those who had other duties followed monitors to the next part of their day.

STRANGE ATTRACTORS

The Maintenance crew offices were in an annex off the living quarters, and a monitor escorted Cali to the gate that separated it from the rest of the building, handing her over to Larry Johnson, who waited for her. He sniffed at her, made a rusty noise in his throat, and loped down the hall, indicating that she should follow.

"Jesse's room is down here," he said, his voice rough with decades of a two-pack a day habit. He stopped at a door, turned to her. "Don't try any stupid shit," he said, and gave a quick knock. "New girl here for you," he rasped.

From within, Cali heard a muffled voice telling her to come in. Larry backed off but kept watching her, wheezing softly as she opened the door and stepped inside. Before she closed the door, she looked around.

She could tell a lot about someone by their office, and she liked to know as much as possible up front. Marilyn's room, for instance, was messy, dominated by a large gilt framed photo of Jesus. The girls called it the Open Heart Surgery photo, because it showed Jesus pointing to his chest, where his heart was visible, bleeding and encased in a thorny vine. Cali wondered at Jesus' blonde hair and blue eyes, and at a world that needed such a god.

Jesse's office was not messy, and there was no fake Jesus picture. The window looked out onto the garden, and the small desk had only a vase with feathers and a large chunk of blue quartz on its surface. One wall had a bookshelf filled with books. On the windowsill there was a snake skin—rattlesnake from the look of it—next to a bird skull. A prism hung from the upper windowsill, shedding rainbows in the room. She took it all in, stored the information for later consideration, then looked at Jesse.

He'd been here less than a year. One of the girls who worked in the offices and knew how to get into systems had looked him up. She told Cali he was 26, unmarried, and used to work at a drug rehab. Also he liked car racing and rock climbing for hobbies. That he was good looking, with a tall, fit body, angular features in his face, startling blue-green eyes and thick, wavy dark hair, was something nobody needed to research.

"Listen, don't try and hook up with him," the girl from the office told her. "He'll transfer you if you do. He don't like it."

"Gay?" Cali had asked. Not that she cared. In some ways it simplified things, but she liked to know.

"Not," the girl said. "Just—well, he's different. You'll see."

As Cali stood in his doorway he sat behind his desk not looking at her. He held a long white feather up to the light, turning it slowly, examining it as it turned, totally immersed in what he was doing. Different was right, Cali thought. But she knew that already.

She'd seen him do this sort of thing before. Once, when she was working in the kitchen she'd seen him standing in the gardens just outside, under a tree near the window. Light shone through the leaves and he held a hand up as if he could cup it in his palm, sip it like water. She'd stared at him, wondering why he did that, until he'd turned to where she stood and smiled. Different.

Now she closed the door behind her hard enough for him to hear it. He held on to the feather, but he looked up at her, waved her to approach. She moved forward and sat in the chair on her side of the desk. He ran his eyes up and down her. She remained silent. He got paid to work here. She didn't.

"You wonder why, don't you?" he asked after a while.

She said nothing, not sure what he meant.

He lifted the feather, then laid it on his desk. "Why I spend so much time looking at things like this."

"It's your time," she noted.

"But you wonder about it. I've seen you wondering. Why don't you just ask?"

"Asking isn't as reliable as watching," she said.

A corner of his mouth lifted. "Fair enough. But I'll tell you anyway. I do it because where I come from, particularity is important." He gestured at the feather. "How the light passes through a feather or a leaf at different times of day. Particular things and moments. Particular people. You, for instance, unique in experience and genetics." He paused, looked at her. "Any questions?"

She opened her mouth, closed it. What wanted to come out was the question where do you come from. Also, what the hell are you doing here, working maintenance at St. Ida's. She didn't ask. "No," was what she said

He spent a moment staring at her. "Okay. Then let's start."

She waited for him to say something. He remained silent.

"Did you want to tell me what to do?" she asked.

"In a while. We get to talk first."

"About what?" she asked.

He lifted a hand, let it fall again. "Just because they put you here doesn't mean I'll keep you. I have discretion in that."

Fine, she thought. He'd have to give her the once over, not just for the job but because work placement supervisors gave reports for parole hearings. She settled in.

"Okay," she said. "What do you want me to do?"

"Turn away from me, please," he requested.

"What?"

"You heard me. Turn away. So you can't see my face."

She turned her head to the right.

"Good. Now tell me what color my eyes are."

Memory and observation test, she thought. Someone was always getting money to test them, and she was good at it. She called up her memory of his eyes. They were complex. A little disturbing.

"Silvery blue," she said. "With bits of gold and green in them."

"Anything else?"

She considered. Of course there was, because the colors seemed to always be in motion, to swirl and shift as you watched, but she didn't know how to describe that without sounding strange. "They're busy," she settled on.

"Pretty good. Most people don't remember the blue, much less the rest of it."

"I notice things." Noticing was a safety issue. Notice everything, be hyperalert to all possibilities of trouble or refuge from trouble. That's how she stayed safe.

"When did you first notice my eyes?"

"When I saw you looking at the tree in the yard."

"Why did you notice, and why do you remember?"

She considered, and decided to go for honesty. He seemed to like that. "Because I thought you were nuts, and I wanted to see how nuts you might be."

He laughed softly. "Look at me."

She did so. He was grinning, the angles of his face softened. "Bullshit," he said.

She scowled. "No it's not," she said. "I thought you were nuts."

He waved it away. "That part I believe. But that's not why you looked or why you remember. What's the truth?"

He was right. She noticed his eyes because they were as beautiful and familiar as sun on leaves. She stared at them just long enough to absorb their properties, so she could tuck this image away in her mind and use it later as a place to hide when she had solitary or Racer had another spell or dreams of her mother woke her in the night. Then the image of his eyes would comfort her, though she didn't know why.

She had other images she used this way. She collected them, used them until they wore out, and then collected more. She kept them in a room in her mind she could enter when she needed to go away. It was right next to the other room, which was locked and marked *Do Not Enter,* where she kept everything she swore she would never view again.

But she didn't want him to know that about her. It was none of his business. He was not a counselor, and she was here to mop floors and rake, not bare her soul. She did what the girls often did at these moments. She kept her mouth shut and let the truth rest in her eyes, which she raised to his. He met her glance, studied it.

"Show me your hands, Cali," he said.

"My—what?"

"Your hands. You work with your hands here."

She lifted her arms, held her hands out to him.

"Turn them over," he said, and she did.

He leaned closer, perusing them. For a moment his face went tight, but it was so brief she wasn't sure if it had anything to do with her hands. He sat back in his chair, looking at her and beyond her at the same time, one finger tapping rhythmically against the surface of his desk.

"They're okay," she said. "My hands, I mean. I never had any problems with them."

"No," he said. "I didn't think so." His own hand moved to a folder on his desk, and he opened it, read a little, then looked back up at her. Whatever had happened was over, and he was back to business.

"Your files say your IQ tests in the superior range. You did good schoolwork, got your GED with no trouble and went on to take some advanced classes in science and math. You did a college level tutorial in physics with Mrs. Henderson before she left. Aced it. You like that kind of stuff?"

"It's interesting."

"Nonlinear equations. Chaos theory. Field Theory. You're smart, right?"

"I guess so."

"No arrests for drugs except the one that brought you here. And you weren't put in rehab. You weren't using?"

"No," she said. "I don't use."

"Just a dealer?"

"That's what I got arrested for," she noted.

"You're claiming innocence?"

"Why not? Everyone else does."

"Your mother testified that you were dealing. That you got her hooked."

"I know," Cali said pointedly. "I saw her statement."

"You didn't contradict her. Or agree with her. You just wouldn't say anything."

"I don't like to waste air."

His finger went tap tap tap on the desk, then was still. "I'd talk to her about that, but I can't. She's dead. So I guess we'll never know the truth."

"I guess not."

He sighed, and went back to her file. She relaxed. That was the worst of it. Getting over the question of her arrest, and why, how could she do that to her mother. Marilyn had worked at her about it for hours.

"You've been doing okay here," he said. "Not too much trouble. Only two stints in solitary involving incidents with a girl called Racer. Your roommate."

"Cellmate," she corrected, before she could stop herself. She hated the bullshit term roommate, as if they were at a college dorm. Another way St. Ida's tried to rehab them, creating illusions they were getting somewhere, had choices about their lives. But the doors were locked at night, and the guards still stood at the electric fence with guns and tasers.

Jesse eyed her, but didn't push it. Apparently he had other questioned to pursue. "You were protecting her," he said.

"I made a few mistakes. I got solitary."

"Right," he said. "You're quite a mix of truth and lies, aren't you? We'll skip it, for now. Your file from Mrs. Henderson said you were an eager learner, but your file from Marilyn says you're impervious to traditional counseling, and unwilling to engage in the therapeutic process. Do you know what impervious means?"

"Impenetrable. Unable to be breached."

"Unable or unwilling?"

"It means I don't like stupidity."

Again, that grin. She wished he wouldn't use it. It put her off her guard, as if he was on her side. But he wasn't, because he went home at night, and she stayed here. He might not be an enemy, but he couldn't be a friend.

"Okay," he said. "I get it. You only like smart truth. I talked with Mrs. Henderson. She confirmed your intelligence. Here's another question. How many dead people do you know?"

That was a surprise. "A few," she said hesitantly, not sure where this might lead.

"From what your file says, quite a few. Your mother's one."

"Yeah."

"And her boyfriend, Keith. And your tenth grade math teacher. And two people died since you got here. A girl named Glory, and your former counselor."

"I'm not counting."

"I am," he said. "It adds up to five. Suggest anything to you?"

"Either I'm unlucky," she noted, "or maybe I bother people."

"Profoundly. Tell me about Keith's death," he said.

She felt the tension creep back in. Nobody ever asked about that. "He did a lot of meth," she said. "I guess that killed him."

"Your mother?"

"Same thing."

"Then what about Marilyn?"

She gave him a good grin, with her teeth in it. "How do I know what she did on

weekends?"

He nodded. "But you didn't like her much."

"Nobody did. She was a perv."

He regarded her for a moment. "Did you wish them dead?" he asked.

She said nothing.

"You don't ask questions and you don't answer either? That'll make it tough to get any work done."

He had her there. "I don't answer questions I don't understand," she noted calmly.

"Alright, then," he said, just as cool. "What I'm asking, it has to do with magical thinking. You know what that is?"

She shook her head.

"It's a therapy term. When you believe you can make something happen by thinking about it. A lot of kids do it. They're angry at someone, or even wish someone dead. If that person dies, purely coincidentally, they think they did it. Then they feel incredibly powerful, but also riddled with guilt and shame."

"I'm not a kid," she pointed out.

"Sometimes it gets to be a habit, and you just keep doing it."

She thought about it, and supposed it made sense. "Okay, but that's for counselors to figure out and this isn't therapy."

"It isn't. But I'm still deciding if I want you working here. So did you wish Keith dead?"

As he asked, she remembered the day. It was cool. Autumn cool. She showed Keith the needles she found, accused him of going back on his word, getting more meth for her mother. "You'll kill her," she said. "You're killing her."

"So what?" he laughed. "I'm on her insurance policy."

What she felt was something she kept in the closed room, and she wouldn't visit it. What she did was drop to her knees. "Please," she said softly. "I'm begging you. Help me get her off this shit."

"Convince me," he'd replied. He unzipped his pants. It wasn't the first time, but it was the worst. It was the moment she knew she'd never again ask for help. Not his or anyone else's.

As put his hands on the back of her head, she wished him dead with all her mind and heart. No. It was more than wishing. She declared his death, stated it as a fact of the universe. She didn't know if it showed in her face, but he pushed her back, zipped his pants quick.

"What? What the hell did you say?" he demanded.

She stood, stepped away, but he grabbed her arm, brought a hand back and punched her. No little slap, but a real punch. She felt the insides of her head knocking around, saw sharp bright points of light. Then his hand was tight on her throat and she grabbed at it, staring until her vision cleared and she saw his eyes.

"You're dead," she whispered, meaning it.

She supposed she passed out because next she knew she was lying on the floor and he was standing over her, looking pale. He kicked her in the ribs, called her a bitch, and walked away.

Later that night, when he was watching TV he suddenly gasped, stood and moved jerkily across the room. He stumbled, clutched at air, and then his knees buckled and he went down. When she put a hand on his chest, his heart had stopped. It was over.

"Yeah," Cali said. "I wished him dead."

"Why?"

"Because he was killing my mother and screwing me," she answered, saying the words casually, as if it didn't matter anymore because it didn't, not really. To her surprise a quick flash of pain crossed his face and went away.

"I'm sorry he did that," he said, meaning it. "How long was it between the time you wished him dead, and he died?"

"Same day," she said. "But I wished him dead about every day."

"Yeah," he said. "And your mother? What was that like?"

Something in her chest constricted, a python wrapping all emotion before it feasted.

She was home alone when the police came and found the meth lab Keith had started, along with the meth they'd stored in Cali's closet. She was already in cuffs when her mother returned, took one look at the cops and started to cry. "Oh, Cali. What did you do?"

They took them both away, questioned them separately. Cali said absolutely nothing no matter what they asked. Silence was easier than partial answers. She was charged with dealing, felony counts. Her father, who hadn't called since he left them, who was remarried to a rich woman, showed up and tried to buy her a fancy lawyer. She declined the offer.

She stayed with a public defender who was young and nervous and said she should take the DA's plea bargain, which was time at St. Ida's, and the possibility of parole or hard time, depending on her behavior. He showed

Cali her mother's statement against her, let her listen to her interview tape. Cali listened, then took the plea.

But she knew immediately and irrevocably that this betrayal was her mother's death. She'd killed her own soul, left any humanity she might have aspired to. Cali didn't wish her dead. She just observed that she already was.

Two days later her mother had a heart attack, and died.

Now Cali looked at Jesse. "My mother died after I pled out the drug charge," she said. "The coroner said it was drugs. The judge who sentenced me said I broke her heart."

"What do you think?"

She shrugged.

"What about the dead people here?" Jesse asked. "Marilyn and Glory?"

"Maybe I didn't wish them dead."

"Maybe you did."

There wasn't a reasonable answer she could give for this. She showed him a smile.

To her surprise, he didn't respond with irritation or impatience. He just held her glance, and there was something about the motion in his eyes, impossible swirls of color. It stopped her smile and made her feel as if she stood on a merry go round turning toward a spiraling center, somewhere dark and far away.

She broke eye contact. Looked out the window. She noticed that her heart was pounding hard. She noticed he was breathing deeply and slowly. She waited for what might happen next.

"You're good at it, aren't you? That magical thinking," he said. "But if it's all about killing, then all you get is a lot of death."

"Maybe," she said, cool as she could be, "it's all therapeutic bullshit."

"Maybe," he agreed, amicably enough. He leaned back, stared at the prism, then turned back to her. "I'm guessing you like outdoors better than indoors."

"When it's not snowing or raining."

"Then we'll start with raking. I'll get you gloves and a suit."

"Now?" she asked.

"I'll show you around first. Then we'll go out."

* * * *

He brought her up and down the maintenance hall, opening closets and showing her where gloves, cleaning equipment, yard equipment was kept. He gave her a jumpsuit and gloves.

"Matching orange," he quipped. "Designer quality."

When she was suited up they went out past the fences to rake gravel in the drive leading up to the guarded entrance. Once they started working she was content, at ease. Here she could stare at the sun-drenched sky, or look down to the road beyond St. Ida's. She could imagine a life beyond these walls.

"I hope you're not inclined to run," he noted drily as they worked, "because I do a six minute mile."

She ran her eyes up and down his form. "Not in those shoes," she said, just as drily.

He laughed. "Yours are worse than mine. And your suit's too long. You'd trip."

She gave him a grin. "I'm not running. Like you said, I'm smart."

"That's good," he said. "I get tired of tackling screaming girls. No challenge, but lots of noise."

"I guess," Cali said, "you never had to tackle Lola."

"Lola," he said. "The girl with enough plumbing problems to enter Guiness Book of World Records? No, I wouldn't tackle her. Not on a million dollar dare. But listen, Cali. Look all you want down that road. Get the feel of it. You should be taking it soon enough."

She kept raking, and for a while the only sound was the crunch of gravel against metal. She savored the sound of his words, liking what they meant and the way he said them. Tibby was right. For now, all the luck belonged to her.

* * * *

They worked for two hours, sometimes talking, sometimes just listening to the quiet around them. St. Ida's was isolated from the nearest city, its grounds encompassing about twenty acres in an area zoned rural/industrial. To the west the grey stacks of a factory spewed smoke, but to the east they viewed a thin ribbon of river. North was a junk yard filled with cars, but south was a pastoral scene of cows and barns. When Jesse called time, Cali was reluctant to go inside. She wasn't tired, didn't care that raking gravel was tedious. It felt good to see things that weren't about St. Ida's.

After they put their suits and rakes away he brought her back to his office, gestured for her to sit and got behind his desk.

He handed her a folder. "Paperwork," he said. "Insurance stuff to cover our asses."

"So I guess you're keeping me," she said.

He startled, gave her a nervous glance. She hoped he didn't think she was flirting. She wanted to stay with this. "I mean—I wasn't sure—" she started, but he waved it away.

"Skip it. Yes, you'll be working here. But not next week. You'll be on a field trip. Here."

He handed her a brochure with a picture of a smiling girl hanging over the side of a cliff on the end of a rope. Cali knew about it this. Girls who were close to release were sent on these trips to test them, to teach them things. Some of them liked it. Some of them wouldn't talk about it. Some of them thought it was stupid.

She raised her eyes to his, but stayed silent.

"You don't ask, but there's plenty of questions in your face," he noted. "Just so you know, I'll be there. I'm a certified climbing instructor, and I get paid extra to do it. There'll be guards, too. And everyone's coming back alive. No matter what."

He stood, and she did likewise. Their time for today was up.

OLD THEORIES PLUS NEW FIELDS

Cali was thoughtful as she walked down annex hall, looking at the brochure. She understood why the girls didn't talk much about Jesse. Different. Yes. He was all that. She was trying to figure out if it would present any danger when she heard the noise.

It started as she crossed the hall between the annex and the dorms, a scream that rose higher and higher, punctuated by voices trying to make it stop. She recognized the voice.

Racer, blowing it.

Cali reacted quickly, running down the hall, turning the corner until she saw the train wreck. There was Racer, on the floor, that sound coming out of her. Betty was there, looking vile and saying things, and Lola and Mindy were nearby looking scared.

Betty pulled out her club and raised it over Racer. Cali was there in a split second, her hand on Betty's wrist, a slapping sound as flesh met flesh.

"That's a mistake," Betty said, a slimy smile on her face.

Cali resisted hitting her. That would get her nowhere. But she felt the burning. Felt the place she went in these moments, so far away from this hall, so different than the memories of beauty she hid in. She swirled into it and it swirled into her and became her. It was bigger than her, but it was all of who she was. It contained time and space and everything that lived within it. She stood at its center and made the thought complete.

"You're dead," she whispered.

And that was all.

As suddenly as she'd left the hall, Cali was back in it, standing there holding Betty's wrist up and away from Racer, who was no longer screaming but staring at her, as were Lola and Mindy.

Before she could drop Betty's arm the hall was full of people—counselors, monitors, a guard. They grabbed hold of her, pulled her away. She didn't resist. Racer stood and started to babble something about falling, about a mistake, trying to make it better. Lola and Mindy tried to disappear and almost succeeded before the monitors told them not to move. All hands were on Cali, even Racer's as she tried to pull Cali away from those who held her.

All she could think of was solitary. Solitary, the small white rooms where you sat and sat in a place of terrible nothing and all those who lived in the room in your mind marked *Do Not Enter* rattled their chains and tried to get at you. In solitary no other voices helped keep theirs at bay and they knew it, came after you, and you had to use everything you could think of to beat them back.

She closed her eyes, taking stock of her inventory, her hiding places. Sun on leaves. Warmth of laughter long ago. Eyes that watched light. And now, a new one—a road that led away, away. Would it be enough to get her through?

Then, she heard a voice.

Open your eyes, it said.

She couldn't identify it. Inside her? Outside her? She did what it asked.

And when she did, she saw blue eyes with flecks of green and gold in oceanic motion, staring at her. Jesse. It was Jesse.

"Let her go," he said, speaking to those who held her.

"Jesse, this is a situation," a monitor said. "We have to—"

"Let her go," he repeated. "We'll straighten it out."

And to her surprise, they released her.

She stared at him. For a moment he stared back. Then he looked at Betty.

"What happened?" he asked.

She opened her mouth to talk, but Racer cut in.

"It's my fault," she said. "I—I fell, and I was scared. I started—I was yelling. And—"

"Quiet now," Jesse said, and something in his voice stopped her words. She stepped back, chewed on her nail. Jesse turned back to Betty. "Tell me," he requested.

"I was walking the halls. Afternoon patrol," Betty said. "I saw this one on the floor. The other girls were standing over her. She was screaming. I thought it was a fight."

"And Cali?"

"She came running around the corner. I reacted. Just a reflex. Then she reacted. Put her hand up, blocking me."

"She didn't attack you, or try to hurt you?"

Betty shook her head. "Cali's okay," she said. "It was just a reflex."

Jesse turned to Cali. "Well?" he asked.

She nodded. "I just put my hand up," she said. "I didn't mean . . ." She shook her head, stayed silent.

She supposed she looked scared. Her face felt cold, as if it had no blood in it. Something was different here. Was it good? She couldn't tell, because it wasn't like anything in her experience here and she had no control over any of it. Betty was lying for her. Jesse was standing up for her, and everyone was paying attention to him. But he was just maintenance. Why did they listen to him?

There was more talk, but she didn't hear the particulars. She looked from Racer, who seemed as puzzled as she was, to Jesse, who was busy with the others. One of the counselors left with Betty. The guard went away and a monitor led Racer and the other girls down the hall. Jesse moved to Cali.

"I'll walk you to your room," he said. "You'll stay there tonight. They'll bring supper to you."

She nodded, moved down the hall after him.

They said nothing until they were in front of the door to her room. Then, as she was about to open it, he spoke.

"Cali," he said.

She turned, looked at him.

"You okay?" he asked.

She frowned, then nodded. Shaky. She was too shaky to answer, but she was okay. For once, her worst nightmare had not come true. But as she looked at him, his eyes seemed to say things she could almost here.

You see, they told her. There's lots of ways to manage things. Lots of ways, and you can learn them.

She didn't know whether to answer this, or not. She didn't know if this was just a different nightmare, about to begin.

"Thank you," she said quietly, and went into her room.

* * * *

When Jesse left St. Ida's that night he was more tired than usual, and had quite a bit to think about concerning his new worker. He was glad to get to his apartment where he could begin to sort it through.

Not that his place was anything special. Living room, kitchen, one bedroom, one bathroom and a spare room where junk gathered with alarming rapidity. But it was one of only three apartments in the building, and the others had older, childless couples so it was quiet, and it was surrounded by overgrown maple trees that obscured the view of factories in the area, and St. Ida's in the distance.

It felt like a haven, a place of solitude and peace. He valued that, especially today when it looked like he was beginning the next leg of the journey that brought him to St. Ida's in the first place. Because of that he wasn't happy when he approached his apartment door and saw a woman standing next to it, even though she was exceptionally attractive. In her early forties, leggy and tall, she carried herself like she meant it, and her sleek honey-colored hair framed a face with alabaster skin and fine features, high cheekbones and cool hazel eyes. But he knew her, and of all the women in the world, Talia Jordan was the last one he wanted to see right now.

"Hello," she said brightly. "I was hoping you wouldn't work late. I didn't relish the thought of waiting here. Where did you find this rat hole?"

"It's an apartment," he said curtly. "Cheap, convenient, and private."

"Why didn't you get something a little more—well, uptown?"

"I like it here," he said. He stepped around her, unlocked his door and went inside.

She followed too quickly for him to shut the door without hurting her. Once she was in, he didn't close it after her. He just stood there.

"How did you find me?" he asked.

She shrugged. "I have my ways."

He knew that. He also knew why she was here, but he asked anyway. "What do you want?"

She tilted her head to one side. "To see you. What else?"

"Something else, so drop the bullshit."

Her brightness went away, cracking against the wall his face had become. "You're unnatural. I always said so. But I won't say anything else until you close the door."

He grimaced, but he did so. She moved to the couch and arranged herself on it, patted a place next to her. "Come sit. We'll talk."

"You won't be staying that long," he replied. "Just tell me what you want this time."

Anger flashed across her face and went away. "Have you found her?" she asked.

"No," he said.

She made small circles on the arm of the couch with her long, fine finger. "I think you wouldn't take a maintenance job there unless it gave you a lead to her."

"I've gotta work, Talia. Times are tough."

"Not that tough. So which one is she?"

He shook his head. "Maybe I'm unnatural, but I'm not stupid. Would I tell you anything at all, after what you did to Mira?"

"Now, dear. That was an accident."

"An accident of your narcissism, and my gullibility. I actually believed you when you said you'd leave her alone."

She stared at him, and he felt her attempt to read him, to pluck information from him. She was good at that, but the last visit had taught him not to let his guard down, not to eat or drink with her, not even to think too much with her around.

That last time he'd had a glass of wine with her, and just that, just one glass of wine, lowered his guard enough to mention Mira, in residence at the rehab in Minnesota where he worked as service staff before St. Ida's. He told her she wasn't the girl they were both seeking, but she didn't believe him. He was interested in her well-being, so she assumed he was lying.

Relentlessly, she went to work on Mira, coming in to the rehab center as a mentor under the auspices of a project grant from Aquarius, her political lobbying and activist group. She gave her services to a program that was hungry for volunteers, for the large donations Aquarius offered, if they liked you.

The girl never had a chance. In less than a month she left rehab, disappearing into the folds of Aquarius. A few months later he heard she'd died of an overdose. He resisted sending Talia a short and bitter note saying I told you it wasn't her.

He left Minnesota, moved to the east coast and took a maintenance job at St. Ida's rather than one in counseling or guidance, hoping that would cover his tracks. But she was nothing if not persistent. Persistent, and gifted with impeccable timing. She showed up today, when he was still thinking about the lines in the hand he'd just seen, and what they signified. He'd make sure she didn't learn anything this time. He didn't repeat fundamental mistakes.

"You know I can get the names of all the girls at St. Ida's easily enough," she said.

"I also know I can leave this job. Go flip burgers somewhere."

"But you wouldn't leave her behind," Talia noted.

"So what does that tell you?" he replied.

She considered, watching his face for any signal of prevarication. He knew she'd see none. After a while, she sniffed. "You think I won't recognize her when I see her?"

"You were wrong last time," he noted.

"I wasn't wrong. I was just . . . exploring possibilities."

"And look where it got you. You have no people skills, Talia. You don't care enough about anyone except yourself to pay attention to others. All you have is a healthy sense of the power play, and that won't help you here."

She pushed her lips into a pout, tried for appealing instead of threatening. "Be reasonable, darling. Aquarius is at a crucial point. We need her."

He deliberately kept his hands still, made sure his body showed no sign of tension, though his heart skipped a beat. "What kind of crucial point?" he asked.

She lifted a hand, let it fall. "Big political changes. Consciousness shifts," she said. "You know perfectly well what I mean."

He did. A shift they'd long been anticipating was occurring. He'd been waiting for it as much as she had, but he couldn't let that show. All the intricate energies put into the world by humans were humming along, playing with and against the human system.

"You don't need me or her for that," he said.

"But you see, I'm worried, about you *and* her. Is she well? Are you well? And I want to rejoice in your happiness when you find her."

"I'll send you an announcement."

"You're saying you haven't found her?"

"Did you get an announcement?"

She eyed him, her glance full of sharp edges that tried to slice away flesh to get at information. He presented a neutral face to her. Nothing was certain yet. She would read that in him.

"Jesse, you can't pretend you're not interested," she said, hanging on to her script.

He laughed. "Interested in what? The Aquarius agenda? I want absolutely nothing to do with Aquarius. Not now and not ever."

"What about her? Would she want nothing to do with us? Regardless of your opinion, Aquarius is doing good work in the world. Creating progressive legislation, controlling corporate interests for the good of the people. She might want to take part in that."

He shrugged. He could grudgingly admit that Aquarius, a group of activist women who worked the political and corporate world with a great deal of unrecognized power, had accomplished some impressive victories for a progressive agenda. They'd gone far to undercut the NRA's lobbying power, and were probably responsible for the renewal of the Glass-Steagall Act, making sure the banking industry couldn't screw its customers the way it would like to. He could also admit his sentiments against Aquarius were personal, though they were based on solid experience, accrued over time. But the last election was a disaster, and the next one might be even more so, and they'd done nothing about that.

"Current President?" he inquired.

She waved it away. "Not enough energy in the group. And that's why I need her. Next election is around the corner, darling. What would she want to see happen?"

Truth, or a trap? Ground or quicksand? Impossible to know, except from what his history with her told him. "I have no idea know what she wants," he said. "I haven't seen her in a long time."

"Then has it occurred to you that Aquarius can protect her better than you could? After all, we're not the only ones looking for her. *He's* still sniffing her out, too."

"Where is he?" Jesse asked, the only pertinent question he had.

"Would I know? He keeps changing identity, using all his cover stories and staying well behind the mirror."

"Then what makes you think he's looking for her?"

She leaned toward him as if sharing a secret. "You know what he's like. He'll never stop trying. If he finds her with you, it's game over. But she'd be safe with Aquarius."

"That's an interesting use of the word safe."

"Since when have you understood her safety?"

Her words were knives, and they hit their mark. Every moment he'd let her down recurred in his memory. And yet, and yet. He did not, could not believe that Talia gave a rat's ass about her well-being. All she cared about was her agenda with Aquarius. Regardless of his past errors, at least he gave a damn.

"Listen," he said, "if I find her, what she does is entirely up to her. I can't control her, nor would I want to. You know that. Right now, all I want is for you to stay away from me—at work and at home."

She twisted her pretty mouth around. "What is it? You want your turn with her first? Want a little fun before we get to business?"

She would read it that way. Let her. It served him. "Sure," he said. "And I think you owe me that much."

"Until when?"

"Until she chooses otherwise."

She pursed her lips, shook her head. "That's too open ended. It gives me all the risk. I prefer more certainty."

"Okay," he said. "It's certain that if I so much as smell your perfume near my home or St. Ida's, I'll stop looking for her, and destroying Aquarius will become my only task." He kept anger and threat from his voice. He didn't need either. She knew what he was capable of.

Her glance rested on him, testing his strength against hers. This was a game of nerves and will. Even if she thought he was close to finding the woman they sought, her first priority would be to keep him from damaging Aquarius. And her arrogance would supercede her fear, making her assume she could still beat him once he found their quarry. So he hoped.

When her mouth relaxed into a smile, he knew he'd hoped correctly. "Have it your way. But when she walks away from you I'm free to do what I want."

"Fine," he said curtly. Not that he believed her. She'd move at her convenience rather than his, for sure. And certainly she'd continue to watch him, keeping her finger on the pulse of his life, but she wouldn't pounce until the mouse was closer to her hand. That would buy him time. He'd have to make good use of it.

He waited. She said nothing more, and didn't move from her spot on the couch.

He opened the door, held it open. "We're done," he said.

"So I see," she said. She uncurled herself from the couch and moved toward him, fluid as mercury. Just at the door she stopped, raised a hand and touched his face.

"You're a handsome man," she said. "I had no idea you'd turn out so handsome. The last time I saw you, you were a boy and now—well, I imagine you'd be quite the treat."

She ran her finger down his face, his neck. He felt a stirring of revulsion deep in his belly. He pulled away from her touch.

"Oh, come on, Jesse. Don't you think it would be interesting? Just to try it?"

"I think," he said carefully, "I'd rather be eaten slowly by fire ants."

Again that anger, there and gone. She winked at him. "Careful what you wish for."

She breezed out of his apartment and he closed the door behind her, stayed with his back pressed against it.

Tomorrow he'd find a new place to live. He'd leave no forwarding address. Of course, she could find him at St. Ida's, but if she did he'd know the war was on, and he'd proceed accordingly.

SCHROEDINGER'S CAT

At night, St. Ida's was generally silent as a tomb. Occasionally a girl would get hysterical with memories she couldn't contain, her weeping like the call of strange night birds. Those within range would stuff pillows over their heads to block it out. But that was rare. The girls of St. Ida's were schooled in silence.

Tonight no one was crying. It was late spring, and they were allowed to keep their windows cracked open to let the warm night air waft in through the bars on the other side. From far away they could hear the sound of spring peepers. There was swampland on the east end of the grounds, though the girls didn't get to go exploring that far. Still, it was a sound that was comforting in its normalcy. They were part of the world, even here.

Cali lay in her bed reading over the story of the goddess Isis for her World Mythology AP class, her reading light illuminating words that bounced around the events of the day. She read how Isis created a snake to bite her oppressor, the great god Ra, and how she resurrected her dead lover, re-membered him. For a moment, she felt own hand curled around Betty's wrist, but as if they stood under the burning desert sun. Her anger and resentment at the power of others burned with the sun, and she saw the oceanic eyes of a man who helped her.

Too much, she decided. Too much bullshit for one day. She closed the book, turned off her reading light and rolled over, waiting for sleep to find her.

In the bed across the room she heard Racer punch at her pillow, make a noise of frustration. Cali knew what came next, and it did.

"Cali?" Racer asked. "You sleeping?"

She debated feigning sleep and decided against it. She was nowhere near tired. Too much was shaken loose today, and dreams might not be the best place to go. "I'm awake," she said.

"I can't sleep either," Racer said. "Hey—thanks for what you did today. That was cool."

"Like they said. Just a reflex. Was she bothering you again?"

"Whispering shit in my ear. That's all." A pause. Not much else to say about Betty. "You hear those peepers? I always liked that sound."

"Me, too."

Cali felt the warm air on her, the scent of it reminding her of catching frogs with her father when he still lived with them in their house in suburbia, when she went to school with friends, and her mother seemed happy. Her father was a scientist, something important in research, and he was always teaching her about the environment, or the stars, or stones or trees. Always teaching her something.

She had loved him, she supposed. At least, she loved the sense of warmth and safety he provided, even if it was brief and illusory. He was tall and broad and dark, and she looked more like him than her mother, though he said she looked most like his mother. His father was a lean no-nonsense British man, but his mother was a soft and round woman born in Nepal, whose lilting accent sounded like singing to Cali. Daadi, Cali called her, and her lessons remained.

When Cali was ten, Daadi took her hand and showed her the lines in her palm. "The women in our family have been reading these lines for thousands of generations, and you are next to do so. You won't understand until you're old, but you will begin learning now. So here, look at this," she said, pointing to a line etched in skin that went up the middle of her hand and disappeared between index and third finger. Cali stared at it, but it meant nothing to her.

"It's the line of true greatness. I've never seen one so strong in any hand."

"Maybe I'll be a movie star?" she asked, which was the limits of her understanding of power at that age.

"No. It means you'll have to give back. A lot."

She wasn't sure she liked that, or even understood it. But to this day she occasionally looked at that line and thought of her Daadi, who died when she was twelve. Now she thought of Jesse, wondering what he saw written there.

"Cali?" Racer asked.

"Yeah?"

"What's the first thing you remember?"

"What?"

"You know. How far back can you remember? Like, when you were little."

Cali propped herself up on her pillows. "Where do you come up with this shit?" she asked.

Racer was always asking odd questions. What was your favorite TV show when you were a kid? Your favorite game? If you could have any kind of food in the world, what would it be? If you were going to win an Oscar, what movie would it be for?

Lola said she was crazy, but she laughed and answered her questions. They were all crazy, Cali supposed, but Racer was crazy in her own way. She had a long history of fights, small arrests for shoplifting, possession of marijuana, trouble in school. Though she was here for the arson at the school, she told Cali they wanted to get her for murder and couldn't hang it on her. As the school authorities dragged her away from the fire in the restroom, she screamed about burning it all down. That day, perhaps just at that moment, there was an explosion in the basement of her home, which killed her grandfather and her parents. The arson squad tried to hang it on her, but there was no physical evidence. Probably a furnace malfunction. Nothing else they could find.

Racer got out of it, as she got out of many things. The shape of her face, her wide blue eyes, her fair skin, always spoke of innocence beyond reason. And beyond any visual illusion, her whole being projected innocence, because she was innocent in some fundamental way. Her internal speed ran twenty-four and seven, so that even in her sleep she twitched and tossed, but she still believed in possibilities, in happy places, happy times, happy endings.

She always thought something good was coming her way, and Cali supposed that was her main problem because when the bad things came instead she'd explode, unable to let go of her own belief. But she continued to believe so hard you just had to protect her, protect her belief. Doing so was protecting your own belief, keeping your own soul alive.

"Come on, Cali. What was it?" she asked again.

Cali thought a minute, opened the door to her own store of visions, and let one out. "Steam. Steam, and warmth," she replied. "Being dried off after a bath."

That was from the time before the divorce and the ratty apartments, before her mother starting getting pills from her doctor to relieve her stress, before her boyfriends. Cali must have been no older than four or five, but she remembered her mother lifting her from the bath, wrapping her in warm towels. Steam rose from her skin, and she was enfolded in a soft towel and safety.

In those days her mother had been a warm and careful person. As a junkie she became cold and sloppy. Makeup smeared, hair uncombed, abs sinking into a small potbelly.

"All junkies are the same person," Keith told her. He was right.

But she'd had those years before, illusions she'd learned to believe in too young to give them up entirely. They were in her cells. They came back to haunt her with dreams of steam and warm towels. Maybe she wasn't that different from Racer after all.

"Was it nice?" Racer asked.

"Yeah," Cali replied.

They were silent, and Cali felt that Racer was absorbing this memory, chewing and swallowing it and making it her own. She didn't mind. They all had their own way of getting through.

"What's yours?" Cali asked after a while.

"It's my grandfather," she said. "I'm sitting on his lap, and he's saying I'm his little angel, and he loves me so much he'll squeeze me flat like a pancake."

She laughed, and Cali could see her hands making motions in the air, gestures that described her state of mind rather than the event she was talking about. She was off on something here. Cali could tell by the energy swirling around her, out of her.

"He lived with us when he got too old to live alone," Racer continued. "We had this cool back yard, and I'd make these little houses for fairies out of sticks and leaves, and I'd put food in, for the fairies to come and stay, right? I wanted fairies around. And he'd sit in this chair in the yard and call me over and I'd sit on his lap."

"Yeah?" Cali asked.

"Yeah. Then he'd put his hands up my shirt, down my pants. And then . . ."

Racer's hands made more gestures. Cali was silent. She could imagine the rest.

"He's dead," Racer continued. "Died in the fire, with my parents."

"Yeah," Cali said. "I know." Just a freak thing that left Racer an orphan. "I'm glad he's dead. If he wasn't I might have to kill him."

"Thanks," Racer said, matter of fact, no emotion involved. That's how they held each other up. Then, quickly, before memory got the better of her, she changed the subject. Another habit of the girls here. "Hey—do you believe in God? Because I was thinking maybe there is one, and he's just like they say, kind of always waiting to get us."

"I think that's Satan," Cali said. "At least, that's what they said in Sunday school. Or maybe I got it mixed up."

"Yeah, but what do you think about God? Because I asked him to get rid of my grandfather, and then, well, the fire thing happened."

Magical thinking, Cali thought. "Did you ask him to get rid of your parents, too?" she asked.

"No. But I was pissed at them, too. For letting him."

Cali thought about it. "If there is a God, he should've killed your grandfather sooner."

"Yeah," Racer said. "You're probably right."

After that they were silent, drifting on the streams of their own thoughts.

Cali was visited by vague memories of Sunday mornings spent in the basement of a church, learning Bible stories. There was a garden, and a woman who was friends with a snake, which apparently was a bad idea. Personally, she liked snakes, so she didn't get it.

Her scientist father didn't go to church, but her mother, raised by a drunken Catholic father and a non-observant Jewish mother, insisted she have some kind of religious schooling. As a result, she was a spiritual mutt, who loved science.

Floating on random connections, Cali moved from religion to science to her father. Before he left them they lived in a nice suburban home, with nice suburban neighbors who cared about their lawns. The woman across the street from them, whom Cali remembered as a flat, broad shape with grey hair, had three cats she worried about obsessively. She let them out once a day, for an hour, and then went up and down the street calling them until they came home. "Harry, Bouncy, Beauford," she would call, "Harry, Bouncy, Beauford." Over and over again she'd call, making Cali and her mother laugh. The woman's voice was strident, fearful.

One day a stray tomcat came to visit, and since Cali's mother gave it food, it stayed in the neighborhood. He was black and white, a long haired cat who liked to stretch out on the tar of their driveway with his belly exposed and his paws curled at his chest. Cali rubbed behind his ears, and that made him purr. Her father called him Schroedinger, and when Cali asked why he told her about that experiment.

"Put a cat in a steel chamber, with a tube of poison and a little radioactive material. If even a single atom of the substance decays, a relay mechanism will trip a hammer, which breaks the vial and kills the cat. Now, without looking we can't know whether the tube is broken, or if the cat is dead. Since we can't know, the cat is both dead and alive—in what's called a superposition of states. That's quantum indeterminacy. What do you think of that?"

Cali dug a toe in the ground and moved it around. "I think it's wrong to keep a cat in a box," she replied, and he laughed.

One day the woman across the street came over to tell them she'd gotten a trap, caught Schroedinger, and released him in a field about 20 miles away. Cali felt bad for him, and hoped he'd find someone else to rub his ears and feed him.

To her surprise, a few days later he was back at their house, lounging in the driveway. Cali and her mother greeted him, fed him, rubbed his ears, and watched him stalk off. They never saw him again.

Later that day they learned that the woman across the street was in the hospital. Schroedinger had laid in wait under her back steps and attacked her when she left the house. She had eighteen stitches in her leg, and twelve in her arm.

Cali found she was more satisfied about Schroedinger's release than sorry about the woman's injuries. Part of her wondered if that was wrong of her, but it was the smaller part. Now, she wondered if that was one reason she was here, at St. Ida's.

"You're going on that field trip next week, aren't you?" Racer asked, interrupting her thoughts.

"Yeah," Cali said, barely awake now, drifting within thoughts of cats who got free.

"I hear it's pretty bad. No bathrooms. Sleeping on the ground. They make you work like hell. That girl over in the west hall—Sequana? She got a bad case of poison ivy."

"I'll be careful," Cali said.

"You usually are," Racer said. "Wish I could learn that."

"Stick around," Cali said. "I'll teach you everything I know."

"Like I have a choice," Racer noted. She yawned deeply, and as quickly as she did everything else, she rolled over and slept.

Cali, cautious even in her approach to sleep, lay awake for some time, thinking of Schroedinger, and what it took to get out of boxes other people put you in, for their own purposes.

That thought, and the random reading of ancient mythology, would invest her dreams with a distant past she was not yet ready to own.

QUANTUM 1: ISIS

IN HER DREAM, CALI WALKED THE EARTH AS ISIS, A WOMAN WHO HELD GREAT POWER IN HER HANDS. BUT ALL HER POWER WASN'T ENOUGH TO KEEP THE GREAT ONE FROM TORMENTING HER. WHEN HE SPIT AT HER SHE FINALLY DECIDED SHE HAD TO DO SOMETHING ABOUT HIM.

For a long time she'd been tired of his commands, of his threats, of his alternate bragging and whining, of the way he scorched the earth just to prove his own strength. He called himself ruler of all, but his powers were no greater than hers. Both of them could move their thoughts into matter. Her companion, the only lover she'd ever wanted, could do the same. The Great One had only one gift beyond hers, and he never used it.

But he used all his other gifts to make the people worship him, to make them see him as a god, because they lacked his particular skills. For her part, she thought they could learn to do what they did, if they were properly taught. She and her companion wanted to help them learn, wanted only to bring greater joy to the land they lived in.

The Great One felt otherwise, and routinely expressed his contempt for her goals. The morning that he returned her greeting by spitting at her she knew his contempt was complete. She'd have to act or he would ruin her, perhaps ruin them all.

She was a woman of great power and great beauty. Lady of magic, Star of the Sea, she who gives justice to the poor, strength to the weak—these were just some of the names the people used for her. If he spit at her, what would he do to those of lesser strength?

Already he'd burned their crops, dried their fields and their mouths, blinding their eyes when they didn't worship him as he wanted. But she would not bow down to him. He was a fool if he thought she would. She knew exactly what action to take.

She bent and put her hand on the place where his spit had fallen. She rolled it into the sandy earth with her hands. She was alone, so nobody heard the sob pulled out of her, or saw the tear that fell into the soil, spit and salt water mingling. She kept rolling it, over and over, her thoughts completing a creature that was new.

It was long, and it moved along the ground without legs, as if by magic. It could curl into itself, devour itself from tail to head, or it could point itself straight as a spear and reach the target it chose, its teeth two points of poisoned intent. It sniffed at the air with its tongue, and its eyes were hooded.

"Snake," she whispered to it, "As I give you life, be my friend, and I will be yours for all of time. Death and antidote to death are contained in you. We will use both."

It wriggled into life, and curled itself at her feet, beautiful as she was. They would travel together for all of time.

The Great One, perhaps suspecting he'd gone too far with her, quickly went even farther. The next day, he sent his servant to murder her lover, her companion, scattering his dismembered remains across the land. When she confronted him, he said it wasn't his doing. His servant had done it. She would have to deal with him.

Her tears were enough to make the river rise, drowning even the Great One's fire. But she could not linger in grief. She went to her sister, who would help her find her lover's dismembered body, help her re-member him. And she sent her newest friend, the snake, to the Great One.

"Bite him," she instructed. "Show him your strength."

So, as he walked about, giving his morning greetings, she watched in secret while the snake's fangs pierced his skin, making his blood burn in his veins.

Immediately he fell down in the road, crying out, "I am colder than water, hotter than fire. Who will help me?"

She moved out of hiding, went to him and bent to where he lay in the dirt, lower than any creature, writhing in pain. "What has happened?" she asked, calm and quiet.

"I am poisoned," he gasped. "Take this from my body, heal me, most gracious one."

Part of her burned with rage. He'd laughed at her ability to heal, and now he wanted it. She could so easily refuse, leaving him in pain. But she had work to do. She would complete this thought.

"I will," she said. "But first, you must tell me your name."

He lifted his head, and she saw the flame of pride in his eyes. "I am sacred, a Great One. I have multitudes of names and multitudes of forms. I make the river rise and the sun burn. I cause the trembling of the earth and the thunder in the heavens. I have dominion over all."

"And none of that is your name," she pointed out. "Nor will dominion or destruction heal you. If you would be free of your pain, you must tell me who you are."

He writhed against the necessity. His name was hidden deep within him, so it could not be stolen. But he felt as if his flesh was pierced by a thousand knives, and he knew she was right. His skills held no sway here, and he could not endure the agony of this poison in his flesh. He would die of it, if it continued. Oh, he would return in new form, but by then, the people might already be following her softer charms.

"I consent that you will search into me, and my name shall pass from me, into you," he said.

He commanded that his boat take them both to a far place, and there his ancient name moved into her. Within it she perceived all his skills: His power to rule, his power to bend the will of others to his. She wanted none of that. But there was one skill he had, one he disregarded as useless, which she plucked from him, and kept as her own: The skill of resurrection. The gift of life. With this, she raised her murdered lover from the arms of death.

She healed him as she'd promised, but from then on into forever, the skill she'd found within his name was hers.

The Great One no longer spit at her, but he would not forgive, nor would he ever forget that he'd needed her for his life. Forever he would think of her with rage. Forever he would track her, attempting to get back the power he'd never wanted, and never used, the one power he wanted to get back.

* * * *

When Cali woke in the middle of the night, she felt the cold wash of scattered images, a residue of fear and triumph. She listened to the song of the night, turned over, and tried for less formidable dreams.

BODIES IN MOTION

Cali was silent in the St. Ida's van that took her and three other girls, Jesse, and two guards, out of the facility on Friday. While the girls chattered and giggled, vying for Jesse's attention, blips of her dream recurred to her. Snakes, and the burning power of determination to destroy and to save. To save and destroy. Much bigger than anything she wanted to feel.

And Jesse was in there somewhere, in the background, a feeling rather than a presence. She didn't try to analyze it or ascribe it any meaning. She chalked it up to her reading, and the unexpected events of the day. But that didn't dull the emotional impact, didn't dispel the rage and resentment that lingered for no reason she could name, a dream hangover she couldn't quite get rid of.

"Hey," Jesse said to her after a while. "You're quiet. You okay?"

She shook off her thoughts, showed him the face she thought he wanted to see. "Fine," she said. "Looking forward to it."

He eyed her, but said nothing, and the van rolled on.

Their first stop was an indoor rock climbing gym, where they spent the day learning the basics. They belayed each other from top rope and from the bottom. They did lead climbs, watched climbing safety films, learned how to place protection, learned what it felt like to fall and be caught. It was all good, hard physical work, forcing them to focus only on the task at hand. By the time they left, the other girls were too tired too giggle.

From there, the van took them to Deer Mountain, where they met guides from a program called *Up and Out*, along with three girls from another facility and more wardens. The guides seemed nice enough. There was a young woman with mousy hair and finely muscled triceps named Kathy, two vaguely nice-looking young men who introduced themselves as Todd and Guy.

Though Cali wasn't particularly friends with the girls who were on the trip, she didn't know anything bad about them. She didn't much care for the girls from the other facility, a minimum security place north of St. Ida's. They flirted with the guides as if it would get them somewhere, and they kept trying to make friends, especially a girl named Darlene with dark spikey hair and tattoos.

But Cali didn't have to deal with them because the guides kept them busy. They spent the morning hiking, with lots of bugs eating at them and lots of instruction about what to do if they got lost. "Don't bother looking for berries," Guy told them. "You'll use more calories picking than you'll get from eating them. What you *should* do is eat bugs." He dug a fat grub from the grass and held it up. "Anybody hungry?" he asked.

He moved closer to Cali, who worked hard not to glare at him. She liked Kathy and Todd well enough. They told her what needed doing and paid attention to the hike. But she immediately distrusted Guy, who talked too much about staying positive and wore a smile she thought was fake.

"No, thank you," she said politely.

"You sure? Don't even want to try?"

She saw Jesse standing behind Guy, looking at her. He shook his head minimally. Permission to refuse this. "Nope," she said. "But maybe Darlene does."

The girls in Darlene's group giggled and made faces.

The first hike wasn't difficult. She breezed through it, and through two team building exercises where they had to figure out how to get through an intricate obstacle course faster than the other team. Cali had Darlene on her team, and had to make sure she was listening. She could see Jesse watching her as she brought Darlene back to attention, nodding at her as he did. Good, she thought. He'd write her a nice report.

Then they made camp, burning hot dogs and opening cans of tuna which they ate ravenously. It wasn't good food, but it tasted great because they were hungry. After dinner the guides led discussions around a campfire. Kathy and Todd took turns asking about their fears, and answering questions about what was next. Guy gave a speech, saying their response to any fear or problem was about who they were, rather than what happened to them.

Cali scowled. That kind of talk made her crazy. Only people who never had anything bad happen said that kind of shit. Guy saw her scowl and turned his attention her way.

"You got something to say?" he asked.

"Nope," she said.

"You're holding back," he said. "Go on. Say what's on your mind."

She sighed, pointed to Jesse, who sat across the fire, his face lit in orange and gold. "See that guy? I work for him at St. Ida's. He gets to write a report about me when the weekend's over. And if my reports aren't good, I go to Bedford."

Jesse's face stayed quiet, not expressing much.

"You think not telling the truth gets you a better report?" Guy asked.

"Where I come from, usually it does."

"That's not how it is in the world," Guy said.

"I guess you don't read the news," Cali noted.

Kathy laughed a little nervously. The other girls went tense, expectant of trouble.

"Go ahead and say what you think," Jesse told her quietly. "All I report on is how good you rake gravel."

Cali looked at him, looked at Guy. "What's the worst thing that ever happened to you?"

Guy told a story about a friend of his who was killed in a car accident when he was in high school.

Cali nodded. "The other night a friend of mine told me about her grandfather having sex with her. When she was four. Now her family's all dead, and she's in St. Ida's."

The group was quiet. Cali figured there were a couple of other girls there who understood Racer's experience.

"This isn't a competition for who has the most pain," Guy said, sounding more angry than empathetic.

"I know. I'm just saying. Giving you an idea of our reality. It's different than yours."

Guy worked his face around to sympathy. "So tell me your reality," he said.

Something about his sympathy reminded her of the slime on top of stagnant ponds. "It's in my files," she said curtly. "I'm a drug dealer who's impervious to therapy."

"There's more, isn't there? Why don't you say?"

"Because I don't know you well enough, and I'm learning to preserve my boundaries in appropriate ways."

On the other side of the fire, she heard Jesse make a sound that might have started as a chuckle, but quickly became a cough.

"I think that's a positive thing," Guy said.

Cali gave him a tight-lipped smile, and mostly he left her alone after that.

* * * *

The next morning they hiked to the areas where they'd be climbing, a harder hike than yesterday, and Cali was glad to work rather than talk. When they got to the cliff they'd be scaling, some of the girls were nervous, but she eyed it with approval. A rock wall didn't ask pointless questions or make stupid comments or have hidden agendas. It was just there, and you had to get up it, which was all about physics, flexibility and focus. Those were her strong points.

They started with a top rope climb, the guides and wardens acting as belayers. Cali was paired with Jesse, which gave her some confidence.

"I'll have you," he assured her. "You just focus on the climb."

She did so, knowing that if the anchor was suddenly split by lightning, he'd still hang on. The climb was just difficult enough to engage her, but not so difficult that she was frightened. She was only a little ways up when Jesse looked down from the height above her, cupped his hands at his mouth, and yelled down to her.

"Can you hear me okay?"

"Yeah. What's wrong?"

"Nothing. I just want you to try letting go."

She looked up at him. Looked down. She was more than fifteen feet up, with good hand holds, feet solid under her.

"Why would I do that?" she asked.

"Check the belayer. Check the rope. Learn to trust it. You won't pendulum here, so it's a good spot."

She shook her head. Jesse called down again. "I have it," he said, and his voice sounded quiet, as if he was speaking softly, standing next to her. "Let go."

She raised one foot. The other foot. Nothing happened.

"Cali, you have to let go," he said.

"Oh. Right."

She took a breath and let it happen, felt the slack taken up, felt herself rise slightly. She counted to three, then found the mountain and grabbed it, found her footholds and put her feet on them. "That's me," she called up.

Jesse's face appeared, looking down at her. "Good job," he called back.

And she continued her climb to the top.

"Well, then," Jesse greeted her when she clamored over the edge to stand on flat ground. "You made it. First one up."

"It's not Everest," she noted.

"Something to be thankful for," he replied.

"Yeah. So now what? We camp here tonight?"

"Nope," he said. "You're going back down. Remember rappelling?"

She nodded. She did.

"You're after Darlene and Jody. Let's check the ropes."

The other girls weren't easy to get over the edge. Darlene whimpered and had to be talked over. Jody lingered at the edge for a long time. Cali, impatient to be done with it, had to wait while they were convinced. Jesse worked with the guides to help out, and she wondered that it took so long when he'd so easily convinced Betty to let her off the hook. If he could do that, surely he could talk two crazy girls into jumping off a cliff.

Finally, they started their descent and it was already late afternoon and Cali was hungry, edgy and irritated. Jesse approached her, checked her equipment, did things to the ropes.

"You scared?" he asked her.

"Try me," she said.

He tossed a nod toward the edge. "Go ahead."

She moved to the edge and leaned back over the side. A strange feeling, to willingly fall backwards off the edge of a cliff, but once you did that, it was much easier than climbing up. And she thought the worst that could happen was that the rope would break and she'd fall and die. She imagined it wouldn't hurt much, and the trip down would be interesting. With one deep breath, she went over the edge and started down.

Looking up she saw Jesse looking down at her.

"You don't care much about living, do you?" he asked.

"Depends on the terms," she replied.

"What terms work for you?"

She was about to answer, but her impatience, her hunger, got the better of her. "Listen, I get it. This is all about trust and finding yourself and that shit, so don't hammer me with it," she said. "It distracts me, and I'm busy."

He laughed, and waved her on.

The rest was just like walking, if you could imagine yourself turned 90 degrees and figure out why you were going backwards. The stone, warmed by the sun, felt good under her. She was aware of strength in her arms and legs.

Another night of eating food with the taste of air and fire in it, another campfire to sit around, with Guy asking how they felt, what they'd learned about themselves.

Darlene batted big eyes at him. "I learned I'm not as bad and brave as I thought."

Guy puffed up so much at this that Cali had to bite her lip to keep from laughing. Instead, she yawned. She was tired, really tired, in the best possible kind of way.

* * * *

The next morning they did an easy climb, but with no top rope. Instead, they took turns being leader and belayer, and this time Cali was paired with Darlene.

"Goddammit," she said softly when she found out.

"What was that?" Guy asked.

"I said I'd rather not," she amended.

"Why is that?"

"Because I don't trust her to hold my rope," Cali said, jerking a thumb at Darlene.

"Trust is always a big issue, isn't it?" He said solemnly.

"When someone's holding you on the side of a cliff it is," she said.

"What will you do about it?" Guy asked.

Cali thought of a number of interesting responses, and deferred all of them. "I won't fall," she said.

On her way up, she noticed that Jesse stayed pretty close to Darlene and she was glad, though the climb was so easy she didn't even come close to slipping. They were allowed to hike down a path rather than lower off, so it wasn't as bad as she thought it might be.

On her turn to belay Darlene, she had her work cut out for her. Darlene needed talking through the climb, Cali telling her the best route she'd found, how to get her foot up onto a hold, where to move her hand next. She came off the mountain twice, without ever yelling the 'falling' command, but Cali caught her both times with no injury. Still, she was more exhausted by this than by climbing herself. It took exquisite attention the whole time, and Darlene did not climb fast. She was glad when they were told they wouldn't climb anymore that day, and instead were led on a short hike to a lake, where they gratefully changed into shorts and hit the water.

It was a hot day, and the water was cool and clear and good. Cali floated on her back, staring up at the sky and listening to the voices of the other girls, distant and muted when heard through the medium of water. The St. Ida's girls splashed close to shore, while Darlene and her group lay on the sand with their faces to the sun, working on tans. Guards stood watching, and the guides swam or watched in turns. She saw Jesse swim out past her, his slow and easy strokes taking him to the middle of the lake while she continued to float.

Then she began moving her arms in an easy backstroke, not thinking of where she was going until she realized she was pointed in his direction. Not to see him, she thought. Not at all. Just to swim out to the clear space, the quiet space.

She hadn't gotten very far when someone started blowing a whistle and she heard her name called shrilly. She flipped her legs under her and tread water, looking toward shore. A guide waved wildly at her. She looked around. Was someone drowning? She stayed treading water, until she heard Jesse's voice behind her.

"You can't go out this far," he said. "Makes the zoo keepers nervous."

She turned in the water and looked at him. He was also treading water. His hair was slick, and his eyes reflected the green of the lake. They were darker in this environment.

"Oh," she said. "Sorry."

"No problem," he said. He raised a hand and waved to the guide, who waved back and turned away.

"I guess I better go in," she said, and rolled onto her back, began to swim.

He came up along side her. "You did a good job belaying," he said.

"Thanks," she replied.

"How'd you know when Darlene would fall?"

"I told you before," she said. "I notice things."

"Good habit," he said, "but you should realize it's not usual."

"It is for me."

"Then you should realize you're not usual," he said.

She couldn't think of an appropriate response. It felt like praise, and something in her tensed against it. Praise meant somebody wanted something, usually. But then it occurred to her that maybe Jesse wasn't usual either.

They swam the rest of the way in silence, and when they got to shore it was time to change and get to their campgrounds for the night.

Talk that evening centered on the climb, more of the 'what did you learn' question and answer session. Cali stayed silent through most of it. The air, the sun, the activity, left her langorous and content as a cat. She heard Guy say something about the next day's climb, but she wasn't worried. She seemed to see the mountain they'd be facing, the route of her climb as clear in her mind as if she'd already done it.

GEOLOGY OF TIME AND INTENT

In the morning, they hiked to the next climb and she saw it rising before her, the same as she'd seen it in her mind the night before. The cliff's craggy grey face rose taller than anything they'd tried so far, small ledges jutting out here and there from its vertical surface. It was a harder grade, but not hard enough to scare her. They'd need to put in protection, but they'd been taught how to do that. Again they'd be working in teams. This time one had to lead, and another to follow.

"Not with Darlene," she said clearly and firmly.

Guy had been talking. He stopped at the interruption and looked to her. "That's rude," he said.

"It's a matter of valuing my own hide over politeness," she said.

He looked away from her and started over. "As I was saying, if you really lack confidence, you can do it on top rope. There's a few different routes up this face, so you don't have to wait too long unless two of you want the same route. And you'll be paired with one of the experienced climbers. If you're not top-roping and you want to try lead climb, you'll do the first pitch."

Cali turned away from Guy, looked to Jesse. He nodded. She would team with him. Her relief was immense.

They each spent some time with their partner discussing the route, the kinds of protection to use if they were leading, how much of it they'd need. She and Jesse worked through it fairly quickly because it all seemed so clear to her.

"You sure you want to lead climb?" he asked her as she was getting tied in.

"I'm sure," she said.

"Okay, but I have to use what you put in, so make it good."

"I will. And—uh—don't drop me."

"What did I tell you before we got here? Everyone comes home alive."

She grinned, and started her climb.

* * * *

She made her way up slowly, found handholds, footholds, found she didn't get dizzy looking either down or up, found she was enjoying this task, which had discrete requirements, specific problems with specific solutions. If a hold was too far, she had to stretch further. If her foot slipped, she'd fall. On the side of a cliff, everything made sense.

Jesse talked her through a few tough spots, and she had every reason to believe she'd make it to the first pitch with no problem. Then she could rest before she belayed him up to lead the second pitch. Tomorrow they'd go back to St. Ida's, and her report would be all good.

The only thing that bothered her was Darlene, on a route to her left, top roping it and making a lot of noise, occasionally stopping and crying, "I can't, I can't." If she fell off, she might interfere with everyone else's route, including her own.

Kathy, belaying her from above, kept reassuring her she was safe, which Cali thought was a bad tactic. What's safe when you're clinging to the side of a mountain? She ignored it, and went on her own way.

Then, about halfway up, she found she was stuck.

She couldn't find a handhold she could reach or a foothold to lift to. Nowhere to go at all that she could tell.

"Shit," she muttered.

"Problem?" Jesse called up.

She looked down at him. "Dead end. I can't reach anything."

"Lower off?" he asked.

"No," she said sharply.

"Okay. Traverse right."

She searched out some holds, found none. "Nothing," she called down.

"Ready to come down?" he asked.

"Go to hell," she replied before she could stop herself. She looked down, saw his face below her, surprised, but grinning.

"Try left," he suggested.

She searched that way for a while, found only dead ends, and then couldn't think anymore of patterns and footholds and handholds. Her right arm began to shake and she willed it to stillness as she clutched the sheer side of the cliff. Nearby, she heard Darlene crying, Kathy calling to her.

She wouldn't cry. Wouldn't give them that satisfaction.

"What do you want to do?" Jesse called up to her.

"I'll keep going," she said, and pushed herself toward something that looked like a foothold. It wasn't and she slipped, felt her rope go taut.

"That's me," she called down.

"Yeah. Listen," Jesse said. "Are you listening?"

She stared at the mountain, at the particular weaving of minerals in the stone that faced her as she faced it. She thought of geology class, but couldn't remember how to name the stone she was relying on. She saw Darlene clutching at a small hold, above her and to her left, still crying.

"Cali, are you listening?" Jesse repeated.

"I'm listening," she said, hearing how shrill her voice was.

"That's better," he said calmly enough. "Go back to your right about ten feet."

"Why?"

"Because I can see things you can't."

She cursed to herself, and did so. "I'm there. Now what?"

"Put a cam in."

"Why?" she demanded.

"Because you're going up from here."

"Where?"

"Put the cam in first."

She did so, taking her time with it. "Done. What's next?"

"There's a hold above you. You can't see it, so you'll have to feel around. It's a stretch, but you can grab it and get your leg up and push up from there. That is, if you want to keep going."

A certain understanding dawned and she turned to look down at Jesse. "You knew that," she said. "You knew I'd have to do this when I started."

"Yes," he agreed.

"Why didn't you tell me before?"

"It's part of the program. See how you'll handle it."

"You didn't think I'd figure that out?"

"Most people don't."

She turned to stare at the rock face in front of her and thought it through. "But if you help me, I didn't do it myself," she said.

"What?" he asked, sounding surprised.

"I won't be doing it on my own."

He laughed softly. She heard him as if he was standing next to her, or standing inside her head. "You never were," he said.

Then she was furious. What the fuck did that mean? Who the hell helped her, ever? Keith? Her mother? Anybody?

She turned her face down to him again. "Fuck you," she said. "If I have to grab a mountain blind to avoid Bedfrod, then I'll fucking do it, but don't give me any horseshit meaning. There isn't any."

He was quiet for a moment. When he spoke, he didn't sound angry. "You sure, Cali?" was all he asked.

"I know bullshit when I smell it."

"I meant about doing it."

"Yeah. That. I'm sure."

"Make your move."

She leaned into the mountain, thinking about what she had to do. There was more noise above her, and she wondered about it, but didn't ask.

"Cali," Jesse called. "You have to let go."

"What?"

"You have to let go of where you are. Otherwise, you can't go up."

She looked at her hands, saw they still clung to stone. She had to let go. Easy enough. She'd dropped over the side without fear. Let go when he told her to before. In spite of that, she continued to cling to where she was, animal instinct telling her not to let go, never let go.

"Let go and reach, Cali," Jesse called. Or maybe whispered. Was he next to her, or below her? She wasn't sure she was thinking clearly anymore. Something strange was happening in her brain, and it made everything sharper, more clear, but less real. Like the dream she had about Isis and her snake. Above her Darlene was still crying, and there was more yelling.

Let go, she told her hands. They wouldn't listen.

"Like this," Jesse said, and she felt his hand on hers, guiding it, swallowing her skin in its strong, cool fold.

Then she was reaching, groping with her fingers, her stomach lurching because she couldn't see. But she could feel and she got her feet to press her up and her arms to work and sure enough there was the handhold, and her leg worked itself up and found its spot and then she was going up again. Going up.

Not too much further, because there was a cleft above her and she'd stop there. It was the first pitch, where Jesse would come up and lead the rest of the way. She focused on the mountain, the stone she was dealing with.

Nearby, somebody screamed like they meant it.

It was piercing, a serious scream, not flirtatiously afraid. She looked up, to her left, and saw Darlene, hanging over the side of a ledge, flailing and then, suddenly, limp and still. She hung in her harness like a rag doll.

There were voices yelling. Guy? Kathy? People yelling, but Cali couldn't hear what they were saying. Then, Jesse's voice, speaking quietly, as if he stood next to her.

"Darlene's in trouble," he said matter-of-factly.

"What she's doing is dangerous," Cali noted, just as calm. "They talked about it at the rock wall. Hanging like that can kill you."

"I know," Jesse said. "But I don't think she can help it. I think she passed out."

"Oh," Cali said. "Well, Kathy can pull her up, right?"

"She can't. There's a ledge between them. Can you do anything about it?" he asked.

She considered. "I'm not sure I want to," she said. "I don't like her much."

"If you don't, she'll die."

Cali sighed. "Okay. I can traverse to her. Haul her sorry ass up the ledge."

"You think so?"

"Yeah. She's small."

"Then you better. Make sure you're protected, okay?"

With impatience, with bad grace, cursing under her breath, Cali moved left. Her moves were efficient, swift and safe, and she was soon on the side of the ledge and just under it, where Darlene hung suspended in air. She heard frantic people talking all around her, but their voices were distant, muted, as if she was in water.

An unknown source seemed to tell her what to do next. Put in protection. Are you secure? Good. Hook your foot up on the ledge. Like that. Good, Cali. Now get your hands under her arms and pull her up. She's small and light. You can do it.

Darlene, feeling the pressure, gasped. Her entire body went tense. She looked up and clutched at Cali's arm, pulling her down in a vise-like grasp.

"Shit," Cali said. "Let go. Don't. I've got you." Darlene whimpered and struggled. "Darlene, it's me. Cali. Look at me. I got you."

Darlene suddenly stopped struggling and stared at Cali. Her eyes were a whirlpool of fear. Cali was dragged down into it, and her own head began to spin.

As if she dreamt, she saw Darlene in a one room apartment. She was pregnant, and sticking a needle in her arm. Then, a flash of a hospital, and a baby screaming, and the baby full of pain Cali felt as if it was her own. She knew everything that would happen in those two flashes. Darlene would serve her sentence, go back to the streets, the drugs, the guys. She'd get pregnant and have this baby who would bear the burden of his mother's choices, bear them in pain.

Cali wanted to let her go, let her die, a dangerous thought to have here, with everyone watching, all these guides and guards and Jesse watching. Jesse watching.

She breathed in deeply, not sure how to stop what she was feeling except that she had to not see those eyes and what lived in them. She jerked her glance away, stared at the stone she was laying on. She studied the way the mountain was put together, the way one stone supported another and that another, layers of time holding each other up. She thought of geology, of time, of stone.

She imagined what it would be like to deconstruct this mountain, to unglue time and loose this one stone in her hand and have that loose other stones, see them tumbling down to the bottom as it all came apart, flying backward to a different age. Would it feel good to break a mountain? Better than breaking Darlene's life? Would it be harder to shift the molecules of stone than to break the thin web that held life in its strands, or was that web stronger than mountains?

"Cali, stop it," a voice said sharply. Jesse. Not angry. Worried. And he was close. Why was he so close? What was he worried about?

"What?" she whispered.

"Stop it." he repeated more imperatively. "Now."

She seemed to know what he meant. She blinked, pulled herself out of the mountain's molecular structure. She took a deep breath, cursed once loudly, and hauled Darlene onto the ledge.

Then Darlene started crying in earnest, and Cali, as if snapped back into this time and place after a long trip elsewhere, heard other voices calling. They said many things at once, none of them coherent, but they were real voices, really calling things.

"What?" she called back. "What?"

From above, Kathy called down. "Good work. Is she hurt?"

"I don't think so," Cali said, then looked to Darlene. "Anything broken?"

"I don't know," she sobbed, and Cali heard the falseness in it, so different from her falling scream.

"Move things," Cali said impatiently.

She sat up, moved her arms and legs, clutched her head. "My head hurts."

Cali called up to Kathy. "Scrapes and bruises. Nothing broken."

"Okay. We can take it from here. You go on ahead. And thanks."

Cali took in a breath, let it out. "Ready to climb," she called down to Jesse.

"Wait," he said. "You sure you can?"

"Yes. Why not?"

"You got any muscle left?"

She looked down over the ledge and saw Jesse staring up at her. His eyes seemed so close, as if he was right next to her, his face close enough to kiss. As if he knew what her muscles felt, every confusion of her heart and soul. She hated that. Hated him knowing that. What might he do with it when she wasn't paying attention?

"You want to lower off?" he asked.

She couldn't say yes. Couldn't ask for relief. Didn't believe in it.

"No," she said. "Ready to climb." She realized her voice sounded desperate, close to tears. She couldn't do anything about that.

"Climb on," he called to her. She began moving.

Making her way off the ledge was harder than getting onto it, but she managed, and began traversing back to where she'd been before Darlene took her tumble. It wasn't a difficult path, but she was tired and thirsty, and her body wasn't following directions as quickly as before. But she couldn't stop until she found her way to the first pitch. Not that far. Not that difficult. She could do it.

She was almost there when her hand grazed something smooth and cool and not stone. She stopped, everything in her going still at this sensation. Her heart beat furiously, as if she knew before she saw it. She raised her eyes slowly and looked where her hand was clutching a crack in the stone.

Snake. A beautiful tan snake with black markings, and a thin forked tongue flicking in and out, sniffing for its future.

She didn't yell. That might startle it. She didn't know if withdrawing her hand slowly would make it strike. The only thing she knew was that it was a rattler. They'd been told to watch for them, that they lived here, though they weren't abundant. But it wasn't here on her way over. Was it? Had it let her pass before?

"Cali?" a voice asked. Jesse.

"Snake," she whispered. "Rattler."

Brief silence. Then, an odd question. "What's he saying?"

She thought she must be going mad. Dehydrated, sunstroke, something. But she listened, and a confused knowledge came to her.

"Something's loose," she replied. "The stone is loose. I made it loose."

At these words, the snake uncurled itself, turned, and disappeared into the rock, melding with it as if it was made of the mountain, just part of its molecular structure torn loose. Cali felt herself breathe again.

She turned her face and looked down to Jesse. She was going to tell him it was okay, the snake was gone, but he was standing with his eyes closed, his lips moving silently as if in prayer. Then, a rumble of thunder, close and fast. In her peripheral vision, a flash of lightning. She heard voices above her, talking loud.

"What is it?" she called, her voice weak and thin. Nobody answered.

Guy was shouting something, his words distant and caught in the wind. "Your call," he was saying to Jesse. "Might blow away, but you call it."

Jesse looked up to her. "You're lowering off," he said. "A storm's coming."

"I can climb it," she called back, knowing it was a lie. The snake had done her in.

He tugged at her rope. "No fucking way," he said.

And she was lowered as if by magic, with no effort, descending against the rock wall, her hands now and then touching it as she floated down and down. She felt ground under her feet, felt the rope go slack. She was standing, but her legs were loose, unreliable, and then Jesse was holding her up, moving her forward.

Above her she heard a snap and a crack. Lightning? She looked up. Not lightning. Where she'd just been, a piece of mountain, a stone held in place for eons, came loose and ripped down the cliff along the path she'd taken. She thought of time coming unglued. Of molecules unhinged. Thought of what she'd been told, that rockfall was one of the biggest killers of climbers. She drew in a sharp breath.

"I got you," Jesse whispered. "You're safe."

Or maybe he didn't say that. She couldn't tell. She only wanted something solid under her, somewhere to sit and not look like a fool.

"Christ," someone nearby said. One of the guides. "Christ. Did you see that?"

She blinked up. Jesse led her to a rock and she sat.

"I didn't think it would do that," she said vaguely, not sure what she meant by either verb or subject. Not sure, but surely knowing.

"That's why I told you to stop," he said, voice tight and trying not to be. He reached out and touched her lip. "You're bleeding."

She raised her hand, touched where he did, supremely aware of him. Of his touch.

"I guess I bit my lip," she said.

"I guess," he agreed.

He gave her his water bottle and she worked to keep her arm steady as she lifted it to her mouth, tasting something rusty. Blood. Her blood. She heard a commotion above and saw people at the top. Darlene, yelling, loudly and with feeling.

"Cali," she screamed. "You saved me. You saved me."

Dark fire coursed through her. She wanted to scream back, scream fuck you. I saw your life. What I saved you for. I saw what you did with the gift. Fuck you. Fuck you.

Then Jesse had a hand on her shoulder. "Everyone comes home alive, Cali," he said quietly, or didn't say, but certainly she heard it.

She drank her water, and was still.

* * * *

Campfire talk that night centered around the fear and triumph of the day: Cali's heroism, how she saved Darlene, and how the oncoming storm saved her.

"It didn't rain, did it?" she asked, not sure what she was remembering correctly.

"The storm moved out. It was just enough to get you out of the way," Kathy said. "I guess the weather gods love you. Not bad friends to have."

She almost opened her mouth to say really it was the snake. Just in time she realized that wouldn't make sense, didn't even make sense to her.

Besides, nobody knew about it except Jesse. At least, she thought he did, unless that whole conversation was delusion. She looked to him. He nodded once quickly, a small move. She turned away.

Everyone was high with what happened, the first high without drugs for many of them. Cali stayed reticent, and moved away when Darlene tried to hug her. She didn't know what she'd feel if that happened, or what she'd do with those feelings.

"Look, it was nothing. Just—that's what you do. Not a big deal," she insisted.

Darlene, finding her embrace repulsed, quivered her lips and made her eyes big. She turned and huddled against Kathy, while Guy patted her shoulder, then scowled at Cali.

Cali took his scowl, made her face expressionless. "Permission to go pee," she said to Kathy, who nodded.

She walked away from the campfire, not sure at all if she meant to ever come back.

* * * *

She found herself walking toward the cliff she'd almost climbed, and when she got to the edge she poked a toe's worth of dirt over the side and listened to it roll down. She thought of routes she'd seen on the map, ways down and out. She was concentrating so hard on that she didn't hear anyone come up behind her.

"You really think you can do it?" a voice asked.

She turned. Jesse stood there, his arms wrapped at his chest.

"Yeah," she said. "I do."

"Not from here. Not without rope."

She pointed to the left. "About twenty yards that way I could."

"You noticed."

"I noticed."

"Okay, so you wait until I fall asleep and try it. Say you make it, which wouldn't surprise me. Then I'll hit the signal for the guards to get you, and you'll be in solitary. No parole recommendation."

She looked him up and down, shrugged, turned away.

Then his tone softened. "You look pretty fed up."

"Yeah," she said.

"Not a lot of tolerance for bullshit in you, is there?"

"Not a lot."

"Because you see too much that's real. It makes you forget you can't see it all. That it's a matter of perspective."

"Don't you start," she growled at him.

"I'm not," he said. "I'm just saying you can't see everything that'll happen with Darlene. Maybe her baby is adopted, and the couple who adopts him has some money and clout, and they lobby for some real legislation to deal with drug problems. The future has a lot of possibilities. It's best to let it unfold."

"If I was doing that, I should have let Darlene fall."

He shifted, rubbed at the back of his neck. "Good point. Why didn't you?"

"What you said. Everyone comes back alive."

"You don't usually take instructions."

"Not unless I agree."

"And you did?"

"Apparently. I don't always know what I mean to do until I do it."

"That's called intuitive thinking."

"Yeah."

A moment passed. A firefly blinked silently by. She realized they'd been talking as if he saw everything she saw in Darlene. As if he knew. And she'd fallen into the trap. That was bad. She wondered if she should do damage control, and decided against it. Best to stay quiet. Silence was her friend. But he wouldn't let it go.

"In case you're wondering, I know what happened today," he said. "All of it. And I know what happened to your mother and Keith and Marilyn and Glory. If you could face this mountain, do what you did today, can't you face what you are? What you can do? Maybe learn to use it to better ends?"

A moment of fear held in suspension. What did he mean? What did he know? He must mean something else because even she didn't believe what she could do when it happened, except that it kept happening. Validity and Reliability were the two key factors in proving any hypotheses. So she learned from Mrs. Henderson. And it kept happening. It was there, solid and reliable.

And so was her own magic thinking, because every time she wished someone dead, the wish came true. Reliability. Validity. But Jesse couldn't know that. Couldn't believe it. Don't panic, she told herself. You know your moves. Use them.

"What happened was Darlene fell," she said. "And I helped her. The rest is bullshit."

She took a step forward, and stopped. She was aware that she was frightened and should resist the impulse to act from fear.

Jesse came up behind her. "You're pretty close to the edge, Cali," he observed. "You're not planning anything stupid, are you?"

She said nothing.

"How much longer until you're out of St. Ida's?" he asked.

"A couple of months, but then I go to Bedford for five big ones, unless . . . ."

". . . .Unless you get recommended for parole," he filled in.

"Yeah. And you're one of my recommenders." With Mrs. Henderson gone, he was also her best bet. She certainly wouldn't get anything good from Betty, and her reports from Marilyn—well, she already knew what they said.

"You want to know what it'd take for that to happen?" he asked.

Her stomach lurched. She knew what that meant. She asked herself if she minded, and realized she did. She didn't think Jesse was like that, and it bothered her that she'd miscalculated. With her back to him, she pulled her sweatshirt off, leaving only the tank top underneath. She heard him take in breath.

"Christ almighty," he muttered angrily, the first time she heard that in his voice. "That's not it." Surprised, she turned around. He was gone. Just gone.

Her relief was so stinging it put tears in her eyes. Like being lowered down a mountain when you know you can't go on but you don't dare say so. Like hands that hold the rope and keep holding it, regardless.

Then she grinned, put her sweatshirt back on, and walked back to camp.

PARTICLES AND WAVES

Monday morning, back at St. Ida's, and the dim rooms all seemed smaller to Cali. Or maybe she seemed bigger. Something had shifted, either here or in her. Maybe everything. Everything except the talk.

Through whatever mysterious subterranean circuits of communication St. Ida's had, they all knew what happened to her on the cliff, and they had plenty of talk about it, with Tibby licking her lips for a description of Jesse in a swim suit. When they'd wrung that dry they were even more gleefully into what happened to Betty, who was no longer at St. Ida's. Though no official announcement had been made, Lola heard she was dead.

"Dead as a doorknob," she announced with gusto at breakfast. "Kicked the bucket, bought the farm, pushing up daisies. There is a goddess, and she loves us crazy chicks."

"How'd she die?" Cali asked, keeping her voice neutral. She'd forgotten about that. Forgotten what she'd done, all of it lost in the complexities of the field trip. She was suddenly nervous about what Jesse would say, or think, or do.

"Heart attack, they say," Tibby said. "Yeah, we knew her heart was bad. Just didn't know how bad. Cali, girl, you're getting a reputation. You put your hand on someone, they're dead. You know that?"

"That's stupid," Cali said. "I'm sure I wasn't the last one she touched."

There were laughs at this, but Racer looked at her with wild eyes, deer in the headlights eyes.

* * * *

Later that day an official announcement of Betty's death was made, and a new guard, equally repulsive but more inclined to look than to touch, was put in her place. Talk moved on to something else. One of the new fence guards, Chuck, was good looking and knew it, and there was lots to figure out about how to use that quality in him. The girls discussed it endlessly. That was a relief for Cali, because it kept talk away from her. But she had another hurdle to leap. That afternoon she was working with Jesse.

She entered his office with some trepidation, keeping all her doors firmly closed. He was standing at the window, looking outside at something she couldn't see. She walked to the center of the room and stood there, not sure what to do next.

"Should I get my suit?" she asked when he didn't speak.

He didn't answer. She waited. He gestured toward the chair. She went to it and sat.

Without turning, he spoke. "Undressing on the mountain—either you mistook me, or you have plans I'm not interested in. Assuming it's the first, I deferred reporting it."

The blow came home to her. He could report her for this, and she'd face Bedford. "I mistook you," she said, with a minimum of inflection.

"Good," he said. He sounded relieved. "Just so you know," he added, "I would never . . ." the sentence trailed away into silence. He took a breath and started again. "I know what happens here, but I don't do that. We're both worth more than that. And it's just not my idea of a good time."

He talked to her as if he knew her. It frightened her more than any gruffness or coercion. She knew those moves. She didn't know this one. He sighed, walked to the center of the room and stood behind her. She hated having people behind her, but she wouldn't give him the satisfaction of turning.

"You heard about Betty?" he asked.

"I heard."

"What do you think?"

"I think she's dead," Cali said.

Silence. It went on for some time. Cali worked hard not to turn and look at him.

"That magical thinking. You ever consider using it for something besides wishing people dead?" he asked.

That was unexpected. "Once I wished for a million dollars," she said, playing it light. "I didn't get it."

"Did you complete the thought?"

She startled at the term. It was one she used to herself, one she understood. If the thought was going to work, it had to be complete. Full and complete. She had to mean it or it wouldn't work. Some part of her had to believe she deserved and would get it. Some part of her.

"What?" she asked, trying to sound blank, innocent of knowledge.

"Did you mean it?" he amended.

She remembered the time between Keith's death and her mother's. She was lying in bed thinking if she had a million dollars she could take her mother away. For a moment the thought was a rippling energy of possibilities. Then, as if she'd swallowed stones, a heaviness shut the motion down. Her mother could, and would, buy a lot of dope with a million dollars. She didn't complete the thought. Her happy ending seemed impossible.

"Sure I meant it," she lied. "Why not?"

"Lots of reasons. Mom might just spend the money on dope. Or you were afraid of actually having a life. Adversity was more familiar, maybe."

Silence. His breathing too soft to hear.

"Maybe I'm only good at one thing," she said, still keeping it light, "and you should always do what you're best at."

Without any sound he was at her side, one hand on the back of her chair. "You're not sure how you do it, or if you can stop it, are you?" he asked.

She shook her head, a barely discernible motion she could later deny.

"Do you want to know?"

He was offering her a gift. Something she'd never be able to talk about with anyone else. Something shining and golden and possible, like a million dollars in the hand. And if she took it? Then what? He reported her for delusional thinking. Magical thinking. His gift was also something she couldn't believe in. Not at all.

"I don't know what you're talking about," she said carefully.

He went tense, as if she'd said exactly the wrong thing, and she had a moment of panic. She'd played it wrong. But what he said next shocked her beyond any measure of her young life.

"Cali," he asked softly. "Am I next?"

She turned to look at him. His face was tense, not with anger. She knew anger. Pain? Something as simple as pain? It made her throat tighten, her pain reflecting his.

"I don't know," she whispered. An admittance of abundant uncertainty. She couldn't always control this thing. She didn't know how it worked. Immediately she wanted to call it back, but he didn't give her the chance.

His hand on the back of the chair worked small motion. "You need to know," he said. "If I'm next, you better mean to do it. Do you understand?"

She absorbed the words, the intent behind them. She almost understood. Know what you can do, and mean to do it. But why would he say that, with his life in the balance? She stayed perfectly still. She'd given enough away.

He released the chair. "I'm afraid it's floor polishing today," he said.

"What?"

"Floor polishing. The machine. Noisy and irritating as hell," he said. He moved toward the door. She rose, and followed him.

* * * *

That day and the next few weeks passed without incident. Her work with Jesse continued, but he seemed more relaxed, asked her no more unanswerable questions, as if they'd resolved something and could move on, though she wasn't sure what it was.

He didn't mention magical thinking or killing people. Instead, while they painted the dorm halls he talked about other places he'd gone rock climbing, or listened while she told him about the various theories she'd learned in AP class, how strange and wonderful they were. He was knowledgeable about most of them, and she wondered once more what the hell he was doing here, painting walls. She didn't ask, but she was used to him seeing the questions in her eyes and answering before she had to.

"I've got a masters in education and counseling," he told her. "I liked teaching, but the administrators were hell. So I took this job. Thought I'd wait and see what I wanted to do next."

"You can do that?" she asked.

"Sure," he said. "Why not? The choices are all mine. And they'll be all yours, Cali."

It was a new thought. When she left here, she'd have choices.

He talked to her about her options for the future, about jobs she might like. He brought in brochures on different kinds of scholarships and college programs.

"How come they never showed these to me in C and E?" she asked. "All they give me is voc-tech stuff."

"Did you ever ask?"

"Well, no."

"Didn't your science teacher ever suggest it?"

Cali shrugged. "Yeah. But then, she retired. It just didn't seem . . ."

"Possible?"

"Something like that," she agreed.

"Can't complete a thought if you don't believe in it, Cali," he said. She didn't respond.

He asked if she ever thought about lab research, or benchwork, and she said that sounded tedious. She never used words like tedious around the other girls. They'd look at her like she was trying to be somebody she shouldn't be, couldn't be.

"Then paint houses and go into the theoretical end," he suggested. "Quantum field theory. You have the math for it."

She shook her head. "It's interesting, but I'm not sure I can buy it. A lot of it sounds like an elaborate story. Chaos theory's more practical. Useful. It makes sense."

"Small choices, huge feedback," Jesse noted. "I guess you would understand that. But doesn't it scare you—the unpredictability factor?"

"No. It just means I don't have to worry so much, since anything can happen."

At that he laughed.

He never talked down to her, didn't look her over as if he knew something she didn't. He treated her like his equal, met her where she was and showed her where she might go next and that was working changes in her. She was less interested in the St. Ida's dramas, less attentive to Racer's state of mind. She looked outward, sensing the possibilities of a larger world.

* * * *

Sometimes they'd have grounds work, and he brought her to parts of the land surrounding St. Ida's she hadn't seen before. He always found good excuses for it. They had to check the drainage pipes. Had to clean out a culvert. They would actually do these things, but they'd spend more time walking around, or sitting and staring at the sky, talking or not talking.

They went to the swampy lands at the east end, and she saw the frogs she'd heard singing at night. He found wildflowers, animal tracks, and named them for her. They laughed a great deal, watching the frogs, looking at birds. Once when they were walking they heard sibilant motion in the grass. Cali looked down to see a garden snake moving smoothly toward her. She stood still, and it curled itself around her foot.

"You're not afraid of snakes," Jesse noted.

"Not unless they're poisonous," she said. "Even those, I don't hate. I'm just careful around them. Mostly I like them."

"And apparently," he said, "they like you."

The snake lifted its head, flicked its tongue out, and moved on.

At lunch one day Tibby mentioned that Jesse had been in her room the night before to deal with a clogged sink. "*Very* clogged," she said, licking her lips. "I wanted to tell him what tool to use to clear it *real* good."

She was about to go into raptures about it, when Racer cut in sharply. "Give it up, Tibby. He already found a fuck."

The other girls were suddenly quiet. Cali looked at Racer, saw her twitching jaw, her tight smile. Cali was at first afraid, and then angry, wanting to jump to Jesse's defense. He's no Betty, she wanted to growl at Racer. It was a new feeling. Before this it was always the girls against the rest of St. Ida's. She cooled down and gave Racer a neutral face.

"He's screwing Hanson?" she asked.

Jane Hanson, who replaced Betty, had the face of a bulldog and was built like a box.

Racer glared at her, then broke into a laugh. The other girls joined in, mostly from relief, Cali thought. It passed, and Cali didn't bring it up again. But she noticed Racer didn't talk to her at night much anymore, and spent more time with Lola during the day.

* * * *

At Cali's next work session, a day full of sun and heat, Jesse stood up when she entered his office.

"It's hot as hell," he said. "Let's get out of here."

She was glad enough to do so, and she followed him to the closet where the suits and equipment were, waited for him to open it. He kept walking.

"Jesse?" she asked his back. "The suits?"

He turned. "Oh. Not today," he said. "Too damn hot. Come on."

When they approached the fence guard Jesse flashed his ID. "We're going to the old church. Repair inventory."

"She needs a suit," the guard said.

"They're all at the cleaners," Jesse said. "Order got screwed up."

The guard barely hid a leer. Cali knew what he thought, and didn't like it much. Jesse walked ahead of her and she followed without speaking, enjoying the sun on her skin, the little breezes that came along to relieve it now and then.

"You," he said, "are more silent than anyone I've ever known. I appreciate it, since I had planning meetings all week with board people who don't listen and won't shut up."

"Quiet's easy," she said. "It's talking that's difficult, if you ask me."

He grunted, walked on.

"Board people are assholes?" she asked.

"It would be inappropriate for me to discuss that with you," he said dryly, and she laughed, and then so did he. "What are you doing in school these days?" he asked.

"World Mythology. Isis, Lilith, lots of goddesses."

"Ah. Well, that ought to be easy for you. Isis created snakes, and they're your friends. And Lilith—did they tell you she was a story the Rabbis made up to explain why humans are created twice in Genesis?"

She frowned, looked to him. "How do you know all that stuff?"

"I read," he said lightly. "And I think it's interesting. All stories intersect over time. Isis becomes Mary, Lilith the Magdelene. I wonder if there wasn't some real people, some real stories at the start of them, and they got changed over time as people told them."

She remembered a game she used to play in grade school, called telephone. One person would whisper a few sentences in someone else's ear, and that person had to pass it on to another, and so on, until they got to the end of the line. Then, when the last person retold the words out loud, everyone would laugh at how much it had changed. "So you think Lilith was . . . . what?"

"I don't know. Maybe just someone who knew too much and got kicked out of town when men decided they liked their women not so smart. Or, maybe it's all the same woman, who keeps coming back until everyone finally understands what she's trying to teach."

She shook her head. "That'll never happen."

He laughed, but it was a nervous sound. "Maybe you're right."

They walked on, up a hill toward a building she'd seen only in the distance before this. He stopped and pointed at it. "Do you know about the bell tower?" he asked.

"No," she said.

"I guess you don't get the guided tours. It's an old church—more than 200 years old. Used to ring bells for services. Now they store stuff in the lower floors, but the stairs to the tower are still good. I thought you might like it, and I really do need to get a repair inventory. Some rich lady wants to pour money into it."

They made their way to it, and entered. When they moved from the bright sun into the cool dark of the building they stood a minute letting their eyes adjust. He shifted, again nervously, and cleared his throat. Something was up, she thought.

"What?" she asked him.

"Some people are making comments about you working with me," he said.

"I know," she said. "Is it—will it get you in trouble?"

In the dim light, she could see surprise on his face. "I didn't think about that," he said. "I was concerned for you. I wanted to warn you."

"Oh," she said. "I took care of it on my end."

"Did you? I think I won't ask how."

"It wasn't a big deal. It's funny, though. With Betty and Marilyn, everyone knew what was going on, and nobody got angry. Like that's just the way things are, and we deserve it. This—it's as if people want good things to be bad."

"Yeah," he said. "Sometimes it is."

She felt shy after that, as if she'd said more than she intended, or he heard more. But he was always hearing more. She should be used to it by now.

He pointed toward the stairs. "Let's go up."

The staircase was stone and curled in tight circles up and up. They went slowly, Cali keeping a hand on the wall as she went, feeling claustrophobic in the dusky small space. When they got to the top, the narrow archway suddenly opened up into a broad, high-domed space that felt like breathing air after a long time underwater.

Cali gave a gasp of pleasure and surprise, and held a hand up. In the late afternoon sky the sun was in the west, throwing gold down on the tops of the buildings below them, making even St. Ida's into something worth looking at. She moved to the low wall under the arched stone opening and looked out at it.

"St. Ida's," she murmured. "But it's beautiful."

"It's a matter of perspective," Jesse replied. "Einstein said creating a new theory was like climbing a mountain. What you saw on the way up is still there, but it's smaller because you have a bigger view."

They stood in silence for some time, both of them looking out. St. Ida's was small at their feet, a still photograph of something diminished by the motion of time, and bodies in space. It tugged at her heart with hope, that most dangerous energy. Cali laughed.

"What?" Jesse asked.

"Makes me think maybe I wouldn't mind being a goddess," Cali said.

He grinned. "Which one? Isis? Or maybe Kali would suit you best. She dances and a thousand live. She dances and a thousand die."

"Sure," she said. "Why not?"

"And if you were a goddess, what would you do?"

"Pretty much what they do now, I guess. Leave it alone."

"Deus Absconitus. You wouldn't try to make it better?"

"Some things," she said. "Less pain, more pleasure. More freedom, too."

"I guess you'd appreciate that," Jesse noted.

Below and away a river rippled silver, snakelike, across the land. She saw a bird flying down over its waters.

"What is it?" she asked, pointing.

He peered, shook his head. "Hawk. Eagle. Gull. I can't tell."

She leaned over to look, moved her foot to put it up on the small step below the opening, but it was worn slick and slightly damp from years of shade and humidity. She slipped, clutched at the stone sill.

He had hold of her quicker than a prayer, one hand on her arm, the other wrapped around her waist. His grasp on her was imperative, and she felt how good it was to be held against danger, held in trust. He would not let her fall. But having grasped her, he went perfectly still, and she knew his stillness as a supreme effort of will. He wanted more, and fought himself not to take it. He wanted more. So did she.

Her body, an instinctive animal, moved before she could articulate its desire. She leaned into him. If it was possible, his stillness increased for a breath of time. Then, a small sound of pain or pleasure, hard to tell which, escaped him. When he let her go, she knew what it took for him to pull away.

It all happened very fast, but she knew. He wanted her, and would not give in to his own desire. Somehow, that was even better. He was a male animal, and if he held himself in check for her sake, it meant more than if he didn't have to make the effort.

"You okay?" he asked, voice gruff and low.

"Yeah. Thanks."

"We better get some notes on those repairs and get back. I've got meetings."

"More talk," she noted.

"Plenty more," he agreed.

On her way down the cool, dark stairs, she tucked the moment away in her store of images, something to get her through rough places, when they came her way again.

* * * *

Cali tried hard not to count the days until her board hearing. Tried not to, and failed. She couldn't help but be aware of it. Racer and the other girls never mentioned it, but she noticed the way they subtly moved away from her. She was becoming a ghost, a memory, someone who got away. They'd be glad for her, she knew, because they all talked about girls that got released, imagined what they were doing, painted pictures of them shopping in malls, eating real food, having sex with guys, getting jobs. They knew half the time the girls who left here ended up in worse places, but that didn't matter. The stories weren't really about who left. They were about hope.

Cali focused on doing well in her last classes, doing her work with Jesse. He gave her easy tasks, and kept her outside a lot. Often he'd appear in the halls when she moved from lunch to class, or class to her room. He'd walk with her, talk a little, his glance everywhere, as if he scanned the horizon for dangers, ready to ward them off. She liked the feeling of his presence. It was soothing and protective, two new realms for her.

Her only real worry was Racer, whose nails were raw and bloodied. Cali suspected something was going on with her and Chuck, the new guard. She saw them exchanging glances as she worked the garden and Chuck watched from his side of the fence. But even that was quickly becoming part of the past. She was a ghost, in a house of ghosts. She floated, trying to keep out of harm's way.

* * * *

On the morning Cali woke up and realized she had only two weeks and three days left, the shit hit the fan.

She'd had a strange dream about being on a mountain. There was a woman there she seemed to know. A beautiful woman. She was calling to Cali, but there were coyotes howling on the bluffs all around them, and she was afraid to move. Afraid they'd see her.

As she decided to go forward, knowing the call was imperative, a foam-mouthed coyote leapt down on her, going for her throat.

She smelled its breath, smokey and sweet. She inhaled it, remembered moments of getting high with Keith, who liked to smoke weed before sex. It sickened her, and she turned away. Then she found she was fighting with her covers and awake, and the same smell filled the room.

She opened her eyes.

Racer was standing near one of the barred windows. It was open, and she was fanning air out of it in the sticky heat.

"What the hell is that smell?" Cali asked.

"Nothing," Racer said. "I was—I got some incense. But I don't like it. Do you?"

Cali sat up. Incense my ass, she thought. As if they were allowed to have incense. As if there was any incense that smelled just like weed. Hell. Racer knew what happened if she got caught with drugs in the room. Both roommates were held accountable.

For Racer that meant solitary. For her, it meant the death of all her chances. She had to stop it, but she had to work it right or who knew what crazy shit Racer would pull.

"Where'd you get it?" she asked, rising, dressing, speaking calmly.

Racer laughed, a little hysterical, more than a little high. "Chuck. You know Chuck? I did him a favor, and he gave me some."

"You fucked him," Cali said.

"Yeah, well. Why not?"

"Because it's stupid, Racer," she said. "Stupid. He's stupid. And dangerous."

"He can't do anything to me."

"Not to you, Racer. To *me*. You get that?"

Racer blinked at her.

Her anger, her fear, got the better of her. "You get caught, I go to Bedford," she said. "My ass is on the line here. *Mine*."

"Shit," Racer muttered. "I—I wasn't thinking."

"Yeah. Where is it?" Cali asked. There was still a chance to get out of this before someone smelled it. Before they came and tore the room apart. Before what her mother did to her happened all over again.

"It's gone," Racer said. "I used it all. It was only a joint."

Cali looked at her, knew she was lying. Her eyes flicked to her bureau drawer. Racer never did learn how to lie. Cali moved to it, pulled out the drawer, tossing it aside. She stuck her hand behind it, felt the plastic baggie, soft and full. She pulled it out, took it to the small bathroom they shared, just a toilet and a shower but it would do.

Racer tugged at her arm, trying to stop her. "Let me keep it. You're leaving, and what'll I have? Some shithead roommate. I *need* it."

Cali suddenly heard her mother's voice when she was stashing meth and equipment in Cali's room. *C'mon, Cali. It's safe. No cops'll come here. Who cares about me? I'm nobody.* But the cops came and they took her, not her mother, who gave her away like yesterday's newspaper. And here was Racer, her face like her mother's, laughing at her.

Fury rose up in her swift and deadly as lightning. She knew what happened next. The place where thoughts would be completed whether she wanted them to or not. She couldn't stop it, couldn't make it stop once it started.

Cali jerked her arm from Racer's grasp, opened the baggie and poured the pot down the toilet, flushed once, twice. Tossed the bag in and flushed again. Racer grabbed at her, babbling, talking too loud, and Cali couldn't stop the anger, the fear. Racer's death wove itself toward completion, Cali's rage growing it strong. It would leap out and kill Racer and she couldn't stop it except one way. One way.

She shoved Racer hard, heard her hit the floor. She whirled back and smashed the mirror over the sink, grabbed a shard of glass. Racer was up, coming at her, and Cali pushed her away, took the glass and slashed at her own arm again and again and there was blood on Racer's face, blood on the floor, on her arm, blood everywhere.

The sight of it made her sick. Made her want only to go away from St. Ida's, from herself, from whatever strange creature she had always been. Her vision curled itself in to a pinpoint of darkness, and she allowed herself to crash into it.

QUANTUM 2: LILITH

Cali dreamt that she walked in the garden at high noon with her companion, the heat of the day soaking her skin. Then, she walked the same garden alone in the cool of the day, her flesh rejoicing in the breezes. But the cool of the day was when the Great One, who now called himself Lord, showed up to talk his talk.

Her companion didn't mind him as much as she did, but then again, Lord asked more of her. From her companion he only seemed to want occasional conversation, discussion about what thoughts would be good to realize here, how to name those things his thoughts brought into being. But he followed her from tree to tree, whispering what he would do to her if she didn't cooperate with his plans. He called her names that sank her lower than the ground she walked on, claiming she belonged to him, to him, to him.

He was wrong. She belonged to no one but herself.

Her companion understood that, and seemed to like it. When she crawled on top of him at night and took her pleasure with him, his eyes filled with joy. When they argued, and she insolently refused to call animals or plants by the names he chose, refused to obey him in other ways, he would break into laughter, gather her in his arms and cover her face with kisses.

"You are my night spirit," he whispered to her.

"And you are all my days," she answered.

She loved her companion, his newly formed body still containing the spirit she'd resurrected when they lived by the river long ago. And she loved the garden. All that lived within it was dear to her, precious pieces of light manifesting in a multitude of forms. Trees and burgeoning flowers, sweet fresh waters, singing birds and the very stones were alive to her touch because whether Lord would admit it or not, her thoughts had called most of them into being. He was not skilled at creating. Only at ruling.

But his petulance increased daily, and he whispered to her that the power she stole from him must be returned, that the job of realizing the world must be his alone. She continued to push him away, but she feared he would kill her body, so she completed a thought of something to remain in her absence. She used her thoughts to make a tree.

It was different than the other trees, its fruits glowing with thick, rich light. She'd put her own wishes for the people into it, that they be well, and liberated from the hold of Lord, who was determined to rule all. Any who ate this fruit would taste her wishes for them, and so gain in consciousness, grow able to care for themselves.

When she told her companion what she'd done, he was afraid. "We have everything we need here," he said. "Why would you disturb it? And he's good to us, as long as we agree with him."

"He's good to you now," she said. "But he killed you once, and will do so again."

"His servant did that," her companion said. "He never meant to hurt me."

She sighed, grieved at his denial, but she could only speak what she knew to be true. "He would keep the people in thrall, to feed his strength. I cannot let that be."

"And I cannot help you," he said. He stalked away from her, but she was not alone. She had another friend who would help. She knelt on the earth, cried out her pain and fears to it, and when her tears had soaked the soil, she rolled it in her hand, and called her old friend, the snake, to her.

Soon after that, she broke with her routine and walked in the cool of the day. When Lord came up behind her, whispering in her ear, she whirled on him, cried out in a voice louder than the rushing wind, speaking his name. His secret name, which she still carried like a knife, hidden but always ready for use.

He reeled back from her, his face filled with rage, his coal dark eyes sparking with fire. He raised a hand against her, but she only laughed. She had her own skills, her own power, and he knew she'd use them.

Instead of striking her, he tossed her from that place. She flew high over the trees until she was far from the garden she'd loved, far from her companion.

* * * *

She went to live by the sea, and learned the names and ways of other night creatures. She knew Lord would make another woman for her companion. He would instruct them both not to eat of that tree, and for a while, they would comply.

But the snake she'd left behind would convince them otherwise, and sooner or later, both of them would listen. Then they would know what Lord knew, diminishing his power. They would leave the garden, and go out into the larger world, where anything was possible.

No matter what Lord said, his power would not belong to him alone.

BUTTERFLY WINGS

Cali dreamt about walking in a garden filled with beautiful trees, their flowers filling the night air with sweetness. But there was someone in the garden. Someone she didn't like much. Someone who wanted to hurt her.

"That's how it is," he said. "Really, there's no escape. You should know that by now."

A strange scraping noise behind her made her turn sharply. She opened her eyes. She was awake, and she knew where she was.

She was in a hospital room, and Jesse was pulling a chair over, scraping it across the floor. By the time he got it settled a few feet from her bed and sat in it, she remembered everything that had happened, and knew she was in deep shit. She tried to swallow and couldn't. Her mouth was dry.

Jesse held out a glass of water, and she sat up, took it from him and drank.

"It's the drugs they give you," he said. "They make you thirsty."

She drank and said nothing. She could think of nothing to say. When the glass was empty she handed it back to him, and he put it on her tray. She noticed her arms were heavily bandaged. She noticed Jesse's face was tight, his eyes puffy, as if he hadn't slept.

"You're a few weeks from the board, and you do this shit?" he asked quietly.

"You don't understand," she said, her voice without emotion. Who would believe her, or care?

"Yes I do," he said. "Racer had weed. You knew what would happen if they found it."

"Did she say that?"

"I *know*," he said, then waved it away. "If you reported her you wouldn't get in trouble."

"She would."

"Hell. Couldn't you take care of yourself instead of her? For once?"

"I'm supposed to just walk away?"

"Yes. This time, this one time, just walk away. *Can't* you?" He ran a hand through his hair, then brought himself up and made himself perfectly still. He could do that, she noticed, and everything in him was hidden. When he looked at her again, his face was stone smooth, stone still, his gaze heavy on hers.

Strange images flashed in her mind, disconnected and unfathomable. There was a garden, rich with flowers. There was the man from her dream laughing and she was wild with rage at him. There was a snake, curling at her ankles, going where she directed. She raised a hand, waved them away. She had to stay with what was important. Getting out of St. Ida's, out of Bedford, out of this.

"You can help me," she said, declaring rather than asking. She wouldn't, couldn't ask. "If you write up something good, they'll listen."

His eyes were full of pain. "I'm not sure I should," he said.

"Why not?"

"Because I know why you cut yourself."

"It was an accident," she said. "I just—"

"—No," he cut in. "You cut yourself deliberately, and we both know why."

A long moment of silence followed. He took in breath, released it again. He stared at his hands, then spoke again.

"If you can't face that, can't say what it means and learn to deal with it, I don't know if I should put you back in the world," he said.

She struggled with this. She knew now what he was after. He wanted her to talk, give a full confession and throw herself on his mercy. But her mouth stayed glued shut on the words.

He made a sound of impatience. "You can't stop holding yourself hostage, can you?" he demanded.

"What?"

"You hold yourself hostage," he repeated. "You want to be rescued and you hate yourself for it. So you hold yourself hostage, thinking that'll force someone—anyone—to hear you scream. You point a gun at your own head, daring anyone to help you, wanting it so bad you'd kill yourself to get it, but you won't ask because you don't really believe it's possible, you've been hostage for so long."

He reached over and grasped her arm, held it up. "You cut yourself to avoid killing Racer," he said. "Say it. Name the truth, and I'll help you."

She shook her head. His hand tightened on her arm.

"Talk about it, dammit," he insisted. "You know what you do. It hurts like hell, and it feels great, like all the energy in the universe moving through you, and you're in a world bigger than most people ever dream of. When it happens, people die, and you didn't want Racer to die. But here's the thing—if you keep on wishing people dead, you'll eventually reach a point of no return. Then you'll lose your best gift, the one you stole from all the gods, and you won't be able to do what you're best at. What only you are capable of doing. Do you want that? Do you?"

She wrenched her arm from his grasp. "You think I'm nuts? Magical thinking? Then put me on meds, in a loony bin. You want me to stop, then go ahead and stop me. "

"I'm not here to make you stop," he shot back. "I'm here to make you do more. You can do *more*, Cali. Much more than kill people. But first you have to talk about it."

His words terrified her beyond naming, like an animal lurking in shadows beyond shadows. The air between them turned yellow with her terror. He knew, and he believed beyond her own belief because these things happened. They just happened, she told herself again and again. They just happened.

His sea eyes regarding her refuted this. They said she could own this. Control it. Use it in many, many ways. She had done so before, and could do so again.

But her dreams of gardens and snakes and trees told her there were consequences for being who she was. If she wanted the prize, she'd have to take the loss. She'd have to return to a place she swore she'd never visit again. Gardens and snakes and trees. Death and grief and pain always at her back. Wordlessly, in a house made of images and emotion without reason, she knew this.

"Leave me alone," she sobbed out. "I can't. I can't. I told you, I can't do it again. Not ever again."

A look of horror passed over his face and was gone. He sat back in his chair, leaned away from her. He put his hands on his knees and stared at them. Time passed, slowly, bringing them back to current needs.

He sighed. "They'll keep you here today. You can get some rest."

"Do I—will I go back to St. Ida's?"

"You will," he said. "For a while."

"Then what? Bedford?"

"I don't know," he said dully. "I have to—to think it through." He stood. "You need rest. When you're rested, maybe things'll look different."

He reached over, touched her face like a blessing, then left the room.

* * * *

The day passed with doctors, nurses, a shrink who interviewed her. She knew how to answer his questions to make it clear she wasn't suicidal. He left looking thoughtful, not telling her a damn thing.

By evening, she was brought back to St. Ida's. When she was led inside the door of the residence the first person she saw was Racer, being led out in cuffs. She didn't know if that was intentional, or just bad timing. Certainly the warden who held Racer looked surprised, and the one who led Cali cursed softly under her breath. She steered Cali away, but not fast enough. Racer saw her, and exploded in true Racer style.

She got her warden with an elbow in her face and lunged forward, ramming her head at Cali, screaming, "Bitch! Fucking Bitch! You gave me away, fucking bitch!"

The warden grabbed her before she hit, but she kept screaming, "I'll get you. You'll see. I'll get you, bitch!"

Cali said nothing. Nobody would believe her, anyway.

She didn't get solitary, and wondered if that was Jesse's doing, but soon enough saw it was more of a curse than a blessing. The girls weren't allowed to make anyone sit alone at meals, and if it looked like that was happening wardens would shift their seats, but they had their own way of dealing with someone they didn't want around.

They let her sit with them, but not one of them acknowledged her presence. Instead, they talked around her, making her a ghost with their words. They talked about how cool her funeral was, and described her violent end in gruesome detail. The knife pulled her guts out and laid them on the floor while she watched, they said. Sad, they said. So sad.

Cali kept her face stony, ate her meal in silence, but every muscle in her body was shaking. She hadn't realized how much she relied on the friendship of these crazy girls.

She went back to her room alone and watchful, not sure if they'd follow, maybe jump her. She was at her door when she felt a tap on her shoulder and she whirled around, ready to defend herself.

Lola stood there, her dark face grim, a hand held palm out.

"Cool it, girl," she said.

Cali dropped back. If this was an imminent attack she'd find out soon enough.

Lola leaned close, kept her voice low. "Stay cool. You hear me? You're almost out of here. Don't blow it. Don't let it get to you."

Cali swallowed back on something bitter that wanted to climb up from the back of her throat. "Lola, I didn't give Racer away."

"Some of us know that. We just gotta play for our own skins. Stay cool. Get out of here. You understand?"

Cali nodded, appreciative of the gesture of faith, understanding that the game had to be played, regardless. Rats were dealt with harshly. That was important. But Lola didn't see her that way. Lola put a hand on her shoulder, squeezed it hard, then turned and disappeared down the hall.

* * * *

With less than a week to her parole board meeting her bandages were off, the stitches gone, and the doctor said she could go back to work placement. For the first time, she wasn't happy about that. She walked toward Jesse's office with a dull sense of inevitability, as if she walked into a building she knew was about to fall.

She opened the door and he ushered her into the room, gestured toward the chair. She sat across from him. When he spoke, he was dry, distant and formal.

"How are you feeling?"

She shrugged. "I'm here," she said.

"You want to talk about it?"

"Not really."

"Is there anything you want to talk about?"

She shook her head. She was made of doors, and they were all locked and bolted.

He considered her a moment, then stood. "We'll be painting in the annex today," he said. "Suit up."

They got their suits and equipment, walked to the part of the hall they were working on, and went to it. They worked silently, not a word passing between them for a full hour. Occasionally he'd look at her as if expectant of some possibility, but she could not meet his glance. Could not make herself produce anything that resembled words.

When they were done and cleaned up, he said, "Come back to the office a minute."

She followed him with a continuing sense of disaster.

He sat at his desk and she sat on the other side. He picked up the stone on his desk and turned it over in his hand, watching light move across its surface. This went on for some time. He was waiting, she thought. Waiting for her to say something. She tried to open her mouth and give it to him, but every time she did an imperative re-doubling of the locks occurred, as if talking presented a danger much greater than Bedford. She sensed something old as blood stalking her, waiting to rend her life.

It became unbearable, and she broke the silence. "What do you want from me?" she whispered.

He looked at her. His mouth twisted a little, then settled itself. "The truth, Cali. Simple enough, isn't it? Just name the truth. Who you are. What you do."

She opened her mouth. Closed it again. She couldn't. Didn't trust him, didn't trust or know herself. She made a fist and rubbed it against the arm of the chair. "Why do you need it?" she demanded. "What for?"

"What would you say if I told you it was necessary, to save the world and all its people?"

"I'd say bullshit," she replied.

"I thought so. Then try this. Because it's the only way you'll be whole," he said.

"What the hell business is that of yours? You're a maintenance man, for fuck's sake."

At this he laughed, a dangerous sound. "Now who's throwing bullshit around," he said. He shifted, and his hand moved to a desk drawer, opened it and pulled out a piece of paper. "I've got two letters for the Board. Here's one of them. Read it."

She took it, glad to see her hand was steady. The words were clear and simple. She was not yet rehabilitated, and should serve out the remainder of her sentence at Bedford. At the sentence that called her 'impervious to therapy,' she choked back laughter, bitter and harsh in her throat.

She closed up on the feeling, took it and stuffed it under the door of the room marked *Do Not Enter*. She had to leave before the wrong thoughts occurred. She put the paper on his desk, stood and walked toward the door.

"You're leaving because you're angry, and you're scared of what you'll do about it," he called after her.

"I'm leaving because this is pointless. You get to make choices about my life. I don't."

"Yes you do," he said crisply. "You know all your choices here. Isn't it about time you owned them?"

There was motion inside her, primordial, slow and certain. He'd said that before. If he was next in line, she better mean it. Choose it clear and true. Talk to him or kill him. Trust him, or kill him. There was a yes in her somewhere, filled with hope, but the no cried out against the danger and she responded more to danger than to hope. And why was he pushing this at her, when he was fully aware he could end up dead?

She turned and faced him. He was standing now and staring at her, one of his hands curling and uncurling at his side. Though she was wallowing in confusion, he seemed to know exactly what he was doing.

"Don't," she said.

"Don't what?"

"Test me."

"Why not?"

She ran her lower lip through her teeth. "You might not like the answers I give."

"I know every possibility, Cali. And I'm ready for any of them. *Now* do you get it?"

She eyed him. "You mean that, don't you?" she asked softly.

"You bet," he said. "Whether you believe it or not, there's a lot more resting on your choice than a few years in Bedford, so I'm ready to leave it all on the field. Now get out of here. Whatever you choose, don't do it blindly."

He turned his back on her, and something in the motion wrenched an unwilling sob from her throat. Tears stinging her eyes, she stumbled to the door, and left.

* * * *

For the next few days, Cali tried to make sense of it, and could not. Talk or kill. Trust or kill. The words became a frantic mantra she repeated to herself over and over until they were meaningless, just sounds emptied of emotion. He'd boxed her in, given her no way out except to face the truth. But which truth? That she could and would kill to defend her life? That she was holding herself hostage? All of the above?

Trust or kill. Talk or kill. Remember or refuse memory of something so terrifying she didn't even dare name it to herself, much less to him.

But trust him for what? To give her what she wanted, if only she'd ask for it? To make the right choice, regardless of what she wanted? What would he want from her after she talked? How could he possibly help her? Remember, he told her. Learn to do more. Remember what? Learn what? Only more terror, everywhere she looked.

On Wednesday, alone in her room and tossing her way toward unwanted dreams, she punched her pillow hard, got up and got dressed. He had night shift on Wednesday. She would go see him. Racer taught her long ago how to pick the lock on their door, so she knew she could get out. She dismissed concerns about getting caught in the halls. She was going, and nobody, nothing in the universe, would stop her.

She stood for a moment, completed the thought. Then she got the door open and walked swiftly through the halls to his office. She met no one. Nothing got in her way.

When she got to his door, she saw dim light creeping out underneath. He was there. Of course he was. Waiting for her. She opened the unlocked door, and stood inside.

He was toying with a silver pen, holding it up and looking at the moonlight glinting against the chrome. He liked small things, small moments, particular pieces of light.

She closed the door. He heard the click and paused, then put the pen down and stood, facing her. She walked to him, and for the first time, went to his side of the desk. She turned her face up to his, realizing how tall he was. She'd never thought of him as a big man, but he was. He could toss her across the room if he wanted, though she knew he wouldn't.

He considered her without fear or rancor, knowing what she'd chosen even before she did. "Thank you," he said quietly.

She clenched her hands. Unclenched them. "For what?" she asked.

"For meaning it. For facing me. We both know you didn't have to. Now go ahead," he said quietly. "Do what you're here for."

"You could stop me," she said.

"By recommending parole because you threaten me? Not on my watch, Cali. There's something to be said for integrity."

One sharp pain constricted her chest, and she breathed it away. "Why are you doing this?" she whispered.

He gave her a shrug, a grin. "It's like rock climbing. I can see things you can't."

She hesitated. Was it a trick? Would the guards come storming in and pin her down? For what? Wishing someone dead wasn't a criminal offense. She could go ahead and do it without qualms. Except that this was different, because he wasn't fighting her. She'd always done this in the heat of the moment, without volition. Now she was owning responsibility for her choice, not acting in blind rage or fear but of intent. And that, it seemed, was exactly what he wanted from her. Nothing more. She needed a gesture, a motion of completion to acknowledge that. She lifted a hand and brought it to his face, raised herself up and kissed him.

The kiss was brief, but he gave it the same exacting attention he gave to light on leaves, his mouth warm and dry against hers. He savored it as if it was a last supper requested before execution. Only this: a taste of her.

The touch of his lips on hers called something new into the room, lending a ceaseless dimension, infinite and boundless, to the space between them. Their smallest click of time was encompassed in a present beyond any counting. The sensation was startling, and she pressed against him, wanting to go deeper in, but he pulled away. He gave her a wry look and shook his head. He wouldn't. Not this way. Not now. Apparently, he'd rather die.

He brushed a finger down her face lightly, then put his hands on her shoulders, staring at her with his motion filled eyes.

"Complete the thought, Cali," he said. "Now, while it's good."

And she did.

Wordlessly, without rage or fear, in full consciousness of choice, fully aware that she didn't know if it was right or wrong, she told him he was dead.

It started quicker than she expected. He gasped in pain, and she tried to back away but his hands held her shoulders, his open eyes forcing her to witness what she'd done.

Swiftly, unexpectedly, sorrow moved through her like an ancient sword. Sorrow? She hadn't felt that with any of the others. She didn't know what to do with it, but it was too late to call back the thought. Too late to change her choice now.

But he was in pain. She hadn't meant that. Not for him. She felt the rebellion of his body, the shrieking in his cells that said no, no, no and would not give in. Strong. He was strong, and he didn't want it, yet he chose it, didn't he? Or asked her to choose it? Or asked her if she would choose it, knowing he had no choice once she made hers. He accepted it, but his body wouldn't give in. His spirit, strong as the light he loved to watch, would not relinquish.

"You have to let go," she said clearly, firmly as he'd spoken to her on the side of the mountain. "You have to let go."

"I can't," he whispered. He dropped to his knees, taking her with him. "Help me."

She was panicked, feeling the drag, feeling herself sink with him. His hands still gripped her, but his eyes had the stronger hold and instinctively she raised a hand, covering them gently.

His hold on her loosened. He slumped to the floor. She knelt there with him, saw him shudder. Saw him sigh out breath one last time.

She stayed kneeling, staring at his body, negotiating sorrow. She wouldn't allow herself tears she didn't deserve. She'd chosen this. She made a gesture with her hand, putting the sorrow away in the room marked *Do Not Enter*. Then, she stood, looked at him one more time, seeing him as a collection of molecules easily unbound. Odd, she thought. Jesse was no longer there. Where had he gone?

She raised her hand and touched her lips.

"There," she said softly. "He's there."

Then she put herself in motion. She went to his desk and opened drawers, looking for the letter he'd shown her. She'd take it, and leave the one recommending parole, if it was a good one.

His desk drawers were neat, sparse, but she found no letters in them. She shook her head. She'd have to trust him after all. Didn't that just figure.

She left the room and closed the door softly behind her. Pain still nipped at her heels, and she kicked it away. Jesse was the kind of man whose heart was clearly determined to attack him, and bring him to his death.

* * * *

News of Jesse's death spread like wildfire through St. Ida's, and even Lola looked at Cali as if she was plague-ridden, disastrous. She didn't care. She'd be out of here soon enough, and wouldn't see any of them ever again. She waited out the remaining time for her board hearing, and entered it with confidence.

When they told her parole was denied, in light of her recent behavior and the absence of any valid positive reports, all she could do was laugh.

PART II

ENTROPY

Rainier Vassago sat at the round table, almost listening to the two men who talked at him. What they said wasn't important, though, and his mind was more occupied with thinking how laughable it was that such men insisted on round tables, saying it created lateral rather than vertical energy and inspire a sense of parity.

As if, he thought. If the table was rhomboid or a cube, where he sat would be the head. Everyone knew that. That's why Tritan Energy Corporation hired him, first as consultant, and now as CEO.

All energy flowed to him, all listened to him as the one voice that carried weight and merit. All eyes watched for what he'd do in a time of change and potential disaster.

Right now, these two men, Harry Bassinger and Joseph Garon, both on the Tritan Board of Directors, talked about profit margins and continuing upward trends. They had no problem with their profits, which were astonishingly high, but they did have problems with their nerves, because they couldn't explain why profits were high, given the current market slump and the current trends toward renewable energy. They wanted Rainier to explain. Wanted him to control it.

He let them yammer on a while, then waved everything they'd said away. "We're doing well because you hired me," he noted. "What else do you need?"

The two men looked at him, then at each other. Harry, an exceptionally white man with not enough hair and a bad case of dandruff, cleared his throat. Rainer settled in. Now they'd get to the substance.

"We were wondering about Aquarius," Harry said.

"Of course you were," Rainier said. "You should have started with that. What do you want to know about them?"

Joseph, in his sixties, balding and paunchy, lifted a hand, let it fall. "We can't track them. Their agenda's all over the place. One minute it's environmental protection, the next it's tax breaks for energy companies. They lobby progressive, but they may support our candidate. You know them, right? Explain it."

Rainier laughed. "What do you think of changing the world through the energy of our thoughts?" he asked.

Harry frowned. Joseph ran a hand along the back of his neck.

"Are you talking about some kind of a retreat?" Harry asked. "Get new ideas moving? You really think that'll help? I mean, we need to keep our guy in the oval office. Election coming up and all."

"Your guy in office is a wreck and he'll wreck us all just to puff up his own ego." Protest erupted around the room, and he held up a hand to silence it. "Doesn't matter. We can keep him if we can use him. What I'm talking about here is utilizing our thoughts to move things the way we want them to go. What do you think?"

At this, Harry looked frightened and Joseph mildly embarrassed. "That's—um—interesting," Joseph said.

"Right," Rainer replied. "Well, you asked about Aquarius, and that's what they're doing. I figured you'd want to know."

"Could you be more specific?" Harry asked judiciously.

"It's science," Rainier said. "E=mc2. There's energy, and there's matter, and we moved between them. Right now, we've got a unique window of opportunity to take advantage of that."

"Okay," Joseph said. "How?"

"The world is turning away from matter, toward energy. You don't carry cash, you just push numbers around computers. We're virtual and digital, all our information carried in bits and light. And after decades of using digital energy, satellite energy, microwave energy, all the bits of energy reaching our brains from our phones and more, it isn't just outside us. It's *in* us. Changing what we can do with our thoughts, changing who and what we are. It's feeding us. Giving us new avenues for power and control through our thoughts. Aquarius is using that. We should be, too."

The response to this was total silence. Rainier wasn't terribly surprised. He was hired to try new things, but nothing too new. Corporations wanted change that fit current specs. If he could help them figure out how to make oil from organic matter, they'd be happy. The idea that the entire human species was evolving because of energy was too much. It was like Climate Change and the Holocaust. It didn't fit into their profit margins, and so was way outside their purview. Finally, Harry spoke up.

"It sounds interesting," he said carefully. "Should we have a committee explore it?"

"No," Joseph said. "We should get one of our people on the Aquarius board. That's what we were thinking of, Rainier. Since you know them, they might accept you. And you can work them toward the bio-fuel side."

Rainier shook his head. "Men in suits don't explore Aquarius," he said. "A woman runs it, and she employs only women."

"I see," said Harry. "But you could—um—get to know her?"

"In the biblical sense?" Rainier asked. Their minds paced the cells of their inch thoughts, and would go no further.

"Your personal time is your own," Harry said. "But if you can find out anything…."

"You don't see," Rainier interrupted. "You're too scared. You always suspected that in spite of all your power and money, women are really running things, manipulating it their own way, and you aren't smart enough to stop them. You try to control their biology, their reproduction, their rights, and it doesn't work. But when you're offered a chance to know what they know, do what they do, it terrifies you. You don't see a damn thing. But I do, and fortunately for you, I'm CEO."

He put his hands on the table and pushed himself to standing. They made noises, and he ignored them. "I'm already working on Aquarius," he said. "I'll take care of it."

He walked out of the room. Too bad, he thought. It would have been good to get some more men involved, but he'd manage fine without them.

HEISENBERG'S UNCERTAINTY PRINCIPLE

Cali tugged at her jacket to close it against the chill October wind as she stood looking at the house. It was a halfway house for newly released prisoners, run by a woman named Ida Bethany, which she found ironic and interesting. She was supposed to live here for the next year. The house was big and old, and needed paint.

She slung her bag over her shoulder and looked down the street. The subway entrance wasn't too far. She could get to Penn Station and be well out of the City before anyone phoned her in missing. Of course, she had no money and no place to go, but she could probably find both of those easily enough. She'd learned a thing or two in her four years at Bedford.

She pointed herself toward the train, then stopped. She asked herself what Jesse would say, and realized he would laugh at her. She turned back to the halfway house.

Consulting with Jesse was a habit she'd developed at Bedford. When she had a decision to make she'd automatically ask herself what he'd say. Not that she always listened to the answer. Sometimes she argued with him and did what she wanted. Sometimes she didn't care one way or the other. But she always asked.

She knew it was strange that of all the voices in the world, the only one she trusted belonged to a man she'd killed, but he'd been right about the important things, and she'd learned a lot from him, though it took her a while to realize it.

This time, she figured he was right to laugh. Why should she walk away? Winter was coming, and this place had food and a warm bed, maybe even a bath. And she wanted to meet this woman named Ida, see if she was a saint after all. She could stay until she got situated, and leave on her own terms. There was no point in hurting herself. No point in holding herself hostage.

Somewhere in her, she thought she heard Jesse approve.

"Get out of my head," she said cheerfully. "I already killed you."

She could afford to be cheerful with him. She was free.

She walked up the steps, knocked on the door. She heard voices behind it. Then the door opened and she was facing a woman with long hair the color of a fireplace flame and a decent crop of freckles on a round face. She wore a sweater that didn't hide the protrusion of her belly. She was pregnant. Very pregnant.

"I'm Cali. Cali Spring. Am I at the right place?" she asked.

"Cali? Oh, sure. I forgot you were coming today. Yes, this is it." She smiled brightly, opened the door, swept an arm out and ushered her in. "Ida's not here, but I know which room is yours, so I can show you. Oh, I'm Lara."

She stuck a hand out and Cali took it, shook it and let it go. Lara gave a little laugh, a small shrug, then opened her arms and hugged Cali quickly and released her. "Silly things, handshakes, right? Something men in suits do. We're not like that here."

Another woman poked her head out from the end of the hall. "Who is it, Lara?" she asked.

"The new girl. Girl," she said, then slapped lightly at her forehead. "Woman, I mean. Cali. Cali, that's Hope."

Cali nodded at her, and she nodded in return, receded back into wherever she'd been. "Come on," Lara said, "I'll show you where you are."

She made a grab for Cali's bag, but Cali got it first. Lara made a tsk sound. "I'm pregnant, not disabled," she said, patting her round belly. "Six months."

"I guess that's good," Cali said uncertainly. Lara laughed again, a bright, inconsequential sound, and walked ahead. She led Cali up a set of old and worn stairs, talking as they went, saying that people never knew how to react to her pregnancy, if they should they offer sympathy or congratulations.

"At least you were honest," she said. "I like honest people, so I guess I'll like you. This is my room. And here's Dolores, and over there is Martina. We've got seven right now, so it's a full house. Ida sleeps up on the top floor. Has the whole attic to herself."

She chattered on as they walked down a long hall, turned a corner and came to a final door.

"This is you," she said, and opened it to a room that seemed spacious to Cali after years of living in cells and dorms. She put her bag down on the double bed, frowned.

"What's wrong? Most women like this room. Close to the upstairs bath, and a nice window, away from the street."

"I don't share a bed," she said. "I'll take the floor."

Lara blinked at her, then her face showed understanding. "Oh, no. This is your room. You don't share it with anybody."

Cali let this sink in, then turned a rueful smile to Lara. "I guess it's been a while."

"Sure. I remember. I'll leave you alone to get settled. Like I said, the bathroom's first door on the right. You have to sign up for tub time, but first day you get dibs, so go ahead if you want. This time of day, most of us are working anyway. When you come down for dinner Ida'll probably be back, and she'll tell you the rest of the routine. You got any questions?"

"Not right now," Cali said. "Thanks."

Lara gave a little wave with her fingers, and left Cali alone.

As soon as she was gone, Cali grinned broadly. This might not be so bad after all. And she could leave when she felt like it. On her terms. She knew how.

When she was at Bedford, Jesse's words kept recurring to her—that she could do more than kill. At first she'd been too angry with him, with herself, to explore the notion. Then there were months of learning to deal with the environment, the people, learning who to avoid, who might offer limited assistance.

She made it clear she wasn't messing with anyone, and wanted nobody messing with her. She'd do her time clean, and wouldn't get involved with schemes for drugs or white gangs or black gangs or any gangs at all. It took some focus, and one dead inmate. That was Dorris, who whispered things at her during rec time. Cali, knowing her capacities better after Jesse, waited until dinner then looked at her, told her she was dead, and went back to her food. Dorris went down within a minute, and nobody bothered Cali anymore.

After that, her anger cooled, her anxiety level lowered, and she began evaluating her situation with a cooler head. She recognized finally that her choice got her here, not Jesse's. She began to understand that her anger was mostly at herself for killing him. Once she understood that, she put it away. It was gone. Done. She couldn't undo it, and she wouldn't waste energy regretting it. With nothing but time on her hands, she thought about the possibilities he'd hinted at, and she began trying new moves.

She started small, thinking of food she wanted. Roast beef and mashed potatoes. Real potatoes with butter, not a box of flakes mixed with tepid water and margarine. She spent some time with this, until the thought felt complete.

Two nights later as they stood in line for dinner, Tanika, in front of Cali, pronounced reverently, "Mother of God and holy shit. I died and went to heaven. Or the cook died and they got a real one."

"What?" asked Rhoda, peering around Cali, who was in front of her.

Tanika pointed at her plate, but Cali didn't even have to look. She could smell it. Roast beef, cooked medium rare, and mashed potatoes with no box smell to them.

She tried other thoughts, staying small, learning the feel of this thing. It was different than before. Without the energy of her rage behind it, she had to focus with greater intent, seek out an open and silent space to let the intent unfold. At first it was exhausting, like digging her way out from under six feet of dirt. A lot of her thoughts wouldn't complete, and that had its own value, forcing her to examine what stopped them, what moved them toward completion.

She learned that failure usually came from either believing what she wanted wasn't possible, or internal interference which kept her from wanting something completely. Once, just to test this, she tried asking for her father. The attempt aborted itself quickly, slamming into the doors marked *Do Not Enter* in her mind. To call her father would be to remember her mother. She did not want that.

In this way she learned that a thought could be stopped if its completion was contingent on something she didn't want. She played with this balance, testing desire against fear, seeing what strength of desire outweighed what strength of fear, and vice versa, seeking ways to bypass the fear and get to the desire.

She also learned that while it was possible to work events and objects, people were difficult at best. Her cellmate, Carla, was a Republican. In spite of the fact that poverty got her here, she talked incessantly about the need for cutting welfare money, making people work for a living. She argued with the other women about it, and though Cali knew little about politics, she tried completing a thought that would turn Carla into a liberal. It didn't work. Didn't even give Carla a headache.

Cali learned that she couldn't shift strongly held beliefs, though she could get someone to behave in unusual ways—for instance, getting the chef to use real potatoes—if she was leading them in a direction they were already inclined to go. She might get Carla to accidentally vote Democrat, if she worked on it, but the cook at Bedford had a hankering to be a real chef, so her thought only nudged him down a path he was already walking.

Changing events was easier, and for the most part, more useful. Weather, she found, was somewhat amenable to shifting, being so dynamic already. As long as she didn't try for snow in August the conditions for any number of possibilities existed at any given moment, and she could get a little rain when she didn't want to go out in the yard, a little sun when she needed it in February. Doing this made her think of her day on the mountain with Jesse, and it occurred to her that maybe the storm that saved her life was more than luck.

She practiced, tested, failed and succeeded in small ways for two years, and then found that her environment was limiting the possibilities. She could maybe try to complete that old thought about having a million dollars, but what could she do with it here? Or could she even believe in it enough to complete it while she was in prison?

She began to think about the possibility of leaving. At first, it seemed remote. How would she begin? Look for a warden to influence? Just wish for it? She could barely imagine it, much less believe it as possible.

She put it aside and worked on other skills, testing the amount of energy it took to complete different kinds of thoughts, because while it was no longer exhausting, it was still tiring. She didn't know if she had enough energy to complete the thought of getting herself out, or where she might get it from. She was perplexed by this problem for some time, and then, for no particular reason, she went back to the store of images she'd salvaged from her time at St. Ida's.

Here was the cat Schroedinger, lolling in the sun, licking his paws. Here was the sound of peepers in the spring. Here was her grandmother's soft hand on hers. Here was sun on leaves, and Jesse's eyes taking it in. Here was Jesse's brief kiss, the feel of his lips on hers, still living vividly in her skin.

And here was energy, apparently in unlimited supply. These images filled her with it as soon as she drank from them, and they never ran out. They were alive and self-renewing.

Having discovered this, she consciously sought other images for her store, and she was never again tired after completing a thought. She returned to the idea of leaving, and this time she felt ready for it. It wasn't impossible. It was just unknown. And she'd have to learn to accept the unknown as also possible.

Three and a half years after she'd arrived at Bedford she opened the thought of leaving. That was all. She didn't try to figure out how it would happen, or do any direct influence. She bypassed all fears or voices that said it was impossible. She just declared herself free, and completed the thought.

The next day, she was offered early parole for good behavior.

By the time she left she found she was grateful for the time in Bedford, because without it she might not have had time or space to understand what she could do. She'd wanted life on her terms, and at Bedford, she'd learned how to get it.

She could hear echoes of Jesse's laughter at this. Embedded in it was a disturbing sense of inevitability, as if she'd gone where he hoped, regardless of her attempts to avoid that path. Maybe she'd learned exactly what he intended: that what you really want will pursue you, in spite of of your protests to the contrary.

* * * *

After she unpacked at Ida's, Cali did take a bath, her first in some time, and she luxuriated in hot water with bubbles from a bright blue bottle on the side of the tub. When she was done, it was dark out, evening coming early in autumn, and she heard sounds of life in the rest of the house.

It had a different quality than the sounds at either St. Ida's or Bedford. At St. Ida's voices were high pitched, frantic. At Bedford they were a constant low rumble. Here there was a variety of pitches and cadences punctuated by laughter that sounded real. Cali dressed and made her way downstairs, followed the voices until she came to a good sized room off a kitchen, where women moved around a large table, setting down plates and utensils and food.

Lara was there, and she flashed her bright smile when Cali entered. "Hey everybody—this is Cali. Dolores, Martina, you met her. Just got here today, from Bedford. St. Ida's before that."

"Oh, God," someone groaned. "You were at St. Ida's? I did a year there. A looong time ago. Is Marilyn still sliming around?"

"Not anymore," Cali said.

"Well, that's good. What a perv. I'm Georgia, by the way," she said, and pointed around. "That's Cheryl, and Nance is on night shift at the hospital. That's the gang."

"You forgot someone," a voice rich as melted chocolate declared, and they turned to it.

The inmates at Bedford told Cali that Ida Bethany was real old, and a little strange, but the woman who stood framed in the doorway between dining area and kitchen was tall and stood straight, looked strong as if from years of physical work, her skin etched with time spent in the sun and the wind. Her thick silver hair framed high cheekbones and alert eyes. Cali startled, seeing them. They were silver blue, with flecks of gold and green. They were sea eyes, tidal and grasping. They were Jesse's eyes.

Ida came up to Cali, put a hand on each shoulder. kissed her on each cheek.

"You're Cali," she said. "I'm Ida. Keeper of this zoo."

The other girls laughed and Ida's face broke into a smile. "That's the official welcome, so now you can eat."

PHASE SPACE

Cali easily settled in to the routine at Ida's. She had a receptionist job at an insurance company, doing work that was neither challenging nor burdensome. She didn't like it, but it wouldn't kill her, so she stayed, for now. She'd learned the value of taking her time.

She did her assigned chores at Ida's, cooking dinner on Tuesdays, breakfast on Saturday, and cleaning on Mondays and Wednesdays. The women were friendly, but gave each other ample space, from long experience of institutional living. For her dinner days she worked with Lara, which she was glad about since Lara could actually come up with a good recipe and Cali knew little about cooking. For breakfast she worked with Nance and Hope, and that was easy. Even she knew how to scramble an egg.

On her first night Ida sat her down at the kitchen table after everyone else was gone and laid down the ground rules.

"No drugs except for prescriptions, which you tell me about. No men on the premises. Curfew's one a.m. on weekends, midnight on weeknights, but you can get out of that if you clear it with me. You make all your parole meetings, and you don't get in fights. If you're inclined to hit someone, go to your room and take a time out, or take a walk or punch a pillow or something. If there's a problem you can't solve, talk to me about it. I also have a list of therapists you can use for free, if you want one. Other than that, do your work and get used to being out again. Any questions?"

Cali thought a minute It all seemed pretty clear, but there was one thing bothering her. "Your name," she said. "You're not connected to St. Ida's, are you?"

She smiled, a slow and careful motion of her elegant face. "When I started doing this I was given a list of facilities to accept women from," she said. "I picked St. Ida's because of my name, so quite a few of the women here went there. Anything else?"

Cali shook her head.

"You'll be here nine months. Take advantage of any opportunity that comes up. Once you're out of here the world won't necessarily be walking up to offer you more."

* * * *

So the days went, and every morning Cali would ask herself if she was ready to leave, and each day the answer would be not yet. The house had warmth, and an absence of drama she appreciated. She figured that was Ida's influence. She was smooth, elegant, yet clearly savvy in the ways of the world. She reminded Cali of a combination of Mrs. Henderson and Jesse. She looked on the women without judgment, stayed at peace with herself and insisted on peace in her house. She got it.

Cali didn't make friends with the other women, but Lara seemed to assume friendship with everyone, and would chatter on as they made dinner together, talking about her past, her ex-boyfriend Danny, the drug addict who used to beat her regularly and whose drug use got her a short sentence, commuted when she turned up pregnant.

"So this baby is, like, rescuing me," Lara said. "I owe him, now. Or her. I'm not sure which it is. And I don't care, so long as it's healthy, except with a girl, I'll worry more. Wouldn't you?"

"I don't know," Cali said. "If it was a boy, I'd worry he'd turn out like all the asshole men I've known. If it was a girl, I'd worry she'd be involved with all the asshole men I've known. Either way, it's worry."

At this Lara laughed. "But if it's a girl, I'll feel it more scary, you know? Anyway, right now I'm just worried about actually having it."

"Yeah," Cali said, stirring the sauce Lara had concocted for the pasta. It smelled richly of garlic and olive oil. Lara's life philosophy was odd, but she knew how to feed people. And her energy did the same. When she was around, the other women laughed more, brightened in some fundamental way. Even Cali did so, though she wasn't sure why.

"I talked to this birthing assistant, you know?" Lara continued. "She said it was, like, possible to go through the whole thing without any pain at all, if you, like, did it right."

Cali shook her head doubtfully "I wouldn't count on that, Lara."

"I don't know. I already meditate. I'm pretty good at it. Like, I can get someplace with it, you know? Come on, Cali. Don't you believe in the power of the mind?"

Cali startled. That was a good kick in the behind. "Sometimes. Other times I think it's a bunch of crap."

Lara brushed her hair back from her face, twisted her mouth into a smile. "You're such a skeptic," she said. "But y'know, you carry a lot of positive energy. I feel it in you. Listen, would you be there?"

"Be where?"

"You know. Like, at the birth. I think it'd be great. You'd be a great coach."

Cali was too surprised to think of an immediate way out. "I don't really know how," she said. "Shouldn't you have people with experience?"

"I'll have doctors and nurses. I'm talking about the right energy." Lara closed her eyes, shook her head, her red hair moving like liquid fire around her shoulders. She held her hand out as if seeing something in front of her. "If I was, like, rock climbing, and I fell, I'd want you underneath me. You'd catch me. I feel that."

She opened her eyes and smiled brightly at Cali, who worked to unclench her jaw.

"Say you'll be there," Lara said. "Come on."

"Okay," Cali said. "Sure."

Lara squealed with delight, threw her arms around Cali, who allowed the embrace but extricated herself as quickly as she could.

"You want more mushrooms in this sauce?" Cali asked.

"Definitely," Lara said. "Always more mushrooms."

* * * *

Cali had been there almost a month and was beginning to think this would be the first normal experience she'd had in her life since her father left, when Ida appeared in her room in the middle of the night.

She'd been dreaming about a mountain that grew up out of the earth, slowly groaning its way skyward, and somehow Ida's entrance was connected with the end of the dream, as if she grew out of it, into the room. Cali woke without surprise or fear and looked at her, standing at the foot of the bed. She wore her usual long pants and simple cotton blouse, and didn't look as if she'd been to sleep at all.

"We'll start now," she said. "You should sit up."

Cali did so. Ida took a seat in the chair next to the bed, pointed to her eyes. "Watch me. Do what I do."

Ida breathed in slowly and deeply through her mouth, then released the breath. Cali did the same.

"Good. Keep it going, and find out where your awareness is in your body."

Cali tracked it, found it lingering at the back of her skull. She didn't say anything, but Ida nodded as if she had.

"Move it to your throat," she said.

Cali did so, and felt a strange stirring there, as if something was coming dislodged. She coughed hard, eyes stinging with tears.

"That's okay," Ida said. "Keep breathing through it. Just old stuff coming out."

Cali recovered, and kept breathing. Ida had her move her awareness through her spine, her arms, her legs, back to her eyes and ears and back down her throat, stopping finally at a center point in her chest. Here, Cali felt something sharp and painful, and she gasped.

Ida ran a studious gaze up and down her. "That's probably enough for tonight," she said. "Not a bad start, but I'm working with pure gold when I work with you, aren't I?"

And she rose and left the room.

* * * *

The next morning, Cali wondered if she'd dreamt the whole thing. During parts of her day she found herself breathing in that same deep way, checking to see how she might move awareness around her body, checking to see where it did and didn't hurt.

That night she tried to stay awake to see if Ida would return, but she couldn't keep her eyes open. She drifted into a dream, and then woke abruptly to the sensation of cold at her back. She blinked up at a a night sky, looked to her right and left and saw she was lying on her back on cold ground, in Ida's back yard.

"What's happening?" she whispered.

Ida's voice replied. "We're working," she said.

Cali turned her head toward the sound, saw Ida standing over her. She didn't question further. It seemed pointless. Ida was working with her. That was all.

"Oh," she said. "What do I do?"

"Arms at your side, palm up. Legs slightly open. Close your eyes, and feel the earth at your back."

Once again, Cali did as she was told. Her back was cool and damp, and for the first time she was aware of the planet that supported her. She felt it perfectly still beneath her, even while it turned at a rate of 900 miles an hour, moving through space at 90 miles a second. Motion and stillness filled her, and she gasped.

"Good," Ida said. "That's good. Now let yourself go."

Cali opened her eyes, stared at Ida. "What?" she demanded.

"Look at your hands," Ida said.

Cali did so. She was clutching grass as if her life depended on it.

"Let go," Ida said. "Surrender. You're part of the planet. Sink into it."

Cali took one deep breath and released it. She deliberately loosened the grip of her hands, deliberately relaxed the muscles in her legs and back and head. As she did, she felt some essential part of herself meshing with the ground beneath her, felt the entire energy of the planet moving through her as she moved with it, dancing in space, becoming part of her as she became a part of it.

"This should be scary," she said out loud.

"Are you scared?" Ida asked.

She thought about it. "No. Not at all. It's just—this."

"What's this?" Ida asked.

"Death," Cali said. "Returning. Going back."

"That's right," Ida agreed. "And you know all about that."

Cali had no idea what she meant, but she was too busy to ask. For a few moments all was silence, while Cali traversed death as if it was a mountain that needed climbing. She found nothing to fear there. It was bigger than she'd expected, but she liked the lack of talk, the absence of bullshit. She didn't know how long she'd been floating in it before she heard Ida's voice, as if from a great distance.

"Come back now," she said.

Cali stayed still, reluctant to return.

"It's important," Ida said more imperatively. "Come back. Now."

Cali moved her hand over damp grass, shifted her back, opened her eyes. "Okay," she told Ida.

To her surprise, Ida's face expressed relief. "Great," she said. "Now sit up."

Cali did so, with a new awareness of her body as it occupied time, and the particular space of Ida's yard. "What's next?" she asked.

"Same as last night," Ida replied.

They went through the same breathing and awareness routine, but this time they went more quickly, and when they got to her chest it didn't hurt as much. Now Ida had her use her hands to push her awareness out and around her. Cali was supremely conscious of new sensations, as if more air was available to her, and as if she could hear a whisper a mile away if she concentrated.

"You're beginning to get it, aren't you?" Ida asked.

"Yeah. But what do I do with it?"

"These are your boundaries. You use them to listen. Sense things. Protect yourself. This'll help you stay alive."

"I don't understand."

"Not yet. But some part of you knows who you are. What you do. I'm just making sure you can take care of yourself when you do it. Let in what you want, keep other things out."

"I keep just about everything out."

"That's a good bedtime story, but it won't work where you're going."

"Where am I going?"

"Either nowhere or everywhere," Ida said. "There's no in between for you. Let's get back to it, shall we? We'll move into core stuff."

She led her back to breathing, and Cali trailed her awareness toward what she wanted. It was surprisingly painful at first, and her breathing grew raspy, tight. She started to cough hard, and Ida moved next to her, put a hand to her back.

"Don't fight with it," Ida said. "Just let it happen. It'll pass."

Cali gasped and coughed some more, until the fit slowly calmed and she could breathe normally. She rubbed water from her eyes, looked at Ida.

"I'm okay, I think," she said, hearing her voice crack.

"You are. You hit some old stuff. Know what it was?"

"Just—what I wanted."

"What was that?"

She couldn't name it. Not here. "Just—someone," she said.

Ida's face went smooth as marble, but Cali saw a muscle in her jaw tightening. "Jesse," she said, pain lodged under her words.

Cali tensed. "You know him?"

"Knew him," she said. "I knew him. He's dead."

In response, the most unfathomable words dropped out of Cali's mouth. "Not to me," she said, meaning it.

For the first time, Cali saw Ida lose her cool. She hissed in a quick breath. Her hands, at her side, made incomplete gestures as if to ward something off. Then they clenched and were still. She didn't say another word. She just turned and walked away.

Cali waited a few minutes, adjusted herself to her surroundings. Then, cold and tired, she pushed herself up and went back to her room.

* * * *

The next day Cali was certain Ida would cut her, or throw her out, but all was as usual. Ida greeted her with casual friendliness, and the other women chatted and laughed as if nothing had happened in the night, as if she hadn't danced with death and eternity and talked about a dead man. All was well.

And Ida continued to work with her, though she didn't mention Jesse again. Cali wondered that she wasn't tired from being woken in the middle of the night, but she felt strangely refreshed and full of energy. She also wondered if Ida visited the other women, taught them this as well, but somehow didn't want to ask. It seemed private, and if she went to the other women, it was none of her business.

* * * *

Shortly after that, one day when she came home from work and was thinking only about Dolores cooking tonight, some of the best enchiladas she'd ever had, she found Lara sitting on the living room floor in her meditation pose, her eyes closed, but tears rolling down her cheeks.

Most of the women here had something worth crying about, and it was best to just let them. Cali checked her steps and was ready to walk away when Lara opened her eyes. Cali was caught by her gaze, which was far away and filled with joy. She thought of Jesse, staring at leaves and sun. She stayed still.

"Are you okay?" she asked quietly.

Lara wiped at her eyes, nodded vigorously. "Sorry. I was doing this meditation I learned. It's called loving kindness. Buddhist thing. It's really, like, beautiful. It's helping me stay calm, y'know? Because of Danny."

Danny was released from prison six months early, and they assumed he'd try to contact Lara. Ida notified the local police and they put extra patrols on the house, but Lara was nervous, especially about what might happen when she went to the hospital.

"That's good," Cali said. "I'm glad it's helping you."

"But you'll still go with me, right? When the baby's born? I mean, if you're at work, you'll leave work, right?"

"Yes, Lara. I will. I already promised, didn't I?"

"I know. Okay. Only—" she slewed her eyes around to see if anyone was listening. "I think if he shows up, you can take care of it."

"If he shows up the cops'll take care of it," Cali said. "You have a restraining order."

"I just feel safe with you. And maybe the meditation'll help. Like, he'll get that energy, y'know?"

Cali shrugged. "Sure," she said.

Lara, whose belly seemed to get bigger by the minute, held out a hand and Cali helped her stand. "You should try it, Cali," she said. "It's really cool. You say you love yourself, and then you say may I be well. May I be peaceful. May I be liberated. Then you start putting it out to other people. To, like, the women here, and Ida, and family, and friends, and then to people you don't know or don't even like. I've been doing it for Danny. Like, I love Danny. May he be well, may he be peaceful, may he be liberated."

Cali made a wry face at this. She didn't think much of wishing Danny well. If she knew him better, she'd probably wish him dead, a more efficient use of energy. "Lara, don't even tell me you think you can fix him," she said.

"It's not like that. It's like, letting him go. You ever let someone go?"

"Not if they did what he did to you."

Lara put a hand on Cali's arm, rubbed it gently. "You have to try it to understand."

Cali tensed. "It's not my thing," she said, her voice more gruff than she intended.

Lara released her. "Okay," she said gently. "But I'm saying it for you, too."

Lara continued to stare at her, her large eyes luminous with clarity and strength. For the first time Cali thought that her meditation wasn't naivete or superstitious mumblings against calamity, or prayers to beg a parental deity for blessings. Lara wasn't innocent. She'd been neglected, beaten, arrested without cause, and her meditation didn't deny that reality. Instead, it was a discipline she followed to move beyond it, to a place where she could have a life on her own terms. Her particular, Lara-like terms, very different from Cali's, but just as interesting. She was working to complete a thought, and it was a thought larger than any Cali had ever imagined.

"I get it," she murmured.

Lara's mouth turned up into half a grin. "You really do, don't you?"

"Yeah," Cali said. "Thanks. I—I appreciate the thought."

* * * *

That night, when Ida came to Cali's room she didn't sit. She stood near the bed, listening. "There's a block," she said. "Can you clear it?"

Cali sat up, shook her head. "I don't understand."

"Something's keeping you from moving forward. Don't you know what it is?"

"Don't you?" she asked.

"Of course not. It's your block. Go ahead and find it."

Cali breathed in, focused her awareness as she'd been doing. It wasn't long before she knew what Ida meant. The room in her mind marked *Do Not Enter*.

"Aah," Ida said. "There it is."

Cali licked at her lips, which felt dry. "Yeah," she said.

"Go ahead and clear it."

"How?"

"Let it go. Release it."

"No," Cali said firmly.

Ida raised an eyebrow. "No?"

"I can't. It's dangerous."

Ida regarded her with a combination of compassion and irritation. "You really have to, Cali," she said. "There's a lot riding on what you can do."

She startled. The same thing Jesse had said, long ago. And she still had no idea what it meant, nor did she want to.

"I can't," she said, even more firmly.

Ida sighed. "Did you try Lara's medicine?"

"What?

"Her meditation. I love myself. May I be well. May I be peaceful. May I be liberated."

Cali wondered if Lara learned that from Ida. Regardless, she'd grown used to following where Ida led, and she took a breath, opened her mouth to say the words. And no sound would emerge. To say it she'd have to mean it. Love herself? Of course she did. Didn't she?

But there was that locked room, and behind it was a self she didn't love, along with the others she'd put there. She thought of Jesse. Was he in there? She didn't know, but certainly the part of her that killed him was there, and that was more than enough reason to keep the door closed. She began to shiver, thinking the air was cool in the room, winter creeping in through cracks in the windows.

Ida's mouth worked hard for a moment and Cali thought she was going to say something angry. Then she offered Cali a brief and rather rueful smile. "I'm not sorry you feel that way," she said. "But we can't go any further until you clear the junk out. Go slow. Make a start. Do what you can, okay?"

"Yeah. Sure."

"Okay." Ida moved over to the side of the bed, put a hand on Cali's head, smoothed her hair and kissed her forehead. "May you be well," she said softly. "May you be peaceful. May you be liberated."

She left the room and Cali fell asleep to dream of mountains that made and unmade themselves while she sat nearby, alone, weeping.

* * * *

Ida didn't visit her at night after that, and Cali found she missed it. The daily routine went on as usual, only now the women were all taking turns coaching Lara with her Lamaze breathing, getting ready for the imminent birth. She had a bag packed and ready, and Ida had a bassinet in her attic ready for use.

Lara spent a great deal of time with Cali, sometimes sitting on her bed and talking late into the night, reminding Cali of Racer, and nights at St. Ida's. Neither spoke about anything too deep or anything to do with the future. Cali understood they were holding each other through a waiting period, days carved out of the counting. It was important to float on the surface of things, not anticipating what was to be.

Cali was actually looking forward to witnessing the birth, with some qualifications. It would be a new experience for her, which might be exciting, but she didn't know how she'd take to the mess and emotional fuss. She hoped it wouldn't be too sappy. Above all, she hoped it would go easily and well, and Lara and her baby would be fine. Sometimes at night she caught herself whispering, "May she be well. May she be peaceful. May she be liberated."

She'd laugh at herself for it, and roll over into sleep and dreams.

* * * *

Breakfast that Saturday, and Cali was in charge of the table, Dinah making scrambled eggs. Everyone was gathered except for Lara.

"Where is she?" Dinah asked. "Cali, go get her."

Cali climbed the stairs to Lara's room, knocked on the door. "Lara?" she asked.

Quickly, Lara's voice replied, "Cali?"

"Yeah. You coming down? Eggs're ready."

A pause. A long one. Too long. Maybe Lara was in labor early and too scared to say.

"You okay?" Cali asked. She moved closer to the door, listening now.

"Sure. I'm just—I'm not hungry," Lara said.

She said that, but Cali heard something else. Fear. Stark, unmitigated, sharp and thick. She moved closer to the door. Lara was saying something quietly, and another voice was answering. A deep male voice. All her senses working, Cali saw what was happening, and knew it wasn't good.

"Suit yourself," she said, staying casual.

She stood where she was, asking herself what she should do. Call 911, she thought. Now. But as she thought it, the door opened, and Lara's terrified face appeared. Behind her a man held her arm, and pressed a gun against her temple.

"Get inside," he told Cali.

She did so, and he closed the door behind her.

For a moment, they were silent. Cali was the first to speak. "Put the gun down," she said quietly, meaning it, intending it with all her will.

The man eyed her, and his hand wavered. Cali calmed herself to complete the thought but from somewhere in that room in her mind marked *Do Not Enter*, old chains rattled. When did a man ever do what he promised? When was this possible? How?

She pushed those thoughts aside, focused everything on completing this thought, but the man turned his gun toward her, screeched at her, "Bitch! Whore!"

Lara, released, flung herself at him, screaming, "NO! NO!" and he whirled back to her, pointed the gun at her and fired once, twice, three times.

Cali lunged forward, hit him below the knees, her entire body in it and he went down, his head slamming against the old metal radiator and he was out cold, gun skittering across the floor.

She heard cries, people running up the stairs and she ignored that, crawled to Lara who was on her back, blood everywhere, her belly covered with it, her breathing labored and shallow. Cali grabbed her hand and she gripped it, turned terrified eyes to Cali.

"Hang on," Cali said. "Hang on. I've got you. Help's on the way."

She went into her thoughts, looked for one to complete, something about Lara living, Lara healing, but nowhere in her could she find any belief in this possibility. She cursed herself for her lack of faith, searched for just the tiniest seed of it, clawing at her past, her present, anything.

Behind her she heard voices. Someone shrieking, Ida, asking for calm, saying something about getting an ambulance. Someone was sobbing. Dolores? She couldn't tell. Voices approached, receded.

"I'm here," Cali said to Lara, whose glance moved to Danny, still unconscious.

Blood frothed at her lips. She moved them, sound emerging. Cali bent low to hear.

"I love Danny," she said, her voice a hiss of air, "May he be well . . ."

Cali felt herself go tight with rage. Lara gripped down on her hand and looked to her with urgency. "Say it," she hissed.

Cali shook her head. She couldn't. She couldn't. Lara's grip tightened, her eyes big with intent and will.

Cali took a breath, let it out. She had to say it, and mean it. Not for Danny. For Lara, who had shown her something new in the world. For Lara, whom she'd failed to save.

"I love Danny," Cali whispered. "May he be well. May he be peaceful. May he be liberated."

Lara nodded at her to keep going, and she repeated it over and over again, she wasn't sure how many times or for how long. She just kept saying it, until Lara sighed out a long breath and closed her eyes.

* * * *

The cops arrived before the ambulance, but it didn't matter. Lara was dead before any of them got there.

Danny was reviving, and at least they grabbed him before he could run or do more damage. They found out later he'd learned about Ida's from a friend of his, who was an accomplished hacker. He'd been watching the house, and when he figured out which room was Lara's, he'd climbed the drainpipe to her window, which she liked to keep open on warm mornings. Two cops took him away and the others stayed to ask questions that had no answers. What was he angry about? Was he doing drugs? Did she invite him in? Was the baby his?

Cali held onto Lara's dead hand while she answered, while the coroner pronounced time of death, while forensic people took pictures. She was quietly cooperative, even when they suggested maybe she let Danny in, maybe she was helping him deal meth somewhere?

Ida stepped in then. She put a hand on Cali's shoulder, looked at the cop. "That's enough," she said. "More than enough."

Cali's lips moved silently. May they be well. May they be peaceful. May they be liberated.

When the police left and Lara's body was taken away, Cali went to her room. Without realizing what she planned, she started packing a bag. She went upstairs to Ida's room, which was empty, since Ida was still downstairs dealing with the police. She moved to Ida's jewelry box and took out some of the better pieces, pocketed them.

When she walked out the front door, nobody noticed except Ida, but that fine lady didn't say a word.

QUANTUM 3: ZIPPORAH

The Great One changed names, changed aspects, and gathered many worshippers to himself. Their energy only increased his, but it was never enough for him. He wanted her energy. Only hers. And so he never left her alone for long. She would return to walk the earth in a new body, thinking he wouldn't care, and for a little while she'd have peace, sovereignty over her life. Then he'd find her, and the struggle would begin again.

Granted, it was partly her own fault. She would not relinquish her gift to him, and she would not leave her companion, who also returned, and who, in spite of their disagreements, loved her as she loved him. They were drawn to each other across miles and years, finding each other in the most unlikely places and ways.

In one return, she chose to do her work in a small way, acting as priestess, daughter to priest of the people. Why would he notice that? She was a Midianite, just as her father was, and she healed as she could, taught who would listen, and lived content. This was enough for her, and though she'd seen nothing of her companion, she'd also seen nothing of the Great One, her ancient enemy. She heard rumors that he was expanding his rule, reaching out to new people, but if that was so, surely he'd have found her by now. She began to hope he'd left for good, or that he'd forgotten her as small, inconsequential.

Then, one day when she was bringing water from the well, a man approached her, and she recognized the strange color of his eyes. Her companion, her eternal lover, finding her again. Though he wasn't of her people, he pled for her hand, and they were wed.

For a while, they were happy living with her people, raising the children she bore him, but then he learned that his people were being held in slavery, by a servant of the Great One.

"I can't leave them," he said. "They must be freed."

She bit at her lip. "How?" she asked, staying calm. "How can you?"

"It's not far. I'll go there. I can heal their wounds, at the least. So can you."

She did not want to go. Did not want to help. Surely, if they went to a land where the Great One's servant ruled, he would not be far behind. He would find them, and destroy all their joy.

He put his hands on her shoulders and looked deep in her eyes. "Will you?" he asked.

She said yes, because she also abhorred the thought of slavery, which, she supposed, was one reason why they loved each other. And so they made their way back toward that place by the river where she'd raised a snake in another lifetime, that land where she'd raised her lover's dead body, and re-membered him. But they did not reach their goal.

They were in the middle of the desert when the Great One's servant appeared, and chased them across the desert sands, intent on killing them both.

Burdened by children and gear, they could not run for long. "Stop," her companion said. "We'll face our death together this time."

She was ready for it, ready to face her own death, but not his. Not again.

When the Great One's servant reached them, she held a hand up. "What do you want?" she asked.

The creature, made only of light and fire, hissed out a reply. "He is ours," he said.

Her throat constricted around impending grief as she knew the truth: The only way to save her lover was to give him away. "I'll make him yours," she replied.

She grabbed a piece of sharp flint from the ground and cut the foreskin that bound him to her. Now he was marked as belonging to the Great One, Lord of his people, who insisted on this sacrifice for all the men he ruled. He might kill her, but he would not kill one of his own.

She touched her companion's thighs with the foreskin she'd deftly sliced, saying, "Now you are a bridegroom of blood to me, for by your blood, I have saved you."

Her companion understood. He also knew her danger, because she was a woman, and could never be fully under the protection of the Great One.

"Leave," he told her. "Stay alive. In some other age we'll make our thought complete."

She accepted this. She'd bought his life, and that was enough. She re-turned to her people, living without him. Occasionally the birds of the air and the snakes of the land brought her rumors of what had happened. Her companion had led his people out of slavery. Plagues sent by the Great One destroyed those who fought him, and they escaped. Then, much later, she learned her companion had died, before he ever reached the land the Great One promised to him. At this, she relinquished her body, choosing to rest in death with him.

In their absence, the Great One gathered power. He grew in strength, fashioning an invisible deity for the minds of the people, feeding off the worship they offered, while even in death she grieved what had been, and what she knew was yet to be.

BOYLE'S LAW

The women of Aquarius gathered in the conference room with its low lighting and minimal furniture. Just deeply cushioned chairs arranged in a circle at the center of the room, a big space, painted blue with a sage green carpet that gave it an underwater feel.

Talia Jordan, seated in the circle with the half dozen women who were most experienced, took them all in with her glance.

"Anybody have anything they need to say before we start?" she asked.

One of the women, a newer one, raised her head. "I think things are getting worse, not better," she said. "I mean, how is it we still got this asshole president in charge? And why aren't we getting him out of here?"

Talia nodded. "It might seem like that, but keep in mind we're working long term, going for big goals, not just getting short term satisfaction. For our purposes, everything is proceeding according to plan."

Another woman nodded. "He's doing our work for us."

"I don't see how," the new woman said.

"The greatest evil creates the greatest good," Talia said calmly. "You'll see. What happens because of him will be the best."

The new woman eyed her suspiciously. "You really think we can turn it around?"

"On a dime," she assured her. "When the time is right, it'll all fall into place. You'll see. But that lives in the future. We need to be in the present. We've discussed that."

One of the other women nodded.

"So what are we focusing on today?" Talia asked.

"We need more funding," one woman said, and two others murmured agreement.

"We'll start there. Anything else?"

"More women," another one said. "We'll do better if we have more energy."

"So we'll start with the money. Let's say . . . twenty million. Work for thirty minutes. When the thought's complete we'll move on to increased membership. If there's a particular woman you know who's suited to Aquarius, focus your energy on her. If not, then just use your imagination."

At this, some of the women chuckled mildly. The energy of the human imagination was their hammer, and with it they were building a new world.

They joined hands, set their breathing in synchronous rhythms, and began, opening themselves to the first thought they'd complete. Money wasn't difficult. There was plenty around. It was just a matter of drawing it close. When they all felt the thought complete and moved on to membership, their work grew trickier. They had to focus on women like themselves, who knew what it took to run the world and wanted the job. Here, without one central focus, they dropped hands and each went their own way. Their breath was synchronized, but their thoughts roamed where they needed to go.

Talia kept track, occasionally going in to one of the woman to steer her away from a fruitless train of thought and toward something more likely. Some of the women wanted to push at those who would never understand or believe what they did, which was a waste. She moved them gently toward more amenable prospects, and if they knew of no one in particular, she brought to mind places like St. Ida's, and Bedford. Aquarian women fell outside the bell curve in both directions. Idealists or cynics, criminals or geniuses, or both.

When she sensed they were all working well, she turned to her own thoughts. She had a particular person in mind and she searched for her, as she'd done for many years. Recently she thought she'd found her. That was right before Jesse died, which was a disappointment to her. Not that she thought he'd help, but keeping track of him was the easiest way of keeping track of where she might be. Of course, she couldn't blame him for dying. She only blamed herself for her own complacency. She didn't believe the girl had it in her, or that he did. She'd been a fool not to get her name before they did it.

But Jesse's death didn't stop her. When she learned of it, she began her own more conventional search at St. Ida's, learning about the girls there. She'd narrowed down the possibilities to three. Two of them she'd tracked, and learned neither was right. The third possibility had been sent to Bedford, but by the time Talia got to her she was out, and had disappeared into the larger world, out of Talia's line of vision.

Talia wasn't panicked. Probably the girl wasn't ready yet. She kept looking, hoping that readiness and finding would occur at the same time. They so often did.

Now it was becoming more urgent to find her, ready or not. The people were changing, accruing all they needed for the next big human shift. She had confirmation of that from a man who understood energy better than anyone else she knew.

For over a century humans had been pouring energy into the world, from electricity, microwaves, radio waves, fission and fusion, the slow stroll of satellites around the planet. Much of that energy only existed because of the work Aquarius did, realizing new technology in the world, and now it was creating new human capacities that few were aware of. There was lots of talk about increases in rates of mental illness, of homicide, of general angst and agitation, but only a handful of people understood why, and she was one of them. She saw all the potential gains and risks at hand, a wild horse ready to run. She would keep the reins firmly in her hands.

Centuries of energy gathered slowly, decades of political maneuvering, all were bringing her to her goal. She was ready. The world was ready. All she needed was this final piece, this young woman who had a gift like no other. It was time call her home.

The focus of the other women on new members might just do it. Their were two members in particular, former residents at St. Ida's, who would help the most—a dark and intense woman named Lola, and a frightening and flighty one called Racer.

Talia opened her thoughts to join with theirs, and if she got more energy than she gave from the exchange they didn't notice. They were both intent on a particular young woman they wanted to draw in. The same young woman for both of them. The one Talia wanted. She listened to their thoughts, and then she smiled.

She sometimes forgot how easy this work was was when you moved in the direction of existing momentum, how difficult when you moved against it. This morning, all moved toward her desire. She quickly found the woman she sought, saw her clearly, drinking espresso at a small café in southern Italy. How lovely.

Talia hated to disturb her, but it was necessary. "Time to come home, Cali," she whispered into the darkness of her thoughts. "Time to come home."

EQUAL AND OPPOSING FORCES

Cali sat in the bar and looked around. She didn't see much prospect for fun. A man in his sixties watched a ball game on the TV above the bar. Two young men nearby were clearly involved in picking each other up. An attractive woman seated at a table ate a burger. The woman caught her eye and smiled, cast a glance up and down her, then went back to her meal.

New York City women, checking out what other women are wearing. Or New York City lesbians, seeking prospects. Though Cali wasn't always drawn that way, if the woman was right she wasn't averse to a good time, especially when she was in the City for the first time in years, and looking for a good one night stand. But the woman wasn't moving forward, and after a long flight Cali wasn't up to being the seducer. She sighed, still not certain why she'd come back.

Two years ago, Ida's jewelry had got her enough money for a cheap hotel room while she looked for work, which she found readily enough at a strip joint. She liked dancing, and liked that she could be as sexual as she wanted, but nobody could touch her. That was very different from recreational dancing in a club, where men groped and grabbed as they pleased.

She'd let her hair grow out again, and took the stage name of Dark Dancer, which she suited to her costumes and routines. She learned how to complete thoughts about really good tips, which was easy since the men were there to part with money, and all she had to do was open herself to increasing the amount she received. Some of the other dancers were jealous, a little mystified about how she consistently pulled in hundreds instead of tens and twenties, but she laughed that off. "We live in a dark time," she said. "That's when dark dancers make out."

It was also a good venue to try for bigger stakes, which she took advantage of when a customer passed her a thousand dollar bill—the first she'd ever seen. She'd focused on him. He was mid forties, handsome, wore an expensive suit. She opened herself to bringing him closer, and he was amenable. When she was done for the night he asked if she'd have a drink with him, talk a little. She did, and from there on in, she had him.

She established a clear line between her work and her personal life, so their dates were just that. No sex for sale. In fact, no sex at all for a few months. Just getting to know each other, though she knew a lot more about him than he did about her. He was CEO of a high-powered brokerage company, and to him, she was just a young woman working off college debt, trying to decide what her real career was.

She made sure he knew she was smart and capable of caring for herself before she slept with him, because she wanted to play this from a platform of strength rather than weakness. Less than a month after their first night together he proposed. A few weeks later they were married, and she moved into his spacious penthouse, stopped stripping and settled in to an easy life. For a while.

She figured he'd want children in a while, and then she'd have to get rid of him. Given the stress in his life, a heart attack would be no surprise, and she was ready for that option. But then, he didn't ask about children, and she couldn't do it. Couldn't kill him. He didn't rouse enough passion in her one way or another to complete the thought of his death. She sighed, thinking of Jesse, telling her she had to mean it. He'd cursed her with truth, she thought.

Just to make sure she could still work her skills, she found and completed a thought about wanting ten million dollars all her own, free and clear of any man. She released it, and waited to see what would happen next.

A few days later she went to the casinos in Connecticut, thinking she'd be in the realm of possibility there, but she'd been disappointed by her take and not sure why she couldn't work the event as she wanted. The only possible obstacle was a lack of real belief on her part, and she thought she was well beyond that. But then again, it was also possible that the thought had been completed in a way she didn't yet know about.

She came home a day early, and was deep in thought about this when she entered the penthouse. It took her a moment to hear the laughter wafting from the bedroom. Walking to it slowly, she listened at the door, heard two voices, both male, engaged in passionate interaction. She smiled.

She opened the bedroom door and saw her husband tied to the bed, being teased with a small whip by a young blonde man. She recognized him as a waiter at one of her husband's favorite restaurants.

"Hi, sweetie," she said. "If I knew we had company I would've brought a cake."

The young waiter left quickly, with a red face. In the ensuing discussion with her husband, he offered a divorce, with a simple ten million dollar settlement.

"Sure," she said. "That's fine with me."

"No hard feelings, I hope," he said.

"None at all," she reassured him.

"Me either," he said. "You've been worth it, Cali."

They parted amicably, and then she had money, freedom, youth and health. She got herself a nice apartment in the village, and paid cash for a house on an island, purchased in such a way as to hide her ownership of it. It made her feel safer just knowing it was there. She anonymously sent a large chunk of money to Ida, and then she went traveling, taking boats, planes and trains to places she'd only read about at St. Ida's or Bedford.

Her guide for Machu Piku knew some of the more interesting villages to take her to, and a great deal about tantric sex practices. The monasteries of Tibet were beautiful, but reminded her too much of Lara so she didn't linger there. The castles of Ireland were mystical, and the guides full of passion for many things.

On a tour of the Great Wall of China she met a touring history professor who introduced to a variety of sexual positions she wasn't sure she'd like to try again. On the beaches of Southern France she learned scuba diving from a woman who could do things with her breath on someone's skin that Cali found enlightening. Then, one day while she was drinking espresso in a small café in southern Italy, she experienced the clear and sharp sensation of being called home.

Home. But where was that? New York State was the closest she had, she supposed, though she had no idea what would make her go back those harsh winters and harsher memories, where she'd broken parole and probably had a warrant out against her for that and for theft. New York meant nothing but trouble to her. Except. Except.

When her espresso was gone the waiter, with his dark eyes and handsome smile, came over and indicated he'd bring her more.

"Grazie, no," she told him. "Vado a casa."

She had to go home. To New York. The closest she came to a reasonable explanation was a sense that Racer needed her. Racer wanted her back. She had nothing beyond intuition to back it up, but she'd learned to trust her intuition.

And now, here she was, in a bar called *Perdition* on tenth avenue, with a woman eyeing her and nothing else in sight. But it would be okay. She'd get her bearings, then look for Racer. For tonight, she'd go to her hotel room and treat herself to a hot bath.

She downed her drink and slid off the barstool, nodded to the woman who'd been watching her, and left. When she got outside she ducked her head down against the cool and damp spring breeze and turned east. In this part of the city that never slept, the streets were quiet. She kept walking.

She smelled the man behind her before she heard him. Heard him before she felt him grab her and turn her around, saw him before he punched her hard in the belly and dragged her into an alley.

Then she was down and the cement was gritty and hard against her back, and he was looming over her. I'll be okay if he doesn't have a gun, she thought, right before she saw the gun.

He pushed it against her head, while his other hand worked his pants. He crooned sickly words at her about how she wanted it, and she stared into his eyes which wiped her out, nulled her existence in lieu of his demands, made her a thing that served his need to have a terrified woman under him so he could get off.

Like Keith, she thought, and her whole being began to spin his death for him, a death worth completing. Before she could do so, there was interference in the form of Lara's voice whispering in her head.

May you be well. May you be peaceful. May you be liberated.

Now, Lara? Now? she asked, though she knew better than to pound against this kind of resistance. Better to go with it, let it wear itself out, then move on. She stared into her attacker's eyes and let the thought reach from her to him. May you be well. May you be peaceful. May you be liberated.

He stopped fumbling with her clothes, and his jaw dropped open. A shudder ran through him. He stared at her in horror, all his leering gone. He pushed the gun into her temple, moving so close she could smell his whiskey breath.

Her heart thumped out panic. I'm dead, she thought. Dammit. Hell. It was the wrong time to fail at completing his death. Absolutely wrong.

But then he made a sound as if he lifted something heavy, wrenched the gun away from her, turned it to his own forehead. With one final intake of breath, he pulled the trigger.

For a moment Cali wasn't sure if he'd shot her or himself. Then he fell onto her heavily. She pushed at him, but he was big, unwieldy in death. As she struggled she heard movement, felt the body shift away and thump onto the ground.

She was out from under and the woman she'd seen watching her in the bar was there, looking down at her. Cali pushed herself to standing.

"Good girl," the woman said. "We better get out of here before the cops come." She took her coat off, put it on Cali. "Wear this. It'll hide the blood."

They left the alley and walked a block without speaking, the woman leading. Cali was surprised at her own willingness to follow, and chalked it up to shock. The woman stopped and hailed a cab. She put Cali in and got in with her, gave an address.

"I don't live very far from here. You can come home with me. I'll fix you up."

Cali eyed her suspiciously. "How do you mean that?" she asked.

"Does it matter?"

Cali shrugged. She supposed it didn't.

The woman laughed. "I meant get the blood off you. My name is Talia Jordan."

"I'm Cali Spring."

"I know," she said, and smiled.

* * * *

Whatever Talia was or was not, she had money. Her apartment was big and well furnished and clean. Talia took her shirt to wash it out and gave her a plush robe to wear while she was waiting. She offered her a bath, and though Cali refused it she looked wistfully at the big tub while she was washing up.

Then they sat on her big comfortable couch drinking what tasted like an expensive red wine while they waited for her shirt to dry. Cali felt herself relaxing into warmth, into physical comfort and safety.

"That's better, isn't it?" Talia said. "No cops now. Not unless I tell, which of course I wouldn't, knowing how precarious your position is."

Cali tensed. She was off her game here. Something keeping her vigilance at bay. She had to be careful. "Nothing precarious about it," she said. "He attacked me, then killed himself. That would show in the evidence."

"But you'd still be arrested for breaking parole. You don't want to go back to Bedford, do you?"

Cali was about to ask how the hell she knew that, but she clamped her mouth shut.

The woman laughed. "You don't ask how I know. I'm guessing that means you're wondering if you have to kill me, too. Not sure yet, are you?"

"No. I'm pretty sure," Cali said before she could stop herself. Her censor seemed to have passed out.

"Not at all. You know I won't give you away. I like what you can do. I'm with the Aquarius Project."

Cali almost seemed to know what this was. Hadn't she read something about it? A bunch of women who did political work? She was feeling more dreamy by the minute, too relaxed to worry about why she felt that way. "The Think Tank?" she asked.

"That's a good name for it. Before I got there the women called it the aquarium. Think tank—aquarium. You see? I suggested Aquarius Project instead. More class, and it implies a goal. I wanted to do some serious work."

She didn't say she ran Aquarius, and so had more power than anyone ever dreamed of. She didn't say it, but Cali heard it.

Talia smiled, sipped her wine, ran a soft, smooth finger down the side of Cali's face. Something in her gesture renewed Cali's confidence and she felt herself inundated with a warm elation, the results of adrenalin and escaping harm.

Talia turned the talk to less personal matters. Good restaurants and bad movies. Places to get shoes and haircuts. As she spoke, she rested a hand on Cali's arm, smoothed her hair. Cali didn't pull away, though she wasn't sure why.

Her eyes were playing tricks on her, she thought, because Talia would go out of focus, her voice distant and filled with echoes. She stared at the wine in her glass, swirled it around and noticed how beautiful the pattern of circular motion was. She smiled at it.

"How do you feel?" Talia didn't ask her.

"Fine," she thought she said.

"Your skin?"

Cali raised an arm, considered it. Yes. Something good was happening there. As if she was being gently stroked. The feeling moved up her arm and to the back of her neck, something warm and slightly moist brushing against her. A mouth, tasting her skin. She thought she should be afraid, but fear couldn't make any inroads against this pleasure.

"What are you doing?" she asked.

"You know," Talia said. "And it will feel good. From now on, it will all feel good."

She didn't remember leaving the room, had no idea how she got into a bed or who took off her robe and the rest of her clothes, but she knew she was prone now, and naked. Hands moved over her, touching her, rousing her. She moaned and moved against them.

"Do you like this?" someone asked.

"Yes," she whispered back. Someone was kissing her, a mouth on her breast, suckling at her nipple, a hand on her wrist, something hot and smooth between her legs. She moved toward it.

"Patience, now. I'm getting you ready."

Ready for what, she wanted to ask, but speech was difficult, so she opened her eyes, saw a woman's mouth on her breast, a man placing himself between her legs.

But she couldn't see his face. It was obscured by a shadow falling between them. Or he was made of shadow and she couldn't see him at all. His hands moved over her and pleasure moved into her.

"Do you want this, Cali?" Talia asked, stroking her, holding her arms. "Do you want him? I'll hold you and you can have him."

She was going to say yes, yes, of course she did. Who would refuse this pleasure? But the man leaned over her and she saw his eyes, coal dark with a burning center. Suddenly she felt herself in danger, and when she turned to Talia, her face became a reflection, a distortion of her own face, something harsh and cold, features melting and reforming with the slow horror of sounds cracked by time.

In spite of the pleasure, terror flooded her, and she sought haven from it. She turned in to herself, seeking the store of images that sustained her.

The first thing she saw was Jesse's eyes, but they were no refuge. They were pools of anguish, of pain and more pain. She saw where she'd killed him. Saw the horror of the killer as well as the killed and knew that choice would hold her hostage as she held herself hostage until she made it right which she never never could do.

And he was trying to tell her something. It was important. Something about returning. Something about not being afraid. Ages of memory and future swirled in his eyes. She saw it all moving there, and she screamed.

For the first time in her life, she screamed and screamed and she kept screaming until her lungs were rubbed raw from the sound of it. She screamed at herself to wake up, to run away. She screamed against whoever was claiming her, and she screamed at what lived in Jesse's eyes and screamed more until she had no air left, and in the silence that descended on her she knew there was no escape. There were only choices that would soon be apparent, leading to equally difficult ends.

In the wake of this realization, she heard small laughter, and then nothing more.

EMERGENCE

"Good morning," Talia said, opening the curtains. "How are you?"

Cali sat up in bed quickly, fully awake and aware of where she was. She clutched the blanket to her, and Talia scanned her.

"I'm not going to jump you," she said. "I just thought you might like coffee and I didn't know how you take it."

No, she thought. Nothing to drink or eat here. Not with this woman. She checked herself, saw that most of her clothes were still on her. That was good, she supposed. "No thanks," she said. "I'll just take my shirt."

Talia tilted her head. "Really? Last night you said you'd come see my office in the morning."

"Last night," Cali said speculatively.

"You crashed so hard maybe you don't remember. One minute we're talking, the next you're almost falling off the couch. I had a helluva time getting you in here. You could barely walk. Then you were making some horrible sounds in your sleep. Bad dreams?"

"Yeah," Cali said. "Nightmares."

"Shock, I suppose. And effort. What you did to that horrible man in the alley takes energy."

"I think," Cali said, "I better be on my way."

"Of course, if that's what you want. After you're dressed I'll walk you out, point you in the right direction. Or, if you prefer, when we get outside, we'll go see Aquarius."

"I'm pretty sure I'll just go home."

"Suit yourself," Talia said.

When they were outside where the sun was shining Cali felt safe again, all her night terrors of strange sex washed away. It was a dream, then. Just a dream, and she was safe. Then, as Talia chatted amicably about how close her office was, and how nice it was to be so close to work, Cali's curiosity overcame her fear.

She turned to Talia. "Okay," she said. "Show me Aquarius."

Tali's mouth curled into a smile. "I thought you'd want to see it," she said.

* * * *

The building was nothing special in a city made of special buildings. Stone and steel, with windows that reflected everything outside, showing nothing of what was inside. They entered it after Talia pressed a palm code pad, and the lobby was large and cool, with a security guard at a desk.

"Hello, Charlie," Talia greeted him, and he nodded at her.

"You work too hard, Ms. Jordan," he said. "Don't you know it's Saturday?"

She laughed. "I know it's a day, Charlie."

He smiled, shook his head, and they moved on to a bank of elevators. Talia pressed the button for the top floor, and they rode.

"What do you actually do here?" Cali asked.

"We think," Talia said. "Just like you do."

The elevator doors opened and they got out. Here, Cali stood and simply looked around.

They were standing in a penthouse surrounded by glass on two sides, smooth marble on the other two. The floors were a deeply grained oak, here and there covered with thick, elaborately patterned rugs. One wall had water falling over stone into a shallow pool of sparkling stone. The other had two Monet landscapes. Not prints. Originals. Some version of Water lilies, Cali thought. Around the room were broad, deeply cushioned chairs in sandy browns. Glass-topped tables with tree-trunks for legs sat between some of them. There were, she noticed, no magazines, no signs of desks.

"Impressive," she said.

"We like it," Talia agreed. "But the individual offices are even better. Come see."

She took Cali down the hall and opened a number of doors which were, she told Cali, the offices Aquarians used for individual meditation, to come up with ideas for the group. Each office was unique. One room had a hanging hammock chair that looked out over the city, and its walls were painted in varying shades of blue that mimicked a sky going toward sunset. Another had the colors of an ocean beach, one chair, and a small fountain with fish in it. A third was painted bright red, and hung with kites.

Cali admired them all, and then Talia opened a set of double doors. "And this is the group room," she said.

She and Cali stepped into it. The space was intensely quiet. The walls were a watery blue, the floor carpeted in sage green, thick and soft under her feet. There were no paintings on the walls, no decorations of any kind. There was a circle of chairs, sand colored, deep and soft, in the center of the room, but no table, no computer, no phone.

"This is where we get our group work done," she said.

Cali, looking at it, thought of many questions she could ask. What work? How is it done? Who is it done for? Who pays you to do it? She asked none of them, because standing there, she understood. She turned to Talia.

"You're magical thinkers," she said.

Talia, who had been watching her as if waiting for this, broke into a broad smile. "We call it Realizing," she said. "Or quantum cognition, depending on how fancy we want to sound. A lot of our new people need the quantum cognition term. They think science makes it more real. They have to be convinced. But not you."

Cali lifted a shoulder, let it fall. "Your new people?" she asked.

"The new people at Aquarius. I'm offering you a job here," Talia said. "But you knew that, too, didn't you?"

"Yeah," Cali said.

"So I'll order in some Chinese food, and we'll talk about it," Talia suggested.

"Wait. First, tell me a few things. You followed me to that bar, didn't you?"

"I did. I was hoping for an opportunity to get acquainted. When you left, I kept following, and it's a good thing I did."

"Because it got me in your apartment?"

"I'm not sure what you mean by that."

"You put something in my wine, didn't you?"

"An herbal thing. To relax you. There's no side effects, except some rather interesting dream states. And it sounded like you were dreaming."

Was that it? Cali wasn't sure, but she supposed it didn't matter. What mattered was laying down some ground rules for the future. "Don't do it again," she said. "Not ever."

Talia's cool eyes ran up and down Cali's form. "I won't have to," she said.

* * * *

They sat in the large open area of the lobby and ate lunch, looking out over the city far below, while Talia told her what her new job would be.

The Aquarius project, she said, was a group of women who did what Cali did, but did it in order to influence world events and affect large change.

"Politics?" Cali asked, shifting uncomfortably. "I don't know much about it, and what I do know I don't like."

"You know what you think is right and wrong, don't you?"

Cali picked up a dim sum, considered it. "This is right," she said. "Being hungry is wrong." She looked around. "This room is right, unless you lock the door and tell me I can't leave. Then it's wrong. And the wine you gave me last night was right. What you put in it was wrong."

Talia crossed her legs, curled back into her chair. "Haven't you ever done something wrong to get at what was right? Unless you consider killing people right."

Cali stayed cool. "I wasn't arrested for killing anyone," she noted.

"I know. You never got caught for that. But the drug charge was bogus, so maybe it works out."

"How do you know what I got arrested for?"

"Aquarius always does its research. And we've found that bad girls are often very good Realizers who just need the right context. So we keep track of young women at places like St. Ida's. I remembered your name from previous searches and kept it in our data banks. I found you just in time, apparently."

"I had it under control," Cali noted.

"In an odd way. How did you get him to pull the trigger on himself?"

"You can't make someone do something they're not inclined to do on their own."

Talia laughed. "I once read a survey where they asked young men whether they'd rape a woman if they knew they could get away with it. Three-quarters of them said they would. Is it possible you were playing tricks on me, getting him to act on his natural inclination?"

Cali grinned. "If so, he's better off dead."

"Your point. But if we're going to work together, you'll have to trust me a little bit."

Cali had to admit she liked the attitude, and the concept of Aquarius, but she was still wary. "If I'm going to work for you, I should know the parameters."

"Of course. I picked you out of a group of girls from St. Ida's based on your peculiar history. I knew you'd be good at this, and we'd love to have you try it. If you don't like it, nobody will lock you in."

That, Cali thought, was a fair offer. But she needed more information. "Can you do this magic thinking—"

"—Realizing."

"—Right. Realizing. *Can* it be done in a big way? I've tried a few things that never got anywhere."

"A group gives you more energy. Of course, everyone's got their own particular skill. Some of the women are better with money, some are better with technology. And there's some things none of us can do. Changing consciousness in someone who doesn't want to be changed is impossible, but you can suggest new ideas to a receptive consciousness, or make a mind move faster in a direction it's already going. You can't Realize something that doesn't exist, but you can build from what does to Realize something better. For instance, there's cars, and there's cars that don't destroy the planet. We're careful about how we use our energy. Strategic planning creates effective results."

"You keep saying the women. No men in Aquarius?"

Her lips twisted into contempt. "Most aren't evolved enough to believe in it, so they can't do it."

She thought of Jesse, but he was an exceptional man, so maybe Talia was right. "But for the women. It works?"

"We've had some failures, and some startling successes—which nobody credits us for, by the way. Our public profile is very low. Anonymous was a woman and so on. And we want to keep it that way. If anyone knew, they'd burn us for witches."

Cali understood the power of invisibility, of machines whose gears you never heard grinding. She approved.

"You like power, don't you?" Talia asked.

"I like being able to name my terms," Cali replied.

"How about naming terms for other people?"

"I never really thought about it."

Talia leaned forward. "Yes you have," she said. "Of course you have."

Cali was about to shake her head when she remembered standing in the bell tower, imagining what it would be like to be a goddess. And she remembered the feel of power moving through her hands, removing Betty from the world, making Racer safe.

"Okay," she said softly.

"Okay is right," Talia said. "You're not someone who's destined to live and die in quiet desperation. Even when you're desperate, you won't be quiet."

"Maybe not," Cali agreed.

"For sure not. But the rest of the world is a different story. People—average people going to office jobs, paying taxes—they say it's all run by politics and corporations and unfortunate gods with unfathomable ends. They think they can't do anything, so why bother trying? Better to enjoy what you can, watch TV, drink a little, have sex and go to sleep. And the thing is, they're right. It's out of their hands. Has been for some time. But they don't know we control the suits and the gods."

Cali felt a shiver run down her spine. Wheels spinning behind wheels. She knew it was true. Had always known invisible hands created visible motion.

Talia, seeing her, laughed. "Even TV was our idea. A way to get the stories we wanted out there, to keep the people amused, distracted so we could work."

"Aquarius—it's been around a long time?" Cali asked.

"The idea of it was always around. Historically this is women's work. I think we're made to do it, our brains structured differently than the male brain. For a while that was understood, and we did what we wanted, but that was way back. Hunter-gatherer days, the start of civilizations. Then men got ideas about wanting to run things. They shifted religions and we were burned, drowned, hung, crushed by stones, run out of town or went underground. We continued the work, but we were isolated from each other and couldn't gather any force. That lasted until just the last century, when we began coming together again. Aquarius is the most recent incarnation, and perhaps the most important. When I took over the helm we organized ourselves politically and financially and now we're ready to do our most vital work."

"What's that?"

"It's unfolding," Talia said. "We're at a crucial time in human history, when energy is moving in new ways, around us and through us. You'll learn more about that. But we all work in the world as well, and I was thinking you'd be a good lobbyist."

"Not something I know about," Cali said.

"You'll learn. It's easy. Just talking to people. It's a way of gathering important information for us, too."

Cali chewed thoughtfully on a piece of shrimp toast. "You act as if you know I'll say yes, and you haven't even told me the pay."

"Besides the power and satisfaction of creating world change?"

"Yeah. Besides that."

Talia laughed. "Our arrangement is simple. You name your price, and the Aquarians use their skills to make sure you get it."

To Cali, that sounded only fair. And it wasn't as if she needed money, but she did value fairness in the workplace. Still, she had some niggling reservations. She'd always worked alone, and wasn't sure if she could play well with others, or if she wanted to. She wondered what happened if they disagreed. With so many magic thinkers in a room, would they cancel each other out? Would they gang up on the one who disagreed, and if so what would that be like? She could imagine it getting ugly fast. As she was turning all this over in her mind, the door opened and someone stepped in, still out of sight.

"Talia?" a voice called. "Are you in today? I wanted to spend some time with the Riverbank thing. I'm a little impatient with it. You know how I get."

The voice spoke rapidly, as if ahead of itself, and Cali thought she recognized it even before the speaker entered into their visual field.

When she did, she was still talking, something about how people really needed to get a clue, and then she saw Cali and stopped mid-sentence, her mouth open.

"Wow," she said at last. "Cool."

"Racer," Cali replied. "You work here?"

"Yeah," Racer said.

Cali turned to Talia. "When do I start?" she asked.

* * * *

Talia left soon after that, saying they probably had a lot to catch up on, and when they were alone Cali went tense and closed, remembering Racer's rage at her. But Racer only talked and talked as she showed off her own office, decorated haphazardly with wild modern art and strange floor lamps whose twisting configurations seemed to reach out and grab for you wherever you walked.

"I'm thinking I have to get rid of one of these," she said, "but I can't decide which one. I like them all."

Cali smiled, relaxing into Racer's enthusiasm. Her energy level, at least, had not changed. "What do you do here?" she asked.

"In the world I'm in charge of protest marches. Get 'em riled up for it, that kind of thing. I like it."

"I can imagine," Cali commented.

"Yeah. The rest of the time I just cooperate with whatever's going on. Put my energy into it, y'know?"

"I know. So. The rest of your life—you're on your own?"

"Yeah. I tried a few guys, and I didn't like it much. Now, well, sometimes I go places with Talia." She ducked her head down in uncommon shyness.

Cali raised an eyebrow. "Talia? And you?"

Racer shrugged. "Sometimes. We're not into commitment scenes. That's not what makes you feel safe anyway."

"But you feel safe with Talia," Cali noted.

"Yeah. Like I used to with you."

Yes, Cali thought. She knew they'd get here sooner or later. "I didn't give you away, Racer," she said. "Honest I didn't."

"Yeah. Forget it."

"Really. It's important. I'm pretty sure it was Jesse. He knew about the weed."

"How would he?"

She could read the rest of that sentence. How would he unless you told him. "He knew things."

As she said it, she remembered the day, his face, what he seemed to know. She missed him, suddenly and deeply, his absence a pain moving unexpectedly through her heart. There hadn't been anyone before or since who knew her so well, and it was lonely not being known. She wondered if Aquarius would change that.

"Well," Racer said. "Dead men tell no tales, right?"

Cali winced. She'd done that to herself, because if he was alive he'd tell Racer the truth and she'd believe it, coming from him. But wishing him back was beyond her powers. She'd have to speak for herself.

"Listen, Racer," she said. "I didn't give you away. I went to the hospital, lost my parole to protect you. What Jesse knew, what he did, I had no control over it. Either you'll believe that or you won't, and I can't control that either. So if you want I'll stay away from you. Or I'll be your friend. You go ahead and decide."

Racer's forehead creased, and then she lifted her pretty face to Cali's and smiled. "I'm thinking you and me should go kick up some dust in this city. What do you say?"

Cali grinned. "Absolutely," she agreed.

FIELD THEORY

"Lola?" Cali asked.

The woman who stood in the conference room doorway could be Lola, with her very black skin and eyes, her tall, strong frame. But her face was softer, and her eyes had a searching quality rather than a hidden one. She wore a yellow and black floor length cotton dress, and a shell necklace and earrings. She looked like Lola, if Lola had suddenly become a goddess. She moved with grace and confidence across the room to greet Cali.

"Who else, girl?" she said. She grabbed Cali and pulled her into a tight embrace, then released her and held her at arm's length, considering her.

"Wow," Cali said.

"For sure. There's a few others here."

"Besides Racer?"

"That's right. There's Ayisha—I think she got there after you left. And there's Sequana, and Adrienne. Remember them?"

Cali nodded. It was like a St. Ida's reunion. "What about Tibby?" she asked. "I'd think she'd be a natural."

Lola shook her head, jangling the multitude of beads at the end of her braided hair. "Didn't make it," she said. "Got killed in a gang fight after she left."

"Hell," Cali said, meaning it.

"I know. Listen, I hear Talia heading this way and I know she wants to get you settled in, so I'll leave you to it, but I'm glad you're here. Me and Racer worked on it, and I don't like to waste my energy."

"That's rule number one at Aquarius. No energy waste," a voice said, and they turned to see Talia entering the room, moving toward them. She nodded at Lola, who grinned, offered Cali a high five and when that was completed, left them alone.

"Ready?" Talia asked.

"Absolutely," Cali said.

* * * *

For her first few days Talia took her through training, teaching her what it was like to work with others rather than alone. As she and Talia Realized together, Cali found that though they might be trying to complete the same thought, it felt different in each of them, and she had to learn to focus on the fundamental energy rather than the thing itself. Her biggest problem wasn't in understanding someone else's thought, but in letting down her own guard enough to be understood.

"You've got to release it," Talia said to her. "Let me know it."

"Tricky," Cali said. "And counterintuitive."

"It's a matter of trust," Talia said. "That usually takes a little time."

Then, one day as she and Talia were working on a thought about a tropical aquarium—something Cali thought would be fun and simple—she felt the result of two minds applying energy to one task. It was like being lowered off the mountain, someone else holding your rope as you made your way down.

"Well, that's *wonderful*," Talia said, clearly pleased when immediately after their work they got a phone call about a donation of an aquarium. "And you'll get better at it as you go along. Let's move on."

Talia also taught her the fundamental rules of the game. Some things were more readily manifested than others. Money was simple, because there were so many natural avenues for that energy to materialize. Objects for office use were fairly easy, and they never lacked for computers or supplies. They'd gotten skilled at developing new technologies, though that took more energy, and a basis in knowledge. They had to understand what they hoped to accomplish with it before they could Realize, and also had to either know how the technology worked, or be able to put the thought into the mind of someone who did.

Cell phones took the imagination of a woman who wanted a portable phone, which she transferred to a man who watched a lot of Star Trek. Ipods took the thoughts of some technogeeks they'd hired, as well as friends at Apple.

On the other hand they'd been searching for better technology to deal with garbage and energy for years with very limited success. Talia said that was from blocked consciousness. "All the power is still behind consumption and waste. Manufacturers. Big oil. A larger consciousness works against us, and we haven't been able to get around it yet. But we're working on it."

"If the price of oil keeps going up, maybe that'll shift things," Cali noted.

Talia grinned. "Exactly," she said.

"What's that smile mean?"

"I told you, we can help thoughts go faster in the direction they're already taking."

"Are you saying Aquarius has something to do with oil prices going up?"

"Now what do you think?" Talia asked.

"Seems kind of screwy to me," Cali noted.

"You're not seeing the big picture yet. Sometimes we influence politics against our goals, in order to create a consciousness that pushes for change. That's a more efficient use of our energy, and we can't ever forget that Realizing is an energy expenditure. When you complete a thought, you're spending from your own account, and you have to keep that account from going bankrupt."

Cali thought about telling Talia what she did to renew herself, then decided against it. She was pretty sure there were things Talia wasn't telling her yet. "What happens if I run out?" she asked instead.

"You die," Talia said, starkly. "We had problems with that. Girls dropped dead or wasted away in strange Victorian declines. Then we figured out what was going on. Now everyone has a regular exercise program, periodic retreats to the spa, a lot of good self care and consciousness of what your energy's up to. You have to keep it coming in when you put it out."

"I'll be careful," Cali assured her.

"I'm guessing you already have a trick or two you haven't shared. Honestly, the group thing aside, I've never seen anyone come in as skilled as you," she said. "I'd be foolish to waste more time training you. You're ready to be in the world. We'll get you some education about strategy. You could use it."

Cali was willing enough to admit that was true. Most of her learning was in the sciences, not politics, which seemed to hold little hope of progress. It was all too complicated, too corrupt, composed of more vanity than sanity.

The current president was an unmitigated asshole, total narcissist, hell bent on his own agenda while the economy and the environment was tipping over the top, and human rights—particularly women's rights—were being set back about a century. It all seemed unmalleable. The impossibility of changing his consciousness or the consciousness of his supporters was clear, and she wasn't into fighting losing battles.

But she hadn't ever lost her love of learning, and perhaps learning strategy was just one more piece to add to her store of knowledge. Over the course of the next few weeks she went with Talia to Washington, DC a good deal, observed who she spoke with, how she managed them, what she aimed for and how she did and did not get there. She was introduced to senators and representatives, shook hands with lots of men in blue suits and learned to remember names. She also grew more familiar with current issues, and who was moving them in which direction.

"This," Talia told her, "serves more than one purpose. It shows us motion we may want to direct, keeps us aware of political change we can use or trouble we can avoid, keeps us in touch with current consciousness. And it gives us credibility, so we aren't labeled as some weird cult."

Cali came up to speed pretty quickly. Most of the politicians she dealt with were male, and they didn't seem much different than the customers in the strip joint in terms of how to persuade them. Self-interest, personal power, vanity and pride were the way in.

But she still didn't understand the strategy Talia employed in choosing what to lobby for or against. There was a bill on the floor to allow oil drilling in national parks, and Talia wanted to make sure it got passed, going against the environmental lobby for it.

"Why?" Cali asked. "It's a bad bill."

"And the people in power want it," Talia told her. "You know the rules. We can't change consciousness. We can only lead people where they're inclined to go at a faster pace. This will make the environmentalists rise up in a big way. We're making it much less moderate, and therefore much less likely to pass."

"Oh," Cali said, getting it. "Really?"

"Really. But it still bothers you, doesn't it?"

Cali shrugged. "I'm a little more direct."

"You'll learn. It's almost always a mistake to appeal to people's better side. They don't believe in it themselves. If you appeal to their meaner instincts in the right way, you'll get further, much faster. You'll see. Listen, why don't you spend some time with Senator Clemens—New York Senator."

"He was shouting against the bill we're pushing," Cali noted. She remembered him. A large black man with a big voice, senator from New York. He had piercing dark eyes and a tensile vigor that had seen him through three elections. He was known as a man to be reckoned with, an old hand at political gaming who served on important committees and was hell on those who tried shit with him.

"He was," Talia said. "That's why we need to keep him placated. He'll like you, and we're trying to track a few things we think he's got going."

"Okay," Cali said. "When do we go?"

"You," Talia said. "On your own. You're ready for it."

* * * *

So Cali went to Washington on her own, and put a call in to Senator Clemens, who was glad enough to give her time when she said she was from Aquarius. He took her to lunch at his club, an old fashioned institution with silent waiters and heavy woodwork on the walls. He ordered a lovely red wine, and relaxed his large frame into his comfortable chair.

"So. What can I do for Aquarius today?" he asked.

"Not much," she said. "I'm new with them, so I wanted to get acquainted. I hear you're the man to know."

He chuckled softly. "They're sending me the recruits? Either Talia's slipping, or you're something special. Which is it?"

She grinned at him. "Talia doesn't slip, so I must be something special."

At this he nodded. "You got that look about you. Like you've seen a thing or two, and remember all of it. But you're not much on politics, are you? You came in very direct, and you're gonna stay direct. That doesn't work very well in this world."

"Maybe not," she said. "But it might save us time."

"That," he said, "I'd appreciate. All right, young lady. You want to know what I got going, or do you know already?"

Of course she'd researched him, using normal circuits and some means that only Aquarius could provide. He'd recently gotten a new energy bill passed and was currently working on Universal Health Care. Rumor said he had a bill ready and from what she'd read it was so simple as to defy argument, and so unlikely to pass nobody could believe he wasn't doing this as anything more than an exercise in getting himself re-elected.

"Talk to me about healthcare," she said.

His eyebrows lifted a moment, and he took a long sip of wine. "Direct?" he asked.

"Yes, please."

"All right then. Universal. Like Canada. No fooling around. It cuts government cost by tens of millions, makes healthcare and prescription drugs available to all at the best possible cost. Nothing else makes any sense."

"How'll you pass it?"

"I can't. But it's right. So help me do it."

Cali shook her head. "It won't work."

"You're smarter than you let on, aren't you? All you ladies are. But if Aquarius supports it, we've got a very big edge. So will you?"

That was a good question, but she didn't know the answer. And she wouldn't lie. Not to this man. She had a feeling he'd know if she did.

"I'm not sure about Aquarius, but I'm for it. I like your other bills, and I like you."

"Aquarius is pushing for the National Park oil drilling," he noted.

"I know," she said. "I objected."

"Didn't get you anywhere, did it?"

"Did the bill pass?"

"Held up. Somebody tagged on some amendments that'll make it tough."

"Huh," Cali said. "Imagine that. I wonder who?"

The Senator gave her a big grin. "Okay," he said. He swirled his wine in his glass. "I get it. Aquarius is a funny place. I been working this health-care thing a few years, studying it, coming up with solutions, and the people who noticed don't take it serious. Everyone else has their eye on what matters politically. Not what the people need. I'm hoping I can make it sound so complicated I'll slide it through while everyone's looking at the Middle East."

Cali raised her glass to him. "You just let me know what kind of help you need on it."

* * * *

Cali returned to New York satisfied with her first solo flight. She hoped to get to Talia immediately about the health care bill, but she was out of town.

"She's working on the Tritan thing," Racer told her. "She'll be gone a couple of weeks."

"Tritan? What's that?" Cali asked.

"Energy corporation. Big money. They're in our way, and they don't like us. Talia thinks they have someone getting in our computers. They can't get in too far, but they've been known to call in IRS audits on competitors, that kind of shit."

"That's not good," Cali said. She knew their money flow might look strange to auditors, given how they managed it.

"Talia'll take care of it. Meantime, she wants you to work with me on a few things. You and me, doing a little agitation."

"Now there's a good idea," Cali said.

* * * *

Racer put her with a young set of activists who were working on endangered species issues, keeping various animal populations at a better balance. This was done indirectly, by determining what the environmental groups needed and seeing they got the funding to cover it. Cali was concerned that Talia wasn't, at the same time, working against oil development in the state, which would probably help a lot of those species, but Racer said she had a long term plan to cover it all.

Cali accepted that, but she wondered if it wouldn't make more sense to work directly with the animals, though she wasn't sure if that was possible. Even so, she liked this assignment because it brought her outdoors, going to the places where the endangered species lived, making sure she knew enough about their environment to create thoughts that would sustain them.

It reminded her of her field trips with her father, hunting frogs, and of her walks with Jesse looking for wildflowers and animal tracks. Only now she was going to Alaska and viewing polar bear tracks, to Antarctica to observe penguin populations and bring back statistics for Aquarius.

Everywhere she and Racer went they were given VIP treatment, the Aquarius logo of a gold sun on purple-blue field opening all doors. Everyone knew they had money—a seemingly unlimited supply of it. All sides of the political fence wanted in on that. She liked the treatment, and the power. She was having fun.

Sometimes, after a trek across a tundra field, she and Racer would go out to local bars and drink too much, dance to the jukebox, flirt with cowboys or rangers. It made them both feel young, and happy.

"You're liking Aquarius, aren't you?" Cali said to her one night after their third round of shots, after they chased away two fat men who tried to pick them up.

Racer beamed at her. "Best thing I ever found. And I probably wouldn't have, except for you, which is why I'm letting you slide on giving me away."

Cali had given up protesting her innocence, but she didn't understand what Racer meant. "I didn't get you here. You were here before I was."

"Only because Talia was looking for you," she said. "That's what brought her to St. Ida's."

"For—me?"

"Sure. She knew about Betty, and Jesse, and Marilyn, and wanted to know who did it."

"She never mentioned."

Racer shrugged. "She will, when she wants to. Anyway, I told her it was you, and I didn't have a clue where you landed. Didn't want to know. But she got me out. Put me in Aquarius. So I owe you one."

"Okay," Cali said. "Then buy me one."

And they ordered more shots.

* * * *

When they returned to the City they settled down to the work of creating thoughts to complete based on what they'd learned in the field. The group working in Antarctica needed a new observation facility, and they would come up with the money for it. The Arctic polar bear needed media coverage, and they had connections at various networks they could influence in that direction, an author they knew who might write a book.

Cali found the work easy, especially when it was done with group energy. But it was still too indirect for her, and too slow. She thought there must be a better way. She decided to try something on her own, to test a hypothesis.

In her travels, she'd learned that the east coast of the United States once had an indigenous species of parrot—the Carolina Parrot which lived as far north as New York. Some birders who felt so strongly about the species they'd weep when you mentioned it.

They were bright green birds, their heads yellow with a splash of brilliant orange. Their favorite food was cockleburs, and they'd flock to farmer's orchards and fields to feed on them, relieving the farmers of a weed burden in the process. But farmers, not realizing the service they performed, saw them as pests, and had no trouble getting rid of them because of an instinctive action of the species: When one member of the flock was wounded or killed, the others wouldn't leave it behind. Instead, they'd gather around their fallen companion, making themselves easy targets. All the farmers had to do was shoot one, and the rest were doomed. Between that, and the way hatmakers liked their feathers for ornaments, they were extinct in short order.

Cali appreciated a creature whose instinct for cooperation had been its demise, and when she got back to Aquarius, she spent some time alone considering its particular genetic code, hearing its call in the woods, imagining it as real.

She didn't ask herself if it was either possible or wise to do this thing. She simply saw them existing again. It would be nice, she thought, to have bright green parrots, splashed with orange and yellow, in New York. Pretty as sun on leaves. She wished for it, felt the thought complete itself, and let it go.

* * * *

Talia returned after almost four weeks away, breezing in to the office and greeting all with smiles and hugs. She was good at hugs, though Cali knew she didn't mean any of them. Having been hugged by Lara, she could easily tell the difference.

"And how are you?" she asked Cali, holding her shoulders and looking at her hard.

"Fine. Spent a lot of time with strange animals, did some work with the youngsters, and I'm ready for what's next."

"You look it. Not tired at all? Watching your energy bank?"

"I haven't been doing anything difficult. Why?"

"I just wondered. Come to my office. I want to go over a few things."

They moved down the hall, and when they got inside Talia's office she closed the door, which was unusual. But all she did was put down her bag and pull a vase from it, unwrap it and hold it up.

"See what I got in Brazil? A new vase. Nice, isn't it?"

It was blue and gold, etched with glyphs. Cali admired it, and spent some time with Talia deciding where it should go. She chatted about what Senator was sleeping with what aide. How the GOP continued to support the current waste of corruption in the Oval Office. Who the democrats might run in the next election. "Waste of time, really. They can't seem to get anyone with backbone."

Cali waited, wondering what it was all about. Then Talia turned a smile toward her.

"I guess you like the environmental work, don't you?"

"Sure. Why not?"

"Yes. Interesting thing I read in the paper on the train. Someone claims they sighted a species of bird that's been extinct for about two hundred years."

That explained the closed door, the nothing chatter, meant to put her at ease, off guard when the hit came.

"Really?" Cali said. "What bird?"

"Carolina parrot. Know anything about it?"

She gave herself time to consider. "Bird people talk about it. Is it important?"

"Why do you ask?"

"You closed your door. You never do that."

"Observant, aren't you?"

"I am. And I notice you didn't answer me. Is it something we're working on?"

"No," Talia said firmly. "We don't raise the dead, Cali. The energy cost is enormous and the social ramifications a potential disaster. A very bad idea."

"That's what I'd think," she agreed. "The guy who saw the bird—he's reliable?"

"He has photos. It's been confirmed."

"You think someone here went on their own with it? Or someone in the world? Maybe someone we want to find?"

"Possible. There's very few people who could actually do it, Cali."

"I know you wouldn't ask me to spy on our own people," Cali said pointedly, "so what *do* you want?"

Talia eyed her for a long moment. "You understand why it's a bad idea, don't you?"

"I'm new here," she said, "but I'm not new to this work. I got it a long time ago."

She could say this cool and easy because she wasn't lying. Not until Talia asked her directly if she did it. Like Racer, she was a lousy liar. Unlike Racer, she was very good at not answering questions. Even better than Talia, she thought.

Talia gave her one more long look, then let it go. "Could be nothing to do with us. I suppose it could even be an error—some escaped domestic parrot. In the meantime, we've got more immediate problems. Tritan is becoming a royal pain."

"Racer mentioned Tritan. I don't know a lot about them. You want me to do something?"

"Yes," Talia said. "Go to a cocktail party with me tomorrow. Wear something sexy."

"You gonna tell me more?"

"Not now. I've got work to do. Tomorrow."

"Okay," Cali said.

She'd grown used to Talia's cryptic moments, though she didn't still like them much. But she had a wardrobe for sexy as well as one for field trips to Antarctica. In that, at least, she felt secure.

QUANTUM 5: THE MAGDALENE

That night, she dreamt she returned again, and her ancient enemy, more powerful than he'd ever been with centuries of worship gathered to him, gave her an illness she could not heal. She spent her days wracked with pain, as if seven demons clawed at her belly, her heart. But her companion found her, and healed her, and she stayed with him, in spite of her fears.

This time, he swore, it would be different. "You are all to me," he told her. "And we have work to do."

He believed it would be better to wrest power from the Great One rather than escape him. If they could find a way to keep the people from worshipping him, he would diminish, deprived of their energy. So her companion believed. So she hoped.

"His hold is strong," she said. "He'll find us before we can complete that thought."

"I have an idea how to avoid that," her companion said.

He started preaching in the name of the Great One, naming himself as his son, and one who worshipped him. But his preaching spoke of their ancient enemy in a very new way. This one was nothing like the petty god who spit at her or the vengeful one who threw her from the garden. He spoke of a being made of love, and told the people all they needed was to love each other.

It was a tricky move. Without changing the name, her companion was changing the being the people worshipped. It might work, if the Great One didn't figure it out before they'd gotten the energy they needed. And her companion had another hope as well.

"Maybe he'll become what we name him, if we can complete this thought."

Was that possible? She knew they couldn't shift a mind that didn't want to move, but could a mind be made new? She didn't know. Neither did he. But they continued their work, speaking to the people of love, healing the sick just as he'd healed her. And she shared with him the gift she'd pried from her enemy's grasp long ago, so that even the dead could be raised.

They worked for three years, and had a large following before the Great One discerned their strategy. Then he sent his servant, disguised as a friend, to move among them and gather evidence against them. Finally her companion was reported to the authorities for traitorous blasphemy, arrested and sentenced to death on the cross, the ugliest death possible. For once, her enemy didn't bother her. He didn't have to, knowing what it would do to her to witness this death.

She stayed with her companion as he was whipped and as he dragged the heavy cross up the hill. She watched as the nails were driven into his wrists, his head crowned with thorns. In the heat of midday, blood crusted on his face and back, drawing clusters of tiny insects to his wounds, and she could not reach him even to brush them away.

For the rest of her life and in many lives to follow she would feel the sun as a cruelty, taste hot wind against her lips as a presage to disaster. It took hours under that hot sun to relinquish his life, and every second was torture to them both. She wished she had the means to kill him quickly, but she didn't yet know how to make that real in the world. She knew only life. Only life.

She cupped that knowledge close to her, and when they took his broken body down she went with him to the tomb, washed him clean with her tears, and with her tears and her love, breathed life back into him as she'd done before.

"Go, now," she told him. "Leave here. Stay in the Ein Gedi and wait for me. I will come to you."

* * * *

A few days later his friends and his mother wanted to go to his tomb, and she went with them, knowing what they'd find.

It was empty. He was gone.

Later, she would find him, and he would speak to his people about the possibilities of life, the importance of love, continued love, always love.

But the Great One had anticipated this, and made good use of it. He would find many who favored fear over love. He would make sure they worked for him, to forget the many lessons of the one who came back from the dead, preferring the fear of retribution, the fear of death, the fear of any loss of control or power.

He would make sure they retained power in the world, which is what, in fact, he loved best.

Though she continued to preach, she was only a woman, and her enemy had spent an age ensuring that men discounted women's words, women's strength, a woman's heart. Her enemy silenced her, erased her, as surely as if she'd never been.

INTERACTING FIELDS

"You can smell the money, can't you?" Talia whispered as they entered the room.

Cali smiled, though she felt twitchy, nervous after her night of strange dreams about desert lands and Jesse and an enemy who pursued her, screaming at her that she was a whore, a harlot. She tried to scream back, then saw she had no mouth at all, and in fact she was slowly, gradually, disappearing, as if someone ran an eraser over her skin. She woke shivering, got up and went to the mirror to make sure she was still there.

At Aquarius, she'd learned to pay attention to such dreams, though she'd gotten no better at figuring them out. She worked to shrug it off, and looked around her current surroundings.

They were in a private home on the upper East side that belonged to a money mogul named Harrison Laraby. He had old money from a shipping concern and new money from oil. The party was to celebrate his engagement to a woman—a supermodel—who would soon become his fourth wife.

Cali dragged up adjectives to describe the place later to Racer and Lola. Lush came to mind. Opulent. Elegant. Too elegant to be decadent, but only just. The ball room, one floor of the house, was done up with gold cloth everywhere, a field of red lilies on the tables, and china in red and gold. Her dress, a soft and simple empire also in deep reds and golds, complimented the room as well as her dark skin and eyes. She looked good and she knew it, and that gave her confidence as they moved around the room.

They were given crystal flutes of fine champagne, and Talia kept them moving as they sipped it. She greeted people, spoke words to one or two she knew. As they breezed past, Talia would tell her who they were. "A Vanderbilt," she said of one lady. "Who thought there were any left? And look—here comes a Rockefeller. Last name of Verstappen now, but still a Rockefeller."

They worked their way into the center of the room, and Cali saw senators she knew. They waved to her, and they exchanged greetings, but Talia wanted her to stick close.

"Maybe if you told me what you're up to I could help," Cali suggested.

"We'll see," was all she'd say.

Cali looked around and tried to determine the target, because clearly there was one. Talia was as watchful as a cat in a field, sensing mice with her feet and waiting for one to come close enough to grab. She wouldn't chase. She was an opportunistic hunter.

As they stood discussing the Dow Jones with a dignified older man who had a heavy German accent, Cali became aware of feeling watched. She studied the feeling long enough to know she wasn't being paranoid, and then she turned to her right.

A man stood stood holding a glass of champagne, making no attempt to hide his interest in her. His gaze moved slowly down her body, undressing her in a leisurely way. He was tall, broad shouldered, dark haired and dark eyed, forty at most and handsome. He reminded her of a stallion, bred for good lines and vigor, with a touch of unmanageability. When his perusal was done he nodded. She returned the gesture, then turned back to her conversation, deliberately dropping her awareness of him.

She was surprised to see him standing next to Talia so quickly, having arrived from the other side of the group.

"Hello, Talia," he greeted her. "They let you in without your leash?"

She turned to him, and Cali saw a split second of anger cross her face and disappear in a smile.

"Rainier, how nice to see you. And without your muzzle. What a pleasant change that must be for you."

The people they'd been speaking with looked a little shocked, and made excuses to exit the conversation, but the man Talia called Rainier just laughed, showing perfect white teeth. Cali knew they'd come here specifically to meet this man. Now she just had to figure out who he was, and what they wanted from him.

"Now look," he said. "You've scared the money away. Maybe you should try being polite and introduce me to your friend."

"If that's what brought you over, I'm sure I shouldn't," she replied.

"Afraid I'll turn another Aquarius woman to the dark side?"

"Actually, I'm more afraid of what she'll do to you. I'm trying to keep up a civil association with you, Rainier."

"Civil. Of course." He turned to Cali and put a hand out. "I'm Rainier Vassago. And you are . . ."

"Cali Spring," she said, but she didn't offer her hand.

He didn't take offense. He just lowered his hand to her arm and touched her at the elbow. "Talia, I'm going to borrow her for a while. No arguments. Let's keep it—civil."

"Cali knows how to take care of herself," Talia said. "But you may have met your match."

She gave Cali a look that told her to use caution, but proceed. Cali thought it would be easier to proceed if she knew what the hell she was after. But then again, not knowing left her free to play it any way at all.

Rainier took her arm and led her toward a table laden with food and wine. "You look like you were special ordered with the china and the cloth," he said.

"Coincidence," she said. "I chose good colors for me."

"You did," he agreed, and stopped her in the middle of the room to scan her again. She was aware of eyes watching them, not all of them friendly. This man roused strong feelings easily, in all directions.

"You know my name," he said, "but you're new to Aquarius so maybe you don't know who I am. If you have any questions, now would be the time to ask."

She looked him up and down, spent a moment reading what she could of him, which wasn't much. He kept the important stuff locked away pretty tight. But she didn't miss the logo on his cell phone case, which he wore tucked at his belt.

"You're with Tritan," she said.

"CEO," he replied.

Yes. Of course. Rainier Vassago. Talia always called him that Tritan man. "You've been trying to close us down," she observed, not sure if it was true, but figuring if she said it with enough confidence she'd at least get a rise out of him.

She didn't. He only smiled. "That's right. And I'm making progress."

"So tonight, with me, you're hoping for what? Argument? Information?"

"Not at all," he said. He reached over, touched her hair with a delicate finger. "I'm hoping for really great sex."

She'd been too busy with work to think much about sex, but his touch woke up something in her skin, made her want pleasure in new ways, and she suspected he knew a few. And Talia wanted her to do this. Cali could feel that all the way across the room.

"Right here?" she asked.

"I was thinking of my apartment. Are you ready to leave?"

"Whenever you are," she said.

* * * *

His car brought them to an apartment building not too far from where the party was, and a doorman let them in with a silent nod. An almost silent elevator lifted them to the top floor, which was all his. He led her into a penthouse where the carpet was thick as a good lawn, and the furniture made for lounging in.

When he closed the door behind them dim lights came on automatically, revealing two red couches in a taupe colored space, a bar at one end of the room. If the party was opulent and elegant, his apartment spilled over into decadence and didn't care who knew.

"Do you want a drink?" he asked.

She remembered her first night withTalia. "No thanks," she said.

"Good," he said, and took her hand, led her through the living room into a bedroom where a king sized bed dominated the room, a thick dark comforter on top. He moved behind her, unzipping her dress. She didn't stop him, nor did she help. He leaned over and spoke softly into her ear.

"Here," he said, "is where I'll take care of you, Cali."

He kissed his way down her neck, slipped her dress over her shoulders and kept kissing, his mouth hot against her spine, his hands playing over her breasts.

She let it unfold, let the heat inundate her. He moved down her body until he was on his knees, and then he turned her around.

"Do you like being worshipped?" he asked, his hands gripping her thighs.

"When it's done well," she replied.

He gave her a smile that was as much a leer as anything she'd ever seen a man get away with. "Kali. She dances and a thousand live. She dances and a thousand die. May I worship here?"

She put her hand under his chin, lifted it slightly, held it firmly in her grasp. She recognized the lie. This sham of worship wouldn't fool her. But she'd play it for both their pleasure. Why not?

"If you dare," she said.

"Oh," he said. "I dare. I absolutely dare."

She released him and he put his mouth against the inside of her thigh, flicked his tongue against her skin, crooning as he moved closer to the source of delight. She stood for as long as she could, and when she felt herself collapsing into pleasure he lifted her, brought her to the bed and laid her down, his eyes never leaving her as he stripped out of his own clothes.

Naked, he bent over her and grasped her wrists in his hands, held them above her head and kissed her hard on the mouth. She moved against him until he moaned with desire, and she felt her own desire rising to meet it. Then he pulled back from her, his eyes coal black in the darkened room, catching light from some unknown source so they seemed to be lit from deep within.

Seeing them, she bit back on a gasp. She knew those eyes. Had dreamt them long ago. Had dreamt them at St. Ida's. At Talia's.

He watched her watching him, and a slow grin formed on his face. "Say you're mine, Cali," he whispered.

She was silent. He moved between her legs, and she felt heat, heat and desire.

"Say you're mine," he repeated, his grasp on her wrist tightening.

"You know better than that," she replied, her voice low and harsh.

He pressed down against her, his eyes flashing with desire or anger, she couldn't tell. Just when she wondering what moves she'd have to make to get out of this, he laughed, touched his lips to her skin.

"Then I'll have to ask permission," he crooned. "May I enter the temple?"

"What if I say no?" she asked.

"Then I rise and fall, a sadder but wiser man."

She heard the self-mocking in his tone, and approved. Felt the straining of her body toward desire.

"You may," she said.

Then he was in her, riding her, and strange images of creatures that weren't quite human danced in her mind.

But her mind wasn't where she was keeping her awareness in this night. She let the creatures dance, and followed her pleasure as deeply as it could possibly go.

EMERGING BEHAVIORS

About 2 in the morning, Cali got up, got dressed, and left without waking Rainier. He didn't seem like the type of man who wanted to wake up to a sleep-tousled woman, and she wasn't a woman who wanted to wake up in a man's bed. She liked her own space.

When she got downstairs his car was waiting out in front, and his driver opened the back door for her. Before she got in, she stopped and looked at him. "Did he call you, or were you waiting?" she asked.

"He called, ma'am," the driver said.

"When?" she asked.

"About half an hour ago. It takes me a few minutes to get the car out of the garage."

She hadn't heard him get up and make the call. That wasn't good. She'd do better next time, if there was one. She nodded, got in, and was driven home, looking out the car window at the City that never sleeps.

* * * *

She was glad to get back to the refuge of her own apartment. The City might not sleep, but she was tired, and dropped into sleep easily, her body feeling as if she'd released some energy she'd held in check for a long time.

As it turned out, sleep was no refuge. Instead it was plagued with dreaming.

First, there was a snake, black and bright yellow. It looked up to her, flicking its tongue out, smelling what would be. It moved forward and she followed it to a door she knew, the door to science class at St. Ida's. She opened it, walked in and took a seat.

There was Mrs. Henderson, giving a methodical lecture on an experiment about photons that made conscious choices, and communicated with each other over space and time. Somebody was asking a question. Racer? Yes, but she had a black mask on so Cali wasn't sure how she knew her.

"Can Cali talk to them?" she asked, and all eyes in the class turned her way.

The question exposed her. Now they all knew who she was, what she could do. They moved toward her, and she put up a hand to ward them off, her fingers creating a wall of static surrounding her.

But the energy didn't just keep them out. It also kept her in, kept her locked in this hot and electric place, with static pinching her skin, scraping her nerves. It engulfed her, and each molecule seemed to contain its own consciousness, its own intent. Whatever this energy was made of, it had purpose.

She sought a door, a way out, and found only a place where the static was less thick. Behind its wavering lines she saw a face she knew, filled with fear and anguish.

"Jesse?" she called. "Jesse?"

No answer. Just more static, and now she was pushing her way through, trying to reach him as the static entangled her, biting her with every move she made. There he was, just behind it, his eyes visible through white sheets of energy. He was speaking and she almost heard words, but they kept breaking up like a bad cell phone call.

"What is it?" she cried. "Tell me."

"Complete . . . Cali . . . make it . . ."

Yes. She understood. Complete the thought. What thought? She couldn't name it. Words eluded her, and she was overwhelmed with a sense of hopelessness. Impossible. It was an impossible thought. Impossible even to name it. Jesse's face grew sad before it disappeared altogether behind the energy that divided them.

She woke, sitting up in bed with a start. "No," she said, quickly and fiercely.

She looked around, expecting to see someone, surprised to find herself alone. She put a hand to her face, touching it to make sure she was awake.

Yes. Awake. It was a dream. Just a dream. But it stayed with her, washing sorrow through her. Jesse. To see Jesse again. To talk with him. She'd wanted that for years without admitting it to herself. And in her dream, for a brief moment, she had.

But he was gone, taking whatever thought she was supposed to complete with him.

QUANTUM 6: THE
DEATH OF PEACE

Every time she returned to a body after that was worse than the time before, as her enemy gathered strength from feeding off the energy of the people and their worship, and learned new ways to control them. His thought of an invisible deity, one only, all powerful and all knowing, drove them in fear. He stalked the earth in whatever form he wanted, moving events to his end. And he found a new way to bend others to his will. He discovered the many advantages of war.

Both fear and longing drove the people into it, as he instilled them with terror for their own safety, or with yearning for something larger than the tedium of their daily lives. They'd race to kill, race to prove themselves heroic, willingly sacrificing their own lives for a cause made in the Great One's name. And there was nothing she could do against it.

She could not shift the consciousness of those who swarmed toward blood without erasing their spirits, and she could not raise her own army and indulge in wholesale murder as he did. The gift she valued most, her capacity to offer life, would be depleted if she did. He knew that. He had won, and all power flowed to him, but he was still not satisfied. He continued to pursue her.

In one return she was a little girl whose name meant peace. He sent his army to trap her and her family in the desert, and his army slaughtered all the men, took the women and children captive, she among them. She saw her father's head shoved onto a stick, carried as the trophy of her enemy.

Then he came to her personally, in a new human form with a new name, but with the same torture in his eyes. He ripped her earrings from her ears and poured water into the ground in front of her while she was so parched she couldn't even cry. "You see you'll never escape," he said.

He kept her in a dungeon, underground, and when she finally died, crying out for water and light, he left her body there, telling her she'd never see light again. She was glad enough to agree. She had no wish to return to his world.

Oh, he'd learned how to manage very well indeed. His armies slaughtered, raped, burned the land in the name of that invisible deity he'd created, saying they brought salvation and eternal life to those they killed. To her horror, they used the loving words of her companion, twisted out of all recognition, to stake their claim.

And he made her null and void, his world making sure the words of women were unimportant, inconsequential. All the gifts she'd given to the people, all her healing and raising of the dead were wiped out as if they'd never happened. She was stricken from the record, as if she never existed.

Many times, in many different returns, she wracked her brain to see if she could find a way to make the people understand what they were doing, but he had skills they lacked. Their thoughts couldn't move energy into matter as his could, and so they felt helpless without him. And when they begged him, he gave them just enough of what they asked for that they'd continue to worship him, continue to believe it was necessary to kill and torture for him.

Why couldn't they learn to use their minds as she did, and so be free of him? At first, she thought fear held them back, but it was more subtle than that. He undermined their belief in themselves, made them dependent on his power, and the skills they needed couldn't be practiced without belief. It didn't take much. Just a grain of sand would do. But he'd made sure they didn't have even that much.

She had no desire to go back to such a world, yet it seemed she couldn't lay still in the arms of death. It wasn't in her nature, and so far her nature was stronger than her grief. Without her volition, her energy leaped into life and took form again and again.

Her companion returned as well, but she tried to avoid him, hoping then their enemy would leave them alone. It didn't matter. Sooner or later their paths crossed. Then she'd have to run from the one she loved, go where he couldn't find her, though his pain tore at her heart. And her enemy pursued her just the same. He took new forms, and every meeting was another lesson in agony.

He stretched her on the rack as a heretic, burned her as a witch. When she dared remove her veil in the holy place men claimed as their own, he had her beheaded. He had her companion poisoned, stoned to death, hacked by the sword, and made sure she witnessed every incident.

He scrambled after her for recompense and revenge, demanding she give back the power he said she'd stolen. She told him each time that he could no longer use it. He'd already traded that particular skill for the power he now had. He could not have both. But he no longer believed her. He would have all in his pocket.

* * * *

At her next return, after a life that ended in the gas chambers for both her and her companion, she chose a simple life. She lived in a city, near a park. She worked as a nurse, staying out of trouble, but she already sensed her enemy tracking her, and knew what would happen next. She would not let it. Enough, she told herself. Enough. She would not, could not do this anymore. She would no longer enter the killing fields. She thought of one last way to escape.

She sought out her companion, and found him teaching children in a nearby school. "Come with me," she said simply. "We have to talk."

They walked in the park, and when they were hidden within a cluster of trees she stopped, turned to him, and spoke. "Bury me here, and don't look for me again," she said. "I'm taking all we know, all we are and hoped for, and I'm locking it away. If I return again I won't remember it or you, and I won't live it ever again."

"No," he said. "Our thought isn't complete."

"And it won't be. We've lost. It's over."

"But you can't," he protested. "It's not possible."

"Yes it is," she said. "I know how."

At this, he blanched. He also knew. Despair.

Like all emotions, despair had its own energy, the only one strong enough to block hers. Before he could offer argument, before he could pull her from the restful arms of her grief, she took a gun from her pocket, put it to her head and pulled the trigger.

How deeply he grieved, how many lifetimes passed in fruitless searches for her, how many times he found her only to have her run away because he spoke of a madness she no longer remembered—all that became his story, his problem.

With her choice to relinquish memory for despair, she believed she'd solved all of her own.

STRETCHING AND FOLDING

"You want a report on Rainier?" Cali asked Talia.

They were in the conference room just after a renewal session, where the women had replenished their energy using techniques remarkably similar to what Cali had learned from Ida. The other women had gone on to their various tasks, but Cali hung behind, to report to Talia about Rainier.

"Go right ahead," Talia said. She was relaxed, rosy from the warmth such sessions generated. "But I'm guessing you didn't find out much beyond the fact that he's good in bed."

"He's good," Cali said. "And you're right. I didn't find out much more."

Talia nodded. "He's done this before. Found an Aquarius woman to seduce, tried to get what he could out of her. I had to let one woman go because of it."

"She told him things?"

"Enough. And she would have told him more."

"What did he want from her?"

"Specifics. What we're working on, how we're working it. And he wants in. He wants to learn how to Realize." She made a face. "Men," she said. "They *think* they can, and they don't understand it takes more than just thinking."

"So what am I supposed to do with him?"

"Same thing he wants to do with you. Find out what Tritan's up to, specifically. Find out his capacities. Also find out if we can turn him."

"Turn him?"

"To us."

Cali blinked at this. A man, in Aquarius? "I thought we didn't hire men."

"Traditionally not, but times are changing, and Rainier is rather special. If he was working on our side instead of against us, he'd be a big help on the energy problems."

"My instinct is not to trust him with his clothes on."

"Mine as well," Talia admitted. "But politics and bedfellows and so on. We should look into it. Keep working him. If anyone can do this without getting hooked, you can. Let me know how it goes. And enjoy yourself. Good sex is very revitalizing."

Talia rose and moved to the door. Cali followed, but before they exited, stopped her.

"Don't you think there's something wrong about—well, using him, I guess."

Talia turned, twisted her mouth into a wry smile. "Do you think he's not using you? Don't make the mistake of seeing him in any human terms, Cali. He's a machine, calculating what he wants and how to get it without giving anything away."

"Maybe," Cali said, "I don't want to have sex with a machine."

"Then why did you?" Talia asked.

Good question, Cali thought. Why did she? Because he was good. Because she was curious, and hungry for it. She remembered Lara telling her she'd left Danny when she realized who you sleep with reflected who you are, and she didn't want to be him anymore. Cali didn't buy it, but like a good scientist, she tested her hypotheses. Was she the same as Rainier? Did she also coldly pursue her own agenda without regard for a moral code? She thought of the room in her mind marked *Do Not Enter*. She thought of Jesse. She thought how easily she complied with Talia's work.

"Cali?" Talia asked. "Are you going into a trance or are we done?"

Cali brought her attention back to the present. "We're done," she said.

"Will you go forward with Rainier?"

"Sure," she said. "Why not?"

* * * *

And she did, meeting him at his apartment a few times when he called. Showing up once or twice when he didn't call just to test his response. He didn't ask about Aquarius, and she didn't ask about Tritan. They didn't talk much at all, in fact. Their interactions were more primal, just washes of pleasure, enormous and unrelenting as the waves on the beaches of Wakiki, which Cali had ridden once. Sometimes he worshipped her, and sometimes he held her as if she was his slave. Either way worked.

She would take this wave, never sure who might drown and who might ride, but once they were back on land, she'd have nothing to do with him. After they had sex, Cali left as quickly as possible. She wouldn't sleep in his bed.

She had other limits, too. She wouldn't go to any public functions as his guest. She wouldn't eat or drink in his apartment. She wouldn't let him come to her place.

"Have it your way, for now," he said in response. "I'm in no rush."

"Are we going somewhere?" she asked.

"What?"

"Not being in a rush implies a destination."

"Oh," he said. "I see. Well, yes, we have a destination."

"Where?"

"Where I want it to be," he replied.

That was Rainier. Flipping between worship and control. Sometimes she would stop him in the middle of lovemaking, force him to be still while she held his face and stared at him. She remembered his eyes from her dreams, and wanted to know why she'd dreamt of him. There was more to know here. Much more.

She groped for answers, trying to see if he was a mirror for her soul, trying to know if she wanted that, if where she was going was the same place he and Talia seemed to already live. He would laugh as if he understood, and move on to wrest more exquisite pleasure from her body, which she allowed him to hold under his sway.

She couldn't say it was without emotion, but the emotion had little to do with human connection. They were each involved with themselves rather than the other. In fact, they were more alone when they were with each other than they were apart, and maybe aloneness was her agenda. The place where she felt most at home. The most accurate reflection of her soul.

But she was beginning to be disturbed by the dreams that followed her sessions with him. Most often they were of static, and Jesse's distant face. He kept trying to tell her something, and with each dream he seemed to draw closer, in increments so small as to be barely noticeable. Each increment took a bite out of her flesh, as if her skin was a rope between them, pulling him forward and fraying with the friction of it.

* * * *

During this time, she went into work one day to find Aquarius in a hubbub—hubbub for Aquarius being that the women were hushed, tense. Cali could feel it as soon as she walked in to the conference room, so unlike the usual pervasive calm of the place.

"What?" she asked Lola, who was sitting in close conversation with Lily and Angela—two old hands, and they both seemed nervous.

Lily looked up at her. "Don't you read the paper?"

"Not if I can avoid it. And I generally can. What?" she asked again, looking to Lola this time.

"Racer led a protest at the UN," Lola said, looking as deliberately closed as she had at St. Ida's. "You know, the thing on climate change."

"Okay. That's her thing."

"There was an explosion."

Cali felt herself go stiff with fear. "Was she hurt?"

"She's fine," Lola said quickly. "It's just—the news is talking about terrorists."

"Did someone plant a bomb?"

"Not that anyone could find," Lola said, with emphasis.

Cali nodded, understanding. Racer, whose furnace had exploded, killing her abuser. Racer, blowing it. Racer, blowing things up.

"But they mentioned Aquarius was at the protest," Angela said. "Talia's pretty pissed."

"Yeah," Cali said. "I'll go talk to her."

"Maybe you better leave it alone, let them sort it out," Lola said.

"When have I ever?"

She touched Lola on the shoulder, a gesture of reassurance, and walked down to Talia's office. She found the door closed, only this time Racer was behind it with her. She knocked once quickly and went inside.

"Did I invite you?" Talia asked, and while she didn't look pissed, she did look peeved.

"Nope," Cali said, and looked around. She let her gaze rest on Racer, who stood as close to the door as she could get, chewing on a fingernail. "I heard you blew something up," she said.

Racer cast a fearful glance at her, and Talia cut in. "Did she? That's what we were trying to figure out. She said she didn't think so."

"Yes you do," Cali said. "I know about it."

Racer kept looking at her, her eyes angry and afraid, waiting to be given away again, Cali supposed.

"I think she did," Cali said, keeping her gaze on Racer, willing her to come clean this time. "It's one of her skills. She's been doing it since she was little. Fire. Explosions. If she gets really tense it happens, right Racer? Something happen at the protest?"

Racer looked daggers at her, but caved in full. "This cop—he was whamming on Mary with his nightstick. I thought he was gonna kill her."

"Okay," Cali said. She turned to Talia. "Like I said, when she gets too tense it happens. Myself, I kill people when I get tense. Heart attacks. Not as messy. Still, I always thought we might make use of Racer's skills. In fact, I've been thinking about that a lot lately."

"In what way?" Talia asked coldly.

"It's about energy, right? She might be the one who can work with the energy issues."

Talia opened her mouth to say something, shut it again. She considered. Cali could almost see the wheels turning in her mind, and wondered where they were taking her. Wherever it was, it probably wasn't the same place Cali would end up, but if it got Racer off the hook, that was okay.

"You may be right," Talia said. "But if she can't control it. . . ."

"She can learn,"Cali said firmly.

"Hmmph. Do you want to help her with it?"

"Sure," Cali said. "I'll work with her today."

"And I'll work with you tonight," Talia said to Racer. "Come back when you're done with Cali. And stop chewing your nails. We'll figure this out." This last said more calmly, with a mild sense of amusement in it.

Cali nodded to Racer, tilted her head toward the door. "Come on," she said.

Racer followed meekly enough, and kept quiet until they were in the conference room and that door closed. Then, she began to babble.

"I didn't mean it, Cali," she said. "Honest to God, I was just there, and that cop was after Mary, and I kept seeing this light flashing behind my eyes. I didn't even think it, really. It just—"

"—happened," Cali said. "I know. Listen, I know. Calm down."

"I thought you were giving me away again."

"I never gave you away, and never would. I knew exactly what I was doing."

Racer moved a hand through her long blonde hair, shook her pretty head. "I guess you did. So what now?"

"I'm thinking it wasn't just Mary," Cali said. "It must've been building for a while. That's how it always was with you. It builds, and then it happens when you're not ready for it. So what got you going before the protest?"

Racer plopped herself down in one of the soft chairs, hunched into herself. "Nothing. I mean, nothing really. Just—I don't know. Talia. She's so busy. I thought—Anyway, it's nothing."

Cali closed her eyes, opened them again, sat down next to Racer and pulled her chair around so she was facing her. "You thought you and Talia had something special, and then you found out she's been having something special with other people?"

Racer shrugged. "There's this man. I don't like him. He comes around late at night, sometimes when I'm there and I can hear them in the living room. She won't tell me who he is. And I guess I thought I was . . . anyway, I thought some things about her. About us. Pretty stupid, huh?"

"Not stupid," Cali said. "You're not stupid. Just, well, you believe in things. But I get the impression Talia's not a woman who ever gets permanent with someone else."

"I wasn't asking for permanent."

"Exclusive?"

Racer ducked her head down.

"I don't think she does that, either. Not exclusive, or even regular. If that's what you want, you need to look somewhere else. Can you do that without blowing anything else up?"

"Yeah," Racer said after a while. "I guess I just had to get it, y'know?"

"I know," Cali said sympathetically. She breathed in and out deeply. "You better stay away from protests for a while."

"I don't think I'll have a choice. Cali, you'll help me, won't you? I don't want to get kicked out."

"Talia won't do that," Cali said.

"She will if she thinks I'll hurt Aquarius. I've been here longer than you. I've seen how it goes."

"How what goes?"

"Talia gets some idea about someone and they're gone. I mean, just gone." Racer lifted a hand, kissed it and blew the kiss away. "Like that. Out of Aquarius, out of town, out of sight. Never hear from them again."

"Where do they go?" Cali asked, not liking the sounds of that.

Racer turned her eyes up. "Just—they leave. You know."

"You didn't mean anything other than that?"

"No. Jesus. Don't get paranoid."

"Right. Anyway, I'm guessing we can manage your incendiary tendencies. It's a bad idea these days. Like I told Talia, we'll find a better use for the energy."

Racer ducked her head down further, then brought it up and blinked, grinned. "Thanks, Cali," she said. "So what do I do now?"

"Some renewal, and relaxation. Take the day off. Go home and watch a movie."

"Yeah," Racer said. "That sounds good." She stood, and moved toward the door.

After she left Cali sat for a moment, thinking maybe she should go talk to Talia more. She rose and moved out of the room, on her way to interfere again, but one of the women greeted her at the door with a message.

"Call for you. A man who won't take no for an answer, and says you wouldn't want him to."

"Who?" Cali asked.

"He said you'd know. I put it through to your office."

Cali went to that room, picked up her land line, used for their secure calls. "Cali Spring for Aquarius," she said. "How can I help you?"

"Come over and let me taste you," the voice on the other end said. Rainier.

She paused just long enough to let him know he'd gotten her. Give the devil his due, she thought. "What if I don't want to?" she asked.

"You want to. You just won't let yourself because you're afraid I'll win."

"Win what?"

"The battle," he said. "The war. You."

"I didn't know we were in a war."

"It's always a war. Between men and men. Men and women. Women and women."

"And I'm the prize?"

"Yes, Helen. You."

"What will you do with me if you win?"

"When," he corrected. "When I win, I'll rule the world, with you as my goddess consort, which you'd enjoy more than you know, if you'd just relax about it. So come over and let me taste you."

She hesitated briefly. Something here beyond memory, beyond desire, and already it was working on her. She knew it. She felt the tug of power and play in him. What would Jesse say, she asked herself and the answer came back clear as the day in the bell tower. Don't go. It's not safe. It's beyond not safe. Don't do it.

But Jesse was dead, and she was alive.

"My car is parked in front of Aquarius," Rainier said.

"I'm on my way," she said, and hung up.

* * * *

When she got to his apartment and knocked on the door he called a quick come in and she entered to see him pacing the room, talking on his cell phone.

He rolled his eyes at her, made gestures to the bar, the couch, inviting her to sit or drink or make herself at home.

"No, Charles," he was saying. "It won't help our interests at all. What you need to do is get Hinkley pinned down." He listened, looking bored, keeping his eyes on her.

Cali debated what to do. Have a drink. Sit down. Take her clothes off. Anyone of those might be amusing. Then, she thought of something better.

She turned, and walked toward the door.

She had the door part way open when a hand suddenly closed it. She turned, and found herself blocked by his body. She didn't hear him end the conversation, close the phone, or walk to her across the thick carpet.

"Where are you going?" he asked, his voice breathless and harsh.

"Somewhere I'm noticed," she said.

He kept one hand pressed against the door, his body close enough that she could feel its warmth. He raised a hand and put it to her face, grasping her jaw. "Being noticed isn't always a good thing," he said. "If you're invisible, you can do what you want."

"I know that," she said.

"Of course you do. You work for Aquarius."

It was the first time he'd mentioned Aquarius since the party. She wondered what it signified, if anything. "This isn't work," she said.

He released her face, keeping her pressed against the door. "Isn't it?"

She shrugged. Talia's agenda was one thing, her own was another, and each were still somewhat mysterious to her. "Does it matter?"

"Not at all," he replied.

He lowered his face to hers and kissed her, his mouth calling up desire. She gave herself to it, let herself fall into the pleasures ahead. They would wrestle for power, for control, and it would all lead to bliss.

She wasn't sure at what point the kiss changed. First, she was only aware of a sensation of being drained, as if he was doing exactly what he said he wanted to. Tasting her. Then he was drinking her, drinking her energy, who she was, what she could do.

Dammit, she thought. The son of a bitch is trying to Realize.

He'd led her to this with a finesse she had to admire, but she wouldn't allow him to steal from her carefully guarded store of energy. Her back was to the door, limiting her movements, so she simply turned her head away from him, pressed a hand against his shoulder to shove what distance she could between them. She felt him tense, then release. She turned back to glare at him. "I told you, this isn't about work," she said.

"It is today," he said. "I've got a proposition for you."

She ran her gaze over his face, read excitement in it. "Go," she said.

"I want you to leave Aquarius and teach me, work with me."

That was a surprise. She thought when the deal finally came it would be about getting information. She didn't expect this, and she certainly didn't expect it today.

"I like where I am," she said. "Why should I leave?"

"Because with Talia Jordan you'll never be more than a grunt, chasing her goals. With me, you'll be partner, consort, Goddess Divine, powerful as you actually are."

He put a hand to her face, and in his gaze she saw what he had in mind for her. No more indirect pushing at the edges of control. No more diagonal approaches to long-term objectives. He liked direct routes to power, and wanted her to help him get them. But she didn't believe in the payoff. He was not a man who shared power.

"Is this how Talia tests her people?" she asked.

His forehead knit in thought, and then he smiled broadly. "You think she hired me to make sure you're loyal? No, Cali. Not that."

"Then what?"

"Cali, I'm shocked. Do you really underestimate yourself that much? With your gifts, and my lust for power, why would you have to ask?"

She stared at him, trying to scent the truth. His eyes were a dark fire, offering her gifts beyond measure in worldly terms. She felt him groping for more than her body, his eyes burning through her. He was doing what Talia did. Leading her faster in the direction she was already going. The direction of power. It tasted sweet to her.

"Maybe I can get more power on my own," she said calmly.

He put a hand to her face, cupped it softly. "Power, yes. Peace of mind, no. Talia seduced you because of who you used to be. With me, you'll have no past. Only a very pleasurable present, and an unbounded future."

Her heart thumped wildly. He was offering her fire, a match to light and drop inside the room marked *Do Not Enter*. She'd become someone beyond it. Someone like him. She felt the pull of that, and understood at last that this is what drew her to him in the first place. He had no ghosts, and he could make all her ghosts rise like steam and leave her. Her mother, Keith, Marilyn, Betty. And Jesse, too.

Jesse. He'd leave as well.

No, she thought. No.

Instinctively, she reacted. She pushed her hand against his groin. "This is all I wanted from you," she said. "Nothing more. And now that's gone, too."

She tightened her hand into a squeeze. He pulled back sharply, out of her grasp. It took him a moment, but he regained his equilibrium.

"Yes, Goddess," he murmured. "Anything you say."

She turned on her heel and left.

BELL'S THEOREM

When she got out into the street she walked for some time, window shopping, going into a restaurant and ordering food, which she found she couldn't eat. She felt mildly queasy, a little dizzy. He'd taken more than she suspected, but he'd also given more than he wanted to. She wondered which made her feel queasy—what he'd taken, or what he gave her. A foreign energy sat inside her, and her body rejected it.

She supposed she should go back to Aquarius and tell Talia that Rainier wanted her to come play in his sandbox, but something in her resisted. She decided to see if she could figure it out before she spoke.

She had her food wrapped, and left the restaurant. To relax, she went to the library, and looked up random bits of information on the internet. She searched for Carolina Green Parrots and learned that a mating pair had been spotted in Pennsylvania. She read the news. She looked at vintage clothing.

She sat in front of the computer, reluctant to move, reluctant to be anywhere in particular. The internet was as close as she could imagine to being nowhere, so she went back to the search engine and looked up snakes in dreams, because in all her dreams of static, a snake would lead the way.

She read that dreaming about snakes meant wanting sex, or fearing sex, or a father conflict, or a conflict between conscious and unconscious desires, depending on who you asked. A link embedded in a paragraph that said snakes were symbolic of death and rebirth caught her eye and she followed it to a site about Isis, who made a snake in order to steal Ra's secret name and power, using it to bring her murdered lover, Osiris, back to life.

She remembered that, from her class on World Mythology at St. Ida's. And she remembered the snake on the side of the mountain. She shivered, queasy again. She raised a hand, flexed it. It was her hand, no doubt, but in it she felt earth, wet and warm, rolling against her palm.

Enough of Isis, she thought. She followed a link on the site to another goddess—to Lilith, the first woman created in the garden of Eden, made equal to Adam before Eve was pulled from his rib. Lilith knew the secret, unspeakable name of God, and she spoke it. So she was banished from the garden and Eve took her place.

"But she left something behind," Cali muttered. "A snake, who served her well."

She clamped her mouth shut, looked up. She was talking to herself. Then again, so was the homeless man in the corner. But what was she saying? Lilith didn't make a snake. At least, it wasn't written here. Still, she knew it was true. Had she read it somewhere else? Lilith made the snake and left it in the garden to tempt Adam and Eve to eat the fruit of the tree. In that way, consciousness would become the property of the people rather than the one who claimed to be their god.

It had cost her, though. Ages of relentless pursuit followed, and her name became the epitome of the evil woman, the succubus. That was the heritage of Isis, of Lilith, of all those first women who took the gift for themselves, against the will of one who called himself master. She knew him. Knew him from her dreams, from doors in her mind marked *Do Not Enter*.

Cali stared at the screen. None of her thoughts were making sense. She called herself back to the present, randomly hit a link on women of the bible.

Here she read about Zipporah, wife to Moses, who circumcised him in the desert when the Angel of Death pursued them. Only Zipporah understood that he did not belong to this god, would not get his protection, unless he was circumcised. She read about the Magdalene, who wept over her lover's broken body, her tears and her hands calling him back to life, back to her.

Cali blinked at the words she was reading. They didn't say any of that. They only said that she went to the tomb with Mary, and found Yeshua gone.

Her thoughts were intercepted by a strange blip of memory. Her mother, drunk or high or both, slapped her hard, called her a whore. "You'd fuck Jesus if he was here."

Cali shot back at her, "He'd be happy to have me."

She shook off the memory. Moved on.

She followed a link on Muslim women and read about Sakina, Hussain's daughter who was captured in Yazid's raid at Karbala. Cali experienced a craving for water in her cells, felt grief and rage move through her. She kept touching her mouth, her hands, her face, as if they weren't hers, or at least not completely hers. As if these stories owned her. As if they resurrected an old enmity between her and an ancient deity who killed and tortured his people to test their fidelity, who burdened women with pain, erased them, stripped them of love and respect and hope. And hope.

Anger trembled in her hands and her mouth, the unsilenced mouth of Sakina, the hand of Isis raising a snake, the mouth of Lilith calling out a secret name, the courage of Zipporah, who could cut when she had to, drawing blood at need.

"I will not be his," she said, speaking for them, with them. "I will not."

But who the hell was she talking to? She believed none of it. She'd long since decided the God they taught in Sunday school was not a myth, but a horror story.

"Stop it," she told herself. "Just stop." She clicked on another link, seeking something to cleanse her of this feeling.

This link led to a site for Kali, and she saw the image of a black woman with a long red tongue, dancing on the prostrate body of Shiva, her consort. He was the only one who could soothe her, keep her wild energy from rampaging out of control. She killed him and raised him, again and again, and they'd dance in frenzy until the ground shook.

This was somehow was better than the others, she thought. Not as painful or fearful. She felt at home with this in some essential way. Even so, as she read, her vision doubled. She danced in her own skin and elsewhere, everywhere, wild laughter slipping off her long red tongue.

She looked away from the screen, pressed her hands together until they stopped shaking. Touched her lips until she was sure she was doing so. Rainier, she thought. The interaction with him had clearly done something unpleasant to her system.

She logged off and left the library, surprised to see when she went outside that it was already night. She felt drained, utterly played out, body, mind and soul. She hailed a taxi, went back to her apartment, got into her pajamas and went to sleep.

This time the dream was different.

When the snake appeared, it flicked its tongue at her, turned and led her directly to the wall of static, dissolving into it. She pushed her hands against it. It nipped at her flesh, pouring over her hands and wrists, encompassing them. She stopped pushing, simply stayed still and waited. I want this, she acknowledged. I want it. She was clear as she could be about that. She'd made a choice against one thing, for another. Without compromise, without trying to determine consequences, she'd chosen.

Then, the dream went away.

She opened her eyes. Looked around. Light from the street planed into the room from her window. And there was Jesse, sitting on the side of her bed, his back to her.

He was staring out the window, where the crescent moon hung high above the buildings. She sat up and looked at her hands. They looked normal. She put them to her face. Her skin was warm, and she was feeling it. But there was a dead man in the room with her.

"You're dead," she said to his back.

"Yes," he agreed without turning around.

"I killed you."

"You did."

She wet her lips. "Then I'm still dreaming?"

"No. That was just a way to get through. Now that you're beginning to remember, I could get here this way."

"Remembering," she murmured, the word resonant with meaning.

"The moon is beautiful, isn't it?" Jesse said. "There's something poignant about a crescent moon. It holds such promise."

They were silent, both of them observing the crystalline outline of it in the dark sky. She scanned his profile. Death hadn't changed him in any way she could tell.

"I guess you're here because you're angry at me for killing you," she said.

"Do I sound angry?"

"No."

"I'm not," he said. "That was necessary. The only way to help. It changed you."

"I thought sending me to Bedford was supposed to do that."

He turned to face her and she saw the motion in his oceanic eyes. They still observed her as if she was leafy and filled with sun. Seeing them gave her an unexpected joy, an anticipation of grace she hadn't felt since his death. She found she'd missed it terribly.

"I didn't send you, or keep you away," he noted. "I destroyed both my letters to the parole board."

She thought about this. "You did," she agreed.

"Coherent superpositions," he said.

"What?"

"We always think there's two choices. This or that. I picked a third way. A coherent superposition in quantum logic."

"Not to decide?"

"More like leaving it all on the field, regardless of outcome."

"Yeah. Are you sure you're not angry?"

"Not about that. I'm pissed about some other things, but not in any lasting way."

"What other things?"

"Rainier," he said. "Mostly Rainier. And it's not anger, really. More like jealousy. Jealousy, and envy."

"Oh," she said. "Well. But you're dead."

"You don't have to keep reminding me. I'm a lot more aware of it than you are." He sighed. "It's also worry, Cali. He's dangerous. You know that."

She nodded. "I had to find out some things."

"Does that mean you'll stay away now?"

"I don't know. It depends."

"On what?"

"I don't know that either." She didn't want to talk about Rainier. There was more to say, more to ask. "Listen, if you're not angry, why are you here?"

"Don't you know?"

She smiled. "First important question I ask you, and you give me another question? Maybe that's why I never asked before. Because I knew you'd do that."

He smiled back. "You're right. Let's try again."

"Why are you here?" she repeated.

He reached over, ran a finger down the side of her face. It was cool and dry, winter air in a desert place. "It's time, Cali," he said. "Everything is changing, and we can complete our thought. But first you have to remember who you are. What you can do."

He cupped her face, drawing her close. She no longer cared what he meant, or why. She wanted only to feel his mouth on hers. She leaned toward him, led by a longing she hadn't imagined possible. Then he gasped. She pulled back. His eyes were large and filled with a fear she'd seen before.

"No," she whispered, but he was swathed in static, fading from her vision, going away.

"Cali, I can't. I can't until you . . ."

The end of that sentence was lost in the sound of a sharp alarm, waking her, calling her into the day.

* * * *

She sat up in her bed, listened to her alarm clock, rose and stumbled to it to turn it off. By the time she got there she was out of breath, as if she'd been running for a long time. She stood by her bureau and let her heartbeat settle back to normal.

She felt close to tears. A dream. So real, and so good and so terrible. It would haunt her for the remainder of the day, and she would long for sleep so she could complete it, fear to sleep because that might be exactly what happened next.

CONTROL PARAMETERS

In spite of her longing, Cali's dreams once again became walls of static and frustration, and she approached sleep with a sense of hopeless resignation. She could neither stop them, nor bring them to any conclusion. She wanted them to go away, and she was terrified they'd leave her, taking Jesse with them. She found no coherent superposition between these two equally painful possibilities, so she kept herself busy with work.

Talia had her on an economic detail, tracking stocks, learning about money flow in the world, which was both tedious and grueling. She understood how to get money. She didn't really care about how it worked beyond that. Talia said it would make her even better at getting it to the places it needed to go. She didn't see it, but Talia wasn't available to complain to.

She and Racer were working on something, and even when they were in the building they spent most of their time in her office. Sometimes she heard them giggling, but when she asked Racer about it she just said, "it's unfolding."

"You sound like her," Cali said.

"Do I? Thanks," Racer replied.

Cali consulted Lola about it, who advised, "Leave 'em alone. They're working something out."

"Do you know what it is? I mean, it's a little irritating to be kept in the dark like this."

"The dark's a restful place, Cali. Relax. Let it be," was all Lola would tell her.

Cali wondered if she was jealous, as if she was the only one who could take care of Racer. Or maybe, she thought, she was just lonely.

That was a new feeling, not one she was used to dealing with. Fear, yes. Rage, and even grief were old friends. But loneliness was out of her ken. She liked aloneness, created it for herself, because connection was dangerous. She liked and enjoyed the women she worked with, liked hanging out with Lola and Racer, and even Talia in small doses, but she didn't let them in. Wouldn't let them know her. And loneliness, she realized, was about not being known.

She wondered what Jesse would say to her, and heard his voice telling her he was willing to call it progress.

"Go to hell," she said in response.

When Rainier called she told him to go to hell, too.

"What?" he asked lightly. "That's what I get for giving you what you want?"

"When did you do that?"

"Last time I saw you."

"What did you give me?"

"A win," he said.

This made her smolder with anger. She'd taken the win, fair and square. And even in thinking that, she knew she was giving him just what he wanted. To fight more.

"If that's how you see it, you can have it," she said, and hung up on him.

When she looked up, she saw Talia standing in her open door.

"What was that about?" she asked.

"Personal," Cali said.

"Was it Rainier?" Talia asked.

"Yes," Cali said.

"That's not personal. He's not just for fun."

"He's only fun if you like snake wrestling."

"It has its moments. What did he want?"

"More good sex."

"And?"

"I told him I'm busy."

"Why?" she asked, a little petulant.

"Because I am. Asian influence on a global economy. Lobbying for things I don't believe in. All that. You assigned me to it. "

She was surprised at herself for not telling Talia what she knew about him. It seemed as if telling would make her feel slimy.

"Are you giving up on him?"

Was she? She couldn't say. "Maybe I'm playing him."

"He's not the kind of man you should play, unless you like high risk sports."

"Don't you think I know what I'm doing?" Cali said.

"Touchy, aren't we? You look like hell, by the way. What've you been doing?"

"What I do in my off hours is none of your business," she said.

"It's so warm and fuzzy, working with women," Talia noted wryly.

"I never think of you as a woman, Talia," she replied.

"Certainly you can't mistake me for a man."

"Not that either."

"Then what?"

"Pure hell," she said, grinning. "How's things going with Racer?"

"Fine. She's got some good ideas."

"Usually. What are you two working on?"

"If you want to know, just ask. Don't be cagey."

"I just did ask. What are you working on?"

Talia laughed. "It's actually your idea. Something you said to her about terrorism not being a good idea right now. We thought maybe we could use that."

"I don't get it," Cali said, but she felt something cold crawling up her spine.

"The more acts of terrorism we have, the more likely we'll keep the same president."

"He's an asshole and a traitor," Cali said.

"Cali, don't be naïve. Who do you think got him elected?"

Her thoughts sputtered in righteous indignation. The current president had raised the deficit a hundred percent, set education and environmental reform back a century, and wanted to take birth control away from women. Racist, corrupt, incompetent, he was destroying the system of government. Why would Aquarius want to inflict him on the world? And was she also saying she was about to let Racer blow things up? She was going to ask, but Mary came in with a question about protocol for a senator they'd been dealing with, and Talia moved to leave.

"Listen," she said before she went. "Don't let Rainier go yet. Play hard to get if you want, but don't burn the bridge. I'll tell you what—leave the economics for a while and go to DC. See some senators, relax a little. We may have a special assignment coming up, and if I put you on it I want your energy at top level."

"What is it?" Cali asked.

"I'll let you know when I'm further along," she said, and breezed away, while Cali continued to fume.

* * * *

As it turned out, Talia was right about the trip to DC. Cali found it was a good distraction, though she drank too much and tried to seduce a young male intern who had nothing to offer beyond a pair of pretty eyes. Fortunately he was gay and politely ignored her attempts. A little ashamed of herself, worried about her own state of mind, she decided to go back to New York, after she took the time to have lunch with Senator Clemens, whose presence she found soothing.

"Who've you been playing with?" he asked, eyeing her over his steak and fries, a lunch he said was neither PC nor healthy, but sustaining nonetheless.

"Young people," she said, poking at her own salad. "And liars."

"Hmph. Well, maybe they're too young, because you look played out. Or maybe that green stuff you eat won't hold you up. Sure you won't try a steak?"

She smiled, shook her head. "I haven't been sleeping well," she noted.

"Bad dreams?" he asked, and without waiting for a response, he continued. "My aunt used to read people's dreams for a bottle of whiskey and a dollar. She taught me some."

"What would she say to dreams about dead men?" Cali asked.

"Depends. Dead lovers? Fathers? Brothers? Sons?"

"Lovers. Well, almost lovers."

"Mm. Means he's not done with you. Still has a thing or two to teach you."

Cali's hand jerked, her fork tossing pieces of lettuce onto her lap. She busied herself with cleaning it up.

The Senator chuckled. "Hit a nerve?"

"Maybe," Cali said, "I'm done with him."

"It sure don't look that way," he noted, but he courteously moved on to talk about politics, which suddenly seemed a lot safer.

* * * *

Cali went back to New York to face more loneliness and global economics, interspersed with static dreams that landed her nowhere. She also returned to flowers from Rainier. Or more accurately, one flower. A very rare black orchid. It came with a brief note that said, "Something singular, for someone singular. I'll see you soon."

She didn't respond. A few days later, he called her.

"You're avoiding me," he said.

"Yeah," she agreed.

"I won't ask why. You already know you can't do that forever."

"Why not?"

"Because we're not through," he said.

"Maybe I am," she said.

"If you were, you'd have hung up by now."

She sighed. He was right.

"Have dinner with me at my place," he said. "I'll have something brought up."

"I won't eat in your apartment," she said. "You know that."

She heard his low laughter. He was amused. "Then just come over," he suggested. "You can feed off me."

"Not that either," she said.

"Scared, Cali?" he asked.

She said nothing. Fear was sometimes an instinct worth following.

"I wonder which impulse is stronger in you," he said at last. "Fear, or curiosity. I suspect they hang in almost equal balance."

"Maybe," she admitted.

"Let's test it. My car will be waiting for you outside the Aquarius offices tonight at seven. Get in, or not, as you choose.'

She heard the click and the dial tone on the other end. She made a rueful face at her phone. Curiosity had always won with her. Always.

She made it a point not to leave the building until 7:20, but when she got outside Rainier's car was still waiting. She walked up to it, turned slightly right, and walked away. After she'd put a block behind her, she hailed a cab and went home.

The door to her apartment was locked. She used her key and entered, closed the door and sighed in relief. Good to be in her own space. Good to be alone. From somewhere near the center of her living room, she heard soft laughter. Her heart skipped a beat. She flicked on the light and looked around.

Rainier emerged from a shadowed corner. "I suppose I lost my bet," he said. "I was banking on curious. Any odds you want."

She didn't tell him he'd won. That curiosity drove her to walk away from his car. She wanted to know what he'd do next. Now that she did, fury moved into her and stayed. How dare he? This was her home. She was violated, trapped, her safety annihilated.

She opened her door and stood back. "Get out," she said.

He laughed. "Or what, Cali? You'll kill me, like you did the others? You won't find me such an easy target."

Of course he knew about that. He knew everything he needed to. "What I'll do is call the police," she offered. "After they take you away I'll make sure the story gets to the media. They'd love a piece about Rainier Vassago's attempted rape on an Aquarius woman."

"You won't have time," he replied. "I'll kill you first."

His words were quiet, but she knew he meant it. If she made a move he would kill her, and whatever method he used, he'd do it clean. Her body would never be found, his involvement with her disappearing as completely as she would.

She eyed him, noticed his anticipation. Was he waiting for her to Realize a death wish, ready to trounce it? Certainly he wouldn't die for her. He was no Jesse. Maybe he wanted to push her toward the attempt, to see if she had any chops. She was considering the option of giving him what he wanted when an unexpected image flashed in her mind: She saw herself clinging to the side of a mountain. Heard Jesse's voice, urgent, imperative. Stop it. Now.

She closed her thoughts and stayed still. He was right. Whatever Rainier wanted, the worst thing she could do was follow where he lead.

"If you kill me, you won't get what you want," she noted mildly.

All his careful watching dissipated. He moved to her, lifted a hand and brushed it across her cheek. "You're right. What I want is to take you out to dinner," he said. "Are you hungry?"

* * * *

She went with him only to get him out of her home, and stayed with him to see if there was more to learn. His driver, waiting outside, drove them without any instruction to Sogna's, an exclusive Italian restaurant on the Upper West side. It was Cali's favorite. Rainier had done his homework.

When they arrived, a waiter brought them into a softly lit private room, taking along a bottle of wine Rainier had ordered ahead. Cali took her seat across from him, staying silent while the waiter opened the wine and poured, waiting while Rainier approved it.

"Your dinners will be out shortly," he said before departing.

Cali looked to Rainier. "You already ordered?"

"I know what you like," he said.

She sipped her wine, watched him watching her.

"What do you hope to get out of this?" she asked him.

"Some plain talk," he said. "And a resolution."

"I'm game," she said. "Talk."

He did so, his tone clear and his manner direct. He wasn't playing anymore. "First, an apology. I've taken an extreme stance with you, but it was necessary. I wanted to demonstrate that I know what you do at Aquarius, and I want to do it, too. Otherwise, you wouldn't seriously consider the offer I'm about to make. Do you understand?"

"Sure," she said. "So what's the offer?"

"I'll repeat what I said before. Leave Aquarius, and work with me."

"Fair enough," she replied, staying businesslike as well. "But you haven't given me a good reason to leave. You got anything different than what you tried last time?"

"Not different. Just more specific. First, Talia's only real power is making good use of her invisibility. The minute her skills are generally available, her personal party is over and she knows it. And that's about to happen, Cali."

She took in his words, but they didn't make sense. "You're saying—what? We'll have competition?"

"That's an understatement. The world is changing. Energy shifts are making your skills more widely available, to men and women. Talia knows it, and keeps the information tucked in her own purse, so she can spend it as she wants. But time is drawing in, and if you don't move soon, everything you've Realized will become the property of men like me."

She stiffened. He was speaking the truth as he knew it. She could smell it. But she didn't understand. More people were figuring out how to Realize? More men?

"Men are getting in the game?" she asked, and he nodded. She considered. Their ace in the hole had always been men's unwillingness to even consider the possibility of Realizing. What would they do now? And why did Rainier care?

"I'd think you'd like that," she noted.

He ran an elegant finger over the fine linen tablecloth, making small circles with his finger as he spoke. "Not necessarily. Men are greedy, needy, and grasping. Not half as much fun to work with as, for instance, you would be. But worldly power is still ours, and we've been using it to keep women invisible for thousands of years. We have a million and one subtle and magnificent ways to destroy you, claim your work, your bodies, your ideas, your names and lives. We can ridicule you out of existence, shame you into submission, dress you up and take you out and then take you home and kill you. Even without Realizing, I can personally wipe out Aquarius with a few phone calls. I can make them so utterly gone nobody will remember they existed. All the quantum cognition in the universe can't save you from that. Only moving toward a larger power and making it visible will."

She believed him. That paradigm was set, and consciousness couldn't be shifted by Realizing. Her life, her work, all the work of Aquarius, could be forfeit if she made the wrong move. But she wouldn't let fear decide. She'd seen wonders in her time with Talia and wouldn't discount them. Neither should Rainier.

She shrugged lightly. "Don't confuse visibility with power," she said.

"Don't confuse invisibility with power, either. It won't serve you well. And if you need another reason to pack and go, you can't trust Talia. She's lied to you."

Cali was about to say so have you, but she couldn't find any example to support the words. As far as she knew, he hadn't. Lacking a solid offensive, she went defensive instead. "What lie has she told me?" she demanded. "She's paying me just what she said, gave me a good place to play and plenty of interesting people to play with."

"I'll bet she also tells you men can't Realize, but have you asked if that's true of her son? Or is that why she traded him in."

Her son? Talia had a son? And what did he mean, traded him in? "That's got nothing to do with me," she said, as if she knew.

"It has everything to do with you. It's one of many lies she's told you, and many secrets she's keeping from you." He leaned across the table, touched her hand. "Cali, you already know what I can offer you, what we can do together. You may not remember it consciously, but you can't escape your dreams, and your body doesn't lie," he said, his tone still clear, but now more intent, directed at the heart of her.

With his touch, she felt a searing flash. He was made of fire, energy stored for eons, waiting to be called into play. She knew that, and was drawn to it, not just because she was like him, though. Also because he was familiar, as if she knew him. And what did he mean about her remembering? Jesse said something about that, too.

He leaned closer, his voice a whisper in her ear. "Would it help if I told you I know how the snake got into the garden?" he said.

The snake. Why did he say that? How did he know about it? She wouldn't ask, because doing so would only be biting on his hook. She made a small gesture with her hand, pushing it away.

"I won't leave Aquarius unless I can take Racer with me," she said, surprising herself with the sentence. She meant that. She'd go nowhere unless she knew Racer was safe.

He leaned back, businesslike once more. "I'll consider it, as a favor to you. But our union will occur either way, Cali. There isn't any escape. You know that. You remember."

Remember. What did she remember? Now was not the time to explore that. Not with Rainier's burning coal eyes staring at her. She needed to respond to current conditions, present needs. But how?

She asked herself a question: What would Jesse do? Jesse, who touched a part of her Rainier didn't know existed. She lifted her napkin from her lap and folded it carefully, put it on the table.

"I think," she said, "that scraps your chance of getting lucky tonight. Or ever again."

She pushed her chair out, stood and left the restaurant.

* * * *

When she got outside, she found she was shaking, and she told herself to calm down. He wouldn't act against her until he got what he wanted. This was just a skirmish in a war he'd pursue further, and so she was safe for the moment. Just for the moment.

She'd take that moment to see if she could figure out how to make herself truly safe, and to figure out what, if anything, Talia might do to help.

GRAVITY

Cali stood outside Talia's office door, and was about to tap on it, when she heard Talia speaking.

"You shouldn't have," she said. "You moved too fast and lost the fish. And now she knows too much."

Not the words, but the sharpness of her tone was arresting enough that Cali paused and listened.

"You can't bring her back," she continued. "We'll go to plan B. And *I'll* manage it from here. I know her better."

The room went quiet. A phone conversation, Cali thought. Probably nothing much, but Talia didn't often express that level of anger. Cali shrugged it away, knocked, then entered. Talia turned her chair and saw her standing there. Her face flashed a brief confusion, which tightened the lines at her mouth and made her look older, and hungry.

"Eavesdropping?" she asked.

"Just waiting 'til you finished," Cali said. "It sounded—intense. What's it about?"

Talia's face settled into more sociable lines. "One of the women tried something she wasn't ready for. I had to give her a little hell."

"Oh," Cali said, but she didn't believe it. She could smell a lie a mile away, and she smelled one here.

"Was there something you wanted?" Talia demanded.

"It's about Rainier. He's mad at me and I think he'll be gunning for Aquarius."

"What's he mad at?" she asked, but there was no surprise in her voice. As if she already knew.

Of course, Talia often knew things ahead of or concurrent with events that should be outside her ken. That's what made her such a good strategist. Cali assumed it was part of the varying levels of psychic capacities Realizing brought out in each of them. Cali, for her part, had a better telepathy and empathy. Talia, she suspected, leaned toward the precognitive.

"Because I wouldn't play nice," she answered.

"He should've known that. Do you know what he'll do, specifically?"

She shook her head. "He didn't say."

Talia waved it away. "We'll manage him. Don't worry about it. It was worth a shot, anyway."

"Okay. But there's something else. Something he said about you. Do you have a son?"

It was the absence of reaction that troubled Cali. Talia didn't look upset, or even surprised, and normally she was hell bent against any intrusion on her private life. Most of the women of Aquarius were like that. Cali thought it was because they were so exposed, so connected, at work. They wanted, as she did, space that was private and safe.

"I *had* a son," Talia said, emphasizing the past tense. "He died."

"Oh. I'm sorry. I didn't know."

"Rainier told you about him?"

"Just that you had a son. And something about you traded him in. He said it as if it was a secret, something he might use against you, so I thought I should mention it."

"He's just fucking with your mind," Talia said. "And maybe trying to get to me."

"That sounds like him. Listen, I'm sorry about your son. Was it—was he a baby?"

"He was grown."

"Oh. An accident?"

"I don't like to talk about it." This, said with finality. "We've got work to do. Conference room in half an hour."

"Anything special?" Cali asked.

"Foreign interests. You'll see. I figured it out last night and wanted to try it this morning. You'd better prep. Group work is still tough on you."

"Wait," Cali said. "You don't look old enough to have a grown son."

Talia tilted her head, smiled. "What we do can keep us young for a long time, Cali. Didn't you know that?"

"I never thought about it," Cali said. "But it's not forever, is it?"

"Wouldn't that be nice," Talia said wryly. "I'll teach you about it sometime. But not right now. Go get ready for the conference. Build some energy."

* * * *

The task was simple enough. Give nuclear power to a small African nation. Seven of the senior Aquarius women were going at it diligently, working to complete the thought, opening the possibilities available in the world and there were many they knew of, having done their research. But then, in the middle of the quiet space, Talia made a sound of frustration and stood, breaking the focus. Groans were heard around the circle.

"Now what?" someone said.

"Cali," Talia said, "come with me. The rest of you keep at it."

They sighed and went back to it while Talia and Cali made a quiet exit, walking down the hall in silence toward Talia's office. When they were inside, Talia closed the door.

"What the hell is it now?" Talia asked.

"What?" Cali said. "We were working."

"They were. You weren't. You're not focused, and it was interfering. I felt it. You knew it. Is it the group thing? Rainier? What?"

Cali crossed her arms at her chest. Talia was right. She wasn't in her work, but not because of Rainier, or the group thing. Not this time. "What you're proposing—I don't buy it," she said firmly. "I can't complete the thought if I don't buy it."

"The others do."

"Kool Aid drinkers," she said. "They don't notice what's in it. They just drink."

Talia pointed her long, elegant finger at Cali. "You're thinking short term, limited goals. You want people to be happy now, even if that destroys them."

"Nuclear power is pretty good at destroying things," Cali noted. "I don't see the point in making more."

"You don't have the complete picture. I do."

"Then maybe you should let me in on it."

"I have, repeatedly."

Talia kept talking, about the complexities of the political scene, about how Cali was too direct in her thinking and didn't understand what was at stake. Cali was barely listening. She'd heard it before, and it didn't satisfy her.

Instead, she was thinking of Lara, so different from her but just as direct in her own way. Just as single minded. She wondered what Lara would make of Aquarius. If she would start them doing the Buddhist meditation, wishing everyone into happiness and love. May you be loved. May you be peaceful. May you be liberated.

Not that Cali believed in that, but if she did, could she complete that thought? Would her belief be enough, wishing happiness on the ten billion who occupied the planet?

"Cali?" Talia asked. "Are you listening?"

Cali blinked at her.

Talia made clucking sounds of irritation. "I said you need to develop some trust in the process, but clearly you can't even hear that as a possibility. What's blocking you? A problem, a question, a bad dream, a bad hair day?"

"Dream," she murmured.

"You're dreaming? What about?"

Talia paid attention to the women's dreams. They were, she said, metaphors of possibilities. Cali didn't want this metaphor put into her hands, however.

"Nothing specific," she said. "Just static."

"Don't you dare lie to me."

"I'm not. The dreams are about static. Ugly, grating static. They wake me up. But it's got nothing to do with today. I just can't do this job. I'll only get in the way."

"Cali—"

"Really, Talia. Isn't there something else I can work on?"

Talia's face screwed itself into displeasure, then let it go. "Well," she said, relenting, "It happens. The most talented Realizers are also the most temperamental, it seems." She ruffled her hair. "There is something else that might suit your talents better. Not a group job. Something for one Realizer. I meant to talk to you about it after the group work."

"Okay. What is it?"

"A special situation. Very important, and very touchy. I've been thinking about it for a while, and I'm pretty sure there's only one way to manage it. I'm *very* sure you're the only one who can do it, too."

Cali felt the flattery, but was willing to believe it. She knew she was better at Realizing than anyone else at Aquarius, except maybe Talia. "Tell me," she said.

"Sit down," Talia said. "No. Wait. Close the door first."

Cali did so, and Talia, seated at her desk, swiveled her chair back and forth, keeping her eyes on Cali. "One of our Senators has become a problem. A very big problem. He's introducing legislation that could ruin our agenda, and wreak havoc on global security. It's potentially devastating."

"Jesus," Cali said. "You haven't mentioned anything like that."

"I didn't want to panic the others. But now . . . well, it's reaching a critical point, and I can think of only one way to manage it."

"What?"

"He has to be removed." Talia was so matter of fact, it took Cali a minute to understand. Remove the Senator. Remove him.

"Have him voted out?" she asked, just to check.

"The election's two years away. We can't wait for that," Talia said.

"What? Impeached? Arrested?"

"Not this guy. He's squeaky clean. Cali, he needs to be removed."

Cali swallowed, tasting something unpleasant. "You want me to kill him," she said.

Talia's expression was a combination of sympathy and determination. "I know it's not a pleasant task. Sometimes our best people have to do the worst work. But you're the only one here who can. The only one with that specific skill."

Ironic that the one skill she'd relinquished was what made her special. "I haven't done it in years."

"You haven't had reason to. But now you do."

"What reason?"

"He's a threat to everything we're working for."

"Worse than the President?"

"Don't start. The President's our best puppet in a long age. He's totally incompetent, and doesn't know it. This man can actually get things done. Every piece of legislation he backs wins. And all of them hurt us. More and more each day."

"I thought Rainier was doing that, and you wanted me to sleep with him."

"If I thought you could get this Senator in bed I'd arrange it. He's too damn moral for his own good."

Cali was beginning to have a bad feeling about what came next. "Exactly what legislation, and which Senator?" she asked.

"The legislation is sweeping. It covers healthcare, environmental issues. Totally upsets the global economy."

"Talia," Cali cut in. "Who is it?"

Talia paused, took in breath and released it. "Senator Clemens," she said.

Of course. Utterly moral. Utterly competent. Imaginative as hell, and proposing a few bills that would change the way the whole system worked.

"Universal Healthcare? The Green Way bill?"

Talia nodded.

"They're good bills."

"They upend things. Destabilize a complex system that's worked for a long time."

"Worked to support the fossil fuels destroying the planet? Work to support the people having no health care? Talia—"

"You're thinking short term again."

"But I know him," Cali said. "I like him."

"So do I," Talia said sympathetically. "But sometimes you have to release negative energy to allow the positive in. That's all you'd be doing. Releasing negative energy."

Cali thought of his particularity, the way his great hands, like the hands of a bear, swallowed hers when he grasped them, thinking of the intelligence in his eyes that saw good and bad and yet were never bitter about it.

"Actually, I'd be killing a man I admire."

"You've done that before," Talia noted.

Cali winced. Did Talia know about Jesse, too? Why not? She knew everything else.

"I can't do it if I don't buy it," she said. "And it'd take a lot to convince me."

"You have to move beyond personal feelings," Talia said. "Listen, do you know that without Hitler there'd be no Israel, no understanding of anti-semitism, and that understanding became a basis for dealing with other issues of racism?"

"Talia, you aren't even saying that Aquarius—"

She waved it away. "It's an illustration, to make a point. You look at this Senator and see good. I see that the change he proposes will create such massive instability the ripples will be felt across the globe, causing violence, destruction. His good deed will result in more deaths than you can imagine, and only your willingness to do the wrong thing, to make that sacrifice for us, can turn it around."

Cali thought of irreconcilable differences, of cats in boxes, of no way out. "Will be, or could be?" she asked.

"From what I can see, will be. And I see a lot."

"You don't know for sure, though. You're predicting the future based on the past."

"It's a damn good predictor. Very reliable."

"But not perfect. And in a dynamic system, small input has unpredictable results."

"It's not my only source of understanding. You're aware that Realizing sometimes opens up other skills?"

"Yeah," she said. Most of the women, including herself, had at least a small share of telepathy or clairvoyance attached to their gift.

"I see further ahead than most," Talia said. "I know where his work is leading. Until you sit in my office, you'll have to trust that's true."

Cali knew the limits of her own understanding. She was a creature of instinct, an old tomcat, sniffing her way home. But Talia knew Senator Clemens only as a political construct, a means to an end. Cali knew him as particular, a singular piece of energy existing in his own right, regardless of Aquarius and its ultimate goals. Nor did she think, when she signed on, that Aquarius engaged in assassinations.

"How long have you been knocking people off?" she asked.

"We don't knock people off," Talia said with disgust. "Don't be ridiculous."

"Talia, this is a hit."

"It's a special situation, Cali. It needs special handling."

"Is it the first time, then?"

Talia shrugged. "It's unusual."

Cali said nothing. She wondered what else she'd learn as she went deeper into the fold.

"Look, what if you knew," Talia said, "I mean really knew I was right—that his legislation is deadly—would you do it?"

"If I knew that, and I couldn't convince him to drop it, I would," she conceded. "But I'd have to see it, and right now I don't."

"Then do some research. Look at the bill, and see how it connects to the larger realm. How it hurts the entire economic basis of the planet. You're smart. You'll see what I mean. I'm going to that Seattle conference tomorrow. I'll probably be gone a week. When I get back, have an answer ready for me."

Cali turned, and was walking away when Talia called her back.

"Cali," she said, and Cali stopped. Waited.

"Make it the right one," Talia said.

PROBABILITY DISTRIBUTIONS

The next day, while Talia was gone and Racer was in Geneva at a conference for young activists, while the news reported an orange alert for terrorism in the City because of recent incendiary events and the President made a speech about the country's response, Cali called some of the more experienced women into the conference room.

"I'm trying something and I want your help. It's pretty easy."

They listened attentively while she explained. They were accustomed to experimenting with each other's inspirations. Some worked and some didn't. It was important to try new moves, though. Valuable for its own sake. Cali had decided on this one after her talk with Talia. For reasons she couldn't articulate, she though it would help her decide what to do about the Senator.

"You want to give it a shot?" she asked, when she was done explaining.

"Sure," Angela said. "Sounds kind of nice."

"Is it for anything specific?" Lola asked, eyeing her a little suspiciously. They all knew that Cali avoided group work when she could, so for her to call a group into session was unusual.

"Just for us," she said. "I want to see if it helps with energy renewal."

Lola, who often felt the drain of Realizing, nodded. "Let's do it," she said.

Cali joined hands with them, started their breathing, and began the mantra.

"I love myself," she said. "May I be well. May I be peaceful. May I be liberated."

The others repeated after her, and slowly she led them through the entire meditation, including Aquarius, the City, the country, the politicians they all worked with or against, and even the President who surely needed some wellness and liberation. She sent their loving thoughts out across the planet and back to their own hearts. It was, if nothing else, soothing. When it was done, the women breathed out easily and smiled.

"That was lovely Cali," Lily said. "But you know, I couldn't actually complete it. It's too impossible."

"I know," Cali said. "But how's your energy?"

"Good," she said. "Very good."

"Then it's useful."

"Yeah," Lola agreed. "Especially since I have to face the auditors next week."

Another problem. The feds were coming to do an audit. Rainier had arranged it, Cali was sure. She figured if she slept with him again he'd call off the dogs, but she was done with him. Too bad. May you be well, she thought, directing it toward whatever auditor might look at their books. May you be peaceful. May you be liberated.

As the week continued, she had the women do the meditation daily. And then, toward the end of the week, she started something else.

It was an accident, really, very unintentional. She'd been taking a NIA dance class, part of Talia's insistence that all the women maintain a regular exercise routine, and they'd done a very intense Chakra meditation at the end. When she left, she felt full of energy, buzzed with it, and she stopped at a bar for a drink, knowing she'd never get to sleep without it. She was having a hard time sleeping lately. In fact, she was having a hard time going home.

After Rainier showed up at her apartment she sold it quickly, at a loss, and found somewhere else to live. It didn't feel like home yet, so she resisted going there. And sleep only brought her static and indeterminacy. So instead she sat at a bar called Oasis nursing a whiskey and her worry about a decision she was afraid she'd already made, regardless of consequences. The man sitting next to her was reading a newspaper and he grunted at a headline.

"Hell," he said. "Terrorism my ass. I'd like about one percent of the money they spend on it and then I could pay for my son's college tuition."

Cali turned to him. "Why don't you wish for it?" she suggested. She was just buzzed enough from the class and her drink to subdue her inner censor, and just curious enough to want to know if Rainier was right. If men could also learn to Realize. If, in fact, it could be taught.

The man turned to her. He wasn't attractive or young, but he had some kindness in his eyes. He looked at her as if she was his daughter. "Okay," he said. "I wish for it. There. You think that did it?"

Cali smiled at him, shook her head. "You have to mean it. Believe it's possible, complete the thought."

"You're one of those new age girls, aren't you?"

"No," she said. "Listen, it's energy. Our thoughts are energy. Electrical energy. Positive and negative ions running across a permeable membrane. You can direct that. It doesn't always work, but sometimes it does. Look, I'll show you."

She put her hand on his, pointed to her eyes. "Watch," she said. "Breathe like I do."

He gave her half a grin. "What the hell," he muttered. "I'm an electrician."

His grin went away when he began to feel what was happening as Cali called the thought into reality, adding her energy to his. Suddenly it seemed easy to work with someone else. Maybe because he had a direct wish, with visible consequences, and no strategizing or harm in it. It was all done out of love.

"Feel it?" she asked quietly. He nodded, his mouth slightly open, his eyes wide. "Okay, then. Complete it."

She loosened her hold on him slightly, pulling her thoughts away, letting his emerge. She felt the moment of completion in him, saw him shudder with his own awareness of it. He really wanted that, more than anything. It was important to him. It mattered.

When it was done, she let him go and turned back to her drink. He sat still, staring at the newspaper for a long time. Then he put some money on the bar, called to the bartender. "Buy her something. Anything. Whatever she wants," he said, and he left.

Cali had no doubt he'd get the money. She was surprised at how easy it had been, and wondered if she could do it with others. She took to going to bars, waiting for the right person to talk to.

She met a man who wanted to win the big lottery, and taught him that he could. She met a young bartender who wanted a new job and instructed her how to complete the thought. She met an old woman who wanted to get the hell out of the City and move to Florida, and she helped with that.

Surprisingly, none of this diminished her energy. When she went home to sleep, her dreams had more singing than static, and though she sensed Jesse's presence within the song, it soothed rather than frustrated her. Just as she'd felt after her night sessions with Ida, she woke in the morning feeling more alive than she'd been in some time. When she went into the office, Lola remarked on it.

"Who's been doing your facials, girl?" she asked. "Because I want some of that."

Cali laughed. "No facials. I'm just taking it easy for a change."

"Well, that's good news. Then you want to catch a movie or something tonight?"

"I can't. I'm busy."

Lola eyed her. "I thought you said you were taking it easy."

"I'm busy taking it easy," she amended.

* * * *

Then another idea occurred to her.

It was after she met a woman with shaggy brown hair who hunched over her drink and a notebook, writing. At a certain point she put her pen down, stretched out her fingers and stared blankly at Cali.

"You're a writer," Cali noted, nodding at the notebook.

"What? Oh. That. Yes. A helluva job."

"Is it? How's it going?" Cali asked.

"The writing's fine. It always is," the woman said. "It's the publishers that're hell."

"How so?"

The woman ran her fingers through her hair, grabbed at one lock and turned it over in her fingers thoughtfully. "One inch thoughts," she said. "Editors say they love my writing, but they have to buy based on what sold last year, what's hot right now. Me, I thought it was about the art, but for the industry the past predicts the present and becomes the future. They say it's just a response to the market, but they're actually creating it."

Cali nodded. She knew this. Sometimes she even lived it.

"What do you want?" Cali asked.

The woman stared across the bar, lifted a hand as if reaching for something far away. "To have my writing read by millions of people, and earn millions of dollars with it." She shrugged ruefully. "I know how it sounds, but it's only eighty percent self-centered. I've got something to say. I want it heard, a lot."

"Wish for it," Cali suggested.

The woman picked up her glass and took a drink from it. "I *been* doing that. Cursing publishers left and right."

"Maybe," Cali said, "you need to wish them well.

The woman looked at her, said nothing.

"Try it like this," Cali suggested. She touched the woman's arm. Breathed with her. Showed her the feel of something you want pouring into the world. "I love the publishers. May they be well," she breathed. "May they be peaceful. May they be liberated."

The woman spoke it after her, breathing, focusing.

"Complete the thought," Cali said. "Make it what you want."

The woman, with enough imagination to understand the nature of the energy involved, did as Cali said, moving the thought to completion.

When it was done, she blinked at Cali. "Thanks, I think," she said. "Is that—um—hypnotism? Creative visualization?"

Cali shook her head. "It's just something humans do. Like using tools or making fire. But it has to be real, and you have to believe it's possible. That the past doesn't necessarily predict the future."

The two women sat quietly for a moment. Cali turned to her again.

"Listen, I want you to keep doing that," she said.

"That—what?"

"The meditation. Only do it for—well, whatever you think needs a little peace and liberation. Start with yourself and move it out to other people. People you love. People you hate. The world. And teach someone else. Okay?"

"Sure," the woman said. "Why not?"

When Cali left the bar she was wrapped in warmth and mild joy. In her peripheral vision, she saw a familiar face. Lola, chatting with some other people, lifting her head and staring at Cali, who moved toward her.

But Lola moved away and was swallowed by the crowd. Funny, Cali thought. She could have sworn Lola saw her.

* * * *

The next day, she wanted to ask Lola about it, but she was out of the office. Cali shrugged it off. That night, and for many nights after, she continued her practice of going to bars and teaching others how to Realize, teaching them the Buddhist chant, instructing them to tell someone else. She had no idea what was impelling her, whether it was a good idea or a a bad one. She only knew she was doing it, with mostly positive results.

One woman called her a perv and a commie. One man couldn't find enough belief to complete his thought, but usually the people she met both longed for and believed in the possibility of their most dearly held wishes. They'd just never had anyone else open that door for them. For each one, she told them to teach someone else, and say the chant.

One night she met a man who wanted a boat. A big boat to take out on Long Island sound, a place to dock it. To Cali that seemed simple enough. Objects were the easiest wished to compete. But when she told him to wish for it and began showing him how he pulled away and shivered.

"That's evil, that is," he said.

That stopped her dead in her tracks. "Evil?"

"If we could all have what we want by wishing, the world'd go to hell in a hand basket pretty damn fast," he said firmly.

"It's not that simple," she said. "You have to mean it. Believe in it."

"Even worse," he said. "If you mean it and believe in it but don't have to work for it, nothing will mean anything soon enough."

Cali pulled up a memory of a story her mother told, about a town in an Irish village that was having a particularly bad year. A leprechaun visited them, and told them he'd give them what they wanted and needed, as long as they didn't thank him or offer him any payment for his work. Of course, the people couldn't do it. They just had to offer something in return for the gifts, and the minute they did, the leprechaun went away.

She was going to tell the story to the man, but he left with a quick backward glance at her, as if she was Satan and he was afraid she'd follow him home. She sat with her drink, thinking about what he'd said. That Realizing could be seen as evil was a new thought to her. If people truly wanted something, and it did no harm, why shouldn't they have it? Wouldn't achieving your heart's desire make you more inclined to be generous, happy, loving and kind, more peaceful and liberated?

She wondered how Jesse would answer, and could almost hear his laughter. Maybe he'd tell her that getting what she didn't want—time at Bedford—taught her the most.

"That was different," she muttered grudgingly. "I had issues."

"So does everyone," she heard him say. "Issues large and small, grand and petty."

"They'd resolve their issues better with a little happiness to back them up," she argued back. "What if it worked that way, too?"

He would turn this thought over the way he turned over a pen or a leaf. He would see it as a generous view. He would say she'd changed a great deal since St. Ida's.

"I know," she acknowledged. "But am I right?"

"Maybe," he'd conclude, "you get your wish, whether you know you want it or not."

* * * *

At Aquarius the next day, Lola was back in the office. After the meditation that had become a regular morning event, she met Cali in the front room as she was staring out the window at the people milling on the streets below. Her thoughts centers on how long she might be coming to this office to stare out this window. Talia would be back soon, and that could mean an end to her employment. She already knew she would not, could not, kill Senator Clemens.

"Cali?" Lola asked, touching her arm. "Can we talk?"

Cali looked to her, and saw she looked serious, worried. "Sure. Go ahead."

Lola gestured down the hall. "My office, okay?"

They moved down the hall in silence and went into that room. Lola had draped the walls in silk fabric of yellow, black and gold, and African masks peered out from the folds, like people hovering just behind curtains. When the windows were open and a breeze moved the fabric, the effect was one of being surrounded by spirits who might whisper to you if you listened. Cali sat, and Lola closed the door.

"This looks serious," Cali said.

"Yeah. Listen, I saw you the other night. At the bar."

"That was you? I thought so, but you disappeared. Why didn't you . . ." She let the sentence trail away. "Okay," she said. "Tell me."

"I wouldn't, but you're St. Ida's, and we keep each other's backs—no matter what Racer thinks. So I did like she said, but I'm telling you about it before there's trouble."

Cali worked her way through all this, and parsed out a question. "You did like who said?" she asked.

"Talia. She asked me to keep track of you while she was away. Wanted to know what you're up to."

Okay, Cali thought. No surprise there. "So, you were watching me? Listening in?"

Lola sniffed. "The bar was real crowded. Noisy. I couldn't hear a damn thing. And even if I *thought* you were teaching some crazy lady how to Realize, I couldn't say that unless I heard it real clear. You understand?"

"Sure," Cali said quietly.

"Good. So what I'll tell Queen Talia is that I saw you at some bars, drinking. Maybe trying to pick up a little fun. But then, maybe I talked to you about how it'd be a good idea to stay home more, and drink less. Not that going to bars would get you fired or anything, because since I been here, nobody's been fired from Aquarius. Women here don't get fired. You get me?"

Cali's forehead knit itself into lines. Lola put a hand on her desk and emphasized her words with her tapping finger. "Nobody gets fired," she said again. "Claro, amiga?"

Nobody got fired. Women left, or were just gone, but nobody got fired. And Talia wanted her to kill a man. "Claro," she replied. "And thanks. Thanks a lot."

"Yeah. You gonna stay home tonight? Because I got this man lined up for the evening, and I'd rather attend to him than you."

"Have a blast," Cali said with some assurance. "I'll be in my bed by nine. Alone."

* * * *

Cali did take a few nights off. Just as many as she thought were necessary to shake her tail. Then, she went out to a new bar, on the East side. Oddly enough, what she'd learned only made her want to do as much as she could before Talia came back, when she'd have serious issues to deal with.

At the new bar, the first person she saw was the writer, scratching away at her notebook. Cali took a seat next to her, ordered a drink. The woman did a double take, looked up, and smiled.

" Hey," she said. "It's the witch woman."

"What?"

"I'm glad I ran into you. Guess what. It worked. What you did. An editor called two days later offering a contract. So I figured you must be some kind of good witch."

"I didn't do it," Cali said. "You did."

"Me?"

"You. And apparently you're good at it. Try something else without me. You'll see."

"I can hardly credit it. This works with other things?"

"It won't make an asshole into a gentleman unless he wants to change, but it's useful in other ways. You have to experiment. But be a little careful."

"Careful? You're talking to a writer. But I get you, and I will be. I gotta tell you, though. I love the idea. No barriers. All the crap of teeny tiny minds out of the way. The whole universe opens up."

"Yeah," Cali said. "It does, doesn't it?"

* * * *

She was thinking about that on the way home, about the universe opening up, when the screech of brakes and a scream called her from thoughts to events occurring around her.

She looked up, saw a car stopped sideways in the street, saw a woman kneeling in front of it, screaming hysterically for someone to call an ambulance. Without thinking, Cali moved to her, knelt with her, and saw a small, collapsed body. A little boy, crushed and bloodless.

The woman turned a hysterical face to her. "Save him," she said, clutching at Cali. "My baby. He ran out. Save him."

Cali looked up. The driver, white as snow, was already on his cell phone. "He's getting help," she said. "Just stay still. Keep him still."

The woman's hand moved on Cali like a talon. "No," she said, her voice a grating of metal on stone. "Do something. Now."

Cali wet her lips, reluctantly put a hand to the boy's neck. She felt no pulse. No motion of life. "Just wait," she whispered. "Wait for the ambulance."

The woman's eyes looked like Jesse's dying eyes, looked like her own eyes when Keith betrayed her. When her mother betrayed her. Looked like Lara's eyes when she died in her lap. They opened doors in her best left closed.

"You can save him," she insisted. "I know you can."

The woman's assurance was complete. She looked to Cali as the centurion looked to the Christ, as the Christ looked to the Magdalene, as they'd always looked to each other.

The woman's grip tightened. "Please," she moaned. "Please. You can."

"Be quiet," Cali said harshly. "Just—be quiet."

And then she was calm, she and the woman both calm as if caught in a bubble of quiet while horns beeped and people shouted things, a crowd gathering around them. But where they were was perfectly still.

Cali laid her hand on the boy. She opened her thoughts to this, to this.

Brief images of his smile, of him playing with a neighbor's child, of him sleeping, having a tantrum, laughing, sulking with a head cold. Nothing special here. Just an ordinary life. The sorrow of the ending might be more than the value of the thing itself, but she saw tears splashing onto him from his mother's eyes.

This child must live, she thought. Not a wish. Not a belief. Just a truth. He had a life, and he must live it. "Look at me," she said to his mother.

The woman lifted her gaze to Cali, who touched her face, catching a tear on the end of her finger. She turned to the boy and pressed the tear into his motionless chest, leaned over and put her breath on his eyes, made the thought complete.

The world blurred, went away. She sat in a blank space where all breath was held in abeyance. She wondered if she'd passed out, but it didn't feel like that. Consciousness wasn't gone, even if all other energy was suspended.

Then, as if she was punched through a wall, she re-entered the world, heard the noise of car horns and people talking and an ambulance siren drawing close. She looked at the mother, who sat very still, staring at her. She turned to the boy and moved her hand over his neck. She felt a pulse. Saw his chest rise and fall with breath. She took his mother's hand in hers and moved it so she could feel it too. Without saying a word, Cali stood up.

The woman looked up at her. "Thank you," she whispered.

Cali touched her head, then turned and walked away.

* * * *

By the time she was in her apartment and in bed, Cali could no longer distinguish between dream and waking. She floated in a realm of possibilities that didn't exist in waking, though she was fairly sure she wasn't sleeping yet.

She lay on her bed, waiting, knowing something must happen. Part of her expected Lara to walk into the room, or Ida. Part of her waited for retribution. Surely she'd stolen the elixir of the gods, broken some primordial law. Surely the Angel of Death would pursue her. None of that happened.

Instead what happened was the feeling of waking up, though she hadn't slept. She opened her eyes, which she'd apparently closed, and she saw Jesse, sitting on the side of her bed, smiling at her.

"Hi," he said.

"Hi," she replied. No dream this time, she thought. Then, what? Hallucination?

He looked her up and down. "That was good work," he said.

"Did I do something?" she asked.

"The boy," he said.

"Oh. That." It seemed apart from her in some very fundamental way. As if she'd witnessed it rather than caused it. It reminded her of a day on the side of a mountain, when she'd agreed that everyone would come home alive.

"Like saving Darlene?" he asked.

She wasn't sure she liked him walking around her thoughts so readily. "It was nothing much," she said.

"You blame yourself for what you do wrong, but you don't credit yourself for your kindness," he said. "You still holding yourself hostage?"

She tightened, irritated, but he laughed quietly. "Okay. I'll leave it alone," he said. "Anyway, it was good. Are you okay?"

"Kind of."

"It takes a lot out of you physically."

"Realizing? It never did before," she said.

"It did when you used this skill. Don't you remember?"

As he spoke, she almost did. A man, dismembered and re-membered. And someone—her?—breathed life into him. She wasn't sure. Memory skirted the edge of knowledge and moved away. She shook her head.

"Don't worry about it," he said. He gestured to her. "Come with me."

"Where are we going?"

"You'll see. Sort of."

He took a step forward and she followed. Her room disappeared and they stood on the air. Then they fell.

The fall was breathtakingly fast. She couldn't talk or think. She waited to hit, and then wake. She'd had this dream before.

But she didn't hit. She just continued to move through air and then she was in a dark place, pinpoints of light all around her as if she swam in a sea of distant fireflies. She looked down and saw more of the same. She looked up and saw even more.

Maybe they weren't moving at all, she thought. Falling wasn't the same when there was no ground to hit. And even if she was falling, she felt held within space, bound up with it, as if she was just one strand of a web woven all around her. She would fall without it, but it would also be weakened without her, and so they both held on.

"See?" Jesse said. "It's all energy. All bound up together. I wanted you to feel that."

"That's what Rainier says."

"I know."

"How?"

"I know him. He's right about the energy, but he's wrong about how it works. He thinks it's all about winning. It's not. It's about connections. Webs. Motion. Can you feel it?"

She could. Whatever this place was, dream or hallucination, within it she perceived directly that she was not separate from other people, other creatures, other objects, from the living or the dead. It was all energy and it flowed between everything, connecting them, weaving them into the vast web of time and space that constantly remade itself, moving effortlessly, with something like joy from one kind of matter to another.

She turned to Jesse, and he smiled, moved to her and then into her, until they were one person, his molecules mingling with hers, ringing against them like small pieces of crystal flicked by a finger's lightest touch. She gasped with pleasure, felt his laughter singing through her cells.

"Well?" he asked, after he moved through and out of her.

"Can I do it, too?"

"Sure," he said. He moved away from her and held his arms open.

She moved into him now, riding within the warmth of who he was, the immense energy of love he contained.

"Jesse," she whispered, though she knew he was more than Jesse. Much more than the name or the man who carried it. He was the renewer, the force that renewed, his fingers green with growth and life even in his death.

"Okay," she said. "Okay."

"Yeah," he agreed. "All that."

She left him again, wanting to see him separate, and in seeing him wanted to draw him to her physically, kiss his lips and feel his hands on her skin.

She reached for him, and was immediately aware of ground beneath her feet. She blinked around. They were standing on a mountain, near the edge of the cliff she'd almost climbed, that had almost killed her.

"We can't kiss," he said gently, sadly. "Not yet."

She ran her lip through her teeth just to make sure she could feel. Of course, it was a dream. It had to be. She occupied a different state than normal consciousness, like solid becoming liquid becoming gas becoming liquid again. Still, when she pressed the edge of her teeth against her lip she could feel it. What did that mean?

"Jesse, where are you when you're not with me?" she asked.

"Everywhere," he said. "Nowhere. Here."

"Where's here?"

"Wherever we are."

"That's pretty unhelpful," she noted.

"I know. It's kind of hard to translate. Don't worry about it. It doesn't hurt except—well, the transition is tough. Listen, Cali. I want to ask you something. Things are going bad at Aquarius, aren't they?"

"They are," she admitted. "Talia wants me to do something. I don't think I can, but I'm not sure if I should. I keep thinking about Chaos theory."

"Nonlinearity? Butterfly Effect?"

"That kind of thing. All the good things people try, they end up in a bad place. So maybe Talia's right. Doing something bad will set it straight."

"You think so?"

"I think it, but it doesn't feel right."

"Instinct. Intuition."

"Yeah."

He rubbed at the back of his neck thoughtfully. "If you need help deciding, look at your hand."

"What?"

"The lines in your hand. You haven't forgotten that, have you?"

She raised her hand, saw the line that ran up the middle, disappearing between her fingers. The line of true greatness her grandmother told her about. The lines in her hand that made Jesse startle when they first met.

"I don't want that," she said. "It's too much of a burden."

"You keep choosing it," he noted. "You already started. Leaving Rainier. Teaching people at bars."

"I didn't think it would be so easy," she mused.

"Easy? You've only been at it a few thousand years."

"What?"

"Never mind. It won't make sense until you remember it all. Anyway, it wasn't possible when you first tried. Most people just couldn't do it. Maybe we're some kind of genetic mutation, and they weren't. But there's been an energy shift since then. A big one." He gestured around. "Radio waves. Microwaves. Cell phone towers and satellites. Humans are sucking up all kinds of new energy and it's changed them. Made them more permeable. What you teach, they can learn now."

Rainier had said something similar, and it made sense to her. The human body ran on immensely complex chemical and electric circuitry. It would react to new energy in more ways than just getting cancer. And she doubted any scientist was researching that angle.

"So what's it mean?" she asked.

He lifted a hand, let it fall. "It means it's already out there. You can't call it back, and there's no telling what it'll do."

"Chaos theory again," she said.

"That's right," he said.

Cali remembered a book her mother used to read to her when she was little. It was called "What if Everybody Did?" and showed different scenarios first done by one person, and then done by everyone. A boy dropped a candy wrapper on the ground. Then everybody did, and all the people were swimming in garbage. A boy uprooted a chunk of grass and then everybody did, and the earth was barren.

So what, Cali wondered, if everybody Realized? She saw scenes of utter disaster, with thought clashing against thought, with murder and mayhem, wars of the mind exploding everywhere. And she saw utter contentment, with gardens and laughter, a sense of ease never possible before, as everyone sent out mantras wishing others well. Like any energy, she supposed it would depend on how it was used.

"I don't want to stop teaching it," she said.

"That's inevitable, given who you are," Jesse said. "But if you need advice, don't go to Talia or Rainier. Try someone you actually trust."

"I don't trust anybody. Except . . ."

"Except who?"

"You," she said.

"Nobody else?"

"Ida," she said, surprised at her own answer.

"Go see her. That is, when you're through holding yourself hostage."

"I wish you wouldn't do that."

His mouth turned up in a grin, but any words he might say were cut off by the sharp and biting sound of static. He startled, looked up. "We don't have much time."

"Jesse, I need to know something. Am I keeping you here? Should I let you go?" she asked, desperate to give him something for his kindness, for his life, his life.

"No," he said, sounding surprised. "Why would you?"

"Because you can't rest, or—or move on, or whatever it is that happens."

He shook his head, looked around quickly. The sound was growing closer. "I *am* moving on. With you. Unless you want me gone."

"No. I want you with me."

"Are you sure? You know what that means?"

The sound was louder, closer, more malevolent. "I don't care," she cried over it. "I don't care what it means."

"Then do what's next."

"What? What do I do? Tell me."

His eyes went wide with pain. Static, heavy and thick, surrounded him. His voice came to her, broken and distant. "You know, Cali," he said. "Complete the thought."

Then he was gone, and she dropped like a rock to the bottom of emptiness, and sleep.

DISSIPATIVE CHAOS

Cali later thought that if she paid more attention to the news she might have been spared a lot of trouble. As it was, she took a few days off and spent them at a Spa where she was massaged, given hot baths and body and face treatments. Nobody made much note of this. The women of Aquarius did that kind of thing often as a way of renewing their energy. It was considered important.

She went back to Aquarius the same day Talia returned, walking in during the middle of morning meditation. Cali heard her the door click open, heard soft footsteps moving toward them. She kept the chant going to its conclusion, though part of her was no longer saying it. Instead she was thinking, I'm fucked. Totally and irrevocably fucked, on so many counts.

When the chant was done, the women looked up and smiled at each other. Angela peered through the dim light and saw Talia.

"Hey," she said. "When did you come in?"

"In time to hear this. That was pleasant. A new meditation?" Talia asked brightly.

"Yes. Nice one, isn't it? Cali taught us. We've been doing it every day."

"How lovely. Makes you good and ready for work, right?"

There were playful laughs, groans, and the women dispersed. Cali stayed seated, and Talia stood staring down at her.

"What was that about?" she asked, and her voice no longer sounded bright.

"I thought it'd be good for them. Things were pretty tense."

"It diffuses their energy, from what I saw. What the hell are you up to, Cali?. "

"Up to?" Cali asked, hoping she sounded surprised, or pissed, or anything other than guilty.

"You've been screwing with things."

"Interesting phrase. You mean things other than men? Like machines, or vegetables?"

"Stop it. You've been teaching people how to Realize."

Cali's heart thumped hard in her chest, as it had when she found Racer with pot. Her world was about to fall apart again. She composed herself, spoke quietly. "You mean the meditation? We're supposed to teach each other that kind of thing, aren't we?"

"Of course not. I'm talking about this." Talia slapped her newspaper down, pointed to a headline. *WOMAN CREDITS BAR MEETING FOR LOTTERY WIN.*

Cali thought about denying it, but figured that wouldn't fly. The story presented a pretty accurate picture of her. She couldn't very well claim it was a different dark-skinned woman with long dark hair who did this. Instead, she played it as a surprise.

"Huh," she said. "It worked."

"Of course it did. What the hell were you thinking of? You could blow Aquarius sky high with this kind of stunt."

"I was a little drunk," Cali said. "I was thinking of Rainer, who wanted me to teach him, and wondering if it was even possible."

"Rainer wanted you to teach him?"

"Yeah. That's why I left him. He was getting pushy about it."

"But then you were curious. And you know what that did to the cat."

"Talia, I had no idea this would happen. I just wondered if other people—just regular people—could do it. Isn't that valuable to know? For when the revolution comes?"

Talia made a face at her, but began to relent. "How much did you do?"

"Not too much. This lady, and a redneck who wanted a new truck. I tried a few others, and it went nowhere, so I figured it's limited."

"Well, you better hope it doesn't get any further than this."

"It won't. How're things in DC?"

Talia eyed her, but she presented a blank slate of a face for her perusal. "Not good," she said at last. "I convinced the auditors to delay another six months, but it took some doing. And Tritan's all over us. What did you do to offend that man?"

"Besides not teaching him how to Realize? And that no more sex thing?"

"Hmmph. Is there any way to repair the damage?"

"None I can think of, but if I come up with something I'll give it a shot. I don't want him on my ass, or yours."

"No. I suppose not. And what about your next task, Cali? Did you do your research on the Senator?"

Talia always did that. Shot at you with what turned out to be minor points, saving the big one for last, after your reserves were gone. And it was a big one. An end point. She could prevaricate about what she'd been doing, but the question of Senator Clemens required either a yes, or a no. She took a moment to find words that were true, and would also do no harm.

"I'm pretty sure I get it now," she said carefully.

"Pretty sure? Just pretty sure?"

"Actually, very sure."

"Well, thank goodness for that. How long before you take care of it?"

Cali shook her head. "That's not what I meant. I can't do it, Talia," she said.

To her surprise, Talia wasn't angry. Instead, she reached over and put a hand on Cali's shoulder. "I know this isn't easy for you," she said. "But Cali, really, I wouldn't ask without imperative reasons. We're weak right now. And—I haven't told any of the others about this, but there's a shift going on. An energy shift."

She startled. What Rainer said. What Jesse told her. "Microwaves and cell phones," she said. "It's changing the human capacity to Realize."

Talia frowned at her. "You know?"

"No. Just—Rainier said the same thing. And then, well, I dreamt about it."

Talia sighed. "Then you understand we have to figure out a way to manage it. Rainier and the Senator could easily be the straws that breaks our back. Do you want everything we've done to disappear?"

What was Talia saying—get the Senator *and* Rainier off their agenda? "Are you asking me to get rid of Rainier, too?"

"Would that be easier? If it is, you can start there."

"*Start* there? Who else is on your list?"

Talia pulled her hand away from Cali's shoulder. "Sometimes the best way to get to the good is to eliminate the bad."

"But if I make poison in an attempt to get to medicine I'll just become . . . a poisoner."

"It's not about you, Cali. Now's not the time to be self-centered."

Yes, Cali thought. It's not about me. It's about Talia, who wants a reliable poisoner on board, and maybe always did. Talia knew how many dead people Cali brought with her to Aquarius, and the long honeymoon here was just a way to establish loyalty and need, get her so enmeshed she wouldn't think twice about killing again. Senator Clemens. Rainier. Whoever was next. Racer was the house arson, and she would be the house assassin. She thought of something Jesse had said to her, long ago: If it's all killing, then all you get is a lot of death.

When she spoke, she stayed calm, judicious. "I'm not sure directed assassination is the right direction for Aquarius," she said. "We can do better than that."

"You want to give people what they want, make them well, peaceful, liberated," Talia said, her face tight with impatience. "We've tried it your way. It doesn't work."

"I've tried killing people. That doesn't work either. Talia, I can't do it. No—wait. I can, but I won't. I just won't."

Talia's face flushed deeply. She dropped her hands to her side. Cali could see them clenching and unclenching. She supposed the sympathetic portion of the program was over. The carrot was about to become a stick.

"Isn't it about time you understood that your mother will never repent, and neither will the world? The sooner we make the revolution come, the better it will be in the end."

"Better for whom?"

"Don't you get it? Catastrophe is the only real force for change. We know that, and we've been setting it up for years. You asked about Hitler? He was one of ours, defeated by another fool like you who thought we needed peace. Believe me, when I made Aquarius mine, I got rid of idiots like that. I got back on track and you won't derail us now. We've got the right president, the right wars, the right economy, plus some environmental and energy crises. We'll have our revolution, and when the dust clears, Aquarius can do what it was meant to do."

Cali thought something was expected of her here. She had a line to recite. "What's that?" she asked softly.

"Rule," Talia said.

The word fell into the room like a stone, and Cali let it settle. She thought of Jesse, heard his words to her. Her decision was as clear as his had been.

"Not on my watch," she said. "There's something to be said for integrity."

That sounded final to them both. Talia said nothing further for a long time. They were each sorting through their options, seeing what was left.

Cali was the first to speak. "Am I free to leave?"

Talia eyed her. "The door isn't locked."

"I mean, am I free to leave Aquarius."

"We don't keep prisoners."

"But you do schedule executions."

Talia shrugged. "Only when absolutely necessary."

"Is mine necessary?"

Talia smiled. Got up and left the room.

Cali stood where she was for some time, waiting for her energy to settle. She knew she'd be allowed to leave the premises, because Talia wouldn't kill her here. Maybe later she'd get Racer to blow her up, or get someone to shoot her. But she had some time to figure out what was next. She went to her office, erased the hard drive of her computer and gathered together the few items she wanted to keep.

When she left the Aquarius building, she didn't look back.

PHOTON CONSCIOUSNESS

The first place Cali went was Washington, to see Senator Clemens. She didn't call or make an appointment. She just showed up, terribly afraid Aquarius would kill him before she could warn him.

She arrived in the the middle of the session and waited outside the Senator's office, stilled herself, took time to arrange her words, practice what she needed to do. When he came striding down the hall toward his office, she was so deep in thought she almost didn't see him, and he was apparently distracted because he didn't see her. He was already at the door when she stood and said his name.

He turned, saw her, raised his eyebrows. "Cali? Did we have something today?"

"No. I just need to talk with you."

"I'd love to, but I'm pretty busy today. Will you be in town for a while?"

"I won't," she said. "And this won't wait."

He looked perplexed, but he gestured to her and she walked with him to his office, working to keep pace with him.

"I can't give you more than a few minutes," he said. "I have people waiting."

"I wouldn't ask if it wasn't vital," she said.

"I know," he said, sounding distracted.

He ushered her into his office and she took a seat, waited for him to sit. "Can you have your calls stopped?" she asked.

He nodded, pressed his intercom and spoke with his secretary briefly. When he raised his face to hers, it was no longer distracted. She had his full attention now.

"Senator, I'm going to tell you something about Aquarius that seems a little, well, fantastic, maybe. But it's the truth, and it's very important that you believe it."

"Go," he said.

She told it all quickly, speaking without emotion. As she spoke, she could see many thoughts passing through his mind as he went from confusion, to disbelief, to a reasoned consideration of what she said. At least he didn't interrupt or laugh at her. When she was done she waited to see if he'd politely ask her to leave.

He didn't.

Instead, he tilted his head, looked at her. "This all sounds like madness, except for the part about them wanting to get rid of me. They wouldn't be the first, you know."

"I'm aware of that. And I know you've learned how to take care of yourself. All I want is the chance to give you another way to do that."

"How?" he asked.

"Give me your hand," she said. When he startled, she amended. "It's not—it's just easier to show you this way."

He shrugged. "In for a dime, in for a dollar," he said, and put his massive hand over hers. She grasped it, feeling the warmth of it.

"Not everyone does this well, but I'd guess you do," she said. "You have to breathe deeply, and focus your awareness."

"Focus it on what?"

"On me, for now," she said.

He did so, and she could feel the way his expansive mind took her in. It seemed a safe place, and she was glad to know it. "Now think of something you want," she said.

"Anything?" he asked.

"Anything."

He relaxed, and a slow smile formed on his face.

"Complete the thought," she said, and felt that he knew what she meant, because something was made complete in the room. The energy was right, and she'd only had to lend the smallest bit of her own energy to the task. She'd been right. He was a natural.

As soon as she released his hand, his phone buzzed. "Sorry," he said. He looked quickly at the clock on his desk, lifted the receiver. "I said no calls," he noted. Then he listened. His face changed, and he looked to Cali. "Bring it," he said, and hung up.

The door to the room opened, and the secretary walked in, bearing a hot fudge sundae, a napkin and a spoon.

"I thought it was strange, but Sally just came back from lunch with it and she insisted," she said. "She said you'd appreciate it, and I didn't want it to melt. Oh—and it's chocolate. They were out of vanilla. Sally hoped that was okay."

"It's . . . lovely. Thank her for me."

"Sure. Sorry for the interruption."

When she was gone, Cali and the Senator stared at the ice cream.

"What you wanted?" Cali asked.

He grunted.

"The chocolate?"

"I don't like vanilla," he noted.

Cali lifted a hand, let it fall onto her lap. "That kind of thing is easy," she said. "Well, not easy, because you still have to do it right, and I was helping. Putting more energy into it, so to speak. But you did most of it, and you see. . ." She let the sentence trail away. The Senator continued to stare at the ice cream.

She felt compelled to explain further, to comfort him somehow. "It's not that different than what we do all the time, really. We wish for things. We imagine them. We find ways to make them true. This is just a more direct version."

He frowned, picked up the spoon and dug in, tasting the ice cream tentatively, as if it might disappear. Then his face opened with surprise. "This tastes real," he said.

"It is real," Cali said. "You made it real. Translated the energy of thought into matter."

He lifted a shoulder, let it fall. "I failed science in college. Twice."

"Do you want me to explain more?"

"Please don't," he requested. "Not about the science, anyway. Just tell me about—well, for instance, can anyone do it?"

"I think so. I'm not sure that was always true, but I'm told there's been a change in—in human consciousness recently. Something to do with all the new ways we use energy now. Now, I think anyone can do some version of it, though there's variations in how much or what kind each person can do. Not everyone can win the lottery. Not everyone can work with technology, and so on."

"What's it cost?"

"Free, as far as I can tell."

He shook his head. "Energy always gets exchanged. So what do you lose when you do it?"

Yes, of course. She so rarely felt that, she forgot it was a problem. "Your own energy," she said. "It gets transferred out of you. That's why it's important not to do it lightly or waste it. It's kind of difficult to do it lightly anyway, once you get it."

"You've taught this to other people? Outside of Aquarius?"

"Some."

"What're they wishing for, in general?"

"Win the lottery. Find a lover. Things like that."

"Nobody wishing for world peace? End to hunger and poverty?"

"There was a man—but he didn't believe it was possible. He kept talking himself out of it."

"Well, we been talking ourselves out of peace on those grounds for a long time. So you think I can use this to protect myself against Aquarius?"

She nodded. "They wanted. . . .one of their people can use these techniques to kill, but she's gone. She won't go after you. There's another who's good with explosions, so you can complete some thoughts to keep safe from that. Of course, they might try a conventional hit, but you can probably Realize some extra protection for yourself easily enough. And there's something else you can do."

She led him through the Buddhist meditation, making sure to include Aquarius in it, and he listened, not watching the clock anymore. He took it all in quietly, and when they were done, he sighed deeply.

"That's quite nice," he said. "And I appreciate what you're doing here, but you do see the potential problems with letting this loose in the world, don't you? If everyone can do it? What if I'm wishing to stay alive and someone else is wishing me dead? Who prevails? Or what if I mean one thing when I say world peace and you mean another? Then there's the whole monkey's paw problem. Like I wish to end world hunger and that happens by all the hungry people dropping dead?"

"I know," Cali said. "I've thought about that. But if you make the thought specific it won't be a Monkey's Paw. As for competing interests, I'm not sure what that does. Maybe the more skilled Realizer wins. Maybe the one with the strongest heart prevails."

"You're still spreading it around?"

"I am," she admitted.

"Then you're like Pandora. The question is, are wishes as bad as fears?"

Cali smiled. Pandora was one of the stories she'd looked up in the library. "In the original Pandora story, she gave all the good gifts to the world. The story got changed when the Patriarchy smashed the matriarchy. New world. New stories."

"I should've guessed. So now, you're putting a different new story in the world."

"No. Just going back to the old ones," she said.

"Okay. But all the gods help you if you're the one to tell it. Nobody's kind to people like you."

"Aquarius is already using it. It's only a matter of whether a select few have it, or if it belongs to the everyone."

He grinned, raised his spoon, loaded with ice cream. "Here's to the people. Long may they wave. But Cali, what about you?"

"What about me?"

"You're not safe, since you left Aquarius."

"I didn't say I left."

"Am I stupid? You were supposed to wish me dead, weren't you? And you said no."

Of course he figured it out. Of course he would. "I couldn't—" she started to say.

He waved it away. "I know. I'm just saying, they can't like you much right now."

"I'll be okay. I've got someone to help me. I'm going to see her."

"She'll keep you safe?"

Jesse wanted her to go to Ida. He wouldn't send her there if he could think of a better place. "She will," Cali said with confidence.

The Senator nodded, reached over and put a hand on hers. "Be well, Cali. Peaceful and liberated. I'll be saying it for you, too."

* * * *

She went directly from Washington to Ida's, with a strange sense of meeting a younger version of herself as she ascended the porch steps. She knocked on the door, half expecting to see Lara's face on the other side when it opened, but it wasn't. It was Ida herself, looking elegant and aged and strong.

"Well," she said, her sharp eyes alert. "The prodigal daughter returns. Here to steal more of my jewelry?"

Cali shrugged. "Maybe I'm here to drop off another check."

Ida nodded. "I did appreciate that. And I really didn't care about the jewelry. I only kept it around in case someone needed it. Come inside."

Ida ushered her in and down the hall to the dining area. Once there, she stood, one hand on her hip, and looked Cali up and down.

"I like your hair better long," she said.

"Thanks," Cali said. "You look good."

"I look old. Good for my age is the proper phrase I think."

"You just look good, Ida."

"Then you must be in trouble. I always look good to people in trouble." She waved a long arm toward the table. "Sit," she said, and both of them did.

Ida stared at her some more. "I understand you're making waves."

Cali frowned. "What?"

"It's in the news, sweetie. The Post. USA Today and of course the Enquirer, which reports you as an alien invasion. They describe you well enough. One paper had a sketch. Not a wonderful portrait, but I wasn't likely to forget you."

Cali didn't see any point in denying it, but she wasn't sure how much Ida knew about Aquarius, or Realizing. "What I do, it's called—"

"—Realizing," Ida cut in. "You learned how to do it even better at Aquarius, and then you had to share."

Cali sighed. At least she didn't have to explain. "I didn't teach that many people," she said.

"But the people you taught will teach other people and they'll teach more and so on and so forth."

"Small input. Large effects. A dynamic system."

"So you say. Fortunately, most people still think it's a hoax. So what will you do for your next act? Raise the dead?"

Cali startled, shifted uncomfortably. Ida's face went tight and suddenly serious. "Look at me," she said, and put a hand on Cali's face, seemed to read it carefully. After a while, she lowered her hand. "That was you, wasn't it? There was a mother. Her son was hit by a car. A stranger helped them. You."

"Hell. Was it in the paper?"

"On a talk show. She was looking for the woman who helped her, to thank her."

Cali shook her head. "Maybe the boy wasn't dead. Maybe I didn't . . ."

"Yeah," Ida said. "You did."

Cali looked at the lines in her hands, wondering what they'd done. Ida reached over and touched her open palm where the long line ran up between her fingers.

"It's who you are, Cali," she said. "It was bound to happen, sooner or later."

"I didn't want it," she whispered.

"Part of you did. And that part always gets you in trouble."

"It does," she admitted. "I left Aquarius. They'll probably try to kill me."

"More than probably, my dear. But that's not why you're here, is it? You can avoid them if you want. You're good at that. But you came to me. So what can *I* do for you?"

Cali licked at her lips, took a stab at telling her. "I've been having dreams about—about someone I knew. He said I should come see you."

Ida's lips tightened into a thin line. "Jesse?" she asked.

"You know him," Cali said, remembering their night sessions together.

"I knew him."

"And do you know it was me . . . that I. . . ."

"You wished him dead," Ida said, her voice without inflection.

"I'm sorry," Cali said softly. "It's the one thing I'd do differently if I could."

Then, before she could stop herself, the whole story was pouring out of her. About her mother and Keith, Betty and Racer, and her fear of going to Bedford, what happened with Jesse, how she'd become someone who could do that and how she'd stopped being that person. She noticed Ida was pale, but she kept going, telling her about about meeting Talia, and Rainier, and the dreams that would neither complete themselves nor leave her alone. When she was done she sat stoically waiting for any reaction Ida might have, however horrid. She was certain she deserved it.

But Ida reached a hand over and put it on Cali's arm, stroked it lightly. "May you be well," she said softly. "May you be peaceful. May you be liberated."

This gesture of compassion pierced Cali at the center of her being. She swallowed bitterness, said nothing.

Ida's hand squeezed her arm, then released her. "The dreams," she said. "Tell me about them."

"I think—I'm afraid I'm keeping him stuck here," Cali said. "If you show me how to stop it, maybe he'd be at peace."

Ida leaned back and her mouth twitched into a smile. "You don't have a clue what you're up to, do you?"

"Not really."

"You're not keeping him stuck. You're calling him back," Ida said.

"I—I don't understand."

Ida laughed. "You can't let him go. You never could. And he can't let you go either, so you have to bring him back."

"What?"

"Complete the thought, Cali."

She shrank into herself. Complete the thought. Bring him back from the dead? Is that was Jesse meant? He didn't want her to send him away. She had to do what was next. This? This?

"It's not possible," she said.

"It is for you. You already did it."

She had. The birds. The little boy. She felt his death in her hands and brought him back, returned his particular energy to his particular matter. But she had no intent in that moment. She had only tears. Jesse was different.

"The boy—he had a body. I could—could call him back into it."

"The birds didn't, and you called them back."

"But Jesse—I killed him. Why would he want anything to do with me?"

"Because even if you're clueless, he knows just what he's doing."

"Well, hell, Ida. If I'm clueless, I shouldn't be messing with this. It's a lot bigger than killing someone. Killing is—is-"

"Easy? Petty? Common?"

"Yeah. All that."

"Are you petty, easy, common?"

She ducked her head down. "Jesse didn't think so," she said.

He'd seen light shining in her and around her. He'd treated her as if she was precious, and that changed her. She remembered the bell tower, when he held her from falling, and held himself against his own desire. He'd given his life so she could have hers back, and now Ida was telling her she could return that favor. Or at least she could try.

"One thing, though," Ida said. "You gotta want it. Are you *sure* about that part? You want him back?"

Cali lifted her head, on firm ground with this. "Yes. I do."

"You understand what it means?"

Jesse asked the same thing, and she'd give Ida the same answer. "I don't care."

Ida eyed her, then sighed. "Okay. Then you'll try, and I'll help. You use a lot of energy for this. You think you're up to it?"

"How would I know?"

"Well, how did you feel after the kid?"

She thought back. "Pretty damn tired. I took a few days off, went to the spa."

"That's it?" Ida asked.

"Yes," Cali said cautiously.

Ida shook her head. "You're the real deal. But like you said, the little boy wasn't very far gone, and you had his mother to help. This is different. You'll be on your own. And Jesse's long gone, and a lot more complicated. It'll take more and you'll have to give back more."

"Give back what?"

"There's no telling until the bill comes due. You willing to take the risk?"

She thought about that less than a second. "Jesse was," she said.

Ida nodded, and a brightness came into her eyes. "So he was. And I suppose he's waited long enough. He was always a patient boy. Patience of a saint, I told him."

"Ida, how did you know him?"

Ida called herself back to the present. "We'll tell that story later. Right now we have work to do. Remember what I taught you when you were here?"

"I use it all the time."

"We'll do a little more. Get warmed up."

So they worked through the night and the next day. Cali was vaguely aware of a shifting in herself and the world, but mostly she focused on what Ida showed her, taking her through the old breathing exercises and adding some new ones. They went along with ease, until Ida pushed her toward the door marked *Do Not Enter.* There, it all fell apart.

Ida clucked at her impatiently. "Cali, you're still holding back. You have to let go."

"Let go of what?" she asked suspiciously.

She tapped at Cali's forehead. "What you keep locked up there."

"That's got nothing to do with this."

"It has memory and knowledge and energy you can use, and you'll need it. If you're wasting your energy to keep emotional doors shut you won't have enough to complete the thought."

Cali stiffened. "I can't. I'm not ready, and it would take too long. I need to do this tonight, before Talia starts on me. I can't tell if she'll . . . what she'll do to me, and I won't be able to manage this, and her."

Ida sighed. "All right. Try this, then."

She gave her a different kind of breathing, one called Dragon's Fire, which generated energy in her. After another thirty minutes of that, Ida stopped her. She ruffled her hair, puffed out a breath. "That's all we can do. It's dark. You should go now."

Cali stood and moved toward the door.

"Wait. You know *where* you're going?"

"Oh," Cali said. "That."

"It's the little things," Ida noted. "He's buried on a hill. A place called Deer Mountain."

Cali startled at this. "There?"

"Yes. There's no marker, and it's a hike up a trail called Waylay. He's near the edge at the top, by a large granite stone, left of an Oak tree."

"I know the place. Why there?"

"He wanted it. Wrote it in his will. There's no coffin. He's just in the ground."

"How do you know that?"

"Because I buried him."

She had so many questions about this she didn't know where to begin. Before she could even make a start, Ida spoke.

"That's the way we do things, Cali," she said. "Back to the earth, where the real energy is. Don't you remember?"

More people asking her what she remembered. It was getting on her nerves. "I don't want to," she said. "Except sometimes, I see a snake. A woman made it, and somehow she's me. Always me. Always fighting with someone who wants what I have, or has what I want, I can't be sure which."

"Maybe it's both," Ida said. "Listen, just so it doesn't leap up and bite you tonight, those things you see—the snake, the woman—they're true. You may not feel it yet, but you should trust the information. It's all real, and it can help. Don't forget that."

"I won't," Cali said. "Ida, thank you."

"Save that for when you come back. But don't come back here. I've got a place in Queens. 42 Parkwood. I'll go there as soon as you leave. Got it?"

"42 Parkwood. Queens," Cali repeated.

"Good. Go now."

When Cali was at the front door and her hand on the knob, Ida put a hand on her shoulder, turned her around, pressed her hands around her face and kissed her forehead.

"Be careful," she said. "Come back to me, no matter what."

"If I can," Cali replied.

"Make sure you can."

Cali shrugged down into herself, and left the house.

LOUIVILLE'S THEOREM

She was driving the thruway toward her destination, almost at her exit, when she realized she was being followed. The car was a dark Mercedes, and she recognized it.

"Shit," she said. "Rainier. God*dammit*."

She put her foot to the gas and sped up, but he kept pace. Of course he did. And now she'd have to make a choice. Keep going on the thruway until he gave up or she ran out of gas, or pull off her exit and let him stop behind her, have it out with him. Before she could choose, he upped the ante, coming close and bumping her at the rear. This leg of the thruway was sparsely traveled at night, and nobody noticed. She sped up. He caught her and bumped her again.

"God *fucking* damn it," she said with feeling. She thought briefly about wishing him into oblivion, but decided it would be a bad way to start her current task. He moved his car alongside hers and pushed at her from the side. She'd have to do something, she thought. Kill him. Or kill his fucking car.

At that thought, her forehead knit. She knew little about cars, except for one or two important bits. Radiators. Gas tanks. Oil. Well, he was the oil expert, wasn't he?

She gunned her engine, got ahead of him, and worked on it. Imagined a hole. Two holes. Now three. But it was almost impossible to Realize and keep ahead of a maniac. She gathered as much of the thought as she could into wholeness, then pulled over to the side of the road. He screeched to a stop in front of her.

She stayed in the car, watching him get out of his car and approach her. She worked as fast as she could to complete the thought, and let it go. Then, when he was reaching for her door, she threw her car into reverse, backed up, got into drive and pulled away, skidding as she went.

For the first time, she wasn't sure if she'd completed the thought. Then, she saw his car behind hers, diminishing in her rearview mirror, disappearing altogether.

A hole in the radiator. A hole in the gas tank. A hole in the oil tank. One of them must have worked.

She turned her thoughts forward, and drove.

STRING THEORY

Cali was shaky when she made the hike that took her to the top of the cliff. She'd lost Rainier, she was sure of that, but the feeling of being stalked remained. It took her awhile to realize that what tracked her was only her former self, the girl who tried to climb this rock and took a part of the mountain down.

She ignored it. She had work to do. She remembered the rock by the oak tree, made her way to it and sat. She stilled herself, gathered herself for her task. For the first time in her life, she wished she had help. Racer, the women of Aquarius, Ida, anyone. But tonight, she had only herself.

"You broke it on your own," she told herself firmly. "So fix it on your own."

She moved her awareness into the place where she did this work, focused her mind on Jesse. As she did, a pang of shame assailed her. What she'd done was so wrong. But her shame was about her, and that's not where her focus should be. This wasn't about her. It was about giving Jesse back what he deserved. His life, which she'd taken from him.

She moved out of shame, and thought of everything good in him. The thought grew, and she opened herself to it, let it spread out and occupy her, began to move toward releasing it. Almost there, she told herself. Almost complete.

Right at the edge of completion, the energy began to dissipate. She tried to hold onto it, but she couldn't, and it simply went away.

"Come back," she whispered. The only response was a small breeze rustling the leaves above her. She stood, clenched her hands and pressed them hard against her temples. "Come *back*," she demanded.

Nothing.

Panic rose in her. It was so easy with the little boy. She didn't even have time to consider whether or not she could do it before it was already done. But his mother was there, with her tears and her complete willingness to believe, and Cali carried no complicated grief in that act. No blocks at all.

She knelt on the earth, pressed her hands against the grass. What was left of Jesse's body was under her, in the cool earth. Long ago, she'd lain on her back on this same earth, feeling the quiet of death, as he might be feeling it now. She knew this place of surrender. Ida taught her how to feel it. And he was close. So close. She should be able to reach him. She started over, felt the build and the movement toward completion.

And then, just at the edge, it was gone again. Where did it go? Where was he, so available in her dreams she could feel his hand on her face, but now she felt nothing at all. Did she use too much energy destroying Rainier's car? Didn't have enough to begin with? She couldn't accept that. Feeling as if she'd done a hard day's work already, she went at it one more time, but got only the same results. More nothing.

But there was something else she could do. Ida told her how. She had to open the closed doors. Release the energy it took to keep them closed.

Just the thought of it made her sick to her stomach. It would be like opening a container left in the refrigerator for too long. Stench and rotting, toxic things would live in it. Best to just toss it away unopened. But she didn't have that option. What lingered in that place had to be opened if she had any chance of completing this thought. Could she do it? Locks freeze with time, and refuse to open short of explosion.

"Chicken shit," someone said, as if speaking in her ear.

She whirled toward the voice. Nobody was there. She lifted a hand, moved it through the air next to her, in front of her, all around her. Something warmer than elsewhere. Something less dark.

"Who is it?" she asked. No reply. Maybe it was something in her own head. She closed her eyes, looking for what she might find within.

She saw only herself. Herself, as a teenager. Someone she'd locked away when she left St. Ida's. A young woman with cropped hair and a face full of anger. A young woman who held herself hostage.

Cali faced her. "How'd you get out?" she asked.

"The door says don't enter. It doesn't say don't exit."

"You never left before."

"I liked it in there. I knew my way around. Besides, it wasn't time. You wouldn't have listened to me. Now you will."

"Right," Cali said. "So why am I chicken shit?" she asked.

"For not opening the door," the girl said.

"I hold myself hostage," Cali whispered. "In there."

"Yeah," the girl agreed.

Her face was angry, but underneath it, she was simply terrified. Why hadn't she known that about herself? That she was terrified most of the time. Cali moved to her younger self, put hands on her face, breath on her eyes. "Let's open the doors," she said.

The girl shuddered, and closed her eyes. Cali felt the ominous shifting and tensed against what might emerge, but it was nothing to be afraid of. Just energy moving around, as Rainier would say. Just ghosts.

There was Keith, exiting without much fuss. She felt rage at his betrayal, horror at what he made her do. He felt nothing at all. He didn't even look at her. He just left.

Her mother followed close behind, and she was shrunken, not who she once was and maybe she never had been. She stopped and looked at Cali for a long moment. She didn't apologize or explain, but now, after all this time, Cali didn't need her to. What she did to Cali, what Cali did to her, that was over. All the drugs and anger, none of it had any intent, which may have been the problem.

Then Glory, Marilyn, and Betty trailed away. Their eyes reflected who Cali had become in killing them, but that was easier to witness than the effort it took to keep them locked in. In letting them go, she could also relinquish her own former ugliness.

When they'd dissolved into darkness, Cali had a sensation of touch on her arm, and turned to it quickly. Just the girl, her former self, looking younger, her eyes softer. "Thanks," she whispered, and she retreated, not leaving, but relaxing into the more complete self Cali had become.

Easy as breath on her face, they were all gone. All but one. All but Jesse. She waited, but he didn't appear.

"Jesse?" she asked.

No response. Wasn't he with the others? Maybe not. She'd told Ida he wasn't dead to her. Maybe he was somewhere else.

Cali opened her eyes. She looked around. "Jesse?" she asked. No answer.

She stood at the edge of the cliff, looked down and saw only more mountain, more earth below and sky above. Where was he? She'd done what Ida said. Shouldn't he be here? Jesse, who studied her as if she was a leaf in the sun and all her strangeness beautiful to him. Jesse, whom she loved, yes, loved because he gave his life rather than asking for hers. He'd earned her love ten times over and more. Even if he hadn't, she would love him for his very being, because he was the kind of man who observed light playing on leaves.

"Jesse," she called out, and heard only the echo of her own voice bouncing off stone.

A sinking feeling. That was it, then. She'd failed. Now what? Go back to Ida? She couldn't. Not this way.

Empty. She was empty now, and alone and out of moves, except for one.

She looked out over the cliff. That was her only remaining option. She couldn't bring him to her, but she could go to him. And maybe that was right. How she felt about living depended on the terms, and she no longer liked the ones available to her.

She moved closer to the edge and peered down. She wasn't afraid. She'd released those whose life and death had been her burden. She was ready.

She sent a farewell to Ida, took in a breath. She was about to let herself fall when she became aware of soft movement in the grass nearby. She looked toward it. She saw nothing, but she heard a voice, a whisper of concern.

"You're pretty close to the edge, Cali," it said. "You're not planning anything stupid, are you?"

Jesse. His voice, unmistakable. Ghost man, still worrying about her. She turned this way and that, seeking him, but saw only the abyss below her and she didn't care because it all hurt too much. She was empty and she was alone, alone, alone and it hurt like hell.

A sound was torn out of her and at first she didn't know what it was, it was so long since she heard it. But it kept coming and finally she realized it was sobs and she was crying as she hadn't since she was maybe thirteen and her mother, high again, slapped her for mouthing off. And she cried and cried and then her mother held her and kept saying she was sorry. She was sorry.

"I'm sorry," Cali sobbed. "I'm so sorry."

Then she was kneeling on the ground, tears splashing from her eyes onto the grass. They were alive creatures, these tears, twisted and wrenched out of her like someone tearing out her veins one by one. They peeled away all surfaces until she was made only of grief, and she didn't know why this was happening, what was happening.

And within the grief, a still, small voice.

"Go ahead," Jesse said softly. "Complete the thought."

"Jesse," she cried out to the night with her grief, with her tears. "I want you to live."

The sound reverberated against the bones of her skull, shattered at the inside of her skin and spread through her like fire on spilled oil. She was on fire from the inside, heat and flame pouring from her into the ground, into the world, her body passageway for what might be. Her tears sizzled on the ground and mist rose where they hit. The mist took shape, and she let it go.

She let it go.

* * * *

A blank space.

She was in a blank space between here and there, fully conscious, aware of motion withheld. A coherent superposition, and she occupied it. Her tears were gone. Sound was gone. Everything was still.

It lasted a millisecond. It lasted an eternity. Then, a punch, like a fist into a wall, and she was shoved into the world again.

* * * *

She was on her knees, on the earth. She gasped, looked up. She saw darkness punctuated by stars. She saw the ground, a burned spot on it near her hand.

She pushed herself up and stood, tried to walk somewhere, she wasn't sure where, but she couldn't control her body's motion and she stumbled and wondered if she would fall off the cliff after all. Then arms were holding her, shoulders she could grasp, and she hung on to them while the world faded into blessed silence and sweet nothing wrapped her in its folds.

She stayed floating in that place for a long time. It was quiet, and she was glad enough to be there, maybe would have stayed there except she couldn't. Voices asked her to return. Voices and sounds of the world. A distant plane. An owl calling nearby. She rode back in on sound until consciousness returned and she knew she was lying on her back somewhere outside.

The air was cool and smelled of grass and trees. She opened her eyes, emerging slowly from the swimming darkness. The first thing she saw was Jesse staring down at her. Her head was in his lap and he was smoothing her hair, watching her with his motion filled eyes.

"You okay?" he asked.

She couldn't find words. She shifted.

"Cali? Are you okay?" he asked again, more urgently this time.

"Jesse?" she tried to say. It sounded wrong. Slurred, as if she'd been drinking.

"I'm here," he replied. He moved his hand over her hair, touched her face.

"Are you . . ." What was he? A ghost? A zombie? A hallucination?

"None of the above," he answered as if she'd asked out loud. "I'm here. Alive. With you."

She rolled over quickly and scrambled to her knees, tried to push up to her feet and couldn't accomplish it. Her muscles were weak and watery.

He was up on his haunches, one hand out to her as if she was a wild animal he had to soothe. "Cali, be still. You need to be still for a while. "

She shook her head no. Words were unavailable, fallen into the void she'd recently visited. But she had to know if he was real. She lifted a hand and he grasped it in his and kissed it. The edge of his teeth was against her flesh and he moaned softly into her skin.

"Cali," he said.

He pulled her to him and kissed her, his mouth full of life.

FRACTALS

When she woke, she was in a bed and she was naked, but she wasn't sure what bed or how she got there or what happened to her clothes. Cool daylight planed across the room, through the slit of dark blue curtains at the window. She lay still, staring at it as consciousness returned fully.

She remembered Rainier and the cliff at Deer Mountain. Remembered seeing her former self, and all the ghosts, and then Jesse. But how much of it was dream and how much was real she couldn't tell.

"All real," a voice said.

She turned her head. Jesse lay next to her, propped up on one elbow, staring at her. She rolled on her side, touched his face. "Do you always eavesdrop on what someone's thinking instead of waiting for them to talk?"

"Not with everyone," he said. "But I always have with you."

"That's kind of rude."

"Ruder than you killing me?" He brushed her hair back from her face, ran a hand up and down the curve between her waist and hip.

"Keep bringing that up and this relationship is doomed," she said.

He laughed lightly, the blue and green of his eyes alive with motion. Real. All real. She put her hand to his thigh and stroked it, heard his breath quicken as desire shivered through him. He drew her closer, put his mouth to hers and kissed her.

She remembered the particular taste and texture of his mouth. The shape of his tongue. The way he took her in, and the way he felt pleasure more immediately and deeply than anyone else she knew. His eyes were filled with wanting her, wanting her. He touched her face, his fingers exploring gently. "You know how long I've waited for this?"

"Since the bell tower," she said.

"A lot longer than that. But the bell tower—that was tough. Tougher than dying."

He kissed his way down her neck, moving his mouth over her body in ways that felt larger than death, and more important. She pulled at him, drawing him to her.

"Not so fast," he said. "It took a long time to get here, and I want to savor it."

He kissed the tips of her fingers one by one, considering each as if it was the origin of light. His fingers played delicate as feathers over her breasts. He put his mouth to the inside of her elbow and lingered there, tasting her. He moved his mouth to her solar plexus, breathing warmth onto it, then trailed down across her belly to her thighs, between her thighs, his mouth against her warm and smooth until she wondered if it was possible to die of pleasure, to drown in it. His hands gripped her hips as she cried out her ecstasy, and then he raised himself over her, his eyes a storm of motion.

"Yes, Cali?" he asked.

"Yes," she breathed back. "Yes. Now."

"Kill me again," he murmured as he entered her. "And again, and again and again."

* * * *

When they were spent of pleasure they may have slept more, or just rocked close in a relaxed state of joy. After a while, she stirred, pulled back far enough to see his face. She touched his closed eyes, moved her hand across his hair, then over the muscles in his arms, his belly. He opened his eyes.

"What was it like?" she asked.

He understood her question. What was it like to be killed by someone you loved more than your life? "Terrifying, and exceptionally beautiful," he said.

"Beautiful?"

"To love that deeply is always beautiful," he said. "Exquisite. Nothing else like it. It's the source of all energy."

"Is that why you did it?"

"Not entirely, though it would've been worth it just for that." He shrugged, touched her forehead. "It was the only way to help you remember who you are. What you can do."

She thought of her recent dreams: Isis, re-membering her lover. The Magdelene, raising a dead a man.

"You let me kill you, so I'd bring you back," she clarified.

"That's right," he said.

"What if I didn't kill you?"

"If you agreed to talk to me, to trust me, I'd have worked with you until you got out, then made sure you were sent to Ida."

"That would've been easier," she noted.

"You were never any good at easy," he replied.

"I guess not. But what if I killed you, and didn't bring you back?"

"That was the terrifying part. A risk I had to take, and worth taking, Cali."

His finger traced the outline of her jaw and she saw a man in an open tomb, and her hand calling him back. Slowly, everything that came before began to weave itself into a coherent whole.

"You . . . knew me," she said hesitantly.

"Always. I wasn't sure if you'd figure it out in time, though."

She had the sensation of motion much larger than she'd ever imagined, galactic, slow and large. They'd participated in that motion, and they were to participate again.

"In time for what?" she asked.

"For what's next."

"What's that?"

"Right now, more of this."

He rolled over and she was under him, his body warm, his back curved over her. She felt him growing hard, wanting her once more, as he'd always wanted her, as she'd always wanted him.

This time he didn't wait. He entered her, moving slowly within her, his hand against her face, his eyes open and seeing hers as he let go of the tight reins he'd held against his yearning, let her feel what he'd wanted from the first time he'd seen her, and how much he'd wanted it. Thousands of years of desire returned to him, to her, and they danced within it like thunder in a storm struck sky. There was particular reality here, and memory like the timbre, the felt sense of a song.

"This is what it's like," she whispered to him.

"What?" he asked.

"To love, and be loved," she said.

"Yes," he said. "Exactly like this."

And then, all words dissolved into the prerogative of the physical, their bodies in motion, speaking beyond reason or doubt.

* * * *

By the time she opened her eyes again, the light from the window had gone violet, and the room was filled with shadow. Jesse was again up on one elbow, staring down at her.

"Is it night?" she asked.

"Evening," he answered. "Blue dark."

"I slept," she said.

"You needed it. Are you hungry?"

"Ummm. Yes."

"Me too," he said. "I could eat a few horses." He kissed her shoulder, kissed his way down her arm, and slid out of bed in one efficient motion.

When he tossed her clothes to her she sat up and looked around. "Are we at Ida's?" she asked as she dressed.

"That's right. Not the halfway house. Her place in Queens. I brought you here. Drove your car. You remember any of that?"

"Not really." She shook her head. "I'm still trying to believe what I did."

"I'm not," he said.

There was a knock on the door. "Come in," Jesse called, and Ida's face peered through the crack.

"You two decent?" she asked.

"More than decent," Jesse said. "Among the best."

Ida opened the door further, looked at Cali. "I hope he's not just bragging," she said.

Jesse, grinning, turned to Cali. "Ida, you know Cali. And Cali, I believe you've already met my grandmother."

UNSMOOTH CURVES

"You're his grandmother?" Cali asked.

They were sitting at her table, having soup and sandwiches, Ida's careful eye on them both.

"This is correct. How do you two feel?" she asked.

"Great," Jesse said.

"Hmmph. No surprise there. You, Cali?"

"Also great, but a little strange," she said. "I'm not sure if it's because of what I did, or what I don't know."

"Ask," Ida suggested.

"You knew about me?"

She nodded. "He told me when he found you. Told me what he planned. I wasn't thrilled, but Jesse always had his own way of doing things and I had to trust it. My job was to start the halfway house, arrange to have you sent here after Bedford."

"And Aquarius? Talia? Do you know her, too?"

"I started Aquarius," Ida sniffed. "That was my job this time around. Talia worked for me. I thought of her like a daughter, and I was happy when she married my son, until her real agenda came out. She married him, and she killed him."

"But I thought she couldn't do that. I thought that's why she wanted me."

"She can't do it the way you can," Jesse said. "She used more conventional methods. What you do—that skill goes with being able to give life, or heal."

"Really? I wouldn't think so."

Jesse shrugged. "Dichotomies contain each other. If you can open the door, you can let people in, or send them away. Talia can't do either. She's good at power, not life. She used her own combination of seduction and torture, then added a needle full of dope. My father died a junkie after I was born."

"That's right," Ida said. Her lips were tight and her face angry. "Then Talia told me I could have Jesse, or Aquarius. If I chose Aquarius, she'd make sure Jesse met a bad end."

"That's a lot to give up," Cali noted.

"Yeah," Ida agreed. I always wondered why she did it."

"I meant Aquarius. You giving that up."

"Not at all," Ida said. "She got the short end of that stick."

Cali looked to Jesse. Ida was right. He was the real prize. But now, she understood something else. "Talia's your mother," she said to Jesse.

"Biologically," he said. "Emotionally I always thought of Ida as my mother. She raised me more than once. But there's some odds we might not be related at all this time around, right, Ida?"

Ida waved this away. "Talia hinted at it. More than one man occupied her bed, Rainier included. That didn't matter to me."

Cali wondered at the long strand of stories that bound Ida to Jesse, bound Jesse to her. She saw a brief image of a man on a cross, and the women who stayed with him as he died. Ida wore a different cut of cloth then, but her light was the same.

"Thank you," she said softly to this woman who was grandmother, mother, and more.

"My pleasure, believe me," Ida replied lightly. "So let's figure out what's next. You won't have much time before there's trouble."

"Sure," Cali said. "After you explain what the hell is going on."

He reached for her hand and took it in his, tracing spirals in the palm as he spoke. "Do you remember what I told you—when you thought you were dreaming?"

She nodded. "You said what Talia calls Realizing, it's been around in some humans from the start."

"That's right," he said. "In the beginning only a few of us could do it. The rest—well, they thought we were magic. At first they called us gods and worshipped us. Later, they called us witches and devils and burned us. But we knew how to move between energy and matter, so you and I, we kept coming back. We had a thought to complete."

Yes, she thought. Her dreams, her new and still uncertain memories, told her this was true. She remembered what Jesse told her, what Talia and Rainier said—energy was shifting, and the people had the capacity to Realize. She'd begun teaching them how to use it. Neither Rainer nor Talia liked that much, and she wondered how old those connections were.

"Rainier—is he. . . ." she let the question trail to silence, not wanting to articulate the power contained in the name of her ancient enemy.

* * * *

"Maybe," Jesse said. "Or it could be someone else. They're all staying in hiding for now, trying to confuse us. They're afraid. If you teach folks to Realize on their own, they'll lose a primary food source."

She ran a hand along the table and considered. "So what I've been do-ing, it might destroy his power."

He nodded. "Might destroy all their power. He never worked alone. You know that."

Cali felt a shiver run through her. As she did with Senator Clemens, she tried to imagine a world where her skills were practiced by any who wanted them. A world where people could get what they needed without butting heads against big powers that shared resources only with the few. Politics, religion, economic practice, would all dissolve, and she had no idea what would take their place, if anything.

Was that good? Was it disastrous? What would people do with it? People expected to pay for what they got. They believed they had to beg at the feet of imperious and capricious gods. If that was gone, what was next? A revolution, on a scale much larger than the discovery of either fire or nuclear energy.

"Maybe Talia and Rainer will get rid of each other, trying to see who gets to the top first," Cali noted.

"You want to wait around for that?" Ida asked.

"What's our options?"

"Keep doing what you've been doing," Jesse said. "Teaching people. If we reach enough before Talia or Rainier can complete their plans we have a chance."

She frowned, suddenly afraid. They'd tried something similar, long ago, and the results were horrifying. She remembered a good man who tried to teach love, and got nailed to a cross. She remembered the way they'd both been subsumed into the dominant paradigm.

"I'm not convinced this is such a great idea."

He traced the line in her palm. "You already chose it," he said.

She did. She chose it instinctively, in the absence of information or memory, and she acted on it. She stretched her hands out on the table and stared at them. "What this does—it could be Paradise, or it could be hell. Or anything in between."

"And we can't know ahead of time what we'll get," Ida pointed out. "The only choice is to let the people have it, or let Aquarius or Rainier call the shots. That's what we got."

Ida had a way of hitting nails on heads. Their only choice was to give the world to a few intelligent demons, or to the potentially loving, potentially murderous mob. She looked at Jesse. His face was full of memory. "Well," she said, "I suppose this is one way of giving Talia her revolution."

Jesse grinned. "It certainly is."

"Okay," Cali said. "So how do we proceed?"

"Like you already started," Jesse said. "Teach the people."

* * * *

They stayed another night and day at Ida's to rest and talk about particular plans. Then they went out, and continued their work.

They started in Manhattan, and went to bars, teaching people they met randomly. Once they felt the energy of it, most were willing to participate. Some reacted badly, but Jesse was adept at getting her out of difficult situations.

But after only a few weeks they were recognized too often, and when they entered a bar a shout of "Hey—it's them!" would go up, and they'd be too crowded with alternating demands and protests to work at all.

They made two important changes. First, they decided to go into the streets instead of the bars. Then they hid their faces. Now when they roamed the back alleys of New York City Cali wore a gold and yellow Sari, the one gift from her grandmother she'd been able to keep through imprisonment and many moves. She wrapped the scarf around her head, draped it across her face so only her eyes showed. Jesse stayed in jeans and t-shirt, but covered most of his face in dark cloth.

Her yellow Sari became a recognizable entity, people looking for her clothes rather than her face, and soon enough their faces were forgotten altogether. Like Superman, they could change clothes and become anonymous, unimportant. But when she put the sari on, the street people moved to her with their madness and pain, their exigent longing, their rage and fear, and they asked her to take it away, to heal them, to make them whole. At least, they thought, they went into the fray prepared.

They went to the places where drug addicts and homeless people slept on grates and in boxes. Schizophrenics were the easiest to teach, they found. They were already halfway there.

"I love you," she whispered to them as they rambled on about their elusive, disturbing visions. "May you be well. May you be peaceful. May you be liberated."

Then Jesse, the healer and renewer, would lay his hands on them, lifting the fog that surrounded their minds, using his gift. They would blink, gasp, stare at their own hands in wonder.

Word spread through the City and people began to use what they were taught and teach others. More papers wrote stories about them, some of them carrying sketches of them, or blurry photos caught on security tapes. Radio shows started cracking jokes about them, and the internet carried videos both created and true about their work. The Village Voice and The Atlantic wrote a serious analysis of the phenomena as an archetypal pattern of desire. Websites started popping up and chat rooms were opened.

Some called it New Age quackery, comparing it to scientology. Others said it was easy, and they could prove it. Everyone wanted to know who these two people actually were, because they never gave names, never claimed allegiance with any church, never asked for money or member-ship. They just did what they did, and left.

Finally, the Times carried a story, buried in the middle of the Metro section, with the headline *KALI AND SHIVA DANCE MANHATTAN*. The story was skeptical, but the names went viral over the internet. Whether they wanted it or not, they were officially promoted to gods.

* * * *

As the buzz in the City grew they began to worry their presence might be hazardous to Ida's health. They packed some bags and went to LA. Jesse's tall frame, the strength of his presence, prevented any overzealous madman from doing harm, and most people were too intent on their desires to be anything other than respectful. They could have worked day and night without stopping, but Jesse kept track of her, making her rest when her energy grew depleted, and his mouth against hers returned her to balance.

"Who are you?" she whispered to him in the night as he held her.

"The renewer. The healer. The one who loves you," he replied.

"Who am I?" she asked.

"My light," he replied. "The light of the world."

She began to understand this had always been true, because as they worked she dipped in and out of their current reality and into many others. The visits were brief, more images than feelings or memory, but they taught her things. She and Jesse were particular pieces of matter drawn from larger energy. That energy, nameless and infinite, returned them to this task again and again, in a variety of forms. It would continue to do so until the thought was made complete, whatever that looked like.

* * * *

When LA got too much press for them to be able to work there, they left and went to Chicago, and from there to Columbus, to Detroit, to Boz-man. In each place, Cali instructed those she taught to teach someone else, and to say the Buddhist chant Lara taught her.

"Listen," Jesse told them. "It's about love. That's the greatest energy there is, and what you'll need most. Practice that. Nothing else matters. Just do what love requires."

By the time they'd worked their way through Colorado and Texas, she was growing disturbed at the reaction to her presence. They treated her like a goddess, and Jesse her consort god, and she knew better.

"You're the one," a junkie in Dallas said to her. His wish was to get clean, and he meant it. That wasn't true for all of them. Some of them just wanted an apartment, a place to live, and that was fine with her. She started where she found them. But this one really did want to get clean, and she helped him complete that thought.

"It's you," he said. "The papers said it. You're a—a goddess."

"No," she replied. "It's you. You're doing it. I'm like you. Just a person."

He shook his head, not believing her. Jesse stepped in, leaning over this man who huddled in an alley seeking his soul.

"Listen," he said. "Are you listening? There's plenty of beings you might call gods or angels but they're not like you've been taught. They aren't above you or beyond you. They're in your heart, in the words of your mouth, in your mind."

The man's eyes grew wide and tears formed in them, as if he'd been told his best friend was dead. "No," he muttered. "No way."

Jesse grasped him more firmly, spoke with compassion and certainty. "*Listen* to me. All our prayers to unseen gods were a way to try and complete the thought. We *are* the gods we longed for, afraid of our own power. Afraid of being alone, of taking responsibility for our own lives. But we're not alone. We have each other, and we'll find no heaven here or anywhere until we learn to take care of each other. Do you understand? Do you hear me?"

The junkie quivered.

"It's okay," Cali said, smoothing his head with her hand. "Really it is. Just say what I told you. You'll see."

They left him, and stopped working for the night. Enough. They'd done enough.

* * * *

When she'd changed they went to a dumpy diner and drank bad coffee, exhausted and unrecognizable as anything divine. Cali turned to Jesse.

"Thank you," she said.

"For what?" he asked.

"What you said to that junkie. I don't want them chasing after us like we're gods. I want it to belong to everyone."

Jesse reached over and took her hand. "Your courage staggers me. It always has."

"Courage?" she asked, surprised.

"Most people are terrified to face that idea. They'd rather be tortured by false gods than accept responsibility for their own souls. Either that, or they have to control it all to keep the fear at bay. Aren't you ever afraid?"

"Yes," she said.

"When?"

"Now," she said.

He pulled back, looked at her. "What scares you now?"

"You," she said. "Loving you."

"Why?" he asked softly.

"It's easy to be courageous when you've got nothing to lose. Loving you, that's not true anymore."

* * * *

They stayed away from Ida's, but in between cities they rested, took the time to read the news and gauge the initial response to what they were doing. To Cali's relief, the stories she found on the internet and in local papers were all good. Lots was written about people who claimed to Realize money for themselves, but it was almost always attached to a particular need.

"Just wanted to pay off the mortgage," one man said. "Anything else, I can earn on my own."

There were articles about people quitting jobs they hated to spend time with family and friends, maybe travel some. And in spite of predictions that the workforce would be decimated by employees leaving in droves, that didn't happen. There were quite a few stories about people who worked because they wanted to do something useful.

The stock market was all over the place, with musical instruments, alternative energy, parks and the arts and social justice organizations skyrocketing while oil and coal tanked. Cali assumed that was because the people who were most amenable to Realizing tended to be liberals.

"It's going pretty well," Ida said when they called her. "Surprising, isn't it?"

"Not to me," Jesse said. "I think most people just want to exist in a relaxed state of joy. They want to live their lives, and laugh and love. But we're not out of the woods. The other side hasn't taken it seriously enough to panic yet, that's all."

"Any word on what Aquarius is up to?" Cali asked.

"Not a peep," Ida replied.

And that, more than anything, made Cali nervous. Talia's strategies were most dangerous when they were silent. Like Jesse, she waited for what might happen next.

* * * *

They continued their work, going to smaller cities where they found less receptivity, but also less noise. A few people said they'd read about it, and figured it was a fad, like hoola hoops and break dancing and the Sixties. Some eyed Cali's sari as if it was a sign of the terrorist enemy. She found that the smaller the city, the better off she was wearing jeans and a t-shirt, especially in some of the back street bars they found.

When they went back to their cheap anonymous hotel rooms, they would reach for each other as if their hunger would never abate. Jesse would stand behind her while she brushed her hair out at night, watch her in the mirror, then take the brush from her hand and drop it on the floor, wrap an arm around her waist and lift her onto the sink counter, his hands moving over her, reaching for her flesh.

And the heat was so compelling she gave herself to it without reserve, let herself ride on waves of pleasure that led ultimately to sleep and dreams of who they were, who they had been, who they might be. "I'm here to feed you," he would whisper. "Take what you need."

But there was a sense of urgency in it as well. Jesse kept her working beyond what she'd have done on her own, convincing her to walk one more alley, one more bar. And when they were alone, he held her as if letting go would mean she'd slip from his arms forever.

* * * *

While they were working bars in Miami Jesse picked up a paper, and saw the front page headline that said *APOCALYPSE NOW*.

"Here it is," he said to Cali. He read her the article, which included interviews with some major religious figures, stating their belief that the two people known as Kali and Shiva were straight out of Revelations. "Whore of Babylon and the AntiChrist," one evangelical proclaimed. "Offering worldly riches in exchange for your soul."

He exhorted all good Christians to run from them, or better yet, shout out who they were wherever they appeared, pick up the nearest stone and throw it at them. His TV show would hold prayer circles to beseech God for their downfall.

More moderate churches and many Rabbis said they were merely con artists, and should be arrested for fraud, but the FBI said they couldn't step been because no money changed hands. The Pope warned his flock about the dangers of false Messiahs, reminding them that their god was a jealous god.

"Well, it's started," Jesse said. "And it'll get worse." He ran a hand through his hair, looking worried. "Maybe now's a good time to take a break. We could go to your island, let the heat simmer down, then come back and do some more."

"Or maybe we should declare ourselves," Cali replied.

He blinked at her in surprise. "What?"

"It's something to think about," she said. "What we do now, it's just enough to get the wrong people pissed off, and leave us powerless. If we went public maybe we could get a little validity in the world. Then we could do this in a bigger way."

"Whatever made you think of that?"

"Lessons from Aquarius," she said.

"And Rainier?" he asked.

"Maybe," she admitted.

He folded the paper, moved his gaze beyond her to a distant point. Memory, she thought. "They'd make us into demons, or gods."

"They already have," she said. "Anyway, it's just one of our options."

"Last time I tried going public didn't work out too well," he noted.

She took his hand, caressed it. "I know," she said gently. "But that doesn't mean this one won't be better. Besides, you can't stop now. You got me into this."

"Yeah." He drew in breath and released it. "Okay. Let's try a coherent superposition," he suggested. "We don't stop, but we try some different arenas."

"What did you have in mind?"

"It's a big world. How about Europe? Africa?"

Cali turned her gaze back to him, full of memory and anticipation. "How about Israel?" she asked.

He closed his eyes, opened them again. "Not yet," he said. "Europe first."

"Okay. I hear Paris is wonderful this time of year."

ARROW OF TIME

Paris was wonderful, a country made for good wine and good talk, where few people had heard the American buzz about them. But Cali was restless, and it was less than a week before she wanted to move on to Italy. Jesse sensed direction in her choice, and he didn't necessarily like it, but they went.

They landed in Rome, and Cali wanted to visit that city first, but Jesse said no. "It's hot and dusty and full of tourists," he said. "Let's go south, see the countryside."

She opened her mouth to say something, then shut it again. Her face was closed, her thoughts unavailable. He was reminded of their days at St. Ida's. But they went south, and wandered the Abruzzi hills, the small villages around Siena. As they sat in trattorias drinking wine and talking with the locals it seemed to Jesse they didn't have much to do here. Many of the people were already Realizing what they wanted, and enjoying it thoroughly. They took the presence of these two American strangers casually, as if it was normal to have the gods among them, eating pasta and drinking wine. Their main concern was keeping the two of them well fed.

"This is good," Jesse said, enjoying the laughter, the sense of abundance. "The way it should be."

"Let's go to Rome, then," Cali said, and under the optimistic influence of the Italian sun, he gave in.

* * * *

Soon enough he saw that was a mistake. Throughout their time in Rome Cali was tense and edgy, distant and increasingly brooding, and Jesse was watchful. They didn't seek people to talk to. Cali didn't want that. They only walked the tourist sites, and at Cali's insistence, stood with the crowd who waited for the blessings of the Pope.

She watched him appear, listened to him speak, saw him move his arms up and down in the Papal blessing. When it was done, and he receded into his confines of stone, she continued standing and looking as the crowd dispersed. Jesse stood at her side, waiting patiently for her to move.

She showed no signs of doing so for some time, and at last he touched her elbow. She startled, turned to him. Her eyes were wild, as if fire burned just behind her cornea. She was far away and long ago, and he tasted burned flesh in the air all around her. He understood, then, what she was doing and why. The flashes of images, the dreams, the knowledge she carried of her past was meaningless without the sense of lived experience. She was gathering memory to her, literally re-membering, connecting thought to feeling. He had the sense that she was preparing for something. He was afraid he knew what it might be.

"Let's go have some wine," he said to her.

She shook herself, gave him a short, tight smile. They moved on.

* * * *

They found a cheap little place outside the regular tourist run, ordered wine and a platter of cheese. The waiter who took their order, a thin man with dark hair and large, clear eyes, watched them closely while Jesse gave it. Cali continued to brood. Jesse let her, but when the waiter returned with a generous plate and full carafe he turned to her, about to ask her what was on her mind. But the waiter didn't leave. Jesse, aware of his presence, looked back to him, and he gave a deprecating smile.

"Mi dispiace," he said, "Ma, tu conosco."

I know you, he'd said. Jesse was about to deny it, but Cali suddenly lifted her head, gave him her attention. "Siedete," she said. Sit with us.

He did so. Jesse poured wine, offering his glass to the waiter.

"No," he said, and then continued in halting English. "You are the ones they call Kali and Shiva, is this not true?"

"It's true," Cali said, touching Jesse's hand. Her gesture said let him talk.

"I know of what you do," he said, nodding. "I read of you in American papers."

"What do you think of it?" Cali asked carefully.

"I think that here it is like bringing your own sun."

"Unnecessary?" Jesse asked.

He nodded. "Long ago, my people learned it is best to live with—with—Dolce Vita. The sun, the friends, the songs. This we learned when empires fell. Do you understand?"

They both nodded.

"Yes," the waiter said. "So what we have is what we want. You can do nothing here. But this woman." He gestured to Cali, sighed deeply. "She is beauty. A goddess. If she was free, I would try to win her to my bed."

Jesse reached over and grabbed her hand. "She's not."

The waiter laughed. "I see this. I speak her beauty not for that. I speak it because I am afraid for her, and for you. You must be careful. Your danger is very large."

Jesse's grip on her hand tightened. "What do you mean?"

The man's face worked around complexities, and then he spoke a rapid fire sequence of sentences in Italian that Cali couldn't begin to understand. Jesse listened carefully.

The man made a gesture signifying completion. "I wish you well," he said to them both, "though I do not think that is what you'll find." He pressed his hands on the table, and with extravagant gestures to them both, he rose and left.

Cali pulled her hand away from Jesse's. He'd been gripping it so hard that it hurt.

"What did he say?" she asked.

Jesse's jaw worked. "He said many eyes are watching us. He said the one you fear is seeking you, and his plans are almost complete."

Cali leaned back, rubbed her hands against her temples. "Jesse," she said, "he's moving. We have to do the same."

"We do not," he said. "You have a house on an island, and we can go there."

"Not the island," she said. "You know what's next."

He moved his arm, an instinctive gesture, trying to sweep away harm. "No," he said.

"Yes," she replied. "And if you won't, I'll go without you."

"Try it," he growled. "I'll track you faster than any god you ever met."

"Then track me, because I'm going."

He leaned across the table to her. "Why?" he asked.

"Because," she said. "It's where it all began. The only place we might be able to figure out how to complete it."

"You're being drawn there," he said. "You sure it's not a trap?"

She lifted her wine, swirled it in the glass, took a sip. "It doesn't matter," she said at last. "I have to go, regardless."

He lifted a hand in a gesture of frustration and understanding. This was inevitable. "Not Jerusalem," he said. "Not first, anyway. Ein Gedi first. The garden."

She nodded. "Then we'll go," she said. "Tomorrow."

* * * *

They took a shuttle directly from the Jerusalem airport to the Ein Gedi, not stopping to see anything at all of that city. After a night of restless sleep in a hotel nearby, they rose to go out into the land.

The first day they hiked through desert canyons where the stones were as softly curved as a woman's hips, and everything smelled of sand and salt and ancient powers whose names were whispered in the wind around them. Cali relaxed.

"This was a good idea," she said.

"I have them once in a while."

They moved from canyons to gardens filled with perfume, where sweet, cool waters flowed over stones into clear pools. Cali stopped to gaze at one of them and he put an arm around her, watching light play on water.

"We've been here before," she murmured.

"A long time ago."

"And we're here to remember why we're doing this. Because this is what we want. For us, and for everyone. What we always wanted. How it was meant to be. A relaxed state of joy. A state of connection."

"Yes. Whatever calls you to Jerusalem, this is stronger. Don't forget that."

They were meant to feel this way, to live like this. This garden, this warmth and liveliness combined, was the foundation of all that mattered, and their long goal. All else was noise, unnecessary and unfruitful.

"Arise my love, and come away," he said, pulling her close. "For lo, the winter is past, and the voice of the turtle is heard in the land."

She moved against him. "When we were here before I tried to tell you, but you believed him instead of me."

"He was good to me then."

"He killed you."

"So did you," he murmured, kissing her.

For the first time in many days, she laughed. "Not as often," she said. "And not for the same reasons."

He cast a glance around, and saw no other human within range. He pulled at her clothes until he found her skin, and reminded her why she returned to him again and again, reminded her of the thread that bound her to passion, to a continuing insistence on life. And if her body felt like a desperate animal seeking shelter in the pleasure he gave, he was glad enough to give her that. Glad enough to give her anything that might save her, save them both.

* * * *

The next day they went to the Dead Sea and floated in its buoyant waters, held up by salt that encrusted land and stone like crystalline sculptures, glittering in the hazy daylight. They stayed all day, relaxing into the cocoon-like nature of the place, barometric pressure and minerals combining to protect them against a burning sun.

Toward evening Jesse sensed a change in her, and knew she was once again thinking of what might be rather than where they were now. He searched for ways to distract her, talking of the birds that flew overhead, of the funny, very round man and woman who floated in the water nearby. She listened vaguely, and stared out over the water, lost to him in both past and future. The sun sank low on the horizon, reflecting in the water as a gash of blood on a darkly translucent skin.

"In spite of all that, we have to go to Jerusalem," she said at last.

He stopped talking, closed his eyes against the inevitable.

When he opened them again, she was already walking away from him. Already occupying a future he did not want to see.

* * * *

In Jerusalem, the heat was like nothing Cali had felt before, the sun an unrelenting presence you could never lose sight of. It spoke to Cali of loneliness and heartache.

And lonely is what they mostly were. The tourist crowd was thin. Easter and Passover, both late this year, had not yet begun, and political unrest kept all but the most foolhardy or committed away. The native crowd regarded them with suspicion and moved on. The bearded Hasidim, the well-suited men and women, the Palestinians in Kefiyas, the Beduin women and the sabras, all glanced with the same careful eyes, then glanced away. Even the beggars in the narrow, crowded lanes got up and moved away when they tried to speak with them. The only ones who gave them more than a cursory look were the soldiers who patrolled the streets with their hands on their rifles. They walked in twos and threes, talking with each other, laughing occasionally, but they never stopped watching.

"I don't like this," Jesse said. "I think we should leave."

"Not yet," Cali said. "They don't know us, and maybe they should.

* * * *

They were like movie stars in Hollywood—gods in a land where deities were a dime a dozen. They walked through the streets unacknowledged, even when she wore her Sari. In the cafes, if they started conversation with someone, their words were greeted with initial suspicion, followed by a quick exit. At the Dome of the Rock those they approached didn't seem to see or hear them at all, and made no response. At the Tower of David they found no one to speak with who would speak with them. At the Grotto of Gethsemane, eyes turned away from them, shunning them, and both Jesse and Cali felt a gloomy darkness moving within them.

"Do they know us and hate us, or do they just not see us?" Cali asked, beginning to doubt her own substantiality.

"I don't know," Jesse murmured. "I don't know."

Cali kept turning toward Golgotha as if compelled to go there. Jesse fought the compulsion, feeling something insidious in it. "It's arbitrary," he reminded her. "A tourist point. Let's go to the Garden Tomb."

"Seeing it again isn't the point," she said. "You know that."

Jesse sighed. "Okay," he said. "Let's get it over with."

They walked the Via Dolorosa, not stopping along the way but just walking, their heads ducked down, their steps slowed by the burden of memory, heavy as crosses. As they approached the top of the hill, they saw the milling clumps of people gathered outside the Church of the Sepulchre. Jesse stopped to stand and stare at the westering sun, wanting something of beauty to renew his spirit. Cali stood with him for a moment, but then she caught sight of a young woman a little ahead, apart from the pilgrims at the church but looking toward them. Her eyes, the only part of her visible under her Burkah, were filled with light.

She was beatific, shining with joy, and Cali wanted to see why. She walked to her, but when she got close enough to touch her, she felt an anguish that wrapped her body like ropes, stopping all motion in her. The woman held ages of despair. She held all grief, all rage, all darkness and light. Feeling it, Cali could not move.

And then, she saw blood.

Blood poured from the woman's face, ran into her mouth, down her neck. As Cali watched, her face became another face, a man's face and that filled with despair. "Why have you forsaken me?" he called out, but nobody answered.

"No," Cali whispered. The vision dissolved, but was quickly replaced by the face of someone she knew, someone whose coal black eyes had a burning at the center.

Images and events flashed within her mind, within her body: She was a little girl in a dungeon, and a man hit her with a stick and she was thirsty, so thirsty. Then she was tied to a pole with a great fire raging against her flesh. She was burning, burning and screaming in pain while satisfied Clerics spoke casually to each other about their dinners. Then, a war-torn ghetto, too many dead and not enough tears to grieve it. Not enough tears in the world. She was dry as old bones.

And always, always that man with his coal dark eyes looked on, waiting for her to break, waiting for her to relinquish, trying with pain or seduction or promises or threats to will her to him. She knew him just as she knew Jesse, from the beginning of time. He'd never forgive her, and he'd use her however he could.

She raised a hand, said one clear and firm word. "No," she said. "No more."

At her word, he faded into mist and was dispersed. Cali stood at Golgotha, looking at a woman with beatific eyes. She saw blood, about to pour out.

"Don't," she cried out. "Don't do it."

Jesse, hearing her, turned away from light and its infinite possibilities, saw her next to the woman in Burkah, her arm frozen in a gesture of denial. The woman shifted her stance. Everything in him tasted fear.

He moved quickly, but the soldiers who seemed to spring suddenly from the ground were faster and got there first. A group of them poured like water toward Cali, then swirled past her and to the woman, surrounding her, rifles raised. They screamed in shrill Israeli. The woman looked at them, smiled, lifted a hand.

And they opened fire.

Jesse flung himself into the air, dove at Cali, bringing her down to the ground and laying his body over hers. Gunshot pinged above them, and he heard her moan beneath its staccato song.

"I can't," she groaned. "I can't. Not again."

What happened next was muddled, disconnected. Soldiers were everywhere, moving, shouting orders. One grabbed him and pulled him up, away from Cali. He saw her lying on the ground, her eyes wide with fear and pain. He saw her turn her head and look at the woman, at the blood pooled around her.

"We're Americans," Jesse yelled in Israeli. "Tourists. My wife. I must see to my wife."

He struggled against the soldiers who held him. One of them, a young man of no more than eighteen, put his face close to Cali's and yelled something. He jerked a gun at her, pointing it at her face. She stared up at him, lifted a hand, and in her mind was a thought she could complete.

She could kill him. Kill them all, all the people who tore at this land like jackals, seeking power and ownership. There was no innocent blood in this place. And with her hand, she could bring them down, dance in the streets until they were cleansed of human greed and fear and stupidity. She could do that. She knew how.

"No," Jesse cried, and she wasn't sure if he spoke to her or the soldier.

Then she felt a hand on her shoulder. Jesse's hand, as if he stood behind her, and his touch was so filled with love, it was like clear water pouring over and through her. "I'll dance with you," she heard him whisper. "Let the boy go."

Incongruous laughter bubbled up inside her. She would dance, and a thousand would die. Or she would dance and a thousand would live. Well, she thought. Oh well.

She raised her hand another inch, touched the soldier's face. "May you be well," she whispered. "May you be peaceful. May you be liberated."

The young man's fingers tightened against the trigger.

"We're Americans," Jesse yelled in frantic English. "Tourists. Americans."

An older soldier pushed swiftly through the group. His quick eyes seemed to see everything at once, and he strode to the young man, put a hand on his gun, spoke to him. Slowly, the young man lowered his weapon, blinked at the other soldier as if he emerged from a dream. They spoke together briefly, quietly. The younger soldier straightened himself and moved away. The older soldier cast a quick glance at Jesse.

"She is your wife?" he asked in good English.

"Yes," he said. "Yes."

He nodded once, knelt next to Cali.

"Are you hurt?" he asked her.

She shook her head.

"Just scared?" he asked.

She nodded.

He jerked his head toward the body of the woman who lay dead nearby. "That one—she had explosives. But we've taken care of her now, so what are you afraid of?"

She licked her lips. "He's here," she said softly.

The soldier's face communicated ancient pain and understanding. "Yes. He holds this land and all its children. We cannot find release."

"Do you want to?" she asked.

He laughed bitterly. "Do you know what Israel means?"

She spoke so softly Jesse could barely hear. "The one who wrestles with God," she said.

The soldier nodded. He offered her a hand, and helped her to her feet.

* * * *

After answering a lot of questions and showing their passports they were released to go back to their hotel room. Jesse got Cali into bed but she remained agitated, unable to sleep. It would eat her, this city. It would eat them both. It had done so before.

"Jesse," she said, "He always kills us."

"This time everyone comes home alive, Cali," he whispered. "You got that?"

She leaned close to him, her chest and throat full of unshed tears. "I could have killed them all," she said. "I feel it in me. I could have."

"You didn't," he said.

"Only because you stopped me."

"No," he said. "You could have tossed me away like an old sock. You chose not to."

"Why?" she asked. "Why did I?"

"You tell me."

She sighed. She knew. Her particular gift could be used for death or life, but not both. She'd already made that choice. He'd just reminded her, with his love, with his healing, with the light he held in his soul.

She shifted. "His power—it's still stronger than ours."

"Not stronger. Just noisier. A god of blow and bling."

At this, she smiled. "Maybe."

"Definitely. How about we get out of here? Find somewhere with less heat and more warmth?"

"Ida's?" she suggested.

He felt relief stronger than he'd care to admit. "Sure. We can grab her up and go to your island for a while. How's that?"

She ducked her head down. "Ida's first. We'll decide the rest once we get there."

* * * *

They were on a plane back to New York the next morning, and the flight seemed almost impossibly uneventful. They collected their luggage, got a cab and watched the skyline of the City come into view.

They were a block from Ida's house when Cali saw the orange glow. She sat forward, staring at it, as the taxi drew closer.

"Jesse?" she asked. "What is it?"

He sat forward with her, and his hand began a fine trembling as he clutched her arm. "No," he said. "Not now."

The taxi went as far as it could, until the street was blocked off and a cop standing at

sawhorse barriers stopped them.

Jesse opened his window and leaned out. "What's going on, officer?" he asked, sounding perfectly calm though Cali could feel the tremor in his muscles.

"Big fire. Explosion of some kind. City's nuts lately, y'know? It's those kooks telling people they can wish for things. Makes people crazy."

"Yeah," Jesse said. "Listen, I live down that way. What number was it?"

"Forty two," The officer said.

Cali's hands clenched. She wondered how Jesse kept his cool.

"Anybody hurt?" he asked.

"They brought a body bag out. An old lady lived there. Somebody said they saw her inside just before it blew. That's all I know."

"Yeah. Thank God it's not my place, huh?"

The cop receded, and Jesse stayed where he was, still trembling.

"Where to?" The cab driver asked at last.

"Hotel," Cali said. "The Regal. It's close."

"Okey doke," the cabbie said, and drove on.

They didn't say anything until they were in their rooms, registered under different names, paying in cash. The door closed behind them, Jesse dropped the bags he was carrying and stood staring blankly around. Cali wrapped her arms around him, and he buried his face in her shoulder.

She felt no grief. Felt nothing only stunned. Her mind was working faster than her heart, and she was thinking, thinking what this meant. She wanted to know who did it. Aquarius? One of Racer's explosions, retribution against Cali on Talia's behalf and her own? Could Racer do that to her? Or maybe Rainier, seeking her, seeking revenge.

She'd think it through later. Right now, Jesse was trembling and she led him to the bed, sat with him on it, let him pull her down and and hang on to her as if she was the only anchor in the universe, and that was okay because she'd clung to him in just that way, knew what it meant to have someone to cling to at such a moment.

"Sleep," she told him. "Just sleep. Sleep."

And after a while, he did.

MOMENTUM

The next morning she woke up alone, and for a moment felt only terror. They'd found Jesse. Taken him away. She had just time enough to tell herself that was stupid. Neither Talia nor Rainier would take Jesse and leave her. Then the door to the room opened, and there he stood.

"Where were you? I was so worried."

"I went to get a paper." He held it up, showed her. In his other hand was a cup of coffee.

"Jesse, that's not safe."

"It's okay. I know what I'm doing." He moved to the bed, sat next to her, handed her the coffee, put the paper down. He rubbed his hands together, warming them. It was a cold and rainy spring in New York, and it felt even more so after the heat of desert lands.

She sipped at her coffee while she looked him over. "How are you?"

"I've had better days," he said. "Cali, you know what this means? They're desperate. They'll do anything. And look at this."

He opened the newspaper and showed her a story on the Religion page. "A skinhead group put a price on our heads. They say you're a terrorist, teaching good American men to destroy capitalism and democracy. The Army of God is hunting us. An Evangelical is offering money if we'll meet with them. They say they just want to talk."

He put the paper down, ran his hands through his hair. He looked very tired. "We have to leave. You can go ahead to the island, and I'll meet you there."

"Meet me? What the hell will you be doing?"

"I have to get her body," he said. "She has to be buried. I know where."

"You can't. They'll be watching, waiting for you."

He put a finger to her lips, stroked them for a moment. "It's what we do for each other. We have to go back to the earth."

What Ida said about Jesse. What she'd done for him. What Jesse would do for her. And it was still dangerous. "But if you claim the body—" she started to say, and he cut in.

"—I called a friend. A lawyer. He'll do the claiming, manage it discreetly. We can meet him, take her where she needs to go."

"A lawyer?"

Jesse shrugged. "He thinks I'm the devil, but lawyers don't mind making that deal."

She saw he was joking, and felt herself grinning in spite of everything. She set her coffee cup on the dresser, and put a hand on his arm. "Are you afraid?"

He nodded, and drew her close.

"Of what?" she asked.

"Of what they might do to you."

"To me? Not you?"

It's you they want, Cali. Don't you get that?"

She put her hands on his face and made him look at her. "I'd rather have it that way. I can't watch you die again."

"Cali—"

"Promise me," she insisted. "If it comes down to a choice, save yourself. Promise."

He didn't stop kissing her until she fell back on the bed with him, and all fears were forgotten in the pleasure they shared. And somehow, she thought Ida would approve.

* * * *

The lawyer met them with Ida's remains on a back road beyond the thruway. She was carefully wrapped in a cotton sheet inside the body bag, just as instructed. He seemed glad enough to turn her over and left without comment, and a pale face.

Jesse drove north late into the night until they were in the mountains and the roads became dirt roads, signs of human habitation dissipating. He drove to the end of a road that kept getting more and more narrow until Cali was afraid it would disappear altogether. Instead, it opened up to a broad space in front of a small cabin, and here Jesse stopped the car.

"Well," he said. "This is it."

"Is it yours?" she asked.

"It's deeded to someone else, but it's Ida's. Has been for years. One of her hideaways."

He took their bags from the car and tossed them into the cabin, got a shovel that was leaning against the side of it, walked beyond the cabin to a spot looking out over a clearing, and began to dig.

"Jesse, stop," she said.

He paused, pulled his shovel up and leaned on it.

"Do you want me to try and bring her back?" she asked.

"That," he said. "I wondered when you'd think of it. But no. She didn't want that. Not this time. She wants to return in her own way, under her own steam."

"Okay," Cali said. "If there's another shovel, I'll help."

He tossed a nod toward the cabin. "On the porch," he said.

She went and got it and they continued to dig, in silence. The ground was wet with spring, and the air smelled of pine and leafy mold. They dug until the sky went from black to grey, and then a shining silver and pink at the eastern horizon. Dawn was rising.

"That's good enough," Jesse said, and together they took her out of the body bag and put her in the ground.

They knelt by the open hole. Cali felt she should say something, some praise for this woman who carried the energy of mountains in her frame, but she couldn't find a praise big enough, and Ida needed no prayers for mercy or reward. She'd made this journey many times, and knew her point of return. Cali would miss her, though. She would miss her deeply.

"I love Ida," she said at last. "May she be well. May she be peaceful. May she be liberated."

Jesse put a hand on her shoulder. "All that," he said. "All that and more."

* * * *

When they finished covering her body with earth they went inside the cabin. Jesse laid down on a cot and fell hard into sleep.

He slept well past noon, and Cali, too restless for sleep, watched him, turning possibilities over and over in her mind. The sun in Jerusalem had been a fire cleansing her of nonessentials, making her options visible with a new clarity. She could not turn back from what she knew. Not anymore. But she still had a thing or two to work out before she knew the right way to go next.

If Ida's death was Talia's work, it was a warning shot, telling them how much she knew, and what she was willing to do about it. Aquarius wanted to control the power she and Jesse were trying desperately to distribute, and the only way to prevent that was to go public, take the reins out of her hands. And if Rainier was responsible, going public was also their best bet. It was the only way to make him null and void for good.

She was no further than that when Jesse woke, but she was glad to see that he, at least, seemed more peaceful. He called her over to the bed and she sat next to him.

"Okay?" she asked him.

"Rough around the edges, but okay," he confirmed. "We better see about getting to your island."

"That's one choice," she agreed. "I've been thinking of others."

"Like what?"

"Like I said before. Go public. Declare ourselves."

He raised an eyebrow at her. "You still have a hankering to be a goddess?"

"Apparently somebody has to. The people seem to need it."

He was quiet. He reached over and put a hand on her arm, bringing her attention to a memory they shared about a man and a cross. She pulled away from him. The vision dissolved. Jesse watched her closely.

"That was then," she said. "There were so few of us, and now there's potentially so many. I think even he can't beat the numbers he'd be facing."

"It's all new to them," Jesse said. "They might just fall back on familiar moves."

Cali knew this was a possibility. "I can prevent that," she said.

"How?"

"Talia said I couldn't raise the dead but I can. She also said I couldn't create a change in consciousness but maybe I can do that, too. We've never tried before."

His mouth tightened into a thin line. "With good reason," he noted.

"Don't say no yet," she insisted. "We could try, and if it works we'll leave and let them take care of themselves. It's a solution, and it would defeat both Rainier and Talia."

"What? We play Deus Abscondito? Go back and mess with their minds, then take off for the islands?"

"We already messed with their minds. What we taught them—we gave dynamite to children. Now we have to show them how to use it."

"You've been thinking about this for a while, haven't you?"

"You know I have. Since before Jerusalem, but that brought it home. We always tried to work from the bottom up, and the top always beat us. This time, maybe we should just go to the top and try from there."

"You told me you wanted this to belong to the people."

"It will. They just have to be taught."

"You're not suggesting teaching. You're suggesting recreating their minds in your image."

"Is mine any worse than his?"

Jesse stared at her. "This, from the woman who made the snake?" he asked quietly.

"It's different," she said. "I'm not like him."

"You will be if you act like him."

"You'd rather I killed them all?" she shot back at him.

He frowned, then spread his hands out on his lap and considered them. Suddenly she was back in his office, the angry and troubled teenager. She didn't like that. Not at all.

"From what I understand," he said, choosing his words carefully, "your intent is to complete a thought of what you want people to be, how you want them to think and perceive. Is that correct?"

"And then I'll leave them alone," she added.

He took this in, considered. When he spoke, his voice had an edge she'd never heard before. "Leave your slaves? Your worshipping minions? Your puppets? What makes you think can once you get a taste of it. Or what makes you think they'll let you?"

"You have no right to talk to me that way," she said, angry now.

"I have every right. I have free will. Choice. My own mind. At least, I do until you make me into one of yours, at which point I won't know any better."

She saw his point, and was angrier at him for that more than anything, but she also had a point. How could they skip off to her island, abandon ship in the middle of these deep and troubled waters? What would it do to the people they'd begun teaching, whose knowledge was so new and fragile?

"Afterwards, we can still disappear. They'll forget us and learn to rely on themselves."

He laughed softly. "Two thousand years later and they're still waiting for me to come back. No, Cali. They won't forget. Unless you wipe out their memory of us, too."

"Okay, then. We'll stay and guide them," she said.

"Rule them," Jesse amended.

"So *what*? So the fuck what? Can it be worse than what Talia or Rainier would do?"

"It will," he said, "because you can actually do it."

Yes, she thought. She could. Talia's schemes were nothing compared to what she could do. Of course, she'd have to give up the gift she'd held close all these ages, have to relinquish the gift of life she was capable of sharing. But if she didn't, she and Jesse would be killed again, anything of love they'd put in the world destroyed, and she'd seen too much of her love being destroyed by those who sought power instead of love. She wondered why she'd never tried it before. And suddenly, an answer occurred to her.

"If I can do it, why haven't I before?" she asked, quiet now, dangerously quiet.

"Because if we use his terms to fight we've already lost," Jesse said, just as quietly.

"We lose anyway. Every time. That's not why. I haven't tried this because you talked me out of it. You kept telling me we could do it *your* way."

"You believed that, too," he said. "You still believe it. So do I."

"I believe I've been used by your belief," she said.

"We're all used. You and I get to choose what uses us."

Her anger bubbled into life. He admitted to this, and stood by his folly. "Go to hell," she said. "This isn't some abstract philosophical question. You're *using* me. You used me to do this work. How's that different from what Talia or Rainier did?"

"You know better." He put a hand on hers. She pulled away.

He raised his eyes, so full of motion, so dear. In them she read his knowledge, full of death. His mouth worked, but he said nothing, and his silence was eloquent.

"You knew all along" she said with wonder. "You called me back with your love and your hands and your eyes, asked me to raise you from the dead so we could lose the same fucking battle all over again. Didn't you? *Didn't* you?"

He made his hands into a temple and pressed his fingers against his forehead. "If that's what it takes," he said softly. "But it's different this time. Maybe it's possible—"

She swept a hand across the room, wiping out his words. "Nothing is possible if we don't accept our own power."

He separated his hands, held them out to her, empty. "We're not here for power. We're here to put light in the world and walk away."

"Deus Absconditus?" she said, her voice cold with rage. "Tell me how that's different."

"Okay," he said, sounding angry in his turn. "It's different because we're doing it from love. Not fear. You get that?"

How dare he? How dare he talk to her about love, when she'd spent countless ages giving that away to him, to the people, to the planet? And the world remembered him, but not her. The world continued to erase her, any way it could.

Not this time.

She made a fist, raised it and hit him on the chest, on the shoulder, hit at him as if her hands were the wings of a wild bird protecting its young against attack. He lifted his arms, shielding his face, but didn't try to stop the blows.

"Fuck you," she cried. "*Fuck* you. How many times have I watched you die? How many times did you leave me for him? Abandoned me, wasted our lives chasing some idea of purity and love that doesn't ever, ever win. *Fuck* you. I raised you from the dead, but who tends my wounds? Who the fuck does that? Who the fuck does something that actually works?"

She kept hitting at him until her throat tightened into sobs she wouldn't let loose and breathless, she stopped. Slowly he lowered his arms. He said nothing, but she saw the truth in his eyes. He knew what came next. That's why he held her as if they had no tomorrows. They didn't. They had only this circle of madness they followed through ages that were all the same. Her mind raced in several directions at once, facing irreconcilable differences. She stood up, staring at nothing.

"Cali?" he asked.

She held a hand up, held him away. "Let me be or I swear I'll kill you again."

She walked to the door, left the cabin. She could feel him watching her, and wondered if he'd go to the door and stand there, waiting for her, peering into the night. She didn't look back to find out.

She walked toward the woods and into them until she was far out of his line of vision, even if he remained standing guard. She sat on the ground, leaned her back against a tree and thought.

She did not belong to herself anymore. She was up for auction to the highest bidder. Talia or Rainier would buy her. The people would buy her. And Jesse—even he would buy her for his cause of light and love. She pushed herself to standing and walked further into the woods, far enough to almost lose herself, wanting only to get out of her own skin, the impossible task—to escape your own feelings. Impossible in this lifetime.

She stopped again, but this time because she heard a noise. She quieted herself. Something walking. Deer? Fox? Jesse, following her? Then, a sigh, human. Not Jesse's. She would recognize that. She peered into the darkness, trying to see. A face appeared, grew gradually clear to her. She blinked in surprise.

"Racer?" she asked.

"Cali?" Racer asked in return. She made a sound like a sob and ran to her, clutching at her arms. "Cali, it's you. I'm so fucking glad."

"How—How did you find me?"

"That woman—Ida. You told me about her, remember? I saw in the paper she was killed. I followed that guy who took her body out of the morgue. Then I waited here. I've been watching for hours."

Racer's eyes flicked this way, that way, bits of light moving in a dark place. It reminded Cali of the day in their dorm when she said she had no more weed. Sorrow moved through her. Racer always was a lousy liar.

"Why?" Cali asked. "Why did you find me, Racer?"

"It's—you're not safe. You have to come with me. I'll explain later. Just come with me," she said. "Honest, Cali, please?"

Cali was called back to an earlier time, when a friend kissed her companion's cheek, and the guards came to take him away.

"Racer," she whispered. "Not you. It shouldn't be you."

"Come on, Cali. Come with me," Racer said, twitching, urgent. She reached over, moved close and enfolded Cali in an embrace, kissed her cheek. Cali accepted it.

Before she felt the needle penetrate her skin, she remembered Jesse. In spite of her anger at him, she wanted to let him know. It would be, she thought grimly, a quick and easy way of saying I told you so. She screamed as loud as she could.

At least, she hoped she did. Whatever drug Racer gave her acted fast, and if she managed a scream, it wasn't a long one.

She fell, and kept falling, into darkness. Into night.

CALCULUS

Cali knew where she was as soon as she opened her eyes. The conference room at Aquarius. She wondered why she was here. Why she wasn't dead. She sat up groggily and saw Racer, sitting in a chair across from her, scowling, her index finger bloody from being chewed.

"What's got you so nervous?" Cali asked.

Racer shook her head. "You shouldn't have given me away," she said.

"I didn't."

Racer shrugged. Cali guessed the notion was just too far outside her worldview. Funny, how people couldn't see what they didn't believe in, as if they were programmed to reject their own possibilities.

"What happens next?" she asked.

Before Racer could speak the door opened and Talia entered. Right behind her, one hand at her back, Rainier followed. Rainier and Talia, working together. Of course.

"Fuck me," she said with feeling.

"But I already have," Rainier said cheerfully.

"At least you kissed me," she pointed out. "Besides, I was talking about her, not you."

Racer went to them, stood between them. Talia put an arm around her and Rainier looked at her fondly. Happy family, Cali thought. Mother, daughter, and the old goat. Or was it three lovers? A thruple. So hard to tell these days.

Talia kissed Racer on the top of her head. "Go sit for a while, darling," she said. "We won't need you for this part."

Racer pulled one of the large, comfortable chairs to the corner of the room. She put earplugs in for an MP3 player, sat back and hummed. Cali wondered if Talia had forced a change in Racer's consciousness. If that was what it looked like, she could now agree with Jesse's objections to it.

"You're with him?" she asked Talia. "Or, more accurately, he's with you?"

Talia gave her a small smile. "You figured it out?"

"Yeah. Just now," Cali said.

They'd scammed her good, she thought. Talia, her ancient enemy, and Rainier, her servant. She chose a woman's body this time, a good place to hide. And Rainier played Red Herring for her, very effectively. Well. Oh well.

"It took you long enough," Talia said a little smugly. "And I thought his last name was a dead giveaway, but he insisted on using it."

"Vassago?"

"The angel who finds the secrets women hold most dear," Talia replied. "An old but respectable name."

"Cute. And what do I call you this time?" she asked. "Ra? Yaweh? Hitler?"

"I was not Hitler," she said, looking peeved. She jerked her head toward Rainier. "He did that."

"Right. I'll just call you Talia, then. Did you really think he'd be able to take me?"

"Not at all. But he deserved a little fun. He earned it."

Yes, Cali thought. He did. "Jesse knows?" she asked.

"Only that I'm his mother," she said. "In fact, even Ida didn't guess. I'm rather proud of that. Then, of course, I hinted to Jesse that his real father wasn't Ida's son, so you could say Rainier distracted him, too."

"Teamwork," Cali noted. "Good for you. So now what?"

"You have a choice to make," Rainier said. He lifted a hand, palm up. "Live, or die."

"That depends on the terms," Cali replied. She shifted, rubbed at her face. She was tired, her energy as low as it had ever been. She was in no shape to take them on, and they knew it. They'd planned it that way. "What do you want from me?"

"Now, Cali," Talia said. "It's not what we want from you. It's what we can share. If we cooperate instead of fighting, we'll all be better off. That is, if you're not too stubborn or full of pride to take our offer."

"Better name it," Cali said.

Talia looked to Rainier, and he spoke. "It's similar to what I offered before, only more immediate. With the trouble you've been causing, the people will need new structures to organize their lives around, on all levels. They'll also need a new god. Or actually a goddess would suit better, given the times."

"Talia?" she asked.

"No," he said. "You."

She let this idea settle in. They were offering her a job? Not only a job, but the one she was considering anyway.

"You look surprised," Talia noted mildly.

"I am," she admitted. "But why not Talia?"

"I prefer working behind the scenes these days," she said. "More perks, fewer hazards. I'm the better strategist, and you're the better front woman."

"And you're a better ally than enemy," Rainier added. "We're aware we've made some errors with you, so we're not surprised if you're skittish, but I'm guessing you've been thinking about this on your own. It really is the best solution for all concerned."

"Maybe," she said. "But I didn't want her invited to the party. Or you."

"Cali, why should we be enemies when there's plenty of goodies to go around, and we can all help each other?" Talia put in. "How many ages did you spend insisting on the importance of connection, of relationship? And here I am, understanding you at last."

Those were words she never expected to hear from the mouth of her enemy. "That sure doesn't sound like you," she said.

"I've been occupying a female body. It's taught me about cooperation and consensus. Funny how the physical can shift the spirit, isn't it?"

"Funny," Cali agreed. "But why shouldn't I just go ahead and do it without you?"

"Look out the window and you'll see," Talia said

She and Rainier led her to a window and pulled back the curtain. In the street below, Cali saw what she could only describe as a mob. There were hundreds, perhaps thousands of people gathered there. Some held signs that said *Kali Our Goddess*, or *Dance, Lord Shiva*. Some had signs that said *Destroy the Whore of Babylon*. Though sound was muted by distance and the barrier of Aquarius's thick windows, she still heard them chanting, shouting, praying, their voices raised for and against her, drowning each other out.

"Jesus Christ," she muttered.

"Some of them call you that. The rest think you're the AntiChrist."

Cali felt her palms grow sweaty. Was she ever afraid, Jesse had asked. Yes. She was afraid now.

"You taught them too well," Talia said quietly. "There's your results. And you can't change their consciousness without—well, you see what it does." She looked toward Racer. So did Cali.

"Yeah, I see," she noted. Jesse had been right. It was possible to change an unwilling mind, if you were willing to make zombies. "But how will you change their consciousness to make them accept me?"

"The usual way," Talia said. "Lots of social media, a great deal of—"

"Propaganda," Cali filled in.

"Well, it works," Talia noted. "Especially when the people are starved for a savior."

"Usually it's a male savior," Cali noted.

"The world is changing. Besides, Rainier will be by your side, the appropriate male conservative guy."

"And you? Will you stay female? Be press secretary? Communications director?"

"I'll do whatever is more fun. And more effective."

Talia's face showed the hint of a grin. Yes, she'd do what was most fun. Use Cali as she wanted, then go back to her old form, perhaps rescue the people from the evil witch. Her ancient enemy, doing what was necessary to retain power.

"Just so you know," she said, "those people down there realize you're up here with us. We told the press we'd hold a conference later, but what do you think they'll do if you say you won't help, and we send you out alone? And which side will do it worse—the ones who hate you, or the ones who love you?"

Cali sighed. A woman's body hadn't changed Talia's methods. She'd offer a carrot, but in the hand behind her back she always held a heavy stick. "So either I play with you, or you feed me to the lions. That's familiar enough."

Talia put a hand on her shoulder, rubbed it lightly. Cali looked at it, felt another hand on her other shoulder, saw Rainier standing next to her, also touching her.

He spoke, his voice close to her ear. "It's not a threat. It's just the consequences of your own actions. But you can take a bad situation and make it better. Greet your people under our protective wings, and let Aquarius be the institution to serve you."

"He's right," Talia agreed. "You'll get all the power you could possibly want, and no old gods on your tail. You can even keep my son, if you still want him."

"What do you get out of it?"

"You'll want to reward your humble servants, who help and sustain you."

"How?"

"What do gods always give? The good life. The gift of life," Talia said. "That's all."

And Cali understood. Her ancient enemy would get back the gift he'd tossed to her so lightly, so long ago. The gift of life, of Realizing a resurrection. Her ancient enemy reclaiming a power he never cared about, and never used.

"Even if I wanted to, it's not possible for me to—to relinquish it," she said hesitantly. "You know that."

"But you can teach us, Cali. And we can learn."

Okay, she thought. Fair enough. Why not teach them, when she taught strange people in bars? But there was more to wonder about. "What about the people?" she asked. "Can I keep teaching them?"

"Yes, of course, within limits," Talia said. "Our goddess is a jealous goddess. If they're good, she gives them eternal life. If not, well, she's pretty skilled at killing people, too."

Control. The old paradigm. A new goddess, using the same old powers.

"Don't mistake us, Cali," Rainier said. "You act on intuition, instinct. We're thinking long-term. The people need time to adjust. Throwing it all at them at once won't serve them well."

"Think of all we can do without our constant bickering," Talia added. "Think of how much easier it will all be."

True, and in some ways the answer to all the problems she foresaw. She could stop fighting, live at peace, liberated from ages of lost battles in a permanent truce. It was even better than what she suggested to Jesse. Why shouldn't she accept it? Two small knots formed in her forehead as she sought answers.

Talia reached over, put a hand on Cali's face and caressed it lightly. "In spite of our differences, Rainier and I are still your people. That mob out there, it's all new to them, but we've been at this since the beginning. We're like you, and we understand you. You should be with your—well, with your kin."

They were her people and she was theirs. Once, long ago, that was so. Only a few of them had this skill, and they were kin of a sort. A fighting family, perhaps. Warring kin. Now they could be reconciled family, if she was reasonable, forgiving. But something at the edge of her thoughts disturbed the pretty pictures they painted. She struggled to find it, name it.

"Rome," she said quietly. "Jerusalem. That was you, wasn't it? You were doing things there." In both cities they'd created events to make her believe she had to relinquish her own power for something resembling Talia's. It was there she first thought of taking over.

"We sent out information. Nothing more," Talia said. "We wanted you to decide with full knowledge. We want this done clean."

Cali shook her head. "You were trying to shift my consciousness. You'll keep trying."

Rainier rubbed her shoulder softly, offering her the pleasure of belonging, of being wanted, valued. "No, Cali. Once or twice along the way we tested you, the same way Ida and Jesse did. They had to be sure of you. So did we."

Everything they said was reasonable. It all made sense. Talia smiled at her warmly. Talia, whom she had admired and liked. Talia, who offered her the world.

She saw it turning at her feet. She felt the pleasure of moving events just as she wanted, with unlimited energy pouring to her from masses of people. Protected by Aquarius, she would stand at the top of the steps and speak to the gathered crowd. They would worship her, adore her. And at last, at last, after years of being powerless to help them, she could heal their wounds, see them live in joy.

That's what this was all about. The people. Healing them. Giving them joy. Using her skills as they were meant to be used. The possibility brought stinging tears to her eyes. She looked to Rainier, and from there to Talia. Waves of acceptance emanated from them, rippling toward her. She breathed in deeply.

Unexpectedly, her breath stopped somewhere in the vicinity of her throat, a raspy, closed feeling. She tried again, but it wouldn't move into her chest. She had a moment of panic, thinking she was drowning, inexplicably dying. Then, she heard a familiar voice.

Breathe through it. It's just a block.

Ida's voice. Hearing it, she was called back to slow, peaceful nights spent in a quiet place. Her back pressed against the earth, knowing death as a friend. She saw Ida's face as she'd seen it then, so old and alive and full of truth. She moved her awareness away from Talia and Rainier and back into her own chest, and she breathed. The body, she thought, does not lie. At least, not after Ida gets through teaching it. Though everything they said was reasonable, she knew something as unreasonable as truth. She gave it voice.

"You killed Ida," she said. "That wasn't fun. Neither was Golgotha, Karbala, or that woman in Jerusalem. Neither is watching Racer play zombie for you."

Talia's jaw twitched, but she held on. An ancient rage made itself known in Cali, demanding her attention, her clarity, her courage. She cleared her throat, and spit at Talia's feet. Talia stepped back, releasing her. Rainier did the same.

"That's the only gift I ever got from you," Cali said. "And now I'm giving it back. I think that makes us even."

Talia brought her hand up and slapped Cali hard. Her head snapped back. She felt her skin smarting, felt betrayal as fresh as it was the day her mother gave her away. She wondered why she couldn't get used to that kind of thing. Why it still hurt.

"Don't play high and mighty with me," Talia hissed at her. "We're being generous, letting you in on something good. Our mistake. For a penny and a cup of tea I'd kill you now. Dead gods are just as good if not better than living ones."

"Go ahead," Cali said. "Get it over with."

"Believe me, we will. We can run this without you, as soon as you give back what you stole." Talia looked to Rainier, gave a quick nod.

He nodded back, moved to Racer, pulled one of the earbuds from her ear. "Racer," he said, "We need you now."

She smiled and followed him back to Talia, while Cali wondered what the hell this was about. Would they make Racer kill her? She wouldn't be surprised.

"What's going on?" Racer asked brightly, still smiling.

Rainier, standing behind her, moved quicker than thought. He pulled a long knife from his jacket pocket, brought it around and slid it across the front of Racer's throat.

Cali gasped. Racer's eyes, filled with confusion, looked to her. Blood poured from her throat and her hand went to it, trying to hold it together as strange sounds, whistling and gurgling, issued from her. She looked to Talia, tried to speak and failed. She looked back to Cali, and her eyes said something about knowing the truth at last. Then she dropped to the floor and lay there, gurgling and writhing as her blood drained away. Very quickly, she stopped breathing.

Talia reached down and put a hand to her chest. "She's dead," she told Cali. "Now go ahead and bring her back."

Cali's initial shock moved into profound understanding. She remembered telling Rainier she wouldn't leave Aquarius without Racer, and they'd used the information well. Before they killed her, they wanted her gift of raising the dead, and they'd figured out how to get it. They'd force her to use it, grabbing knowledge of how it was done in the process. They'd used her love as their weapon, knowing it was the only one she had no defense against.

"You win," she whispered.

She knelt down to Racer, put a hand on her chest. Tears fell from her eyes onto the wound at Racer's throat, mixing with the blood. Tears for what Racer did to her, what she had done, unwittingly, to Racer, tears for what would happen next, for all of it. All of it. She dropped all consideration of strategies and consequences and attempts to save her own life. She let them go, and focused on Racer, put breath on her eyes and completed the thought that would bring her back to life.

Talia and Rainier leaned in, grasping her by the shoulder, gauging the energy she used to Realize this. If they felt how much it took from her she doubted they cared. Talia, her ancient enemy, wanted this back, and would have it regardless.

Cali felt herself go away into the blank space and return, dizzy with effort. It wasn't as tough as Jesse. Racer was only recently dead. With blurred vision Cali saw the wound was closed and Racer was breathing. She stood, stumbled back away from her.

Talia and Rainier ignored her as they knelt in front of Racer, putting their hands on her, feeling what had occurred. Let them, she thought. She finally understood something else—something they didn't have a clue about.

They could glean all the mechanics they wanted from her field of energy, but they couldn't do this unless they changed their own consciousness. Neither one of them was capable of shedding a tear, or acting with love, and this gift was utterly dependent on both. Without tears and love, without real joy, life was a thought that could not be completed.

In that, Cali felt something like pity for them. They were large in the world, and would soon get larger, but in themselves they were very small, and very afraid. Well, she thought, maybe feeling this shift would change them. Or maybe she'd given enough power to the people to overcome them, in some distant day. In any case, she could do nothing about it now. She stood in back of them, put a hand on each of their heads.

"I love you," she said to them, her voice low and clear. "May you be well. May you be peaceful. May you be liberated."

They were so involved in crooning over their take, they didn't pay any attention to her at all. Cali released them and moved slowly and carefully toward the door. She'd shown them what it was like to love. Now she'd leave, and let them choose what to do with it. Deus Absconditus. She could do that.

When she opened the door and walked out, they didn't follow her. They knew there was only one exit, and they didn't much care if she took it. She was expendable now.

* * * *

Cali rode the elevator down to the bottom floor, walked across the lobby and stood at the glass entry doors, where she saw the people, the reporters, the cops, gathered in the streets behind a barricade at the bottom of the steps. They couldn't see her through the mirrored glass.

She heard them screaming for her to save them, for her to be destroyed, and all her fantasies of power or an easy peace were dissipated. She'd get neither. What was left was either to cower here until Talia and Rainier came down to announce they'd struck a bargain with the new goddess, or go outside and face the screaming mob. No choice at all, really. Not anymore. She wouldn't be used as letterhead for the deity of her ancient enemy. And she had one more gift she could give the people, a small drop of humanity in an infinite ocean of fear and hate. It probably wouldn't make any difference, but it was all she had left. As she chose to give it, she sensed Jesse's frantic searching for her, trying to stop her.

"I know," she said, a little apologetically. "But you might as well admit you knew we were headed this way all along."

She felt his sigh of resignation and frustration. He knew. Within her flesh, her bones and blood, she held one small and final truth to share, a shining piece of wisdom to offer with her life. With her life.

She opened the door and stepped outside.

* * * *

Screams rose from the crowd as they saw her. They pointed at her, crying out, their words nothing but noise to her ears. There were police, but they just stared at her with everyone else. She wondered if her clothes were torn and her hair a mess. Maybe she didn't look like what they expected. Maybe she did.

Someone—Talia, she assumed—had set up a microphone at the top of the steps. She thought of what she might do just by talking to them. She had the bully pulpit, and maybe could use it to change the consciousness of this entire writhing mass, except that she didn't think it had consciousness. She wondered, in an idle and intellectual way, if that would make it easier to impose her will on them.

But if she did they were all lost, herself included. She would belong to Rainier and Talia, a machine set on its course to serve their ends. Though that might not ultimately be a bad thing, it certainly wasn't her thing. She was a particular piece of matter, and she wasn't here for that. It wasn't written in the lines of her hand.

Some distance away, she felt Jesse reaching for her, trying to stop her. "I hear you," she said, "but you might want to turn away now. You won't like the next bit very much."

She ignored the microphone and stepped forward. Words wouldn't help her. Only her body could shed the light they needed to see.

She went down another step and stood there. Just stood there, looking at the faces. They were old and young, male and female, black and white and all shades in between. They were terrified and enraged and ecstatic and crying and laughing. They were mean and ugly and beautiful and kind and thoughtful and totally without reason. They were lonely and afraid, fiercely independent and courageous. They were everything, all energy pushed into these particular pieces of matter that were capable of knowing themselves almost enough. Almost.

She went down one more step, and another beyond the barriers, onto the street.

Hands swarmed her body, pulling her into the writhing mass, and she didn't fight them. Only one tick of terror engulfed her, as she thought obliquely of a story she'd read in the news, about a woman who passed out, and her dog kept licking her face to wake her up. He licked it raw, and when he smelled the blood, he began to feed.

It's going to hurt, she thought. A lot.

When she accepted this, the terror went away. It was pointless. They had her now. She could feel them pulling at her, muscle ripping from bone, her flesh torn by nails and teeth. Some were trying to hurt and some trying to help, but they were all pulling, ripping at their own irreconcilable differences, ripping at hers. She felt herself lifted from the ground, many hands like an ocean current moving her this way, that way, voices crying out with hate and love and mindless noise. She was passed from one set of grasping hands to another, and each tore more deeply, more completely into her.

Yes, she said with her body. This is how it is. We try and fail and work and pray and in the end what's real is this. Our willingness to give ourselves to each other. To feed each other. To know and be known by each other. Our willingness to be love.

They lifted her up and pulled her here and there, and the agony was more exquisite than her memory of thirst or fire or the rack. She dissolved into it, all her energy going to them, dispersing into their souls. She knew she was losing it when she thought she saw Lara standing among them, smiling. She smiled in return, then looked where Lara pointed. To Jesse. Yes, of course. Jesse would be here.

She gave him one last smile, then turned back to those who tore at her.

"I love you," she told them, clarity of purpose giving her voice strength. "May you be well. May you be peaceful. May you be liberated."

And they continued to feed on her flesh, on her love.

BODIES AT REST

When Jesse heard Cali's scream from the woods, faint and brief but unmistakably hers, he'd run out just in time to see his car explode. He was tossed back by fire and sound, and lay on the ground asking himself if he was dead again.

He wasn't. Not dead, not injured. But he was stranded, and he had to get to Cali. It could only be Racer who took her, and he knew where she'd go, knew that wasn't good.

He stood and ran, racing the two miles to the road. He would have kept running, but a better thought occurred to him and he stood at the side of the road waiting. Not many minutes passed before a young man in a GT whizzed past him, then stopped.

"Don't usually do this," he said to Jesse. "I'm not even supposed to be on this road. I just wanted to see what it was like over this way."

"Yeah," Jesse said as he pulled himself up and into the passenger's seat. "I need to get into Manhattan. Fast."

The young man drove at top speed and brought him as close as he could get to the Aquarius building, two blocks away where the road was cordoned off. Jesse ran the rest of it, then pushed his way through a crowd that seemed to extend indefinitely around the building. By the time he was in the midst of it, Cali was already moving into the mob.

He saw her open her arms to them, felt the prayer breathing on her lips, and was stung by a moment of love and pride so intense he thought it would crush him before the crowd did. But he also knew what came next, so he pushed on, hoping to reach her in time.

Impossible. Impossible to breach this swarming mass of matter in motion. It had lost particularity. It was one body with too many arms and legs and torsos for him to manage. He felt himself lost in nightmare, unable to get anywhere. Cali disappeared from view, swallowed by the beast.

Then there was a wild screaming, rising above the cries of the crowd. It went on and on, and all turned to its source. A woman, anonymous and nondescript, stood at the microphone on the steps, shrieking into it until all eyes looked to her.

"What are you doing?" she cried. "Don't you remember? Don't you?"

The crowd went perfectly still. They were a drop of water suspended from the end of a leaf. Light shone through them.

"Love one another," she sobbed. "That's all. Don't you remember?"

Someone sighed. A sibilant breeze of understanding moved into them, making them ripple and shimmer. They understood. So did Jesse.

This was the end of their task. Just this. Everything he and Cali had done through the long ages, all that happened to them, all the pain and defeat, was meant to make this moment possible. All for this. Only this. One small moment of awakening, a wrenching shift in the dominant paradigm, at just the right time.

The people stopped the killing, and knew it as wrong. They remembered. They understood.

It might last no more than these few seconds, but they chose it, and so it was a seed of possibility that could grow. Cali had taught them their strength, and they were beginning to claim it as their own. She'd shown them love, and they'd seen it.

She'd done it. At last. At last. Her task and his, their long journey, their thought, was complete.

Jesse stood still, feeling the burden of ages rolling off his shoulders. The woman at the microphone covered her face with her hands and sobbed. The milling mob split off into individual molecules, each one busy with their own particular thoughts, their shame, their sorrow and confusion. One by one, starting from the outer edges of the crowd and moving to the inner, they dispersed. Nobody looked at anyone else. Nobody spoke at all.

The police stood in a magnificent stupor, not sure what their role was with an orderly, self-dispersing crowd. Something was wrong here. Some law had been broken. The law of entropy, perhaps. Or the law of things in motions staying in motion. But actually, Jesse thought, they'd met an equal and opposing force. They'd met Cali Spring.

He was able to get through as the crowd thinned, revealing those who were trampled in the initial frenzy, wounded and dazed. He kept moving, seeking her.

"Cali," he called softly, then more loudly, "Cali. Cali!"

His worst fear was that she would be gone. Just gone. Taken by Talia, by some maniac, or ripped to pieces by the crowd. He was pushing forward, refusing to accept his fear, when he felt something at his feet. Small motion at ground level. He looked down. It was a snake, and it moved with purpose toward the prone body of a woman. It curled around her head, and seemed to dissolve into the ground. Jesse took a breath and moved to her.

One of her legs was twisted into unnatural posture. Her right arm was bent the wrong way at the elbow. Her face was bloodied and bruised. He knelt down, gently touched her cheek in the only place he could find that wasn't cut.

"Cali," he said. "Oh, Cali. What a mess. What a fucking mess."

A cop came close and spoke to him. "You a relative?" he asked.

"Her husband," he said.

"We'll get an ambulance. Take her to the morgue."

"No," he said.

"Got to," the cop said. "It's the rules."

"Then go," he said. "Christ almighty, just leave me alone with her."

They did so. Jesse bent to the broken body he loved without end, seeking her soul as he had for all of time.

OBSERVATION INFLUENCING OUTCOME

It was dark, and it seemed to stay dark for a long time.

Cali didn't mind. Wherever she was, it was quiet. No noise. It felt almost like the old days, when she ruled her own life alone.

But then she realized she wasn't alone. She saw people. Two people. They were below her, on the ground. There was a snake nearby and he lifted his sleek head, beckoning to her. She felt laughter rise in her. She knew him, and he always had some surprise.

"Is this a trick?" her thoughts asked him. He flicked his tongue out, raised his body up another inch. He wanted her to come closer.

"Okay," she sent her thought to him. "I'll play."

She drifted down until she was just above him and the two people near him. One of them was very broken, and the other was sobbing. What would make someone sob like that in this peaceful place?

"What a mess," he was saying. "What a fucking mess."

That was true. The body he cradled was a mess, broken and bloody. The snake, curled nearby, drew her closer, asked her to look at this, to touch it. She reached her thought toward the body, feeling something like compassion for it and for the man bent over it. Some energy poured out of him that drew her. It was sweet, filled with the strength of light. She moved closer yet, and touched the body.

A mistake.

The moment she touched it she was caught, pulled into it, and it hurt like hell, stealing all peace, swallowing it whole. She gasped in pain.

The man held his breath, held her. "Cali," he said. "Cali."

Yes. That was her name. And she knew him. He was Jesse. But he was supposed to be far away.

She choked out words. "How—How did you get here?"

"For fuck's sake, Cali. I let you kill me and bring me back. You think I can't conjure up transport when I need it?"

She wanted to laugh, but everything hurt horribly. "I can't," she groaned. "Let me die."

"Quiet now," he said. "This time, everyone comes home alive."

She wanted to tell him he couldn't. He was the healer, but her wounds were too deep, too encompassing. Before she could form the words she felt his touch moving things here and there, a deep warm energy flowing through her. Her heart constricted with the ache of reconnection, re-membering. He always remembered. Always.

"Okay, girl," he murmured. "We've done it before, and we'll do it again." And he kept working, while she endured the return of her body to the land of the living.

He fixed what needed immediate attention, then called a halt. She had more wounds to tend, but he couldn't do it all at once, and he couldn't do it here. "Let's get you someplace safe," he whispered.

He lifted her in his arms and stood. He walked, going fast and avoiding cops. He hadn't gotten far when there was sound from the microphone. He turned and looked. Talia and Rainier stood on the steps. Talia pointed at him.

"There he is," she called urgently into the microphone. "Don't let him take her."

Jesse cursed soundly and kept walking. Talia was the master of the last minute strategy, the improv. He saw police moving his way, their hands on their guns.

"Fuck you," he muttered. "Shoot me, then."

Cali gasped. He looked to her, and her eyes were wide.

"Racer," she said hoarsely. Then, "Run."

He responded, but he couldn't move as fast as Racer's angry thoughts.

What happened next was quick and bright and explosive, and not a part of anybody's plans.

SCALE

Senator Clemens sat in his office in Washington, DC, and read the news reports from both the internet and the Post, which all agreed that a terrorist group was probably responsible for the bombing outside the Aquarius Project building the night before. Fortunately, it had been evacuated earlier because of the purported presence of the woman known as Kali, allegedly in the building with Talia Jordan of Aquarius, and Rainier Vassago of Tritan.

Unfortunately, Mr. Vassago was not available for comment, being dead. Investigators believed one of the explosives was planted directly on him. Ms. Jordan was unconscious from wounds sustained during the incident. Doctors said her condition was critical, her injuries severe. They didn't anticipate any comments from her for some time, if ever.

Many people in the crowd were injured, but they had all been treated and released. The woman called Kali remained missing, and eyewitness reports of her varied wildly. Some said she was carried away by her companion, popularly known as Shiva. Some claimed to see her raise her hand and cause the explosion. Some said she walked into the blast with her companion. Some said she wasn't there at all, it was just mob madness.

Another contingent said she walked among the crowd healing the wounded and raising the dead, and always a small snake slithered at her feet. One man who'd been trampled in the crowds swore that when Shiva passed by him, carrying Kali in his arms, he lifted his hand to touch the hem of Shiva's shirt, and he'd been instantly healed. He'd gone to the rally screaming *Kill the Whore of Babylon*, but he felt differently about it now.

A prominent Christian leader, when interviewed, said God had intervened, defeating the AntiChrist and Whore of Babylon, and surely the Rapture was at hand. The President, in his press statement, said the incident highlighted the need for renewed vigilance against terrorists. The FBI had no comment. They were still investigating.

24 Hour news stations sought out those who had previous meetings with Cali and Shiva. A best-selling author said she would certainly continue to do as Kali instructed, and she'd teach others to do the same. They would say the chant Cali taught, seeing it as a thought worth Realizing. A man who had a brief meeting with Kali in a bar disagreed.

"New Age bullcrap," he said. "Nothing's free. Not ever."

Buried under the primary stories, a few reports described how Cali gave herself to the crowd, and how an unnamed woman stopped the violence by sobbing out words of memory and love. Most of the articles closed by saying the truth about Kali and her companion might never be known, but all hoped the City could return to normal now.

When he finished reading, Senator Clemens chuckled to himself. He took the time to re-read the parts that specifically mentioned Kali, though he had a busy day and was already holding off one appointment in order to savor what he learned.

The appointment was with the last holdout against his Universal Healthcare bill, a man who was coming to say he'd changed his mind after a meeting with someone who'd met Cali, and taught him a thing or two.

That was good, but there was a lot more work to do. He had bills on new emissions standards for factories and power companies, and a plan to put solar panels on all public buildings, plus a lot of private ones. Also a plan to impeach the current president, while supporting someone altogether new for the Oval Office. A woman of both substance and color. Other senators said his ideas were just wishful thinking. In response Senator Clemens only grinned and said, "Yes, indeed. They are."

When he was done reading he sat back and smiled. He called to mind the face of a young woman whose dark eyes were deep as the night sky, with distant stars sparking at the edges. He stretched out his thoughts to her.

"I love Cali Spring," he said. "May she be well. May she be peaceful. May she be liberated."

And then he went back to work.

INITIAL CONDITIONS

The beach was quiet, and filled with sun. Small birds ran along the shore, and light played along the surface of the water. A man stood watching it, absorbed by its motion. He was tall, broad in the shoulders, dark haired, and his eyes reflected the color of the sand and the sea. He looked simultaneously tired and relaxed, as if he'd recently released a burden he'd held for a long time.

Behind him, a woman approached. She was barefoot, and her long dark hair hung loose over her browned skin. When she reached him, she put a hand on his back. Without turning, he reached around and grasped it in his.

"The light?" she asked.

He nodded. "Look at it, leaping."

She stroked his back. She couldn't see his eyes, but she knew light and motion were buoyant within them. After another moment, he turned to her, put his hands to her waist.

"How do you feel?" he asked.

"Good," she said. "Like light, leaping."

He kissed her neck, her shoulder. He moved his mouth across her skin just for the feel of it. Warmth rose in her. The warmth that never left them entirely.

But she had something to discuss first. They'd begun that discussion earlier, then he was distracted by the light on the water, and insisted on coming out to see it. Discussions could happen any time, but the light would never look exactly this way again. It was particular to this moment.

She understood. The renewer needed renewing, and this was how he found it. She let him go, and left him alone with it long enough to take it in, then she came out to lay certain matters to rest.

She put a hand to his face, raised it to hers. "We did our job, and it's more than complete, but we'll still have to go back eventually. I have to find out a few things."

"They're dead," he said. "You already know that."

They'd watched the whole drama rise and fall on the internet, and laughed with the people who lived here and thought the fuss in America was amusing.

"You look like her, this Kali," a bartender at a little dive near their home said to her when she was first well enough to go out. He showed her a blurred photo in the paper. "You look just like her. Funny, yes?"

"Funny," she'd agreed, and he'd ambled away.

"Rainier is dead," she said now. "Talia's still alive."

"With a variety of tubes in her," he noted. "And for as long as she's neither dead nor alive, we don't have to worry about her coming back, in any form. Nor will he come back without her to tell him what to do."

"That's all fine, but the stories are still alive. They don't die."

The papers still reported it. People waited for her return. They'd wait for a thousand years. Two thousand. There was precedent. And eventually Talia would die, and take a new form, and bring her servant along. He knew this was all true, but found it impossible to worry about it here and now.

"It could be years," he said. "Decades even. By then, the people will know a lot more about how to use their own skills."

"It's not *just* about Talia," she replied. "It's Racer. I have to know if she's alive or dead."

"Can't you ever let her go?" he murmured into her hair.

"You know better. Besides, I think we owe her one."

He could agree with that. Racer's explosive tendencies saved their lives, giving them time to escape. She'd made it possible for him to get here with Cali and heal her fully, spending his days in watchful vigil of her recovery. Now, though some shadow of her wounds still lingered, every day brought new light to her face.

"We owe her," he admitted. "And we'll pay our debt. But right now I wouldn't let you go back on a million dollar dare, so you might as well settle in to some joy for a little while. Do you think that's a thought you can complete?"

She took a breath, let it out. He was right. They'd cast their small and vital piece of light onto the streets. And Racer, if she was alive, would take care of herself.

"Then distract me, for a little while," she said, and he heard the lightness, the happiness in her voice.

He smiled, stroked her skin. "Yes, my chatelaine, my lady, my love, my forever wife, my most precious leaping light."

He kissed her as he spoke, then lifted her, carried her away from the sand to a blanket nearby, and laid her down on it. In this position he could fall into her dark eyes and find bliss. She could fly into the light of his eyes and know joy.

"Jesse," she whispered.

"Yes," he whispered back. "Again and again, yes, Cali. Forever yes and yes again."

They'd have to return sometime, but not now. For now they were here, where light played on water. They would stay here, for a little while.

For a little while.